Of Glass and Lavender

The Ascension Rising Series

K. R. Rainbolt

BOOK 1

To my momma. Thank you for always having my back and believing in me when I didn't believe in myself. I love you.

AUTHORS NOTE

Hey all you tortured souls. I'm happy to have you here. I have a few things to note before you dive in. This is a slow-burn, dark-themed, paranormal, 'why choose' novel. While this book doesn't contain any heavy spice (though it's not lacking in tension), the following books in the series will. If you think you may need a bit more information on the cautions/triggers of this book, please check out my website.

Said website: krrainbolt.com

If you're ever confused about something/just want to know what something means, I've included all translations and general information at the end. I'm also a lover of lore, and if you ever want to know more about the Natural world than you can find in this novel (random stuff that isn't necessary to the plot, but is fun to learn about) then you can also find that on my website.

That's all from me! Kick back, relax, and enjoy the read.

CHAPTER 1

AALIYAH

"Alright, pick a hand," I said, caving into Grigen's contagious giggles and dazzling little smile.

The grin took over his entire face, brightening his wide aqua eyes and filling them with the kind of limitless joy that only a child was capable of. It was a look that never ceased to make me melt. The kid was too cute for his own good, and he knew it. It was part of what made him so easy to love.

Adorable.

I pressed both hands behind my back, hidden from view as I shifted on my feet and subtly listened for the telltale sound of the shop's oak door opening. A few more moments passed without the distinctive muted ring of the old bell that sat above the entrance, and I relaxed slightly. It was rather late, with the evening sun peeking through the clear windows, bathing the room with an orange glow. Closing time was only a few minutes away now, and while I didn't really expect to see anyone, I couldn't stop myself from scanning the space and checking that I hadn't missed a random customer coming into the humble little herb house I called home.

The area was small enough to see everything from the cash register, so it only took a few seconds to trace the entire store and note that it was still empty. Two rows of short storage racks stretched across the center of the room, perpendicular to the desk where I stood. We'd crammed their chipped white shelves full of teas, herbs and other valuable plants, all sorted with an air of organized chaos in see-through glass jars. They gave the room a distinct sense of clutter while also filling the space with a comforting earthy smell, and I took a deep breath, expecting that warm scent I'd grown accustomed to. Instead, a sweet floral fragrance that bordered on sharp made my nose burn. I squinted at its foreign potency as I continued my leisurely perusal of the room.

The faded gray walls, packed full of little trinkets from Eliza's many trips to the sea, were also empty of customers. Shells, vials of sand, and even a few fishbones littered their shelves. Several other pieces, like charms and ornaments, were strewn about as well, but the stock changed so often that I had never been able to keep track of all we had. Authentic gifts from a Siren were a hotter commodity than one would expect. Some Naturals liked to use them in potions, humans liked how they looked, and some just wanted to say they had something from the deep. Eliza had a hard time keeping up with the demand, and she'd been traveling to the coast more and more these last few weeks to boost our stock.

Finally, after scanning the room one more time just to be sure, I let out a breath of relief and turned my gaze to the only other person in the room.

Prince.

Like always, he was situated against the far wall, near the door. He was tucked against the tea sets, standing under a ray of the evening sun. I would have been more surprised if he hadn't been there, his presence as usual as my own. The regal way he stood, arms crossed over his broad, semitransparent chest, reminded me why I'd picked that name for him. My knight in astral armor. My best friend.

My Prince.

He smiled when he noticed me, nodding toward an impatient Grigen, who was still bouncing on the balls of his feet. Prince said nothing, and he couldn't even if he wanted to. The dead couldn't speak after all.

Grigen tugged at my shirt, pulling my attention to him, his smile still resolutely in place. He glanced at the stairs, giggling again while covering his mouth. That mischievous light in his eyes was so endearing I nearly gave him what was in my hand without him winning it first.

"Did you pick one, GeGe?" I asked again, chuckling as his expression turned serious.

Face scrunched in concentration, with the tip of his tongue peeking through his lips, he looked around the room. He took a deep breath, taking in the smells of the teas and herbs around us. He must have noticed the subtle difference in the air, his face twisting up at the unfamiliar sweetness. Grigen's nose was sharp, a trait inherited from his Dragonkin father.

"Left, Aunty Ali. Left!" Grigen said after a moment, the twisting hum of the word 'aunty' missing the distinct sound of a fully developed 't'.

He continued to bounce on his feet, clenching his hands together in front of him. It made his long brown hair bob, stray strands falling over his eyes, which he quickly batted away.

"You sure that's the one you want?" I asked, trying and failing to stay straight-faced and not give the answer away.

He took a second to consider his options again. Then, his nose twitched, flaring wide, before his smile grew, showing off bright white and slightly pointed teeth.

"Yes!"

I couldn't help but laugh at the dramatic exasperation in his voice as I pulled my hands from behind my back, holding them closed in front of me. Then I opened them both, showing an empty right hand and a small chocolate kiss in my left. Grigen's glee was contagious as he laughed. He reached out and picked up the chocolate, holding it close to his chest.

"Make sure you eat it *after* dinner, okay? Your momma wouldn't want you to ruin your appetite." I ruffled his hair, turning back to face the counter as Grigen bolted up the narrowed stairs that led up to the living quarters. They creaked and groaned under his slight weight, and joy clung to his words as he screamed, "Look, Momma! Aunty Ali gave me a chocolate!"

I laughed at his outburst, my hand covering my mouth to muffle the sound as Eliza's exasperated sigh echoed down the stairwell, followed by the booming rumble of Dezen's laughter. I was going to get an earful for that later, but the sound of Grigen's joy was worth every second.

I shook my head, searching for Prince, and I found him still standing against the wall on the far side of the room, his eyes on the setting sun. His prominent jaw, shadowed by the whisper of what had been stubble when he was alive, accented the serene smile on his face. It was the kind that inspired contentment, and I took a second to admire him as I leaned over the counter. He'd worn that expression a lot these last few weeks, and it made the butterflies in my stomach flutter every time I saw it. His grin, lopsided and amused, widened into a full-blown smile when he caught me staring. I rolled my eyes as his eyebrow rose and his head shook with joking admonishment.

"You would have done the same thing," I said, grinning when his head fell back into a silent laugh, his transparent form flashing with each false breath. He drew out the motion, ensuring it was as exaggerated as possible.

There was no color in his figure, just minor details that had clung to his soul when he died, like his heavily worn T-shirt and thick jeans that looked charred at the bottom. He floated away from the wall, swagger in his 'step' as he came toward me. I snorted, and it only made him smile wider. He was like a black and white hologram with a sass complex, and he unwittingly proved that thought when he winked and tilted his head toward the staircase. I laughed again before taking a deep breath and settling my thoughts. I'd forgotten about the sharp floral scent that had caught my attention earlier. It was familiar, almost sickeningly so, and it drowned out the warm aroma of the herbs. Now that Grigen wasn't here to grab my attention, I couldn't keep my thoughts off it.

I tapped at the counter, trying to push back the uneasy sense of *wrong* surrounding the smell. The dread came almost too easily as I recognized what was coming, and pressure built in my skull, burying into my skin.

Again? But I'd been doing so good...

There was no use questioning it now. I had little time left before it happened.

Before the *Rend*.

I rolled my neck and closed my eyes, trying to abate the feeling for as long as I could. Over the last few months, I'd learned that this feeling wouldn't just disappear. Not until it was over. So, I took a deep breath, forcing the smell to fill my lungs. The pressure expanded until it was a steady thump, my body jolting with each pulse, and all the peace I'd constructed broke down. I rubbed my forehead, pushing away the oncoming headache brought on by the *Rend*. I flexed my hands and moved my weight across both feet.

Prince was in front of me now. I could sense him without having to open my eyes as the chill that followed the dead became more intense. His anxiety settled in the air, making my skin tighten as his previous joy faded. It left a sour taste in my mouth as his panic built, and he asked me to look at him with everything but words. I ultimately caved, opening them and giving him my best fake smile.

"I'm okay," I said, stumbling over the words.

I smiled through it, refusing to ruin our moment of happiness until I couldn't hold it back anymore. But he didn't look convinced, always in tune with what I felt. It was a magic power that was just Prince. He'd known me for so long that I often wondered if he knew me better than I knew myself. No, I *knew* he did, especially now, as I remembered so little from before six months ago.

Prince got my attention, his form flickering slightly as he pressed his palms flat against each other, before dragging them apart. The newish gesture in our makeshift language only took a second to register.

Rend?

I moved things around the counter, reorganizing the chocolate bars and removing invisible dust off the faded oak. It was something to draw my attention, to keep me distracted as I nodded in Prince's direction, flinching when his face fell. There was a pinch in my ribs, the burn spreading down my arms and back. It ached like a hand was grabbing at my insides and toying with my organs. I swallowed hard and couldn't find the will to keep moving, my hands stilling on the cool counter as the faintness made it almost impossible to stay standing. Prince leaned in, his face as close as possible without risking touch. I flinched again, the pain expanding until it was unbearable. The sharp ache spread to my chest, and I reached up to grab it on instinct, trying to dull the throbbing.

"I'm okay," I mumbled again, more for myself than him, choking on the breath that came after.

Prince's panicked expression flashed across my vision. It was hard not to focus on the desperation on his face, on how his hands flexed as if wanting to reach out to me. I wanted him to. It was all I ever seemed to want, all I could remember wanting. He'd been my constant, my best friend. He was the first person I'd remembered after that first *Rend* six months ago, and he was the one I'd sought after I crawled my way out of a shallow grave. I'd remembered him before I even recalled my name.

The soft aroma that was becoming a bane was suddenly all I could smell, and the more I breathed it in, the more familiar it felt. It was on the tip of my tongue, its name hiding in my subconscious, like it was just out of reach.

Lavender.

The pressure came to a precipice, my body humming as the *Rend* overwhelmed me. It was like my skull was trying to split in two and, for a moment, time seemed to stop. A burning tug at my insides replaced everything before my pain disappeared, and I felt nothing at all. My eyes rolled back, and without time to collect my thoughts, I was abruptly watching myself.

Watching my body from the outside.

My hands, semitransparent like Prince's, were reaching out toward *me*. The once colorful shop appeared warped, the landscape black and white, like an old noir movie. I couldn't move, couldn't speak, or breathe, though I'd gotten used to that fact. It wasn't a shock anymore, and even the numbness was familiar as I did the only thing I could while waiting for the *Rend* to pass. Watch. The slow tick of time dragged for what seemed like an eternity as I watched the world around me move. I focused on my body, recoiling as it hit the floor, the echo of it resounding in the air over and over. I urged the *Rend* to end, silently begging that it would pull me back before Eliza heard the crash so that I could pretend this was all a bad dream.

Pretend I wasn't getting worse.

Of course, fate had never been on my side, and it wasn't long before

Eliza came down the stairs. The drag of her movements forced me to watch her pained expression for even longer. Though I couldn't see the color, what I recognized to be her vibrant red hair bounced as she moved, the aqua eyes she shared with Grigen widening as she saw me on the floor. It was her anguish, and the scream on her lips that always hurt the most.

Prince moved in front of me, the lag of time outside this plane of existence not affecting him. He kept his distance, as he always did. If he touched me, even when I was like this, it would likely result in him fading away and crossing over to whatever came after death. Though we'd never had it confirmed, it wasn't a risk either of us was willing to take. So he just smiled, the melancholy he tried to hide finding its way into the air. The static atmosphere of the world seemed to hug my limbs like an old friend, as if comforting me. Embracing me as I waited for this nightmare to end. It always took forever; minutes, or hours. I could never tell how the time moved, only that it was far slower than the world of the living.

Without warning, like a rubber band pulled too taut, my semitransparent form snapped back, slamming into my body, causing me to jerk forward. My head bounced off the wooden floor, just as Eliza tried to stop it and I gasped, strangled by the air attempting to force its way into my lungs.

"Aaliyah," Eliza said, the panic in her tone unyielding as she helped me up, bringing me to sit against the counter.

Lavender. It was more pungent around Eliza, masking her natural scent of seawater and spring air. I sucked in a breath as understanding returned to me.

Her new perfume had been the catalyst.

My head continued to pulse, eventually falling in sync with the beat of my heart, shaking my entire body. I smiled the best I could at Eliza, her trembling expression meeting me.

"I've got you, Ali," she whispered, knowing what was coming as well as I did.

I grit my teeth, trying to force the discomfort away, but my body didn't care, and the pulsing didn't stop. The *Rend* had done its job when it killed me, and now it was time to remember. The pressure dragged me along into a memory I wasn't sure I believed and a life I still wasn't convinced was mine.

I opened my eyes to a kitchen with checkered walls that stood stark against yellow countertops. The small room held a comfort that I couldn't quite describe, something that reminded me of a calm summer day. There was something in the air, a sweet, almost delicate scent, that had me looking around. The walls seemed to warp as I moved, as though trying to keep up with my wandering gaze.

It felt wrong.

A woman's smile greeted me as I turned, her thin lips tilted into a warm grin. My mind clung to her, and for a moment, nothing else mattered.

Mother.

I stared up at her, watching as she kneeled beside me, and her button nose turned up with joy as she realized I was there. Her hair, which extended down to her lower back, was a silky white, and I dug my fingers into it as she lifted me from the ground, pulling me close. The smell I'd been searching for clung to her.

Lavender.

The heat of her skin warmed me as she swayed with me in her arms, dancing us around the room as she crooned one of her foreign melodies. I leaned into her warm embrace, relaxing to the steady beat of her heart under my ear. She continued her simple moves, holding me close until footsteps echoed around us. They were loud; louder than they should have been, and just like the walls, the sound seemed to move; warped and delayed. I could see it in the air, almost clear enough to touch.

A man stood in front of us with his arms crossed over his broad chest. The stiff posture contrasted with the laxity of the rest of his body. His face held a warm smile, and his eyes crinkled at the corners, their red hue shining dimly in the room's low light. He had his black hair brushed back, not a strand out of place. I reached for him on instinct, overwhelmed by joy.

He felt like home.

Father.

I closed my eyes, leaning into him. He smelled of warmth and cinnamon cookies. Everything I knew love to be. But when I opened my eyes again, I was no longer in my father's arms. I was once again level with the checkered counters. I glanced around the room, and my eyes grew heavy and clouded.

Was I crying?

My gaze ultimately landed on a pile of white and red, something I realized in my core didn't belong, before I even registered what it was. Laid against the wall, body strewn haphazardly, was my mother. She was unnaturally still, and her violet eyes were closed. It was like she was sleeping. I moved toward her, taking small steps to not wake her. She had her hand extending toward something. No, someone. My father was to her left, his hand extended out to her the same way, his pale skin crudely painted with sick black lines.

Something pooled under the both of them, painting the white tiled floor and my mother's hair red. It was surreal, and at first, I questioned what it was. Maybe paint or cake batter? I didn't want to believe it could be anything else...

Because it couldn't be their blood that was crawling toward me.

An eerie screech filled the air, the sound so loud my ears burned. What seemed like arms wrapped around my waist, dragging me to a cold chest. A hand, as chilled as the body, covered my mouth.

The room fell silent, and I realized the eerie, desperate sound had come from me.

I'd been screaming.

The image stayed burned into my mind, even as my eyes shot open, and an expanse of darkness greeted me. The pressure in my head ebbed away.

"Ali, for the love of *Himal. Answer me,*" a voice above me hissed.

The familiar tone was crisp and clear as it rang in my ears, chasing away the black haze that had surrounded me. A tear-stained face came into focus sharply in the low orange light.

"Eliza?" I croaked out, my vocal cords protesting against my attempt to speak.

Eliza heaved an indigent cry, pulling me into her arms and crushing me against her chest. My entire body ached to the point where even holding onto her hurt. There was a brittle stiffness in my bones, one that didn't abate even as I began breathing again.

"How long?" I asked, unable to say much else.

It was always like this after a *Rend*. My energy was drained, and my body was left feeling like I'd fought a train and lost. I took a deep breath, taking comfort in the smell of lavender that clung to her.

"Three minutes, at least," Eliza said, her voice muffled against my shirt.

I closed my eyes, swallowing the panic that surfaced with her words. Three minutes. Dead for *three* minutes.

"What caused it, Ali? You haven't had one in days."

I tensed at the stark hope in her voice; a hope that I couldn't say I shared anymore. The guilt I felt was sour on my tongue, and I struggled to find any words. Eliza had faith that these episodes were going to go away, that one day I'd stop having them, and I *had* shared her hope for a while, at least. After she first found me those months ago, I also wanted to believe that I would get better with time. But then the *Rends* just kept happening, becoming a relentless reminder that the past I had ... was anything but good. It made me not want to remember any of it, even the good parts. I glanced at Prince, who still looked stricken by the *Rend*.

Yet, they never stopped, and I doubted they ever would. Just another grim reminder that I was dying. I swallowed and pushed down the thoughts I didn't want to have.

"Lavender," I said, still breathing in the reminder of my mother I didn't realize I had.

Eliza cursed above me, jerking back, staring down at her shirt with a twisted glare.

"Damn it, I knew it was a bad idea," she said, a look of guilt on her delicate face. "Carter found it at the market last week."

I remembered Carter getting back late a few days ago but hadn't questioned it then. He often went out in search of things, odds and bobbles. I'd learned from Eliza that it was a trait that most Dragonkin shared: the need to collect items of interest. In Carter's case it was scents, and he often found little gifts for Eliza, often shiny or glittering, and always harboring a different pleasant smell. I hummed, understanding.

"You had no way to know, Liz. It's okay," I whispered, leaning back into the counter.

The chill of the wood seeped into my skin, only adding to the damned ache that didn't want to fade, and I shivered. Eliza frowned again.

"I'll get rid of it," she said, turning away.

Her eyes closed just as I grabbed her hand in mine. She was warm—warmer than any human could be—and I sank into the feeling of that heat.

"No, don't," I blurted out, smiling the best I could at her confused look as I flexed my hand. I let go of her and wrapped my fingers around my upper arm, trying to mimic the comforting warmth of my mother's soft touch as she'd danced us around our kitchen. "My mother used to wear lavender perfume."

I hadn't known before, but now that I did, I never wanted to lose it again. I remembered so little about my parents that I held each memory of them close to me. Even if it didn't end as well as it began.

"Not a terrible memory, then?" Eliza asked, her eyes widening.

Her surprise stung, though I really should have expected it. I'd remembered so few pleasant memories during my *Rends* that I could count them all on one hand. Each of them had been with either my parents or Prince. When he arrived at the compound, coming up with our first word so he could talk to me, the little games we used to play to pass the time. Small things, ones that couldn't entirely bury the chill of my glass cell or the haunting peal of Doctor Castillion's laughter. But it made the less pleasant memories more ... bearable.

I tensed, straightening my spine as I swallowed my response.

"Aaliyah?" Eliza pressed, her tone breaking off into a whisper.

I shook my head, fighting the instinct to stay quiet.

"It was nice. To start with anyway," I said, pulling my knees to my chest.

Prince took his spot next to me, mirroring my position with a worried look and a tilt of his head. His pointer finger dragged from his lips to his left ear, a nod following his serious expression. *Tell me*, he asked, but I didn't know what to say. It shouldn't have been so hard to talk about, not when at least *some* of the memory was good. But the parts that weren't ...

My mother strewed across the ground. My father's broken expression.

... really weren't.

I shuddered, and nausea made my stomach roll as I turned my attention to the floor.

"You don't have to say, Ali," Eliza said, drawing me out of my head.

She pressed her forehead to mine, humming a soft tune under her breath. It was melodic, and it drew me into a calm sway. Her *Siren's Call* seldom left me this relaxed, and I reveled in it while I could. Her gift still came as a shock sometimes, even after half a year with her. When she first found me stumbling through the woods looking like I'd just walked off a horror movie set, I hadn't believed her when she said she wasn't quite human. I hadn't known what being a Siren meant until we got to town. When she'd sung with that hauntingly melodic voice that somehow held every answer and every question I had. Everyone around us had turned away as though we weren't even there.

I hadn't known of Naturals then, or I hadn't yet recalled hearing about them. Sirens, Ghouls, Banshees, Hemomancers, Dragonkin, and so many more ... I couldn't dream of remembering them all. Each of them shared the fact that they were species with human sentience that didn't classify as human. It was a definition that I'd come to loathe and hold hope in as we searched for answers I wasn't sure anyone had.

What was I? And would knowing even help save me?

"We're going to fix this, Ali. I promise," Eliza said with a nod, dragging me from my thoughts. Her red hair bobbed as if she was underwater, giving her an almost ethereal beauty.

"I know, Eliza. It's just hard."

Her eyes narrowed, and she opened her mouth to speak. I knew how Eliza worked, and I also knew that she would likely tell me it didn't have to be so hard and that I had her to lean on. She'd said it before, and I knew she would always have my back. But I didn't have the energy to hear it right now, with the reminder of my parents' deaths so fresh. So, I didn't give her the chance to say it as I leaned into her, hugging her close.

The ache still sat heavy in my muscles, but I pushed myself to stay still as Eliza's haggard sigh ran over the top of my head, and her arms circled me. She gave the best hugs, the kind that enveloped you and made you feel safe. So even as I worried my limbs might revolt and try to find their way off my body, I held her.

"I didn't say I was going to stop fighting," I said before pausing again. "I have too much to live for to give up now."

"You're damn right you do." Her voice echoed, bouncing off the walls as she pulled back, still gripping my shoulders lightly while watching for hints of pain that I bit back with a smile. "Grigen would kill me if 'Aunty Ali' weren't here to sneak him chocolate."

I smiled at her mimic of her son's developing voice, unable not to at hearing Grigen's nickname for me. I shrugged, rubbing the back of my head—the joy of listening to Grigen's innocent laughter had always outweighed the guilt of giving him sweets.

"He asked so nicely..."

Eliza shook her head as it tipped back, and she gave off a short laugh.

"You spoil him. I think he loves you more than me."

Our conversation still sat in the air like a weight, but at least now we were both smiling. Her words lifted across the room, and I could hear her attempt at distraction in them, pulling me away. I was thankful for it, grateful for her.

"Besides," her eyes glimmered as she pulled back from me, sitting with her legs crossed on the ground, "I think I found someone who might be able to help."

I perked up at her words, though dread pooled in me at the same time. "You said that about the last one. You know, the human in the wizard hat?"

Eliza's face lit up a brilliant red that nearly matched her hair. "Hey, that was Dezen's fault! He was in charge of finding Ericetis. Being a Sorceri himself, a *Hemomancer* at that, you'd think he knows what a real Chronomancer looks like," she huffed, mumbling something about magic users before her smile turned confident.

Sorceri were some of the most interesting Naturals I'd come across. Technically, they weren't Naturals at all. At their core, they were humans that could do things others couldn't. Magic, as Eliza's second husband, Dezen, often called it. His power came from blood, and though I'd never seen him use his Hemomancy in person, I could always feel the touch of his power in the air when he was around.

Eliza finished her mumbling and sighed.

"Besides, I don't have to guess on this one." Her smile dropped, and an uncharacteristically serious expression took its place. "He's the real deal."

She pulled her arms to her chest like she was trying to hide. Her posture had me tensing, and a cautionary hesitancy kept me from talking.

"His name is Archon Sewire. He's a friend of my *baba*. If anyone can help, it'll be him."

Archon Sewire, I hadn't ever heard her mention that name ... I mulled over Eliza's words, flexing my hands. I hadn't met Eliza's *baba*, her grandmother and matriarch of their small Swell, not in person anyway. But I knew of her, knew how much Eliza looked up to her. Besides that, the only thing I could say with certainty was that she didn't know what I was either. And that thought didn't fill me with much hope as Eliza looked to me for a response.

"Why haven't we gone to see him yet, then?" I asked tentatively.

"Well, he just got back into town for one. He's also notoriously reserved," Eliza said with a sigh, tapping at her lip as she leaned onto the counter next to me.

She glanced at the stairs as if waiting for someone to interrupt the conversation. There was no more echo in her voice, almost like no one else could hear it, even if they tried.

It made me nervous.

"My *baba* got me in touch with him as a favor. He can't say no to her." I narrowed my eyes, and she smiled sheepishly. "Something about a blood pact. I don't know, and I didn't ask."

Eliza shivered, her expression twisting into a grimace. It was all I needed for my nervousness to blow into a panic. My hands grew numb where I gripped my thighs, and I desperately rationed my breaths so it wouldn't spiral into an attack.

"And *you* think he can help?" I asked after a pause, the roaring beat of my heart echoing in my ears. Her word meant more to me than her *baba, Dezen or Carter.*

I glanced at Prince, taking in his expression. He looked tense but didn't refute her, and at his sharp nod, I knew he agreed as well. It was another of those things that Prince knew, another question I would never get an answer to.

"I think it's worth a shot," Eliza said. A pregnant pause surrounded us. "We don't have a lot of options left, and my *baba* speaks nothing but praise ... mostly."

The gnawed panic in my gut didn't leave. Instead, it expanded, tearing at my lungs and burning down my throat, causing me to freeze. I glanced at Prince again. His jaw was clenched like he wanted to speak, to tell me what we were missing. Something that he couldn't sign to me with our limited vocabulary. So he did the best he could, crossing his arms over his chest in an 'x'. It was a symbol that I knew well, one I'd seen in my first memory.

Danger.

"What aren't you telling me?" I asked as I jerked my head back to Eliza, and she hesitated at my question, her expression conveying her desperation. "E-Eliza?"

"He's a Djinn," she blurted out, her face going crimson.

I froze, my mouth opening in surprise. Of all the things I'd expected Eliza to say, of all the Naturals that he could be...

"A Djinn?" My hands flew up, going to my hair on instinct, and my startled laugh had Eliza frowning. "You're kidding me!"

Eliza straightened her back, an expression of utter certainty on her face. The confidence I admired shone in her eyes, burning like liquid fire in the aqua depths. My breath stuttered, and I found I couldn't catch it.

"We can't," I said, shaking my head, instantly looking at Prince.

His face was still twisted in a dark glower. I could sense his worry, his trepidation and his rage. The intense emotions burned in the air, so heavy I could feel them as though they were my own. But he was sure as well, the truth as bitter as the rest. Archon *could* help, but at what cost?

A Djinn.

"When you first told me about Naturals, you gave me a list to avoid at *all* costs."

Eliza went to speak, but I cut her off.

"On that list were Demons, Fae, Vampires and Djinn," I said, counting them off, my lips trembling so badly it nearly stopped my speech before it left my mouth.

I recalled that conversation so vividly that I doubted I'd ever forget it. Eliza was everything I aspired to be: confident, loving, kind. But, most of all, she took things head on, without hesitation. So when she'd sat me down, ashen in the face with a haunted look in her eyes ... I knew to listen.

Djinn were known for their trickery and deceitful words, but that wasn't what made them dangerous. No, it was what they could do with those words that made Eliza wary. One wrong sentence, or a wrong phrase, and they could tear you apart. A Djinn could grant wishes, but you never knew when they would or how literally they'd take your words. And they were at the *bottom* of the list, the least dangerous of the ones she avoided. It was probably why Eliza was even considering Archon.

Not that it made me feel any better about it.

"Yes, I told you that, and I still stand behind that list." Eliza's exasperated sigh only spurred me on.

"And you want to go see one?" I asked, and if my confusion reached Eliza, she didn't show it. Instead, there was just that confident look that made me want to agree against my better judgment. The kind that caused me to realize why people went to war for Sirens.

"It sounds a lot stupider when you say it," she said in a whisper, though not backing down on her stance.

"Maybe that's because this is a bad idea, Liz," I said, groaning at her unwavering conviction.

Trying to argue with Eliza was like expecting a brick wall to move. My head throbbed, the after-effects of the *Rend* making it even harder to deal with. As if she realized that, Eliza sighed, pressing her thumb on the space between her eyes. She was silent for a moment, her expression shifting. She couldn't hide her emotions to save her life, and I found it comforting now as she sought to break one of her few rules.

"There has to be something else we can do, someone else we haven't talked to," I said, rubbing at my achy temples.

"There isn't. Not anyone we'd want to talk to, anyway."

I bit my lip and considered my next words. I wasn't as familiar with

Oakridge as Eliza was, but I knew more than most. I knew there were others in town that we could have gone to, other Naturals on her list of those to avoid. I didn't know their names or anything at all about them ... I only knew that they were here.

And what they were.

"But you're willing to talk to a Djinn?"

Eliza stiffened, her head twisting toward me like she already knew what I was going to say.

"I don't understand. There are Vampires—"

Eliza grabbed me by the shoulders before I could finish, turning me to face her. I was so startled by the movement that I yelped, pulling away with a jerk, my back slamming against the cabinets. Eliza looked so stunned that she jumped back, falling on her palms as regret covered her features.

"Oh *Himal,* I'm so sorry, Ali. I didn't mean to grab you like that," she started, shaking her head and laying it in her hands. "Vampires are ... out of the question. I can talk to Archon because of my *baba,* but Vampires are a different story."

"Why, Eliza? What's so different between them and Archon?" I asked, biting my lip.

She'd never straight told me why, but I knew that of the Naturals on her list, Vampires were the ones she *hated.* Curiosity got the better of me, and I couldn't stop the question. Eliza froze, turning away, hesitating to tell me before she sighed.

"Vampires and Djinn aren't comparable, not like that anyway. Djinn may be powerful, but we can kill them." Eliza paused, her expression taking on a look I recognized all too well: repressed fear and an inability to think of anything else. Something had happened, something I had a feeling I wasn't going to like.

"Vampires differ from most Naturals, Ali. They're powerful, ruthless, and practically immortal. Hell, the only way you can really kill one is direct sunlight." Eliza's face grew pale, and she was shaking as she spoke. "And they know it. They draw people in with their good looks and charm, then kill without mercy because they can. So, even if we found one that would talk to us without tearing out our throats, there's no guarantee anything they say would be true. It's just not worth the risk."

I grimaced, taking one of Eliza's trembling hands in mine.

"What happened, Liz?" I asked, so quiet it surprised me she even heard it.

Eliza, the woman who had become a sister to me, who had taken me in and given me a home, smiled even when tears brimmed her eyes. She let out a haggard breath as pain flashed across her face.

"A Crypt killed my parents and most of my Swell."

Whatever I'd expected, didn't even come close to the reality. I froze, my mouth opening though I couldn't get any words out.

"I remember Mom begging to know why," she explained.

"The man, their leader or just another lackey, I don't know, said 'because Siren blood tastes best when they're scared.'"

Again, I was at a loss for words, so stunned by what I heard, I could only squeeze Eliza's hand tighter as she finished softly, "Carter's mom was killed by one while walking home one night. Drained her dry, then left her on the stairway to their family home. He found her there."

The message was clear enough, but it was only hammered home when Eliza's lips thinned into a dark scowl, her eyes glowing so brightly they almost looked white. A flicker of her power pressed against me, and I stiffened as it slid across my skin like it was looking for a threat. Eliza took a few deep breaths, and the feeling faded.

"I don't know. Maybe not every Vampire is a monster, but I haven't found one that isn't. Everyone I know has a story about them, has a family member or a friend they've lost. They'll tear you apart if you give them a chance, Ali." Eliza wiped her tears on her shirt, the long-sleeved silky material doing little to help. "So I won't let them near you to find out. We can do this without Vampires. I know it."

I nodded numbly, turning toward her the best that I could. The pain was fading, and the headache that pulsed in my mind was less severe now. Eliza reached out for me again, pulling me into another hug. Even after six months with a very huggy Eliza and an even huggier Grigen, it still felt strange. She sagged into me, her grip holding me to her like a lifeline.

"I'm sorry, Eliza," I said, pulling back with a forlorn smile.

"It's fine. It happened a long time ago." She clutched at the necklace she always wore, a small golden shell. "Thanks for listening, Ali. I didn't mean to drop that on you."

"That's what friends do, right? We help each other."

Eliza looked like she might cry again, reaching out to grab my hand.

"You're damn right. Which is exactly why we're doing this." Like someone had reignited the fire, Eliza's eyes shifted. Any vulnerability that had been there before faded, and only the determined Eliza that I'd grown to love as a sister stared at me.

"Doing what?" I asked, watching as she all but jumped to her feet.

"We're going to get you some help," she said as she rushed around the counter to the small closet by the loose tea.

She pulled out two coats, warm enough for a trip out in the late fall weather. I recognized mine clutched in her hand, the soft brown fake fur shining under the evening sun. I furrowed my eyebrows, tilting my head at her as she ran back to me.

"I really hope you don't mean what I think you do," I said, just as she looked at me with a mischievous grin, one I knew Grigen got from her.

"Do you trust me?" she asked, shaking off the coats.

"Of course I do, Eliza. But that doesn't mean—"

She cut me off with a pleading look, halting my words.

"Then get up. We have somewhere to be," she said as she pulled me to my feet.

I struggled to stay standing next to her as my knees buckled. The after-effects of the *Rend* still lingered in my bones, and she had to steady me to keep me upright. She helped me put my coat on, and I humored her, if only to keep her focused enough to listen to reason.

"Eliza, you realize it's almost sundown, right?" I asked, shaking off the ache in my limbs.

Black spots danced in my vision, and I leaned onto the counter to stop from falling back down. Eliza sent me a look of apology, lessening her grip and helping me gain my bearings before she glanced at the stairs again.

"I know. Which is why we need to go now."

I pulled out of her arms, stretching my hand out at her when she reached for me. I shook my head.

"Now? As in, to *Archon's* now?" I asked.

"Yes," she said matter-of-factly, and like a train barreling full-speed ahead, she didn't let up. Instead, she grabbed my outstretched hand and pulled me toward the door with fierce determination.

"You want to go to a *Djinn's* house, in *his* territory, at *night*?" I tried and failed at shaking her off. "Where is my Eliza, and what have you done with her?"

"This is serious, Ali."

I laughed, unable to stop myself. "I can see that, oh wise and all-knowing, Eliza. Which is why I'll ask again ... What have you done with *my* Liz?" My retort had her throwing her head back with a frustrated groan.

"We don't have time for this. We need to leave before the sun sets, Ali."

A chill shot down my spine. "When did you have the time to set this up?"

"Earlier today. I figured I could set up the meeting and deal with the consequences later," she said. "I wasn't sure when we would have this chance again. Who knows when he'll be back in town, especially with the Eternium so close."

I faltered, biting at my lip. She had mentioned the Eternium before, a gathering for the leaders of each Natural race. She would have to make an appearance since her *baba* was the Siren Eternal. Dezen and Carter were in similar situations, though I didn't know what their connections were. I hadn't asked about the details, and from the sound of it, Eliza had little to tell, as it would be her first one. She'd told me it was a ball of sorts, where all the heads of the races met and mingled, telling stories, sharing secrets, and hashing out Challenges if anyone thought an Eternal needed to be replaced.

Suddenly the thought of talking to Archon now didn't seem so terrible. I'd forgotten how close the ball was, and once it was going, there would be even fewer places for us to go asking about me. I didn't have the time to wait.

"Okay, fine," I said, shaking my head, pushing back the dread that bubbled in my chest. "Where are Dezen and Carter? Are they ready to go?"

As much as I didn't like the idea of going out at night, I knew they could protect us. But, of course, her husbands were forces of nature, though what else would you expect of a Hemomancer and a Dragonkin? I expected her to call them down, but Eliza just grinned sheepishly, opening the door and motioning me outside.

"They don't know," she said, turning back to glance toward those same steps Grigen had shot up earlier, as though she was waiting for Dezen to come running down. Her panicked looks at the stairs all made sense now.

"*What*?" I hissed out, all but screaming. "What do you mean they don't know? We can't go outside alone right now. It's almost dark!"

"You aren't alone. You have me," Eliza said, as though that took care of all of our problems.

I let off a frustrated groan, planting my feet, not letting her drag me further. Her eyes narrowed, and her eyebrows rose. There was a bright flash, and then Prince started clapping beside her, choosing his time to appear as strategically as possible.

His head nodded toward her in a *you're the boss* kind of way.

The ass.

"And *you* have *me*," I said, waving at myself with an exuberant flourish. "Want to point out anything else?"

"I'm a Siren. We'll be safe, I promise," she said while crossing her arms over her chest.

"That doesn't explain why Dezen and Carter aren't coming. We'd be safer with them there, Liz," I said, trying to get the logic across to her.

But she didn't listen, her head shaking.

"We can't, Ali," she started so faintly, I almost didn't hear her. "Archon made it clear that if we brought any males into his territory, he wouldn't help."

My hackles raised, and I narrowed my eyes.

"And that didn't seem at all suspicious to you? What if he's setting us up, or worse?"

I swallowed the thoughts that came with that sentence. It hurt to even think of it, of the metallic tables and Dr. Castillion's twisted smile. The experiments and the agony that always followed them. I couldn't take a risk like this ...

"Eliza—" I started, stuttering over her name.

"I know! I know it's a stupid plan, but it's the only one I have left," Eliza cried, her voice cracking.

Prince tensed beside me. His expression was carefully blank, but I knew him better than to think him calm. I felt it in the emotions he couldn't quite stomp down. He didn't like to show anger, not around me, especially not so soon after a *Rend*. Not when he'd seen everything from before, and I knew that even if he could talk, he was more likely to tear out his vocal cords than he was to tell me about the times I couldn't remember. He would save me that pain if he could.

"I can't watch you die, Ali. I can't, not anymore." Her voice cracked, and her *Siren's Call* leaked into her words.

"I don't like this, Eliza," I stated with as much finality as I could muster. I understood my situation. I saw what was at risk and knew what I could handle... And this wasn't on that list. "I know you're trying your best to help, but I don't think this is the way."

Not when getting to Archon's home meant crossing Oakridge at night.

"Dezen and Carter can't find anything else. No one in this *district* can find anything else. Nothing on what Natural you could be or why the *Rends* are happening to you," Eliza said, her hands going to her face, running over her pale skin. The bags under her eyes were more pronounced now that I could see her in full color again, and when tears brimmed them, my resolve cracked.

"You've become a member of our family, and I'll do anything I can to protect you, Ali. I've tried everything else. Called everyone else. I wouldn't have even suggested it if my *baba* wasn't so confident in him. He's an Eternal, the head of the Djinn. So, if *anyone* knows what's happening, or what you are ..." I knew what she was going to say before she said it, and it ached all the more when she managed to get the words past her trembling lips. "It's him."

I stared, using the silence as a time to think. My breath quickened as though my lungs were desperate for air. I looked at Prince, always hunting for the comfort of his presence, and his soft, crooked grin. I couldn't have missed the way he winced as he nodded, how he tensed as though the movement physically hurt him.

"It's my last chance?" It was a question I'd been pushing down for the last six months. I continued staring at Prince, his smile falling and his head dropping in defeat. Then, Eliza's shaky nod confirmed it for me as the final nail in the coffin.

This was it.

I pushed down my fear, straightening my spine even as my legs tried to fall out from under me.

"Then I guess we better get going."

Eliza's eyes brightened, and I could see some stress drain off her shoulders. The evening sun was setting on us, and we likely had some ground to cover. Ground we would have to walk, thanks to Eliza being vehemently against vehicles. The only time I'd ever seen her in one was when Carter was driving.

"His home is on the far side of Oakridge, past the Calico Bridge," Eliza said as I leaned into her, unable to keep my weight on my legs. "If we hurry, we can get there before sundown."

She held me up, making sure I stayed standing. Then her hum started again, breathing some strength into my legs.

"Century Side ... you know that's Vampire territory?" I winced, forcing the steps I didn't think I could take.

"That's why I have this." Eliza produced two vials from her pocket. They were small, and each held a clear liquid.

"Concentrated nectar from the Zinnia flower. It won't hurt them, not permanently anyway, but it will slow them down long enough for us to get away if it comes to it," she said, handing one to me. "Which it won't, by the way. No one would dare take me on."

I clutched my unoccupied fingers into a tight fist, grounding myself. Eliza winked before flashing me a smirk, and I tried to ignore the way her expression faltered.

"Come on," she said. "Let's get this over with."

I nodded, taking a deep breath, letting the smell of lavender calm me, even as dread settled so firmly in my stomach I could barely move.

"Yeah. Let's go fix this mess."

CHAPTER 2

ADRIAN

"Any last words, Fally?" I asked, flashing my best grin at my rather disgruntled elder Crypt mate.

Fallon narrowed his eyes but was otherwise unflinching at my words. He held his pool cue loosely while watching me measure up my last shot. Laid out in front of us was a pool table, a beautiful dark oak with a red cloth top. Left on it were three striped billiard balls and the eight ball. I leaned forward, readying my stance as I prepared to win my third game of the night.

"None that you'll find pleasing to hear," Fallon scoffed, raising a sculpted brow.

"Oh, come on now, you've got to have *something* you'd like to say. I'm inclined to remind you what's on the line." I practiced my swing, a small hiss coming from the wooden pool cue against the skin of my hand. "How long did it take you to get the *Mona Lisa* again? If my memory serves me right, I believe just a touch over two hundred years?"

It had been a goal of Fallon's since his turn, and he'd finally bribed the curator at the Louvre several years back to trade it out for a counterfeit. The man, a Gargoyle Imp with an affinity for rare gems, had budged for only *one* offer. He was now the proud owner of one of only twelve Painite gemstones, a price Fallon was all too happy to pay to receive such an exclusive piece of art. Art that would now find a home on the wall in my room until Fallon could win it back, and though he tried to hide it, I caught the slight twitch of his upper lip: a dead give-away for agitation.

Other than that, Fallon didn't move, and a normal person would have thought that he was perfectly content, if not slightly bored. In fact, the only reason I could tell he was angry at all was the murderous look in his eyes, and a hundred years' experience of poking at the hotheaded beast. That lime green was so vibrant and *absolutely* furious. I chuckled, hitting the cue ball as I called the back-right pocket. The eight ball sank exactly as planned, and I stood up straight, gesturing toward the table with a roll of my hand.

"Then that's round three," I said, lifting my arms above my head, stretching out tense muscles as I winked at a still-glaring stone-faced Fallon.

Oh, I could do this all day.

"What do you say we go again?" I asked, egging him on, all the while knowing he likely wouldn't pay me any mind.

Fallon had never been one to fall for my goading, and today was no exception. Instead, he walked away, hanging up the pool cue meticulously on the rack across the room before strolling over to the couch and taking a seat next to Eirik. Fallon sat with refined grace, his white suit glaringly bright, the lightness of the material making his perfectly styled blond hair seem almost white. Not a single piece of him was out of place. Not a hair, not a thread, not even a wrinkle. It was as unnerving as it was insufferable. How could someone stay that *perfect* while getting their ass so firmly handed to them?

I sighed, leaning against the pool table that graced our home's 'game room', or leisure room, as Osiris often called it. It had taken me years to convince Osiris to replace the dreadful armory that had been here, moving all the ancient gear to the basement and firmly out of sight. The room was quaint, with gray walls and the stone accent Eirik enjoyed. The carved squares were of varying shades of gray and white. Even I had to admit they fit rather well, giving the room and the rest of our house a far more modern feel than we had originally gone for.

There was enough room to hold several entertainment pieces,

though much of the space was barren. There was only the single pool table that I currently leaned on, which was by one of the side walls, and a grand piano under the room's crystal skylight. And, of course, how could I forget the blood-red couch that was plastered directly in the center of the floor? It was part of a dreadful matching set, with one in our library and the other where Fallon and Eirik currently sat. They stared straight ahead, their thoughts far away from this room, likely avoiding thinking about why Osiris summoned us for a chat.

Fallon shuffled, and I knew immediately what his plan was when a twisted grin tugged at the corners of his lips. He pulled a single piece of chocolate from his suit coat, the familiar shiny paper telling me it was *the* chocolate. The Aldovin delicacy that he hoarded like a Dragonkin did gold.

The sly bastard was more upset than I thought.

He unwrapped it with care, neatly placing the silver foil in his suit pocket, before he popped the chocolate into his mouth. All while smiling so cruelly, I *nearly* cried. It was the only thing he wasn't willing to place up for the bet, no matter how much I begged, pleaded, and offered. Fallon wouldn't risk losing even a piece to me, not when they were no longer produced. He'd picked up his final batch the last time he was in Australia some four years ago, essentially buying out what they had left of the company's stock.

Damn the stubborn man's sweet tooth.

Eirik caught my gaze before glancing between Fallon and I, watching the interaction with veiled interest as he sipped on his drink. It was a harsh honey mead he'd made a few summers ago. The dark ink around his left eye—a Celtic dragon with a twisting body and geometric patterns—flexed as his lower lip raised, giving away his stake in this match between us. His rolling sky-blues caught my attention, and I didn't miss the way they flared with hints of a challenge ... a challenge to rile up Fallon some more. My smile broadened.

Game on, old boy.

"Come now, Fallon. You can't just leave me to my boredom when *you* were the one who wanted to play," I said as I turned toward him again.

That got some movement, Fallon's eye twitching as his glare turned deadly. Fallon liked his expressionless mask and used it well most of the time. Though his ill temper was easy enough to coax out if you knew where to prod.

"You've only lost the aged Brava Wine, a counterfeit *Mona Lisa*, and the *real Mona Lisa*. What *else* do you have to lose?" I asked, leaning forwards. I glanced at the wrapper in his hand, smiling as he scowled. "Besides your pride, of course."

"I think I've had enough of your games for the evening, Adrian," Fallon said, the crisp, frigid words laced with buried aggression.

He opened another chocolate, eating it leisurely. Dragging out my torture. *Definitely* struck a nerve. So I smirked and blew him a kiss.

"Translation, 'Oh, Adrian, I simply can't take the idea of losing again, else I might cry,'" I said, mockingly throwing my head back and covering my face with my forearm. Eirik's silence finally broke, and the giant choked on a laugh.

Jackpot.

"Fine. You want to play again? Why don't we take this to the training room?" Fallon growled, his teeth clenched.

I threw my hands up in exasperated surrender and sighed.

"Now, no need to be a sore loser." I put my cue next to Fallon's before taking my spot by the pool table again, claiming my victory before it turned into a brawl. "We can always try again later. I have wanted that Picasso, the one you keep above your bed, for ages."

I tapped at my lip, dodging Fallon's swiping blow with a laugh and a flourish. Pool, I could win. But you didn't fight Fallon when he was calm, let alone angry. The bastard could throw hands with the likes of Nero—meaning I didn't stand a damn chance in hell.

The sound of a door opening drew our attention, and Osiris marched into the room, looking every bit as irritated as I expected he would. His black hair, which was always crisply pressed against his head in what I could only describe as a 1920s' gangster look, was disheveled. The scowl on his face dropped the room's temperature, and the briefest hint of his *Charm* spread. His ill mood, so heavy in the air that it felt like a living thing, nearly strangled me.

"Evening, Osiris," I said, tipping my head at the oldest of our Crypt.

He barely looked at me, walking swiftly over to the still-open bottle of mead on the counter. He poured himself a drink and took a sip, his face twisting at its sweet taste.

"Took you long enough," Eirik said, stretching out on the couch, downing the rest of his glass. There was tension in how he sat, his hands flexed and his shoulders tight.

Ah, so the mock calm was done then. I straightened my back, crossing my arms over my chest. It was a serious time. Therefore, no time for a joke about Osiris's dreadful-looking black pinstripe suit that *screamed* gangster.

His theme for this decade really wasn't doing it for me.

Osiris shook his head as he walked to the piano, taking a seat on the dusty duet bench. He picked at the stained ivory keys, never pressing hard enough to make any sound.

"So, what was the answer?" Fallon asked, impatience bleeding into his words.

He grabbed his drink, which was sitting on the end table next to him. He sipped it, much more inclined to admire the sweet flavor. Osiris didn't answer for a time, choosing instead to peer out the window at the mossy pasture we had made into our yard. His eyes were far away, and the look in them was the most troubling.

Nothing. No worry, no question. Just nothing. It left a sour taste in my mouth; watching Osiris slowly sink further and further into this pit of numbness and sorrow. But I couldn't pull him out of it. I'd tried, Gods had I tried ... but nothing I did would ever be enough, and the only one that stood a chance was the same one that'd caused the numbness in Osiris.

"The Eternium ball is to go as planned."

My head dropped at Osiris's words just as Eirik's growl echoed. I tapped at the pool table, desperately trying to keep panic at bay. Neither Fallon nor I had ever been to an Eternium ball, the event only coming up once every quarter millennium. A gathering of the heads of us Naturals.

The Eternals.

And as the Turned of Sebek Ra, the Vampire Eternal himself, we were expected to show.

"Fuck," Eirik said, that growly tinge clinging to his words. "Two

Eternals have died in the past month, and they *still* want to hold their ball."

The beast inside of him flexed, moving behind steadfast sky-blue eyes. It sent a jolt of fear down my spine, the kind you only got in the presence of a predator. Even after all these years, his beast *still* terrified me, despite me being part of his Crypt. I didn't want to even consider how I'd feel if I were facing the Viking giant as an enemy.

"And Sebek? I'd assume he's even more volatile than normal with the Eternium so close," Fallon asked.

If the news scared Fallon, he didn't show it. Instead, his expression was relaxed, and his posture laid-back. Even his hair didn't have a damn single golden strand out of place. Once again, I found that fact *infuriating*.

"Xander said he was last seen in Prague. Still, he likely has eyes on us even with his distance," Osiris said, unblinking, so used to the wrath of our Maker that he'd grown numb.

I wasn't as lucky, as the panic that had started when Osiris entered the room crawled up my throat, catching any response I had.

"Bastard's probably even more uptight, with you in line for Challenge and all." Eirik leaned forward, pressing his hand to his scarred neck.

His words had Osiris tensing, and a chill took up the air. The power that came from Osiris nearly choked me, and his *Charm* that had been barely there before was now overwhelming. I recoiled, barely able to stand as a tense, brooding energy filled the room.

"So cold in here all of a sudden," I said, forcing a laugh at the end.

I emphasized the word cold, rolling my neck as I reached out, hand extended in front of me. I focused on the dead candles around the room as I took a deep breath, letting the *Flame*, the gift that those of our blood held, sizzle beneath my skin. Its spark crawled along my veins before ending at the tips of my fingers. The wicks lit with a snap, and heat seeped back into my bones as the gift warmed me from the inside out. As expected, Osiris closed his eyes when he realized what he'd done. The overwhelming feeling in the air faded, and Osiris sighed.

"You're getting better with the *Flame*," he said, tapping at the window.

"You could say that." I leaned in, giving Fallon my best smile as I spoke again to Osiris.

"Don't tell Fallon, but I've been using his paintings as target practice," I whispered, grinning wider when Fallon snarled, his icy mask slipping enough for his anger to come through.

"Adrian." Oh, if death had a voice.

"Calm down, Fally, I jest." I smirked.

"I don't understand why you goad him," Osiris said absentmindedly, taking another sip of his drink, not bothering to turn toward me.

"Someone's got to. Otherwise, his face may get stuck with that dreadful scowl." I imitated the expression, laughing as Fallon rolled his eyes.

Silence took over, and even my push to lighten the mood couldn't eliminate the feeling of desolation. A topic long since ignored, like most things that could cause ire in our home, was rearing its ugly head, and it seemed Osiris didn't like that fact.

The Challenge.

Eternals fought for their place to rise above the rest, and Osiris had just hit the age mark to call for a change of leadership. Though, he had no intention of calling for a Challenge. The thought of mingling with the leads of the Races had never much appealed to our eldest brother. If anything, Nero had been the one that would have fought for the spot.

But that didn't mean Osiris wouldn't be seen as a threat to Sebek's carefully crafted throne. Sebek no doubt knew this as well, and that thought was making the approaching Eternium that much more straining. There was a strange tiredness surrounding Osiris, one that made my skin tight. There was none of the panic that Fallon, I, or even Eirik were feeling. Osiris was startlingly ... calm? He was in a position that would make most Vampires tremble and count their days. Sebek had allowed no one to reach the age for Challenge since becoming the first Vampire Eternal over five thousand years ago. No one had expected Osiris to be an exception.

"So, what does this mean for us?" Fallon asked, finishing his drink.

"He'll be watching to see what we do, to make sure we don't damage his reputation before the ball," I chimed in.

"Meaning, we need to make an appearance *before* the Eternium."

Osiris sighed as he spoke, rubbing the area between his eyes. "We need to remind others in the community of our presence."

Silence settled over us again and understanding took over. The kind that drowned the room. I'd been dreading this since I first reported to Osiris about Pennsylvania's status a few weeks ago. I'd hoped we wouldn't have to use this.

Because it was about to go over like a lead balloon.

"What do you have planned, Osiris?" Fallon's suspicion showed in the way his eyes narrowed and his shoulders tensed.

"Adrian began searching a few weeks ago for suitable events, in case something like this happened. He found only one that met our conditions."

"But?" Eirik asked, catching the hesitation in Osiris's voice.

Eirik had known Osiris for well into a thousand years. So, I would've been more surprised if he *hadn't* picked up on how our eldest was stalling his words.

Osiris began tapping at the piano keys again, before he sighed. "It's an auction. One of Darius Verslini's."

I'd been prepared for blowback the moment that I'd learned of the auction. Though nothing could really prepare you for the unfiltered rage of a Vampire with the blood of a wolf. Eirik's snarl filled the room, the spark of our *Flame* lighting along his skin as his emotions spiraled.

"I thought he left the territory after his dispute with Nero,' Fallon said, ignoring Eirik's rage, only making our Norseman brother angrier.

Eirik glanced between Fallon and Osiris like they'd grown extra limbs.

"He did. He returned a few years back with the permission of Sebek, and he's likely the eyes our Maker has on us. I wasn't aware he'd started his dealings again until Adrian reported it," Osiris said.

"You jest," Eirik said, a deadly calm to his voice, one that betrayed the sharpening of his jaw and the push of the wolf behind his eyes. "We aren't going ... not there, Osiris."

"We don't have a choice, Eirik. We need to give a public appearance, or it could lead Sebek to pay us a visit before we're prepared for one." Osiris's accent came up when he said Eirik's name, twisting the syllables to hold a distinctive early Egyptian tinge.

Eirik stood from his seat, eyes narrowed in a challenge. Osiris didn't move. Hell, he barely managed a blank stare as he continued to sip his drink.

"Darius's auctions are cesspits. It's why we got rid of him in the first place. You can't seriously be considering this." Eirik's words caused Osiris's jaw to tick, though he didn't speak again. "We go somewhere else."

"It's the biggest gathering of Naturals in the area for the next several months. Adrian confirmed it," Osiris said, nodding his head in my direction.

Eirik turned his volatile glare on me, and I smiled sheepishly.

Thanks, Osi.

"It's true. Several prominent Naturals will be there," I said.

"How many?" Fallon asked, tapping at the arm of the sofa, his cold, expressionless mask back in place.

"Six Packs, three Clutches, and a few rather high-profile solo Naturals. I couldn't really get a good gauge on Swells, though Waterborne Naturals are harder to track down with them living in bodies of water, you know?" I paused. "Though, we'll be the only Crypt."

"No," Eirik growled.

"Eirik," Osiris started, standing, brushing off the non-existent dust on his suit.

"I said no. No auctions." Eirik's hand shot to his neck again, and the snarled words burned us all.

Osiris's mouth snapped closed, his jaw tensing at the sight of the scar that had led to Eirik's turn. Neither Fallon nor I knew exactly what happened, though we didn't need to. The rest of his scars were telling enough.

Just another thing that wasn't spoken of, another beast you didn't need to prod.

"I know it's not ideal," Osiris whispered, his hands pale and, as always, clenched tightly as Eirik walked toward him. He wasn't scared, at least not of Eirik, no matter how much he snarled and growled.

Eirik was just too close.

"Not ideal Osiris? It's fucking disgraceful. Against everything we stand for!" Eirik took a step back, his movement directly contrasting the snarl in his voice. "Nero wouldn't have agreed to this."

Nero's name, like a curse of silence, stopped all conversation. No one spoke. No one moved, and the pain was palpable.

"You're right. He would have laughed in my face at the thought," Osiris said, the words barely a whisper. "Know this, brother. I don't like it either, but it's this, or we face *his* wrath."

The ultimatum was enough to make my body tense again. Eirik was much the same, his teeth grinding as his face sharpened further, nose dragging to a harsh point, and jaw cracking as his beast lingered close to the surface.

"He's already waiting for a wrong move, anything to justify culling his line. *Us,* Eirik. We cannot afford to give him any more reason." The sharp tone that defined Osiris bled into his words, cutting in their intensity.

There was a surety in how he spoke. Sebek *would* destroy us before he allowed Osiris to take his title. Hell, he'd cull us just for the fun of it. At his best Sebek was a loose cannon, and we were about to deal with him at his worst.

The room fell silent, leaving us to our thoughts. Moonlight shone down on Osiris, the effect seeming to age him. He looked tired, sipping at his drink while tapping the piano keys that he hadn't truly played in decades. He'd always preferred to duet. Though, the only one who could keep up with him had been Nero, and since his death, Osiris hadn't done more than touch the keys.

"Sebek will kill us all," Osiris finished, a startling calm to his words. Like he not only expected it, but he was ready for it.

Eirik tensed, and his snarl morphed into a resigned scream. I knew Osiris had convinced him then. Eirik wouldn't put us at risk, not willingly.

"I know what I'm asking, Eirik, and you know I wouldn't call for it if I didn't think it was unavoidable." Osiris's words struck a chord, one that had Eirik faltering.

His intense rage evaporated from everything. Everything but his eyes. There, his beast still swirled, itching to come to the surface and take over.

"Fine," he said. "But we save one."

I swallowed hard at the ramifications of his words.

Only one, because you could only *buy* one. It was the rules, and we weren't in a position to be making waves right now. So, they wouldn't be swayed. Not even for someone as old as Eirik; as old as Osiris.

"Agreed," Osiris answered immediately.

Eirik didn't appear settled. If anything, his face twisted more, his eyes closing as he grimaced, hand reaching for his neck again.

"All in favor?"

We all nodded, standing tensely for only a moment. Eirik was out the front door between one breath and the next, the wood straining as it slammed.

"Well, let's get this shitshow on the road," I said, trying to lighten the mood.

I stretched my arms high, forcing a grin at a stoic Fallon, who had just swallowed the rest of his drink. He muttered something under his breath that sounded distinctly like a curse pointed in my direction.

I could only laugh when Fallon raised a disgruntled eyebrow.

"Shotgun," I called out as I *flitted* down the stairs, and toward what I could only hope wasn't a terrible evening.

Chapter 3

Aaliyah

I ground my teeth, focusing on the crisp pain that came with it as the familiar sense of panic nipped at my heels. It was the same panic that had followed me like a plague for the last six months.

We ambled down the dimly lit streets far slower than I would have liked. There was an unnerving quality to the chill in the air, or at least that was what the goosebumps on my skin were telling me. The sun had set behind the horizon, and its absence left a distinct feeling of fear in its wake. I walked a little faster because of it.

"This is a terrible idea," I ground out, glancing back sharply between Eliza and Prince as they worked to catch up with my stiff pace.

Well, Eliza did. Prince just floated my way, doing his best to keep my spirits up with his flashy expressions and swoon-worthy smiles.

The streets on this side of town were narrow, and the buildings seemed to age with every step. The old brick crumbled like the crunch of leaves under our feet. Fall had come to Pennsylvania, and the trees had started to change color, painting the ground an orange-red. Any other time I would have taken a second to admire the colors, but right now, it just left a distinctly hollow feeling in the pit of my stomach. The kind that made me want to run in the exact opposite direction.

"I don't like it either. If you have a better idea, I'm all ears," Eliza admitted, sighing as she spoke.

Her nose twitched as I glanced again between her and the silent Prince. She didn't turn to look at him, not when she knew she wouldn't see him there. When we first met, she didn't believe me when I said I could see Prince and others that had passed on. Even less when she learned what else I could do to them. That I could basically *unexist* them, for lack of a better term. She still seemed skeptical sometimes, but that didn't stop her from being as supportive as possible.

Case in point, *this mess.*

I knew she sometimes tried to see Prince like I did. But no amount of her *Siren's Call* would make her see ghosts. I was alone in my gift to see them, and alone in my gift to set them free. Sometimes, it felt like I was just alone.

I shook my head, guilt building at the stray thought. I glanced at Prince again, watching how he walked with that soft swagger, his entire form radiating confidence. Like a god or a king.

A Prince.

He tilted his head and gestured toward Eliza, as if to say *What's up with her?* The flare of his arms and that lopsided smile I loved so much helped calm my nerves. I couldn't help but smile back at him, my heart speeding up as his grin expanded, reaching up to his colorless eyes.

I shook my head, relaxed by his ease as I stepped closer to Eliza.

"I don't, but that doesn't make this feel any less *wrong.* It's like we're walking into a lion's den." I shuddered, unable to stop the clench of my hands as Eliza stepped toward me.

I was still quick to jump, quick to slam my jaw closed whenever someone or something moved a little too fast. They were habits I'd yet to break, habits that didn't feel like they should be real.

"Archon is the last person we'll have to ask. He *has* to know what you are, and he wouldn't do anything to upset my *baba*, not when she's still the Siren Eternal," Eliza said with a certainty I didn't feel.

"Then why are we meeting now of all times, Eliza? He didn't want you to bring Dezen or Carter. It's past sundown. Not to mention Fellow Manor is on *Century* Side." I swung my arm toward the darkest part of Oakridge, which we were currently walking toward. "I'd like to reiterate, that's Vampire territory. You told me as much several times."

I could see Eliza's argument brimming just behind her closed mouth, the twitch of her lip and the cross of her arms giving her away.

"What about this guy makes you so sure he's worth this risk?" I asked, not giving her time to start her rebuttal.

"He's a Djinn. They can't *outright* lie," she said, rubbing her face.

Even in the dark, she glowed. Her scarlet hair, long on the left and buzzed short on the right, was bright against her pale skin and deep black winter coat. She was like beauty made flesh, and the way she spoke made me want to say yes, no matter what she was saying. The *Siren's Call* did that even when she didn't want it to.

"And he's got over three thousand years of experience under his belt."

My eyes widened, and I found myself stunned, mouth falling open.

"Three *thousand*? There's no way," I said incredulously.

No one could be that old. Right?

"It's true. My *baba* knew him when she was a little girl," Eliza said, and I started walking again, listening as she hummed under her breath. "A lot of Naturals are like that. Old age isn't something that can kill most of us."

It was strange to think about as I settled my hand over my chest. My heart beat heavily under my palm. I hadn't given much thought to my future, not when there was a very real possibility that I wouldn't have one. But I let myself, for just a moment, consider what meeting Archon could mean for me. Maybe I was a Natural. Maybe I would never have to let go of Eliza's quick wit or Grigen's smile.

Hope flared in my bones, and it almost made me sick. I moved quickly, just as Eliza spoke again.

"This has to work. He *has* to know how to make you better. You were dead today, Ali." Her voice cracked at the end, ending her tune. "You were dead for three minutes. How much longer before you don't snap back?"

She began humming again, a melancholy sway to it this time. I didn't have an answer, not one I wanted to voice out loud. Eliza's soft melody calmed me, helping me to relax. I didn't have a rebuke for her, not when she was right.

"Speaking of, how are you feeling?" Eliza asked, inching closer until she was walking next to me.

Prince took up my other side, keeping a reasonable distance between us. There was no pressure in my head, and my heart wasn't thundering. No building *Rend*, not yet anyway.

"I'm fine, for now," I whispered, holding my coat closer, comforted by the fabric.

I shoved my hand into my pocket, wrapping my fingers around the small glass vial that Eliza had given me.

"No pressure?" Eliza pressed, her arms crossing over her chest.

"No, not right now."

"Alright," she said, a relieved breath helping to lessen the stress in her shoulders. Eliza hesitantly glanced around the dimly lit street. "Are there any other spirits around?"

I took a deep breath before looking around the area. Spirits had a particular feel to them. They were cold, and that chill was typically the first thing I noticed when they showed up. But it was nearly impossible to sense a new one with Prince here; his familiar chill dulled that feeling, so I had to rely on my sight alone.

"None that I can see, no," I finally said, scanning the empty streets.

"Well, that's a good sign, right?" Eliza asked, letting out a breath, the condensation visible now.

It was getting colder the longer we walked, the crisp Pennsylvania fall air setting in. I nodded, turning back to gauge our quickly darkening surroundings as I recognized where we were. During the day, this little road was bustling, but now, there wasn't a soul in sight. We stopped and just stared at the crossing point that led to the Century side of town.

Calico Bridge looked like it hadn't been touched since it was built. The old oak structure sat over the small stream that ran through Oakridge. The town split here, literally. The houses on the other side seemed ancient compared to the weathered buildings we had passed so far. Cracked streets and flickering street lights only made me want to turn back more. I could see the dark and crumbling brick of the buildings from where I stood. What lurked just beyond them? *Who* could be lurking? A soft breeze blew crumpled leaves around us, mixing with the sound of the stream.

I took a deep breath.

I forced a step, and the creak of the bridge caused me to pause as the hair on the back of my neck stood at attention. I searched for Prince, hunting for my safety net, and he looked at me with a sideways glance from my left, with his eyebrow raised and expression tense. He glanced between me and the other side of the bridge as though expecting me to keep walking.

I didn't want to move. Something about it felt *wrong*.

"Everything okay?" Eliza asked, obviously not feeling the same thing I was.

I forced myself to take another step, cursing when that overbearing sense of panic didn't ebb. I wanted nothing more than to turn back, head home, and pretend this was all just a bad dream. I wanted to hope that we'd missed something, that Dezen and Carter were holding onto one *last* option. That there was more left to try, or someone left to see. But I knew there wasn't. This man, Archon, was my last chance at figuring this out. At understanding why my soul wasn't settling. At figuring out what I was.

And why I kept *dying*.

Because if he didn't know, I wasn't sure what I would do.

My steps were slow and dragging, but eventually we found ourselves on the other side of the bridge. The air was physically cooler here, as though I'd walked into a different season, and even in my thick fall clothing, I shivered.

"You're fine," I said to myself as I picked up a steady pace. It was another habit I found I couldn't shake. "It's just the dark. That's all."

Eliza shuffled behind me, catching up with a huff just as a twisting dread settled in my stomach, and a prickling awareness that we were likely being watched made me shiver. I glanced at Prince again, and his mouth twisted with worry as he watched me. His hands flexed, and he looked around, tracing our surroundings for what was making me panic. Even Eliza stayed quiet as she searched the dark. Uncharacteristically, she let me continue my rant, her entire focus on the dimly lit streets.

"Just the dark," I whispered.

I had to squint as I watched the alleyways. The streetlights on this side of town were far and few between, an obvious inkling of those that lived here. Humans knew to stay away, their instincts telling them that whatever this path held wasn't worth it.

Much like mine were telling me now.

I trudged on, focusing on the road as a towering building slowly came into focus in the distance. Its extensive structure stuck out like a sore thumb, with long, arching walkways between towering spires. It was grand in every way you would expect a castle to be. I could see the regal hedges from here, and the dark brickwork was masterful. It was lit softly with yellowed lights, more brightened by the moon than anything.

That had to be it. Fellow Manor.

I took in the sounds of the wind in the trees, their leaves a bright mix of color, slightly dimmed by the dark; the unique crunch of leaves under my feet.

"Just the dark." Another mumble.

It made me feel better, less alone. I clutched the vial of Zinnia extract in my pocket. The crunching sound of leaves increased until the sound was almost aggressive in my ears.

I froze.

The sound of leaves crunching did not.

I flipped around as fast as I could, barely catching Prince's startled expression and Eliza's gasp. The surprise action made me slide backward, my feet nearly tumbling from under me. A startled cry bubbled up my throat, caught just behind my teeth.

A man stood just feet away. He was tall, easily towering over us. White teeth were on display, with what looked like a lit cigarette bit between them. The tiny bud lit up his face enough for me to catch the stubble on his jaw and his slicked-back brown hair. Smoke came from his nose, rising over his face. I jolted on instinct, forcing myself back another few feet, dragging Eliza behind me. His face, shapely in a way that most would call attractive, held an expression that made me want to puke, and the leering way he looked at me felt all too familiar.

And like fate couldn't *stand* the thought of giving me a break, pressure built in my skull. I clenched my teeth, biting down my panic and a wave of nausea.

Now is not the fucking time.

"Good evening, ladies. Was wondering if you might be able to help me? I'm a tad lost, you see," he said, taking a step toward us.

There was a drawl to his words that cut at his vowels, making him sound less intimidating. He wore a deep brown suit with a red under-shirt. The collar was ruffled and unkempt, much like the rest of him.

Eliza gripped my shirt from behind, trying to move me out from in front of her, but I didn't budge. I couldn't, not with how the man was looking at us. I didn't want Eliza to endure it. I wouldn't let her. So, I held firm, doing all I could to stay standing under the man's brutal regard and the pain of an upcoming *Rend*. My legs trembled, and agony speared through my skull.

"We can't help you. Leave us alone." I couldn't muster anything else, and what I hoped was a snarl sounded more like a cry.

My right hand, still clutching the vial in my pocket, tightened as Eliza tensed behind me, and Prince moved to stand next to me. With clenched fists and a murderous expression, Prince glared down at the man who couldn't see him, as if willing that to be enough to ward him off.

He gave me the strength to keep standing.

"Are you sure? I could really use your help," the man tsked, his head shaking.

He took another step forward, and I staggered back, gripping Eliza's arm with my free hand. He sighed, raising his hands disarmingly.

"Maybe we got off on the wrong foot. I'm Curtis," he said, waving at himself with a flourish. "It's a pleasure to meet ya both."

He stuck his hand out slowly, reaching it toward us. Black ink curled around his fingers and arm, poking out from under the red of his shirt. It looked like snakes were crawling up his skin and reaching out to grab me. That smile never left his face, and I struggled with what to do, caught between forced silence and a curse.

"She said to leave us the fuck alone, you creep," Eliza sneered.

She trembled behind me, and that pull in her voice slid across my skin, making my mind muddle. The man in front of us didn't seem affected. He just continued to smile as he pulled his hand back, throwing his arms up in surrender. Eliza noticed, letting out a sharp breath, her *Call* ending abruptly.

This was bad.

"Alright, alright. I'll just get help from someone else. Sorry to bother you, ladies."

His lips pulled back and exposed sharpened teeth, canines long enough to tear apart flesh.

From the smugness in his eyes, I'd say he knew what Eliza was, and knew that she wouldn't have any effect on him. I took another step back to create distance between us and him as our game of cat and mouse continued.

"Do have a good evening," he said, tipping his chin at us.

But he didn't turn to leave, only smiled again. His predatory gaze followed us, and the distinct feeling of being hunted crawled down my spine. It was like he knew exactly what I was thinking. My breathing was spiraling now, and I tried to recall what Eliza had told me about calming my panic when it came up.

"*Leave,*" I snarled.

Something akin to a shock lit up my spine, and the surrounding darkness seemed to close in, covering my sight in a haze of black. The pressure in my head raged, and I forced shallow breaths. But that damned haunting smile never left his lips, and though I braced for his next step, nothing could have prepared me for when he hurled himself at us. Curtis' movements were fast and calculated, far from the sluggish way he'd been standing. He reached us before either of us could react, his hand grabbing my hair, pulling hard enough to rip strands from my head. I didn't scream.

Never make noise.

The mantra started in my head, roaring along to the sound of blood pounding in my ears. I moved as he had, quick and efficient, as I smashed the vial into his head with enough force for the glass to break. Shards sank into my skin, and he screamed. He released my hair, stumbling back, holding his injured face.

They get more violent when they hear noise.

I was already running, dragging a dazed-looking Eliza behind me, unfortunately away from the bridge that led to the other safer side of town. The sound of feet on the pavement echoed in my ears, and I glimpsed Prince beside me, urging me to run faster.

"Better hope you're fast, bitch." Gone was the kindness that Curtis had been forcing into his words.

The malice in his tone had me picking up my pace, and for a second, it was like I was flying. I took a corner hard, trying to lose him between the buildings. I could hear his footsteps behind me, gaining on us.

We were fast.

He was faster.

His fingers found purchase on my shirt, and I came to a jerking halt. He ripped my breath from my lungs as he dragged my legs out from under me. My head throbbed and ached, a mix between pre-*Rend* and the impact, as I realized I was on the ground.

I turned, noticing Curtis hovering over a struggling Eliza.

"So you're the Siren, eh? You'll fetch a good price." His words froze me to the spot, nearly stripping me of my will to breathe.

"Fuck you!" she screamed in his face, thrashing.

She didn't take in his words, not like I did. That unprecedented pressure pulsed in my head, and I staggered to my knees. He knew what Eliza was; he said *the* Siren.

He knew we were going to be here.

That thought had me dragging myself to my feet. I wobbled, but didn't hesitate as I threw myself forward, and wrapped my arms around his neck, wrenching him off Eliza with everything I had. I dug my hand, still full of glass shards, against his bleeding face and anywhere else I could reach. Blood flowed from my mouth as I bit my lip hard, and pain spread up my arm from the tear of the glass, but I refused to let go. I only dug in harder as he screamed.

"Run, Eliza!" I yelled, struggling to stay on the agile man's back as he stood fully.

Eliza jerked to her feet, moving to come closer to us, to fight. I could see the determination in her eyes. I shook my head violently, fighting back the will to let go as Curtis dug claws into my arm. It was nothing. The pain didn't faze me, not anymore. It was just another scar to add to the list, and I would add however many I needed to get Eliza out of here.

"Eliza, NOW!"

She was crying. I could practically feel it in the air, but she still didn't move, hesitation and desperation keeping her still. My arms strained, and the man slammed against the wall closest to us, stealing the breath from my lungs again. I wrapped my legs around his waist, anchoring myself to him. Again, my arms screamed for me to let go, and I knew I couldn't hold on for much longer. Tears built in my eyes as I caught Eliza's gaze. The family I chose. She needed to go, to run, to get help. I gritted my teeth.

"Do it for Grigen!" I cried, and the agony that stretched across her face would haunt me for the rest of my life.

She didn't want me hurt, but she would do *anything* for her son. I saw the moment she cracked, and a sigh of relief crawled through the sobs I couldn't stop. Eliza choked on her cry as she turned away from us, running down the alley.

"I'm sorry, Ali, I'm so sorry." Her words echoed in the small space, and then she was gone, bolting down the road, away from us.

She disappeared from view.

My arms gave out, and I released a shuddering breath as the man ripped me over his shoulder, slamming me to the ground. My head, still pounding with the pain of an upcoming *Rend,* split into agony. Then he was over me, so close I could feel his breath on my face. He smelled of smoke and ash, the scent making my nose burn. I didn't open my eyes. Fear held them tightly shut.

He gripped my jaw in a relentlessly bruising hold, dragging my head to center, and my eyes only shot open when his nose skimmed across my skin. His one open green eye glowed eerily, an unnaturally pointed pupil sharp against the color. He snarled down at me, digging his bloodstained claws into my neck.

"You've got some talons, you little bitch." His voice was like glass on my eardrums, and I tried to shrink into myself, ripping away from his grip.

The pressure in my head pulsed, bouncing along with my erratic heartbeat. I forced myself to stay conscious as I struggled in his hold, trying to buck him off. I wasn't winning this fight, and unless I changed tactics, I doubted I would.

"Well, guess you'll have to do. You little freak." I froze as adrenaline surged through me.

He spit to the ground, painting the concrete an ashen black. It sizzled, ringing in my ears. I glimpsed the mangled side of his face, where a slow trickle of blood flowed from the still-open, glass-filled wounds.

I took a deep breath before stilling entirely.

There were still shards of glass in my palm, and I opened my hand, pointing it away from him. I forced myself to stay calm, feigning a struggle so he would move to better immobilize me. That's when I would strike. I doubted it would feel pleasant for me either, but it might give me a better chance. I took a deep breath.

"Now, that wouldn't be a very nice thing to do." The man's honeyed voice made me jump, and I went cold when his head shook condescendingly above me. "You wouldn't want to add any more glass to my pretty face, would you, doll?"

I froze again.

He must have seen me move or seen me unclench my hand. Or did I say it out loud? I trembled as I tried to sink further into the ground.

"Didn't see it, darlin'. *Heard* it. Your thoughts are as clear as day," he snarled as dread pooled in my stomach. "Two young women alone on this side of town, awfully dangerous, don't you think? Wandering unprotected on Century Side."

I couldn't find words. He knew what I was thinking. I could see it in the calculating way he followed me, like he knew what I would do before I did.

"We're not alone." I choked down my panic, trying to think of a better lie to tell, but nothing would escape past my frozen lips.

Eliza had told me about Naturals like him, people who could read thoughts. Carter, one of her husbands, was one of them. The quiet man could search your soul, exposing what you didn't want others to know.

Dragonkin.

Curtis rubbed at his scruffy jaw, scratching in contemplation. "Ah, you know my brother."

I recoiled, finding none of Carter's likeness in this monster's eyes. The cruel anger in his words told me he didn't much like the connection.

"Never met him," he continued, "the deserting bastard. If I'd known that Siren was his little thing, I would've fought harder to catch her. Shame." A puff of smoke escaped his nose as though to prove his point, and I was too sick to my stomach to even consider words. "See? No point in lying to me, darling. Now, remember, imaginary friends don't count."

Of course, he was talking about Prince. This wasn't happening.

I jerked as he held my arms above my head with one of his much larger hands, his other reaching behind him. He snapped my hands together with some kind of rope. It wrapped around my wrists, binding them to the point of pain. It smelled of dirty magic and gasoline. Prince was at my side, his face stricken in a silent scream as he watched in horror. Unable to stop what was happening. His pain devoured me, and his guilt drowned me.

"Don't worry, *Prince* can come too." There was a dark, mocking tone in the man's voice as he lifted off me, pulling me into his arms effortlessly.

I dug my nails into whatever skin I could get hold of, the glass in my right hand shredding my skin and his. A hollow sob left me when he brushed off the aggression with little interest. I grew desperate, thrashing as he carried me out of the alley and into the dimly lit street. Someone had to see me, had to see what was happening.

But no one did, or if they had, they didn't care enough to help.

I wrangled my knee to his chest, and Curtis grunted. The unruly growl that slid over me caused me to stop in my tracks. His eyes skimmed over me, a sick look coming over his face. Then, before I could register what was happening, a sharp pinch bit into my arm, and I watched in horror as he pulled back a syringe.

"Didn't want to do that." His angry mumble clouded my thoughts.

My mouth went numb, and my lips tingled. I could feel it settle under my skin as I tried to pull away from him. Panic welled in my chest as my adrenaline spiked. It forced the drug through my veins, making me dizzy, delirious almost. As though my limbs weren't my own.

In what seemed like a matter of seconds, we were back on the main road, the dim streetlamps barely casting our shadows. I could feel the drug taking hold, pulling me under its seductive spell. The man had me in the back of a pickup before I recognized what was happening. He reached under the seat, pulling out a terrifyingly familiar object—duct tape.

I kicked at him, my legs barely making him move before he gripped my ankle and squeezed with enough pressure to bruise it. He jammed a rag into my mouth, the taste distinctly sour, before covering my mouth with a long piece of tape. He didn't spare me a second glance as he slammed the door, walking around the front of the truck with confident strides. I looked around for anything that might help me, a weapon or something to cut the rope. My head was heavy, and I could barely keep it up as I fought back the impending unconsciousness.

His door slamming made me jump, pulling me out of my thoughts. He didn't glance back at me, as though he knew I wouldn't be able to get out of the bindings, and pulled up a small phone, flipping the screen open as he started the truck. He brought it up to his ear, his face stern for a few seconds. When a smile split across his face, I knew that whoever he was trying to contact had answered.

"Why, good morning, you lazy fuck. Glad you could answer my call." There was a pause, and I did my best to hear what the person on the other end said, but couldn't quite catch it. The sound was too mellow for me to pick up.

"Angry? No, just cut to fucking hell. The tip was right on. Found them just past the bridge."

There was another pause, and I could hear a mumbled reply on the other end. The smile never left Curtis's face. "'Bout that. The Siren got away."

And just like that, Curtis confirmed what I'd assumed in the alleyway. It felt like my heart stopped, and a rush of panic came back to me. I was being watched, and I ignored it. I had felt off about it, had known it was a bad idea, and I *ignored* it.

Archon had set us up. *And I fucking ignored it.*

Curtis's face curled into a snarl. "Hey, it wasn't my fault. The other one fought like a fuckin' banshee. Had a vial of Zinnia on her, would've lost them both if I was a fang." He turned to glare at me.

"Well, maybe this wouldn't have happened if you had come instead of sitting on your fucking ass." He rolled his eyes at whatever the other man had said. "Whatever, man, she's going to be a hit. She's a beauty, white hair, violet eyes. The scars are kind of jarring, but you know how those rich bastards are." I jolted at his words, and the man chuckled as though it were all a joke to him. "I know more than a few Naturals that would like to add her to their *collection*."

Curtis turned to give me a sickly grin, and bile rose in my throat. I barely fought it down as he turned back, placing his hands on the wheel in front of him.

"Don't worry, darlin'. I'm sure they'll take good care of you." That same snicker in his voice made me tremble.

I felt exposed, almost like I was back under the knife. This man could dig into me all the same, cut me open and dance among my secrets. The truck was now moving steadily down the road. The movement made me sick, and I had to fight a new wave of nausea.

The air grew chilled, and goosebumps lined my arms. I knew without hesitation that Prince had made it into the truck, his familiar chill cutting through the lull of whatever drugs now coursed through me. He looked bloodthirsty, a snarl marring his usually calm features. He said something I couldn't read on his lips; perhaps in a language I didn't understand. But I didn't need to hear the words to know what they meant.

If he could've, he'd have already killed Curtis.

"We can have the doc check her out when I get there. She should be awake by the time it starts or awake enough to stand, anyway." The man on the other end of the phone didn't seem thrilled about waiting, but Curtis only smiled.

I zoned out, staring ahead at Prince and his intense eyes. What would they have looked like when he was alive? It was hard to guess. I could imagine them blue, shining brightly against his pink-tinged face as he laughed, the smile lighting them up. A vibrant green, glowing in the dark of the night, twinkling with joy as we lay under the stars. Or maybe a soulful brown, with hints of gold in them you could only see if you got close enough?

The only thing I knew for sure was that they were beautiful.

The thick scents of leather and dirt settled in my nose, and I leaned into it—a slight comfort before facing my next hell. Tears welled as I struggled with my bindings, an effort that only served to make my wrists bleed under the strain of the rope.

At least Eliza wasn't here. Had she made it home okay?

I closed my eyes and tried to calm my erratic breathing. I had to do something, anything, to pull into myself and fall away from all this. I didn't want to think about what was going to be waiting for me when I woke, or how bad this idea had been, or how *stupid* I was. I'd felt it the entire way here, that sensation of dread. Felt it as sure as I'd felt the eyes on me while I walked. I should have fought more and convinced Eliza that there were other options.

Because I was stronger than this.

The pressure finally climaxed in my mind, the *Rend* drawing me away from my body just as consciousness left me. How much more would I have to fight for my freedom?

This wasn't what I expected from death.

Chapter 4

Osiris

We had barely stepped out of the car, and already I wanted to turn back and deal with whatever consequences would come from angering the *mighty* Sebek. The rough stench of shifters sat heavy in the air, their unsavory scent killing my already thin patience. One would think the ill-mannered heathens would at least *try* to bathe before coming out in public.

"Is it too late to change our minds? I'm all for a slaughter. Sebek be damned," Fallon said, only half-joking as he crossed his arms and finished, "A dead body can't make a report."

"The dead speak well enough," I said. "If we make a scene here, it will get back to him. He has a knack for knowing when his name has been sullied." I rolled my head from side to side, trying to loosen my shoulders.

Eirik stepped up to my left, taking in my lax stance. His eyebrow rose, though he didn't comment. Instead he shoved his hands into his suit pants pockets. The black material strained as he walked forward.

"Let's just get this over with," he ground out past clenched teeth, effectively ending the conversation.

I approached the door to *The Devil's Details*, unable to mask the scowl at the sight of it. It was the only building for miles, placed so far into the thick Pennsylvania trees that one could only find their way here on purpose or through wickedly bad luck. The canopy of leaves shrouded it from the moonlight, and no lights were visible from inside. Windows weren't commonplace for Vampires or establishments that they frequented. It wasn't good for business if a patron were to burst into flames or if someone were to stroll by and see what was happening inside. See the *auction* that all these Naturals were here for.

That *we* were here for.

It made me tense, knowing how many others were likely in the black-bricked building. I pulled absentmindedly at the cuff of my shirt. While the fabric did well to limit the amount of skin I had exposed, it felt like a crutch, a weakness. I couldn't stop myself from pulling at the offending article, from wanting to limit the skin that these barbarians could touch, even accidentally. The thought of being in close quarters with anyone in this godforsaken establishment brought a sour taste to my mouth.

Curse these wretched events.

I clenched my fist, coming to a stop, almost physically unable to walk any closer. We weren't innocent by any means, but even when Eirik, Nero, and I had been in the prime of our violent days, we never sank so low as to barter on flesh. Betting on people's lives made me sick and Eirik even worse. He practically radiated tense energy. I had known he wouldn't take the news of our appearance here lightly, even less so when he would have to deal with these shifters and their fictitious way of life. He snarled beside me, as if the sight of the building alone was enough to send him into a frenzy. His beast, the part that made him *Úlfheðinn*, hovered just below the surface of his skin, ready to slash out at a moment's notice. His braid was pulled tight, and his tattoo shone against his brutal expression. It was the look of a Norseman on edge, and if he glared any fiercer at the unfortunate bouncer we found ourselves in front of, the man might just burst into flames.

It would be the highlight of my night.

I turned my attention to said shriveling shifter waiting to greet us at the door. He hadn't said a word to us, too busy gaping as he stood as tall as he could manage, though if his physical shaking were anything to go by, I would say we scared the poor boy.

Shame.

He was doing his best to keep his dignity intact. His eyes were steady, and though I watched him swallow harshly, he made no move to fall to our considerable force. Instead, he caught my gaze, eyes widening when he saw my particular defect. My eyes had always drawn attention with their two distinctly different blues. I waited for him to glance away, scream or cry as he realized who I was. Instead, he just continued to stare until I finally stepped toward him, using great care not to recoil at how close I'd gotten. The blood drained from the man's face, and as if suddenly realizing what he was doing, his head shot down with an audible snap.

"Vivas." My voice was crisp, low, and holding the push of a *Charm* as I tapped at the clipboard clenched between the bouncer's fingers.

The added bit of force I laced into my words had the man stuttering as he scanned the list of names, though I doubted he would find it there. We hadn't called to inform Darius of our appearance. We didn't need to. He wouldn't dare turn us away, not even with the chance that we weren't who I said.

The man's hair, ridiculously long and midnight black, was in a bun at the top of his head, like a 'hipster,' as the humans said. The amber hue of his eyes flashed brightly in the night's lingering darkness, showing his shifter heritage. He stuttered, swallowing down his fear as he tried to find the correct thing to say, all while glancing between his feet and my own, trying not to meet my eyes again. The odd coloring was something that was always noticed, and most *knew* I hated when people stared. The fool's indiscretion wouldn't cost him his life this time. I didn't have the time or energy to bother with him.

Adrian cleared his throat behind me, stepping up to stand by my side. He had his arms crossed behind his back in what was supposed to be a disarming manner.

"So, are you going to be letting us in?" Adrian's brogue spoke to his European heritage. The accent was thick as he waved toward the door. Despite his time spent in the States, the lull of the American drawl had yet to take hold of his words.

The doorman only shuffled out of the way, his tail firmly between his legs, so to speak. I strode past him, unwilling to spare the man another glance. Fallon eventually took up space on my right side. He glanced around the room before settling on me.

"Didn't have to scare the poor boy like that," Fallon rumbled, his voice a resounding echo as it bounced off the walls, and more than a few jumped to get out of our way.

Fallon practically bled power, a feat for someone so young. It was likely a surprise to the other Naturals in attendance, most not having seen him in the flesh before. We had expected it when we first sensed the new connection to our bloodline. Sebek had been well over five thousand years old when he turned him. That wasn't the only reason for it, though. Fallon had always been a bit of a brawler, and he could hold his own against Naturals far older than himself. What I wouldn't give to see him and Nero spar again. It had always been a sight to see.

That was the power of our blood. It was why our Crypt was so feared, why we only had to appear once in a blue moon to appease our volatile Maker.

"Should've done more than scare him," Eirik grumbled from somewhere behind us.

I couldn't help but agree. If it were Nero dealing with that shifter, his crass nature and sharp tongue would have likely put that bouncer in his place only slightly faster than he would have snapped his neck. Had *Nero* been here, we wouldn't have been at *The Devil's Details* at all. Hell, he would have burned it down as a warning to those wanting to trade in flesh, like he had the last one. He was surefire, and I could have used that tenacity tonight.

This was where my thoughts always seemed to linger. *What would Nero do?*

I ignored the scrutiny of the onlookers as we continued our trek through the building. We hadn't made a proper appearance since the last Eternium ball, well before losing Nero. This was the first time most of them were formally seeing Adrian and Fallon, the first time they had seen any of us since our loss. So, while I wanted nothing more than to snap at them to look away, I allowed it, stifling a sigh as we walked through the room and found a table at the front of the stage. I flicked the reserved marker off, sending it toppling to the ground, not bothering to check the name as I sank into the chair. I couldn't even pretend to be graceful. I was at my limit, drowning. In what, I wasn't sure. Agitation, fret, boredom? I should have been terrified. Should have the same level of stress that the rest of my brothers had.

But, in truth, I wasn't even worried about the ball, not as I should be. I was tired of dancing around a Maker whose best trait was that he preferred to pretend we didn't exist. And I was tired, so tired of the guilt of a death I couldn't take back.

Just *tired*.

I tapped on the metallic table, settling myself with the soft echo as I surveyed the room, noting the interest still on us. Endless faces looked on, none of which I cared enough about to remember. Instead, I could feel their fear, nearly taste it like pollution in the air. That was how it was, how it was supposed to be. Sebek had *made* us to be feared, and if we had any sense, we would keep true to that statement. At least until after the ball, when he was less likely to tear out our throats for speaking wrong.

"Fucking dishonorable worms," Eirik snarled, eyeing one table.

I spared a glance. Its occupants looked like shifters, Lycan, like him, from the look of it. I vaguely remembered the man at the head of the Pack, his face paling when he noticed us. Edvin Crustava. He was a pathetic sack of a man. So, it was unsurprising that he would be here, of all places. His balding head peaked out past wily white strands of hair, his frame near bone thin. It was his eyes, a vibrant green full of anticipation, that finally made me feel something.

Anger was that unfortunate emotion.

I turned back to Eirik, and I could practically see the wheels turning in our master tactician's mind as he scanned the room. He looked the part of a brute Norseman, at well over seven feet tall, with scars and tattoos covering nearly every inch of his skin. For the most part, that was precisely what he was: *brutal*. But his mind was just as sharp as he was strong. It was likely that he already had several plans to eradicate everyone in this building and get us out without a trace.

"Calm down, Eirik," Fallon said, crossing his arms over his chest as he followed our brother's gaze. "You're making a scene."

"No, a scene would be planting that wretch's head on a spike, then scattering his body parts around the room," Eirik said, so calmly it was like he was discussing tea, not dismemberment. "This is just me contemplating it."

Eirik leaned back, taking another slow appraisal of the growing crowd.

The space felt smaller than it was, tables packed closely together, though the few surrounding ours had scooted away, giving us a wide berth. It was the opposite of what one would expect of a bar owned by a Vampire, with its crisp white walls with old Victorian arches, a white aspen floor, and silver tables. The only splashes of color came from the stage. Harsh brown oak covered it, with blotches of deep red standing against the shiny finish, bringing attention to the velvet curtain that hid the prizes of the night.

"Now, Eri. You agreed to play nice," Adrian chimed in, though he looked no more pleased than Eirik.

Eirik growled, eyes flashing red, then back to blue. His mouth opened, likely to use that silver tongue of his to tear into Adrian, but he didn't speak. Instead, his nose flared, the sound of his harsh breath echoing softly around the table before it too halted. Eirik's eyes cleared for only a moment, surprise taking over his features as he looked around the room. It took only seconds for the sky-blue to morph into a harsher hue, darkening like a clouded sapphire.

"Something wrong?" Adrian asked, his eyebrow raising when Eirik didn't respond to his quip.

Eirik didn't seem to hear Adrian speak, his head still tracing the crowd of Naturals. Some were taking notice, or their focus had never left us. Their attention poked and prodded, before it sank into my skin, feeling distinctly like touch.

I gripped the sleeve of my suit coat, pulling it to cover more of my wrist.

"Do you smell that?" Eirik asked, still searching for something we couldn't see.

He took another deep breath before his eyes clouded over completely, going red and staying that way. The bloodlust sparked confusion, and Eirik looked almost shocked by it. Curiosity got the better of me as I pulled in a measured breath as well, immediately realizing that a soft scent permeated the area around the table. It was sweet, delicate and addicting in the way it glided across my tongue. For a moment, the stress of the evening faded. I wasn't thinking about the room filled to the brim with people, Sebek's rage, or even Nero. There was no *numbness,* only peace and ...

Lavender.

It sparked along my skin, almost out of nowhere, scorching me until the ache of my fangs sizzled at my gums. I had to physically will them away with a harsh press of my tongue against the roof of my mouth.

Strange.

I took a calming breath, intent on purging the scent from my lungs. Unfortunately, that didn't remove the scent. Instead, it forced itself along my skin, into my pores, digging into every inch of me. The unmistakable sound of fangs falling into place and tearing through gums echoed around the room, and that I had to take a second to check if they were mine was troubling enough. Gazing around the table, I focused on Adrian. He looked at me, stunned silent at his display. His typically copper eyes shone red, the entirety of them consumed with the color. Again, I glanced around the table, each of my brothers showing the same startled expression.

"What the fuck is that?" Eirik's voice was roguish and hard.

He was trembling, honest to *Ra* trembling. His scarred hands shook as he tried to fight off the impending bloodlust, and his mouth curled into a snarl like he was barely holding back his fangs. Like he was moments away from ending up precisely as Adrian had. I ran my tongue behind my teeth, putting pressure on the roof of my mouth to subside the overwhelming scent. It didn't work. If anything, it seemed to worsen as the feeling refused to leave me. The murmuring of those around us faded, but I knew their eyes were still on us.

It seemed our discomfort had drawn a crowd.

I turned, forcing my glare at the nearest server, desperate to sample the wine that was driving us mad. It *had* to be the wine. Darius had a knack for his exquisite drinks, often exotic, much like his *auctions.* The waiter question all but sprinted to our table, whispering words of apology as he set the drinks in front of us with staggering speed. His fear should have amused me, but it only made me want to glower at him again.

"What is the special today?"

The server jumped at Fallon's crisp tone. The scent of his panic forced its way over me, drowning out the sweet smell that had been so consuming, and fury blinded me at the loss. The poor busboy struggled to find words as he bowed low at the waist, practically knocking himself over with the force of it.

"It-It's Mr Verslini's special blend, sir. A mixture of Oreads Nymph and Briar Phoenix aged for seventy years. He pulled it from the reserves as soon as he h-heard you were here," he said.

I barely heard his words, and I couldn't find the time to spare him even a glance as I peered at the glass. Some years ago, we had lost our taste for blood wine, its familiar fulfillment slowly fading until it barely curbed our thirst at all. We had resorted to donors every few months to get by, using wine only for the taste. If this 'specialty blend' had somehow relit our ability to gain sustenance from blood wine, then I would need to buy Darius's full stock before we removed him from the territory again. It *had* to be the source of my current dilemma. It would be a pity if it weren't, as I sincerely did not wish to kill the busboy.

It would get my favorite suit bloody.

Not taking a moment to smell the contents, I brought the glass to my lips, and I expected bliss, like the sliding of sunlight across my skin or a fine-aged whisky. Instead, there was only the bitterness of ash. It was putrid, and I had to force myself to swallow as the sourness sat on my tongue and washed over my senses. As I pulled the glass away, my silent anger matched with the growl of Eirik that rumbled over the table. The rage I felt was different from the numbness that had become my life for the better part of the last hundred years. Emotion was trivial, unneeded.

So why was I so *angry*?

The busboy stopped breathing beside us, his face going a harsh red as he registered our displeasure, before he promptly passed out. His body slumped to the floor, his tray clattered to the ground, and the rest of the drinks stained the white aspen red.

Just *wonderful*.

The foul liquid barely curbed my thirst, and I dragged my hands across the table, trying to gain control over my spiraling bloodlust. Again, I glanced up, taking in the conditions of the others.

Adrian was as pale as snow, his fangs standing against his skin and his eyes glowing a dangerous red as he focused on his hands. Like a ticking time bomb, he continued to sit, fighting the bloodlust the scent had brought.

Eirik was barely any better. His scarred hands clenched tightly onto the steel table and the metal bent where his fingers dug. His eyes were as red as Adrian's, and he passed me a look of agony as he again sought the source of the scent.

Of us all, Fallon looked the least unhinged. His face was a sheet of glass, carefully concealed. To those that didn't know him, *truly* know him, he would have appeared unaffected. His hands, however, told another story. There was blood pooling on the table beneath his tightly clenched fists. The nails of his right hand dug so deep into the palm of his left that it surprised me they weren't peeking through the other side. His fangs had yet to drop, but based on the sweat sliding down his neck, I'd say they wouldn't be long.

What the fuck is making this smell?

I glanced around the room, *convinced* we couldn't be the only ones in agony. Staring around the room, however, I realized something. No one else in this infernal building seemed to be affected like we were. Instead, everyone was looking at us like we had gone mad. Most weren't even paying attention to the auction that had started only feet away. If we left now, who knew what they would think of us?

Who knew what would get back to *him*?

No. No, no, *no*. This was a disaster. If Sebek got word of weakness, he wouldn't hesitate to deal with us. Knowing his unyielding volatility, he would cull us, a feat he had likely been planning since I reached the age of Challenge. I couldn't let my brothers perish because of something as simple as a scent, not again.

Never again.

I focused on the stage, *desperate* to get my mind off this crippling feeling. I stopped breathing entirely, something I'd never had trouble with before. I'd grown out of the habit of breathing some three hundred years ago. It wasn't like we needed to, our bodies didn't need oxygen to function. Yet I struggled to keep from pulling in another lungful of that tantalizing smell.

"Now, my dearest friends." Darius's voice was sickeningly sweet, and it pulled my attention to him.

It echoed around the packed room, and my desire to bludgeon something increased nearly tenfold. His name alone made me want to tear out his throat and watch him bleed under the yellow stage lights. His chubby face was lit up rather unflatteringly, and he had his shaggy brown hair greased back against his head, the color standing proudly against his shit-colored brown eyes. His maker must have been one cruel bitch, to have turned him how he was—all thick fat clinging to a short, stocky body. If I remembered right, he was barely over three hundred years turned. If I were to take to the stage it wouldn't even be a fight. He would be in pieces before anyone in the room knew what was happening.

"I have an extraordinary gift for you tonight," he whispered into the mic, gesturing toward the closed curtain.

My will slipped, and I took another slow breath. The scent hit me hard as my head lolled back, and I took a moment to appreciate the unique ensemble. My attention flicked to the stage, to the blood-red curtains behind Darius. The faint sound of another heartbeat roared in my ears, and I finally pinpointed where the smell was coming from. I felt the dilation of my pupils, hidden behind the red sheen of my eyes, as blood pounded in my veins. My body was primed and ready to strike. Every muscle in me seized, begging for the hunt, demanding the kill. I felt like a fledgling, completely and utterly lost to my base instincts. Eirik growled next to me, the sound low and hollow. The table beside us physically jumped as its patrons scrambled away from the furious display.

"A woman, no records on file, a virgin, both blooded and other-wise." Darius's cruel smile made me sick, but the cheers from the crowd did one worse.

They made my mind scream for a slaughter.

I barely caught the end of his sentence, waiting rather eagerly for the revelation. I knew I shouldn't. These auctions were what was wrong with the Natural community. They were nothing more than breeding grounds for filth.

But we could save one. We agreed on it beforehand. Betting would go against our moral code, would go against everything we tried to stand for. But setting her *free?* That we could do. Though, that thought didn't make me feel better about the clench of my jaw and the fangs I couldn't hold back, or the bloodlust that swallowed my base instincts and sought for me to stand and give chase.

"Little thing wouldn't even give us a name. You can pick one for her. If she lasts that long."

Darius's chuckle was like razor blades on my eardrums, but I couldn't seem to focus on it. I couldn't even find the will to be angry with him because behind him was a woman, held tightly by another man I recognized. Curtis Hadfall. He was one of the many sons of the current Dragonkin Eternal. He gripped her arm tightly as if expecting her to run, and from the bandages around his face, I would believe it.

She was small, so small I doubted she'd even reach my shoulders. They had bound her hands so tightly that the ropes were stained a bloody red. Duct tape obscured her mouth, and when she lifted her head, her eyes bore right through me. They were a brilliant violet, shining and marvelous. She practically glowed, ethereal down to her soul. I found I couldn't stop staring. Terror mixed with sheer determination on her face, and I jolted back at the sight. Emotions that hadn't graced my mind in centuries flared to life. Concern. Curiosity. Anxiety. *Need.*

She was a fighter, and the realization that we were monsters in her world made me sick. The bloodlust didn't waver, but a sour feeling settled in my chest over it. She didn't keep her head up for long, as her eyes jerked over the crowd. I could feel her gaze sinking into my skin before she quickly glanced to the floor, clenching her hands tightly as she pulled at her restraints. She jolted beside Curtis when he leaned in and whispered something in her ear. Eirik growled beside me, fury radiating off him.

They had stripped her down into the usual pieces of clothing: a pair of white underwear and a near-see-through blouse. It was something to draw the monsters to the surface. I was disgusted with my reaction, with the way my blood rushed at the sight. She was a pale white, the kind that lacked any color at all, like she had never seen the sun.

And the scars, the thin white lines covered every exposed piece of her. It was easy to tell they were old. Most of them faded and pale. The pained ache caused by seeing them, finally overpowered the arousal that had come with the bloodlust, and I forced my eyes closed to quell the reaction I shouldn't be having. Question after question ate at my curiosity, solidifying my want with each mystery. Her scent hit me again, and even in my long life, nothing of the sort had ever graced my tongue. That was a feat not easily accomplished.

I needed it.

I needed *her*.

"Can I start the bidding at one million for our little glass doll?" Darius's whiny voice again filtered over the crowd, and the need to kill him intensified.

It intensified *greatly*.

I glanced back at my brothers, their eyes following her every movement, glued to her. It was Eirik that turned to me first, and I expected the hunger I saw lurking in his red depths. He had long since torn off the offending piece of the table he had been using as an anchor, and his claws were now dug deep into his thighs, red lines poking through the gouges in his torn suit pants. The pain that sat firmly on his face, however, was what grabbed me. Torture wasn't new to Eirik. He had endured more than any man should, and yet above his hunger, his lust, he wanted to save the girl. I couldn't say I didn't agree with him either.

I pulled the others' attention as my *Charm* bled into the air, and their attention drifted to me with sluggish movements. Adrian only nodded, the movement jerky and borderline painful, before he snapped his head back into the direction of our boggling obsession. Fallon was far more hesitant, and I could see the restraint in his eyes.

The barely controlled restraint.

He picked fights and could hold his own against the likes of Nero and Eirik. He was hotheaded and always ready for a brawl, but he never truly lost his composure. He prided himself on it.

He *lived* for it.

Fallon stared at me, hiding his hunger behind a crumbling wall of self-control. Seeing that he was all but salivating, I realized precisely how fucked we were, and I knew I should worry. But I didn't, couldn't.

"I don't think this is a good idea." The words were grated and stifled on Fallon's lips.

If I hadn't been watching him, I would have assumed it wasn't Fallon who had spoken. His words held neither his characteristic bravado nor his typical chilled charm. Instead, he looked scared, and with a haunting understanding, I realized I felt the same. A mere girl brought the Vivas Crypt to their knees, and she'd done so without so much as a word. She was, logically, something that we should avoid.

Eirik snarled at the words that fell from Fallon's lips, the sound all-consuming, the low reverberation running through the table.

"We can't give her to these bastards. We agreed to save one." Eirik barely spat out the sentence, his teeth grinding hard.

There was a sharpness to his face, his skin pulled taut. The beast beneath his eyes snarled, and that sound found the real world through Eirik's harsh growl.

"Then pick a different one, you terse bastard," Fallon said, his face never losing that laid-back expression.

The tightness of his tone and the choked way he spoke to Eirik said enough about how bad the situation was.

"No," Eirik growled just as fiercely. The word was rich and heavily influenced by Eirik's *Charm*, though Fallon wavered little. The table next to us must have felt it as one dropped from their chair, their gasp echoing in my ear.

Sebek will hear of this.

"If we don't save her, then who? Look at her, Fallon," Eirik said, glancing between the stage and us.

Darius's voice echoed again, calling for another bid. Eirik must have noticed as well, his eyes narrowing. I glimpsed Crustava raising his hand.

"I am aware, but Eirik—" Fallon bit out in a harsh whisper, unable to finish his sentence as Eirik snarled low.

The start of a shift was clear on his face, not like it had been in the leisure room earlier today. Then, he had been angry, and his wolf always came to the surface when emotions ran high. But he was in control of the wolf, not the other way around.

It didn't feel like that was true right now. Eirik looked like he *might* shift, like the wolf was planning on forcing it. If he did, Eirik wouldn't be the one making decisions. Eirik didn't notice, or if he did, he was too lost in whatever this bloodlust was to care.

"*Lítár hana*," he said through clenched teeth, in thick ancient Norse as he pointed to the stage, to the defiant woman who had captured our attention.

Look at her. Fallon hesitated to obey the stiff direction but eventually turned. His face twisted, teeth grinding as his eyes flashed red.

"You would leave her to them?" I chimed in, hoping to sway him.

He turned his icy glare toward me.

"We're going to leave the rest to them. Where's your righteous indignation for the others?" Fallon asked, his voice holding all the calm he likely couldn't feel.

He was right, of course. We had set out to save one, one of however many Darius had. It was the rule, only one successful bid per table. Not even my age could sway the rules, not here, not when a show could lead to negative attention. Though it seemed we were causing a scene either way.

Darius called another bid, and silence met the room.

We were out of time.

"We need to make a choice," I said, and Eirik was already speaking as I called the vote.

"Aye," he said, once again looking at me.

Blood-red eyes swallowed the typical sky-blue. I wouldn't have been surprised if it wasn't the most emotion the Norseman had shown in the last hundred years.

"Yes," Adrian chimed in from his spot, his face twisted into a grimace as he focused on not breathing.

I dragged my attention to Fallon, holding on to what little control I could as I waited for his final verdict. I refused to go against one of my brothers. We hadn't made it this far by turning on each other. When we did something, we *all* had to agree to it. So if Fallon shook his head, that would be the end. My nails dug into the skin of my palms as I waited anxiously, watching closely as Fallon's jaw clenched. I could see the turmoil beneath his skin as he struggled with his decision.

"Fucking dammit," Fallon hissed the words through gritted teeth as his head bobbed slightly, barely noticeable, but it was enough.

I flung myself out of my seat, the screech of the metal chair against the wooden floor echoing in the room. I couldn't find the will to care that the auction patrons were staring at me like I was the newest freak show at a circus. Instead, my gaze landed on Darius. He looked like a ghost whose skin might spontaneously combust, and after what I was about to say, it just might.

"Twenty million."

CHAPTER 5

AALIYAH

"Twenty million."

Those two words echoed off the walls before bouncing back and strangling me. I couldn't see him, the man that called out the bid, his hauntingly melodic voice getting lost in the seemingly endless crowd. They'd roared and screamed every obscenity, shouted things meant to tear and gouge. But the moment those two words swept over the floor? Everyone in the room fell silent, like they were as terrified of the man with the commanding voice as I was.

Twenty million. That was how much I was worth. My life, my freedom. *Me.*

The lights above burned my eyes, making it near impossible to gauge any details about my surroundings. The numbing disorientation was only made worse by the lingering effects of the drugs in my system, and the terror that still clung to my limbs. I did everything I could to gain my bearings as panic set in, forcing deep breaths as I tried to focus on something, anything, to get my mind off this place.

Twenty million.

Curtis leaned down from his place next to me, so close I could feel the heat from his breath. I barely took notice of it, too numb to breathe, let alone think.

"Better get a good look, doll," he said, running a finger across my cheek, forcing my head toward the table directly in front of the stage. "The Vivas Crypt got your bid, and I have a feeling they're the type to play with their food."

I flinched, unable not to as Curtis spoke. I didn't really take notice as Curtis stood straight again, gripping my arm tight enough to leave bruises. I was too focused on what I saw, the men who sat at the silver table. They looked ravenous, feral, and it *terrified* me. I felt the fear in my bones like it was instinctual, and it gave me a chill that made my teeth clatter, and goosebumps rise on my skin. I shook, unable to look away.

Vampires. The men at that table were Vampires. I could hear Eliza's warning, loud and clear, ringing in my mind like a mantra. I clenched my battered hand, and the ache of the still-open wound barely kept me sane enough not to burst into hysterics.

They draw you in with their good looks and their charm.

I hadn't understood then, didn't realize how much sway they had with only a look. Didn't understand that terror clung to them like it did those at the compound.

They'll tear you apart if you give them a chance, Ali.

Monsters.

These men fit Eliza's description. They looked like wild, barely controlled beasts. Their eyes were blood-red, covering every inch from white to iris, glowing even against the bright lights of the stage, sticking out in the crowd. The color seemed to shift as if agitated, provoking an eerie jolt to shoot through me. I knew they'd sealed my fate when Darius practically tumbled over himself to confirm the bid. The squeaky pitch of his voice expressed his blatant excitement. I pulled against Curtis again, glaring at his smiling face as I fought against his bruising hold. I wouldn't lose myself again. I would die first.

"Sold to the Vivas Crypt!" Darius's scream was shrill, and it only made me struggle harder.

The skin at my wrists tore as I pulled desperately at my shackles, trying to jerk away from Curtis, even knowing I didn't stand a chance. Curtis laughed, *laughed*, as I struggled, holding my arm with an unrelenting grip. Just as I was about to slip into a complete breakdown, something flashed in front of me.

Prince. *My* Prince. Always there to hold me together, even when I didn't feel like there was anything left to save. His expression was calm, with a slight smile gracing his lips. That look was the farthest from what I'd expected, what I'd grown to know. He glanced over his shoulder, looking at the table that held my buyers, the very word making me sick. Surely when he saw their faces, their blatant bloodlust, he'd understand, and he would be just as furious as I was.

But when he turned back to me, that same look was on his face. Calm, collected, even *soft*.

What was happening?

He raised his hand, using his pointer and middle finger to point at his eyes. He was trying to tell me it was *all clear*. I looked at him in disbelief, part of me questioning if the man in front of me was *my* Prince. He smiled again, pressing that same hand over his heart, pinky and ring finger down. I choked on my gag, tears finally coming up, cracking the numb exterior that had taken over. It was our sign that he would always have my back, that I could trust him and that he would always protect me.

Forever. It was our sign for forever.

"Better get you back there and ready for pickup," Curtis said, dragging me away before I could come to terms with how Prince was acting.

He was the last thing I saw before the door to the tiny back-stage room slammed closed and I was locked in with Curtis, who still didn't let up on his grip. If anything, he squeezed tighter, and the pain shot up my arm, wrapping around my throat, trapping my scream in it.

Never make noise.

The mantra, like a broken record, repeated in my mind every time I got hurt. A reminder of how angry Castillion used to get when I'd scream. I hated it on regular occasions, but now it seemed to burn even worse. I *wanted* to scream, fight, and cry.

But I couldn't even give myself that.

The room was small, only a few paces between the muted gray walls, with only one other door on the far side. There was no furniture, only cold stone stained with dusky brown blotches beneath my bare feet.

The door at my back clicked, opening behind me, and Curtis practically threw me to the ground as he pulled Darius in for a firm embrace. A shock went through my body as I fought back another cry, my arms screaming in protest as the impact rattled my bones.

They get more violent if they hear noise.

I pulled myself to the wall with quiet movements, desperate not to draw their attention, and when I finally hit the cold concrete, I stifled a sigh of relief. At least now they couldn't get behind me.

"Did the Vivas Crypt just bid? At my auction?" Darius was screaming incredulously, shaking Curtis, who held a similar expression.

"I told you she was going to be a hit, Darius. I *told* you. This could be our in with them, a way to make amends!" Curtis said as he turned toward me, greedy wonder in his eyes.

"Yes, you're right. They obviously enjoyed themselves, and with Nero no longer in the picture, they must be more open to our way of business. I'm sure we can come up with something." Darius squealed like a child opening a Christmas gift, not a grown man who had just sold somebody like cattle. "We might even get an invitation to Eternium!"

Curtis rolled his eyes, body tensing as he turned back toward Darius. I was glad to have his gaze off me as I took a few seconds to search the room again. But it was still empty. Completely and utterly empty. The only thing I could think to do was rush to the door on the other side of the room. I glanced at Curtis, his maimed face doing nothing but adding to his intimidating stature.

Instead of running, though, I froze. I cursed myself, pushing myself to move so harshly I shook. Yet nothing happened. I just stayed pinned to the wall like a coward. I hated myself in that instant, hated Curtis and Darius and the men that bought me. I bit down on my tears, choking on them.

"Fuck the Eternium," replied Curtis, his gaze flicking to me. "It's not as glamorous as you would think. Bunch of pompous asses drinking fine wine and congratulating themselves for fucking off for the last quarter millennia."

Curtis's attention sank into me like a brand, freezing all thoughts I had. I was unable to move as that sick twisting smile spread across his lips, showing that he'd heard everything. If I ran, he would enjoy every second of catching me.

"Though maybe we can convince the Vivas' fangs to share their new toy. After all, I went through all that trouble to get her." Curtis spoke like one would about a meal, and the hatred that had bubbled up inside of me thundered through me like a storm.

How many times had they done this before? How many women had gone through this same torment? It made me sick to my stomach, and all I could do was panic as Curtis turned toward me fully. No matter how far into the ground I sank, I couldn't get him to look away. A whimper slipped past the gag in my mouth, sounding more like a gargled cry than anything.

"Curtis, perhaps you shouldn't ..." Darius whispered, but Curtis paid him no mind as he walked up to me briskly, the smile never leaving his face.

He stepped close, the toes of his boots brushing my thigh, and the overwhelming stench of alcohol flooded my nose. He looked paler than he had at the truck, sickly. His brown hair was stringy, and the longer he lingered next to me the more he smelled distinctly like rot. Someone had covered his left eye with a small bandage, that side of his face obviously mangled.

I raised my head a little higher at that.

"Come on, Darius, live a little. I won't do anything permanent. I just want to make sure she's ready for them." Curtis reached out, and I slammed myself hard against the wall, evading his grasp for only a second.

In my panic, I instinctively searched the room for Prince, until the feeling of being trapped built inside me, pressing against my organs and muddying my blood. A numbness swelled in my chest until there was no more room left to breathe, and I came to the burning realization that Prince wasn't here. He hadn't followed from the auction hall.

I was all alone with these men. Truly alone.

Curtis lifted me effortlessly, putting me on my feet with my back against the wall. He forced my head up and seemed to stare straight through me as he assessed my face before he glanced down. The pupils of his copper eyes dilated, the round shape morphing into a sharp diamond as they glowed. If he felt my body quake, he ignored it.

"What made them like that, doll? What about *you* made the infamous Vivas Crypt crack?" Curtis leaned in close, running his nose across my neck. I froze.

"You smell normal."

Instincts that didn't feel like my own kept me still. I couldn't run, even as I begged my body to do something. I stifled the cry that built in my throat as he ran a tongue along my neck.

"You taste normal ..." Curtis said, his laugh shaking my body as I tried to pull away. "Sour, even."

Everything in me screamed to move, to fight. But I couldn't respond, the fear paralyzing me. Castillion's voice echoed in my head, bouncing around my mind, fraying what was left of my nerves.

Such a good girl, Glass. I knew you wouldn't run.

I choked on the memory that had come to me in Curtis's truck. Castillion had left my cell open, had taunted me with freedom, then broke every bone he could when I tried to claim it.

"Curtis, that's enough. Osiris will be here any moment, and I don't think he'd be—" Darius's words tapered off, drowned out by the voice of my old tormentor blaring in my mind.

We're going to have lots of fun, aren't we, Glass?

He'd stared at me for hours, taunting me, telling me everything he would do to me when he was finally given the okay to do more than just get my blood and run his tests. He'd had the same expression Curtis did now.

Like I was something he could take.

Curtis lifted his hands to my chest, and the spell that kept me still broke, snapping like dead wood. Castillion had stolen a lot from me, my childhood, my life, but I knew he'd never gotten this.

And I would die before Curtis got it.

My knee shot up, finding the area between his legs. He released a startled gasp, dropping his hands as he stumbled away from me. I tried not to wobble as I pushed past him, my body groaning in protest as I threw myself at the door on the opposite side of the room. My bare feet thundered against the ground, and my heart roared in my ears, drowning out all other sounds.

I had to get home.

My bound hands had barely touched the handle before something yanked me backward. Large fingers gripped my hair, and I didn't have time to cry out as my spine hit an unyielding wall. The motion was savage, and it ripped my breath away.

Those same fingers stayed buried in my hair, and pain exploded in my skull as the hand tightened. I couldn't stop the whimper that slipped out at the sight of the door fading slowly to black.

Too slow.

Chapter 6

Osiris

"Did that really just happen?" Adrian asked, a look of muddled confusion on his face.

He glanced at the thin metal door that led to the stage room where the auction had taken place, rubbing at his neck. We were in one of the small waiting rooms now, having been ushered in just after they dragged the woman offstage and the curtain had dropped. Much like the rest of the building, the room held white walls with some Victorian flare. The only thing in it was a single black couch, the scent of stale blood covering what was left of the gentle lavender that had taken over our minds. The floor, a cold gray concrete, gave off a distinctive echo as Eirik paced.

"We bid," Eirik said, stopping just long enough to reach up to his neck, his hand running over the jagged scar there, before he began again.

Rational thought had come back shortly after the auction officials had placed us here. The room was closed off from the rest of the building, and it hadn't taken long for the air to clear until there was only the barest hint of *her*. So, though it was still there, the bloodlust was less, and the more time we had to wallow, the more it came crashing down on us. I sank into the couch, cringing as my hands rubbed against the coarse leather.

We had bid under a charade of kindness that only masked the blood-lust that still drove our instincts. We had *bid* with malicious intent exactly as the rest had, though at least they had the gall to admit it, and the thought of that burned. Bidding on a life we had no right to dictate, craving something that wasn't ours to take.

How shameful.

I sucked hard at my gums, and my fangs gave way with extreme protest, pulling in and leaving dull teeth in their wake. My eyes settled next. The red sheen that had covered them faded, and a painful ache lingered behind them. Adrenaline still soared in my blood, leaving a chill behind as it slowly dissipated. The cold from unsatisfied bloodlust sank farther into my skin, burying deeper than expected. The uncomfortable sensation further cleared my mind.

It was such an intriguing feeling, the cold mixing with need until they were one. I took a deep breath, thoroughly disappointed by the lack of sweet lavender in the air and equally disgusted with my want for it to return.

"We did," I said, finally answering Eirik's strangled words.

"What a cluster fuck," Fallon said, his head buried in his palms.

"Any thoughts on a plan?" I asked, running my hand through my hair, tugging at the black strands with a harsh pull, trying my best to think at least somewhat rationally about what our best option might be.

"Kill everyone in the building and hope notice of our behavior doesn't reach Sebek before the Eternium?" Fallon's voice was harsh, holding every bit of fury in his body.

His eyes, which had narrowed into two thin green slits, closed as he struggled with keeping that forced laxness in his body. He didn't breathe, not that we needed to.

"Too late for that, Fally," Adrian whispered from his spot by the door. He was leaning against the wall, ear pressed to the chilled surface. His eyes were closed; and his focus entirely on what was happening on the other side. "Most that didn't claim a bid have already left."

"Then we hunt them down. Make a show out of it," Fallon snapped back, flexing his hands. "If nothing else it will clear this damned bloodlust."

Adrian opened his eyes at that, rolling them at Fallon's emotional outburst. They didn't happen often. In fact, I could count them all on one hand. The anger he tried to shove down came up as his emotions built, and I could see his need to brawl in those small tics that most wouldn't notice. His glower shot to me, tracing my spot on the couch.

"What do you have to say about this, Osiris? Awfully quiet after that declaration in the auction room." Another hiss and grumble from Fallon made me sigh.

I expected his volatility the moment he agreed to the bid, and it was hard enough to reason with him when he was calm, the stubborn man, but when he was like this?

Practically impossible.

"We retrieve her and go home. We can figure out the rest from there, in *private*," I said.

That calmed Fallon's fight enough for him to roll his eyes, and grab a candy from his breast pocket. Eirik stopped his pacing, though he didn't let go of his neck or the small fake silver chain around it. The solidarity that we were in this together pulled them back enough to see reason. We lived together. We fought together. We bonded together. We were the only family we had, as broken and dysfunctional as we were. We couldn't lean on each other if we broke that trust, and I wouldn't fail my brothers again. I would never repeat the mistake that cost Nero his life.

"Well, I don't think we'll have to wait much longer," Adrian said, pulling away from the wall to sit next to me. He leaned back, the leather crinkling beneath him, rolling his neck as a smile slipped seamlessly onto his lips. "Sounds like the cavalry's here."

As if on cue, a knock sounded at the door and in walked a young man. He kept his head down, black hair obscuring the top part of his face. He tilted forward into a shallow bow before straightening. It only took one look to know he was a type of Waterborn Natural, though I couldn't quite decide what branch. Small blue scales crept up his neck from out of his crisp black suit, and the smell of salt overwhelmed every other scent in the room.

"Darius sent me to retrieve you for pickup, *Challe* Vivas," the man said with a monotone drawl. His words made me tense, and I narrowed my eyes in warning, though the man didn't move.

Challe. One in a position of Challenge. Most would be more than happy to hear the term and revel in its advantage. This man didn't know the extent of my hatred for the word seeking to tear apart my family, so I said nothing of it.

"The rest of your Crypt is welcome to wait here for testing. But only one of you is allowed in the back for pickup," he said.

Eirik snarled, the deep growl so loud that it boomed off the walls. The man, again, didn't falter or move from his stiff position. He was likely so well trained that things like this no longer fazed him, and a hint of remorse covered the rage, if only for a second.

"Please follow me." The man gestured toward the door, ignoring Eirik's stunned glance and my own scrutiny.

He turned, and just as quickly as he came, opened the door for me to follow him. I took a deep breath, once again greeted by the subtle aroma of lavender. It ignited my senses as it had before. Though it wasn't nearly as overwhelming, my gums still ached, and I could feel the surge of adrenaline in my blood soar to life. Guilt again crept along my consciousness, and the man's words sank in. I glanced around the bare room and the small, plush black couch that graced it. It was as scrubbed clean as one could make it, the distinctive scent of bleach covering far less pleasant smells. Though some things couldn't be erased, and now that I had time to breathe in the room's air, I realized that the sour odor of fear coated every wall, every surface from the couch to the floor.

"There will be no testing. She'll spend no more time here," I said as her eyes appeared to me again like a phantom flashing across my subconscious.

Violet, vivid, and full of the fury one would expect. The thought of them made me tense, and I found it difficult to walk through the open door. I had been alive far too long to feel out of my element and had thousands of years of experience to rely on. So for me to be anything less than self-confident in a situation like this was ridiculous. *Why*, then, was I finding it hard to calm my erratic heart? Why was I more worried about her thoughts of me than I was of Sebek's inevitable reaction to our appearance tonight? It was as boggling as it was terrifying. It was a challenge I couldn't stop myself from wanting more of.

"Of course, Sir Vivas," the man said, emphasizing the word 'Sir.'

So, he had sensed my dislike of the title he had started with. He once again gestured toward the open door. He was perfectly cordial, though I could hear the growing agitation in his tone.

"We'll meet you by the car, Osi. Try not to get lost." Adrian's voice, smooth and playful, rang in my ears, and his nickname for me made my eye twitch.

I had grown used to his quips after he refused to stop with them. He thought they drew us closer together. No one else dared to use them besides him, and since he was our brother, we allowed it. Adrian's natural charm was out in force, and it was apparent he was trying to defuse the situation. A goofy smile landed on his lips as he turned around, clapping Fallon and Eirik hard on their backs. Neither of them so much as grunted at the impact. The smack resounded throughout the room, and their blank glares landed on our youngest brother. They walked through the open door, heading for the front entrance.

I watched until they disappeared from view, then turned, following my escort through the auction room and toward the back of the building.

"You can make your payment just beyond the stage. Pickup is the door on the left just past the desk," the man said, bowing again. "Thank you for your patronage."

Then he was gone, the thick scent of salt the only trace left of him.

I hurried toward the back where I had been directed, to where they housed the pickup area. It took everything in my power to not *flit* there. While it was faster and more convenient, moving at speeds that most other Naturals couldn't see drew too much attention. The force of moving itself was likely to knock things over, and people could always seem to tell when a Vampire was *flitting* near them. Their instincts told them to run, causing their blood to pump faster for us. So even though it pained me to walk casually, I did. This night was already a disaster. No need to make it any worse.

The back of the auction house was as Victorian as the rest of the building. Long crimson curtains over crisp white walls. The counting desk stood tall, the aged mahogany coming up to my chest.

The payment process itself was painless. A swipe of plastic and the transaction was complete. The ability to flaunt money so easily was still strange to me, and I found I missed the days when wealth meant castles and a calling of men at your back. When loyalty was one's most formidable form of power. Now it was all suits and deceiving smiles. These days lacked the class of the past.

The man that had taken my order practically beamed at me as I put away the card. If he noticed my foul mood, he didn't comment on it, his wrinkled face lighting up as he reached out and grabbed my hand before I could think of moving away. The feeling of his skin against mine nearly sent me into a frenzy, and the seductive power of rage boiled in my blood. I didn't have the chance to stop the shudder that moved its way through me, and I couldn't keep my carefully trained facade in place.

Panic seized my spine before I could stop it, and unwanted memories crawled their way up my throat. Had I started the touch, I could have stilted my reaction, and acted like a Turned of Sebek should. Thoughts of my weakness mixed with furious, indignant hostility inside of me. I longed for more cover, for my skin to be hidden behind a wall of cloth. But gloved hands were a crutch. They were another way for your enemies to attack you or, even worse, *judge* you. I bit down hard, the grind of my teeth echoing in my ears as I shoved back the need to remove the man's arm from his body. It seemed money made these people forget who I was.

I let a dark smirk settle over my face as I leaned down, keeping the man's hand firmly placed in mine, even as the contact left a sickening feeling in my stomach. I needed the front to confirm that I was as bad as Sebek in his feeble mind. That my wrath wasn't worth calling our Maker. Even if the act of doing so made me physically ill.

The man's gray eyes dilated, and I could see the exact moment he realized his mistake. His breath picked up, and he began to tremble uncontrollably, covering my weakness with his own fear. I tilted my head to the side, giving him a fanged smile before releasing him. Its intended effect was supposed to be a show of mercy. To show what I could do to him. In reality, I ripped my hand away, so intent on removing his touch I nearly tore his arm off with it. He threw himself to the side. So eager was he to get out of my way, he tripped over his own feet.

The feel of his fear consumed me, and slowly that sickening crawl of disgust faded. It drew my mind away from our guest as I walked to the door that housed her. I willfully took a deep breath in an attempt to level myself. The mystery woman's scent on the air calmed me in ways I never thought were possible. My stomach settled, and panic ebbed from my limbs. I could hear her hidden just beyond the threshold. Mere feet away. Even now, she was all I found myself drawn to.

Muffled sounds slipped through the cracks of the door. Darius and Curtis were speaking of something, though I didn't bother focusing on their words. Instead, I flexed my hands as I hunched down, trying to seem less intimidating. The girl had been terrified when she saw us earlier, a reasonable response considering we likely looked no better than savages. I grimaced, tugging at my sleeves again. We would have to work to rectify that image. I didn't think I could handle having her fear directed at me again. The very thought of it caused my chest to burn and a dull ache to settle there.

I reached for the handle of the door that separated us. My priority was getting her out of this squalor and to somewhere she could feel safe. As I was about to turn the intricate handle, gold against the door's white, I heard something that made my blood go cold. Ice slithered through my veins, and rage reignited in my belly.

The crack of a slap echoed through the door, and the sound sent me into a vicious spiral. The gagged whimper that followed destroyed any hope of an amicable solution. I practically ripped the door off its hinges as I tore it open, not even bothering to turn the handle. The lock gave way from the pressure I put on it, and splinters of wood shot out around me.

Curtis hovered over her, with his hand raised like he was going to hit her again. Confusion blended with surprise on his sharp features, and his fury was palpable in the air, as was his pain. Though most sickeningly, past all that, was his arousal.

"Release her."

The explosive force of my *Charm* wrenching itself to the surface had Darius whimpering as he stepped back. At the same time, the *Flame* came to life in my veins, running like a loose spark along my skin as I dug my fingers into Curtis's throat, ripping him off her, as he also scampered back from the press of my command. The *Flame*, like it had its own mind, crawled across Curtis's skin, up to his face. It did little damage, his Dragonkin blood making him mostly resistant to fire, but the heat was enough to make him scream. I tried to focus on him, keep myself as calm as possible, and avoid a bloodbath. Until I heard a body crumple to the ground.

I turned, my gaze catching hers as she hit the hard floor, her body going limp. Her eyes were blank as she tried to register what had happened, and the blooming red that lit up her cheek had me visibly shaking. Blood slipped down her face, dripping off her chin, past the gag he had placed on her.

"Please, *Challe* Vivas," Darius started from across the room, his voice cracking on each word, fear clouding the room and souring the taste in my mouth.

His use of the title was meant to placate and soothe. *Challenger Vivas.* I hated it, hated every syllable that reminded me this life was never mine, that Sebek would always dictate it. Darius was pressed so close to the door leading to the stage that he practically melded with it. He swallowed before continuing.

"Curtis meant no disrespect. Your purchase tried to run, and he was only subduing it for you." Darius's words had me snapping my attention to him, stopping his speech with just a look.

No disrespect.

"Curtis Hadfall struck *her*," I said, squeezing the neck of the squirming worm under my hand. The monster didn't see her as anything but a sale. "A woman under my protection, through my right of the bid."

The deadly calm of my words caused Darius to jolt.

"A mistake, surely. I beg you to forgive my foolish partner for his transgression," Darius said, desperately looking between me and a still-struggling Curtis.

I squeezed harder on his neck, tapping at the vein beneath my finger without breaking eye contact with Darius. I could kill the Dragonkin so easily, have both of them gutted before either could scream. But I held back, trampling down the disgusting feeling of Curtis's skin and the sick look on Darius's face.

"It is a mistake that I will not tolerate a repeat of. Your operation in my territory is over, *Darius* Vercelli," I said, hissing his name like a curse. "That you returned at all is enough to make my blood boil."

My hatred for the name alone was enough to make Darius go pale at my words, his mouth opening and closing rapidly. He wasn't the Darius I knew all those years ago, before my turn, but the namesake was enough to condemn him to me. His auction had been the final straw over a hundred years ago and that he returned was just another insult. I let up enough for Curtis to gasp for air, though I couldn't find the will to release him yet.

"I implore you to reconsider. Surely that is too cruel a punishment, over a blood bag no less," Darius said, trying to appeal to my nature, the same one he shared.

As though the thought of her blood would make me see reason, and it did, just not how he thought it would. I heard her ragged breathing, the scent of lavender clouded by the sour scent of fear. It sparked blood-lust; it sparked curiosity. Things that I could find inside of the two men that dared to disrespect my Crypt in such a way.

"Surely you wouldn't close one of the most influential Natural Hotspots in Pennsylvania over such a minor discretion. Curtis barely touched her, and her face will heal," Darius said again, raising his hands, trying to act like he wasn't shaking.

That icy rage held me prisoner as I turned, fully facing Darius without letting up on my grip. The arousal in the air was all too apparent now. I hadn't thought Curtis would be stupid enough to act on it.

"Touched her?" I whispered, once again clenching Curtis's neck.

The thought of him *looking* at her that way made every instinct I had in me scream. I knew he had been taken with her, but if he *touched* her? I held back, just enough to keep from killing him on the spot. She was right behind me, watching me. I could hear still her sharp breaths, still scent the sourness of fear in the air. I couldn't make this worse by killing Curtis in front of her. She already thought me a monster. I didn't want to confirm it for her.

"I misspoke. Please let me explain," Darius stumbled over his words, catching his mistake, trying to gain more time to find an excuse I didn't have the control to hear.

I cut him off, swinging my free hand out in front of me.

"I am past my limit for patience tonight, Vercelli." I heard her shuffle. A pained gasp caught in her throat, and my hand tightened around Curtis's neck until he began to choke. "Did he touch her?"

"Yes. Her chest." He couldn't lie, not when my *Charm* was shattering his will and forcing his truth. The red sheen that had faded away after the auction covered my eyes again. "But, only clothed. He wouldn't have disgraced you or your Crypt by going any further, *Challe* Vivas."

I wasn't listening as I again faced the struggling Dragonkin beneath my hand. Curtis cowered as he stared at me, looking like he was going to beg for his life. Part of me wanted him to. I wanted to hear his cries for mercy as I tore his limbs off and ripped him apart. His face was a sickly pale white, and trails of blood fell from his nose and the corners of his eyes. I could see his veins move under his skin, fluttering unnaturally because of his increased heartbeat. The stutter of it was perplexing. There was no way I'd done this much damage, yet he was already at death's door. The fool. I wanted to drop him and his useless body to the floor, to let him die the same way he seemed to live.

Pathetically.

Had he not reached up, dragging his hands across my exposed face to get away, I would have. But the feeling of his fingers on my skin, the touch almost feather-light, caused me to snap. Everything that had led to that point compacted, burning down to my bones. My left hand was in his chest before I could take a moment to think about my actions, before Curtis could so much as whisper an apology. I wrapped my fingers around his heart, clenching my fist as it beat viciously against my palm, before I ripped it out with sick satisfaction. Curtis stared at me as if surprised I held his heart in my hand.

"Useless," I sneered at him, the word like acid on my tongue, as I threw his heart to the ground, his body quickly following as I released my hold on his neck.

His blood coated me, a harsh ashen red, ruining my favorite suit. Not even his death sated me, I realized, as I stared at the useless sack of flesh that had molded to the ground. He had deserved far worse. I turned my wrath to Darius again, daring him to make a move. *begging* him to. I wanted more blood. I wanted to hear him scream for what his partner did.

"You are to be out of my territory by first sun," I said, brushing my hand against my suit coat, serving only to spread the blood.

Darius's face lit up, twisting with rage as he looked between me and the body that was now on the floor.

"Do you have any idea what you just did?" Darius asked, looking as disbelieving as he did terrified.

"I do," I said, scowling as Darius jolted, mouth agape.

"You killed kin of the Dragonkin Eternal. A son," Darius continued to mumble, and the sound was nearly enough for me to go after him as well.

Like Eternal Teviticus didn't have hundreds more. Sons who weren't cowards that dealt in flesh.

"Perhaps you didn't hear me. I said *I know* what I did."

Darius stopped talking, eyes firmly on mine, wide and unblinking. "I'll send my regards to Eternal Teviticus and tell him to pay for my dry cleaning. For the trouble of his son's blood on my suit."

I didn't throw out empty words. I would be in discussion with Teviticus, and he would likely do just that. I was above him in age, in power, and I was now in line for *Challenge* despite how much I loathed it. He would bend over backward to continue being on the Vampire Eternal's winning side, the worm. Not to mention Curtis had been a bane to the Eternals since his hatch, and having touched something that was no longer his, I was well within my rights to seek revenge.

I didn't look toward the wall, toward the eyes that were still on me. I could feel them tracing my skin like the blood that dripped down my hand, splattering on the floor. I could taste her fear in the air, and it culled my rage, making me realize I still saw red. I took a deep breath, pulling back on my fangs and letting the red bleed away.

"You have till sun up, Darius," I said.

"You can't do this. I've got permission from the Vampire Eternal to sell here!" His words, high-pitched and whiny, did little more than irritate me further.

"And I have rescinded your permission as head of the Pennsylvania Sector," I said, turning away from him and toward the bundle on the floor, huddled in the corner by the door I had destroyed.

"You'll regret this. Just like Nero—" The sound of my brother's name on his sullied lips tore into my skin, and I cut off Darius before he could finish.

"You do not speak his name!" I snarled, and Darius's mouth snapped shut, his entire body trembling as the force of my words shook him. My *Charm* snapped against his skin until he was gasping for breath. "The only thing I regret is not removing you sooner, you worthless parasite."

I turned, staring one more time at the man that was quickly approaching the same fate as his partner.

"Now get out of my *fucking* sight." There wasn't any *Charm* in my words this time. I didn't need them. "Or die like Curtis."

I dared him to move, practically begging him to give me a reason to rip out his throat. But he backed off, one hand held up in a defensive position, the other trembling as it landed on the door leading to the stage; though not moving to open it. I made no move toward him, and he was out the door before I could have stepped forward. He wasn't worth it, not now that I had far more pressing things to be dealing with.

Like cleaning up the mess I just made.

My resolve shattered when my eyes landed on the slight frame curled into a ball on the ground. I looked down at myself with barely concealed revulsion.

"Fuck."

I ran my clean hand across my jaw, somehow still managing to smear blood across my lips. The ashen taste, much like the wine from earlier, burned my throat like it was acid. It tasted nothing of a regular Dragonkin, and I let the question of *why* distract me while I contemplated my next move.

This was already going worse than I would have hoped. I didn't want to be a monster in her eyes. Yet all I had done so far was prove I was precisely that—a mess of broken pieces held together by a nature just as sinister. Part of me wanted to walk away now, to save her from the fate we had planned for her. She was light even in the face of the darkness that this building held.

Yet, I couldn't stop myself. I knew in the pits of my blackened soul that I was too selfish for that. I desired to sate my curiosity, and I only hoped she could come to forgive me for that.

I inched over to her slowly, crouching down to her level. I tried not to move too quickly as I reached my mostly unbloodied hand up to her face. Of course, it wasn't intentional. I could still feel the lick of nausea hugging the back of my mind from mere moments ago. But for reasons I couldn't quite discern, that wasn't deterring me.

I had never in my life wanted something as desperately as I wanted to feel her skin. That I should desire to touch this girl after centuries of avoiding the feeling of it was beyond intriguing. I should have *Charmed* her and got her to the car with haste, but I couldn't stop myself. The need to bring her comfort practically consumed me.

Her flinch shouldn't have hurt as much as it did. It was the flinch of unwanted contact—a burst of understanding tinged with regret pooled in my mouth. She practically jumped out of her skin to get away from me, though she didn't make any noise. I fought my frown, trying to keep my gaze level with her. Catching her eyes was both the best and the worst decision of my life. Hers searched mine as if looking for the pain she was sure I was waiting to deliver. As if she *expected* it.

I reached up again slowly, holding her gaze as I pulled the tape away from her mouth. The pain caused by removing it reflected in those beautiful violet eyes. A rag fell from her mouth, covered in her blood and the sour scent of gasoline. I desperately wanted to run my fingers along the scrapes on her cheeks to soothe the battered skin.

So strange.

I kept a tight leash on the bloodlust that still clung to the back of my mind. Although it was still there, pushing me to lean forward and sink fangs into her, it was less now, and my fangs stayed hidden in my gums. Her eyes bored into mine, still searching. Finally, I cleared my voice the best I could and spoke, trying to level her nerves. At least a bit.

"It's going to be okay," I said, hiding the husky tone of my voice behind my worry.

Her expression hazed over for a moment, and I took that time to assess myself. I couldn't very well carry her like this. I shrugged off my suit jacket, using a clean part to remove most of the blood from my left hand. I didn't bother to lift it from the floor.

I wanted to ask her if she could stand or walk, but my instincts took over as I pulled her into my arms. She was so small against me, like a porcelain doll. The bare skin of her legs sat against my right hand, and I reveled because for the first time in a very long time, the feeling of someone else's skin against mine didn't revolt me.

I held her a little closer.

She shook relentlessly in my arms, as though she were trying to decide whether she wanted to fight my hold.

"I've got you now." The words tumbled from me before I could stop them. "Sleep."

I didn't want to force my *Charm*, but she needed to rest. And I needed her to stop looking at me like that. Because if she didn't, I might have gone and ripped off Darius's head if only to satiate my need for violence for a moment longer. She seemed startled as her eyes slowly drifted closed, and her head fell back against me. *Hope* was the last thing I saw, buried in those violet depths before they were stolen away from me. It made my chest tighten, and I held her a little closer.

Ah yes, we were *fucked*.

Chapter 7

Fallon

What a cluster fuck.

The bloodlust was all-consuming, and the gnawing endlessness of it made rage settle in my stomach. My throat burned at the thought of that tantalizing delicacy just below the mysterious lass's skin. I shoved away the raging desire, and forced the tremble in my hands to stop with the only thing I could think to use.

Pain.

My nails sank deep into my palms, and that sweet, insistent ache was barely enough to keep me from acting on the impulse to chase. To kill.

I needed a good fight, and I wouldn't be getting one here.

"You alright, Fal?" Adrian asked.

I could sense his gaze on me as we left the building, his anxiety building as I continued to walk. I barely heard him, barely heard anything but the soft flutter of a heartbeat that was too far away. The girl's eyes flashed in my mind as if taunting me. Then dragging me forward into a pit of loathing acceptance. To thoughts of *her*, my sweet Aislinn. Of blood against a barren ground, and the weak flutter of a pulse dying under my fingers as I tried to force myself away from a failing body. I ground my teeth, trying to get my fangs to pull back into my gums.

The chill of the night didn't faze me as we stopped in front of Osiris's coveted *custom-made,* four-seater McLaren. The sun was still a few hours from rising, and its heat had long since departed from the cold earth. I ground my teeth again as my nose flared. Even outside I couldn't seem to purge the scent of lavender mixed with dark chocolate from my system. My head tilted forward, and my eyes slid closed for only a second before they shot open. I glanced around the nearly empty parking lot, sucking in a harsh breath when I realized I'd lost my sense. Exposed. Vulnerable. Those were not words that I used to describe myself, not now.

Never again.

I wanted to curse this mystery woman for this distraction, for tearing down the power I had over my instincts. Why did she have to stare at me with eyes that begged to be saved? And curse me for being unable to leave the lass to the fate that would have awaited her.

A hand settled on my shoulder, and I knew by the heat that seeped into my skin that it was Eirik. He said something I was too lost in my thoughts to hear.

I could only see Aislinn, her sepia skin and endless black eyes. Hear her voice, berating me for wanting to leave the girl to her devices when I knew we had the means to save her. Aislinn had a gentle soul, one that was deserving of far better than what she got. Far better than I'd been for her. She would have been furious had I left the girl stranded in the hands of a beast far worse than us. That reason alone was why I'd agreed to the bid that still felt sour.

What a *damned* cluster fuck.

"Fallon." Eirik flipped me around, finally dragging me to look at him.

"What?" I bit out, jerking out of Eirik's hand and taking a step back.

Eirik looked less than sure at my response. His head shook, and a worried expression spread across his face. The emotion was barely there. A twitch of his eyebrow and the twist of the scar that stretched over his face. The dragon tattoo that surrounded it appeared to coil like a snake preparing to strike as his eyes narrowed. The sky-blues swirled with the flecks of his beast that had slipped to the surface, darkening the hue. It was a giveaway for Eirik, something that let you know his beast lingered close to the surface. You didn't spend two hundred years around someone and not pick up on their ticks, on what made them *them.*

"What?" I raged, feeling more cornered out in the open than I had inside *The Devil's Details.*

There was strain on the Viking's face as his jaw clenched. He struggled to say something more, something to encourage or spur me on. I knew he wanted to tell me to pull myself together. But he didn't. He'd never been one for motivational words, though he tried. I knew why. We all did, which was precisely why I said nothing else.

It was hard to fill someone's shoes, especially someone like Nero.

I clenched and unclenched my hands, unable to keep my eyes off the door to *The Devil's Details.* This was a fucking mistake.

"What do you think is taking him so long?" Adrian all but groaned his question, his impatience showing as he leaned back on the car. There was a distinct lack of tension in his voice and a mischievous mirth in his eyes that I hadn't seen in years.

"She's probably scared," Eirik answered, finally leaving me in peace as he turned his attention to the door.

I bit my tongue, nodding at Eirik. She had every right to be scared, and she should be. We were unnatural. Dead.

And we bought her like savages.

Her hands were clean and unstained.

Blood against a barren ground, in my mouth, on my skin.

I could still feel her stare from her spot on the elevated stage, filled with rage, panic and fear.

More. I always wanted more. The Maker's call couldn't be denied, no matter how much I screamed at myself to stop.

"We need to get rid of her."

A distinct sound of indignation followed my words. I wasn't sure if it came from Adrian or Eirik, but one thing was certain. They didn't like my idea.

"Why would we do that?" Adrian asked, scoffing at my suggestion.

He didn't avert his attention away from the building. Instead, he studied the crisp, black brickwork, tracing each detail as if it would make Osiris move any faster. His disregard for the situation made my blood boil.

"Are you daft?" The bite in my tone had Adrian jerking his head to face me, his brow raising. His confusion drew on my frustratingly volatile emotions, on my fury. "We took her against her will. *We bought her.* We agreed we would save her, not trap her in another hell." I nearly choked on the words and their implications.

Bought. We *bought* her.

Monsters.

"We paid for her freedom, and you have the gall to ask why we'd *let her go?*"

Adrian's face twisted into a scowl, and he went to say something, to quip back, but I was already moving.

"And what about you, Eirik?" I seethed.

Eirik's entire body flexed as he shot me a pointed glare. He already knew where I was going with this. The pain in his eyes was blatant. I could *feel* it. It burned me, digging into my skin like that damned scent. It tore me down until I was nothing but crumbling ashes.

"Do you feel the same? Do you want to *keep* her? You saw the scars."

I heard Adrian protest in the background as Eirik recoiled and reached for his neck, his hand hovering over the scar that tore through the skin there. I didn't know exactly what had happened. The damned bastard wouldn't tell us. None of our elder brothers had been very forthcoming about their pasts, but in this case, I didn't need him to. I knew enough to prod to get my point across. I gritted my teeth, pushing the building guilt down with determination. He needed to hear this, to understand that whatever this girl did to us in there was trouble. My nails dug into my palms again, and the pain kept me silent as Eirik spoke.

"No," Eirik said, voice sure, even with the growl that sank into the end of the word. He scowled, and part of me sank, drowning in his confident tone. "We agreed to save one, and we did. Our intentions are nothing like—"

"Nothing!" I half screamed, cutting him off as I grabbed his shirt, dragging him down to eye level.

He was taller than me by several inches, and his eyes went wide before he could register my movement. I took him by surprise, and the

Viking snarled as his *Úlfhéðinn* swirled in his ocean blues. I hoped he could see my intensity, my desperation.

See the fear I couldn't find the strength to voice.

"You were both as bloodthirsty as I was in that room. Fuck, Osiris was foaming at the mouth!" I said, jabbing my hand toward the door. Internal conflict raged inside me; I yearned for Osiris to open the door but dreaded what it might mean for the future.

The mention of our brother had Eirik settling, a knowing look on his face. He'd seen it too and had felt Osiris's power swirling around the room. He'd seen the volatile emotions in our eldest brother's eyes, the pure, undivided interest. The girl having that kind of power over him was dangerous in more ways than one.

"Tell me, what had you intended for her then? Did you want to hold her close? Tell her she was *safe*?" I hissed the word.

Safety was a joke meant to make fools feel comforted in their short, dreary lives. Safety was an illusion that we broke the moment we bid. Eirik's eyes narrowed, his head turning away from my steadfast gaze. I couldn't tell if he was agreeing or getting ready to fight. It didn't stop me, not when panic nipped at my heels, and everything drove me to get out of this situation.

Blood against a barren ground.

"No, I didn't think so." I released Eirik's shirt as I pulled back, my fingers numb from how tightly I'd been holding on. I crossed my arms over my chest, trying to drive away the anxiety in my stomach. "You wanted to tear out her throat. You wanted to see if she tastes as good as she smells."

There was a distinctly calming tone to my words, one that didn't match the intention portrayed.

"You wanted to destroy her, and you would have loved every second. Just like I would have, just like I want to *now*." I admitted my weakness, admitted to what I desperately wanted to hide.

I said the words, choking on the panic they brought—anything to get them to understand that this was a mistake.

"It's not like that." Eirik's confident tone wavered as he glanced between me and the door.

I could see resignation slowly overcoming the bloodlust, and while I was glad he saw reason, something else jumped to the surface. He tapped at the scar on his neck again before his hand fell to his side, clenching into a tight fist. An emotion I wasn't expecting shadowed my rage, one I couldn't cope with.

Regret.

"Then, by all means, open my eyes, Eirik. Tell me so I can understand why we're risking the ire of Sebek for a girl none of us knows. Why we're willing to let someone unknown into our lives, so close to what could be our downfall," I said, and Eirik didn't respond. His jaw clenched tight, though the swirling of his eyes didn't stop.

"What do you suggest, Fal?" Adrian's calm voice jerked my attention away from Eirik.

I froze, unable to plan a sentence that my mind found acceptable. I wanted to tell Adrian we should let her go, return her to where she'd been taken from. Or to her home. To anywhere but near us. But I couldn't force the words out, even as I screamed in my mind that it was what we needed. Something held me back, kept me from saying what I knew to be best, strangling me with what I craved but didn't want to admit.

"I don't know," I said.

The pain in my palms no longer held back the things I felt, and I could no longer focus on anything but the desire that burned in my blood.

"You've gone mad, brother," Adrian said, his head shaking, looking disappointed.

"She's dangerous," I choked out.

Adrian scoffed, his eyes rolling as he leaned back onto the car, the metal groaning under his weight.

"Dangerous, Fally?" Adrian asked in a mocking tone.

I grit my teeth.

"Dangerous doesn't have to mean the danger of the body." No, she was dangerous because of what she could do to our sanity, to our carefully constructed peace since Nero's death. "She brought us to heel, all of us. That is a threat. You cannot deny me that, Adrian."

He didn't look fazed by my statement. If anything, he seemed at ease.

"Why'd you agree to the bid, then?"

I jolted back, unable to form the words to defend my actions.

I bid because she destroyed my will to fight my instincts. I bid because the thought of missing out on her delectable scent had me ready to tear apart everyone in the room. I was prepared to go to war if it meant I could steal her for myself, if only for a moment.

I was a monster. I *bid* because I was a monster.

"Something changed your mind. Something pushed you to agree," Adrian said.

Adrian knew me like he knew the back of his hand. Of all my brothers, he and I had bonded the most thanks to how similar our turns were. He knew nightmares still haunted me because they followed him as well.

"I agreed to keep the peace," I managed.

"No, that's not it. You felt it too, past the bloodlust." Adrian stepped toward me, his copper eyes glowing in the darkness. "You're scared."

It wasn't a question. It didn't need to be because he knew. He feared the same thing I did, a feeling our brothers couldn't help us with, even with all their experience. Losing control and falling to the *Maker's Call* that still held us.

Blood against a barren ground.

"I'm afraid," Adrian said, breaking the silence. "But I've also never felt more alive."

His words jolted down my spine, and I almost felt numb for a second.

"You agreed to the bid, Fallon. I won't let you go back on your word. Not now. Not until we've at least spoken to her." By the burn in Adrian's eyes, I knew then that I'd lost. Eirik once again placed his hand on my shoulder.

I couldn't get out of this.

"This is a mistake," I tried.

"No, Fallon," Eirik interrupted me. "We've already decided. We will speak with her."

Like that, the conversation was over, and a silence that felt foreign bit into my consciousness. Aislinn's face skirted across my mind. Her soft smile, how her eyes would light up when I returned home. Turmoil raged inside of me, threatening to spill over my mask.

Only when Eirik turned away, facing the door to *The Devil's Details* again, did I drop my mask enough to take a slow breath. The girl's scent, barely there, washed over me like a calming wave against the sandy beaches of my childhood home. My fangs burned in my mouth, and I briefly considered *flitting* to the house to avoid occupying the tight space of the car with her.

Could I do this? Did I even have a choice?

Monster.

"You know, you have far more important things to worry about, Fally," Adrian started, a glint of mischief in his eyes. He hadn't turned away from me as Eirik had. "Like how you're planning on winning *The Lisa* back from me."

Adrian, always the peacekeeper. I scoffed but found it impossible to not drop my shoulders. He had a knack for getting on my nerves. But he also knew me, and I could see his need to distract me, to keep me from slipping into the past, as he knew I would.

"We should do pool again. That was fun," Adrian said, sighing wistfully as I shook my head.

"Why would we do that? It's my choice, and I think I've had enough of betting on pool," I replied.

The only reason we played it to begin with was because it had been Adrian's turn to pick our game. His sheepish smile told me he'd been hoping I would forget.

"I choose chess."

Adrian's smile morphed into a shocked glare as he gasped.

"Absolutely not. That's not fair!" he said, pointing at me. "I just won *The Lisa*. At least give me a chance to hang her up first."

"Don't worry, *brother*," I said, shaking my head at Adrian's indigent huff. "We can play tomorrow. That will give you some time to come to terms with your defeat."

"Damn it, I shouldn't have said anything. Fine! Chess it is, you supercilious bastard ..." Adrian said, crossing his arms. "At least give me a piece of chocolate to soothe my battered nerves."

"If you win tomorrow, then you can have one."

"Oh, stop *teasing*. Now you're just being cruel." Adrian leaned against the McLaren with heavy exasperation, the sound of the bowing metal reverberating as he did.

"And you need to stop pouting," I quipped back, and he continued to point his mocking glare in my direction. It lacked heat and had done precisely as he wanted it to. It distracted me, and I found I wasn't upset with that.

"I'm not pouting. I'm trying to figure out how to become a master of chess in oh ..." He glanced at his wrist and the non-existent watch there. "Forty-five minutes."

I had another quip readied when the sound of a door opening stopped my words flat. I tensed and was again reminded of the predicament we found ourselves in. The heady scent of lavender and rich chocolate took over again. I huffed, ignoring the cold, all my focus on the door as Osiris stepped into the crisp air, a bundle in his arms. His flit was crisp and clean as he appeared in front of us, moving so sharply that I barely saw it. Though there was far more to see than just that.

Like the blood that coated him. It had a sharp taste, like the dying embers of a fire. It matched the scent of the one I'd caught just after the lass had made it on stage.

A Dragonkin.

"You smell like shit," Eirik gracefully supplied, huffing when Osiris raised an eyebrow.

The harsh Norse drawl clung to his words sharply, a growl lingering in the air after he finished speaking. I didn't have to see his eyes to know that his beast was lurking behind them, using the proud Norseman's eyes as his own. My skin tightened like prey, which in this case, wasn't entirely wrong. Wolves were dangerous to Vampires, and our instincts knew it even if I knew Eirik would never turn on me.

"I take it things didn't go well then?" Eirik asked, moving to take off his suit coat, laying it against his arms.

Osiris stared at Eirik with blinding, unchecked emotion. His arms tensed, and he looked between us. It made that sick feeling of wrong crawl up my throat again, and I almost protested before Osiris spoke.

"Darius is to be out of our territory by sunup," Osiris said, turning his attention to Adrian. "Make sure he is, Adrian,"

The malice sat easily in Osiris's eyes, a direct contrast to the lowered tone of his voice. Adrian only nodded, seemingly unsurprised at how our eldest was acting. Just as quickly, Osiris's expression grew soft, and his posture relaxed as he stole a glimpse of the lass in his arms. He held her, his skin against hers, *unflinching*.

It was difficult for Osiris to touch us, his family for centuries, with cloth between our skin. Seeing him so at ease with a stranger felt wrong. Yet he held her close like he was basking in it. He'd killed someone tonight, likely going against what was no doubt Sebek's word by turning Darius away from the territory. And now, he held her like it was all he wanted to do.

I turned toward the car, hopping into the front seat before any protest could be made, too distracted by the panic in my stomach to care about whatever else they had to say.

We were monsters. Bloodthirsty, broken, and held together by what was left of Nero's memory. This girl, she was going to break us.

And there's nothing I can do to stop it. Worse of all, part of me doesn't want to.

Chapter 8

Eirik

The car door slammed, and Adrian sighed.

"Well, I take it I'm not going to get to hold her, so I'll go comfort Fally," he said, shaking his head as he smiled. Osiris shot Adrian a questioning look.

"He's still a touch upset about the bid. Though, not in the usual Fallon way ..." Adrian's voice trailed off.

The usual Fallon way was to throw a punch first and deal with the consequences after. Even I had to admit that Fallon's outburst was concerning. He was cold, calculating, and he never backed down from a fight. Until tonight. There had been genuine fear in his eyes, fear I hadn't seen since his turn. A sliver of guilt formed in my chest.

Nero would've noticed, would've known what to do. But we weren't Nero.

"I think he's scared about the *Call*, Osiris," Adrian added, giving our brother a pat on the shoulder as he turned to get in the car.

Osiris's eyes narrowed again, his worry expanding past the woman in his arms as he really looked at Adrian.

"Are you—?" Osiris asked, his thought getting cut off by Adrian's easy laugh.

"No. I haven't felt the pull since we were first in the auction hall. I don't think Fallon has either, but it's got him scared. Just keep that in mind. He's probably going to be a bit more temperamental than normal."

Then he was in the car, and I could hear his quips with Fallon begin again. They were closer to each other, able to relate with their similar turns. It helped them stay grounded.

I turned, facing Osiris as he realized I was the only one left outside the car. It was obvious he struggled with himself to walk closer to me.

I couldn't blame him.

I clenched and unclenched my fists, keeping my arms steady with my suit jacket draped over them. A content sigh fell from my lips when she settled into my arms, and her body seemed to sag into my own. I wrapped my jacket around her frame, all but drowning her in the fabric. The coat reached down to her knees, swallowing her. Even after she was covered entirely, my beast didn't settle. I could feel him crawling around in my head, nipping at my control as he tried to fight his way to the front of my mind. His agitation was palpable, and I didn't understand this almost panicked desire to comfort this girl. *Úlfhéðinns* were territorial of their family, which I knew well, but for this feeling to be swallowing me so completely over a stranger, over someone whose name I didn't even know?

It was strange, but my beast didn't seem to care.

When she shivered again, I pulled her closer and glanced at the car. Shiver bumps lined the skin I could see, and it seemed my body heat wasn't enough to ward off the cold. I kept her close as Osiris opened the door for me, his face still holding that sickeningly sweet *smile*. In reality, it was a tilt of his lips, barely shown at all.

But damn, if it wasn't the most we'd gotten from him in years.

It was a damn frigid day in hell for him to be fawning over anything that wasn't his whisky collection. The sight of it left a strange feeling in my chest—a mix of ire and elation. I hated that the emotion sat so smoothly on his chiseled face like it was meant to be there. Even though he'd smiled *kindly* maybe three fucking times before this, and not a single one of those times was in the last hundred years.

I grumbled as I forced my large body into the car, taking every care not to jostle the girl in my arms. When I was firmly seated and Osiris got one last look at her, the door closed.

Her gentle scent washed over me, far less consuming than it had been at the auction but still strong enough to make me want to drop fang. It settled me, my beast curling into a slumbering position behind my eyes as we stared down at her. My chest swelled with heat and emotions that weren't quite mine as he watched her with an admiration that left me as confused as it did calm. A rumble bubbled up from deep within me, as my beast made a melody meant to bring her comfort. I half expected her to jump out of her skin at the sound, even with the *Charm* that made her sleep. Though the beast intended no harm in it, it didn't sound friendly. Especially not to a young woman, even a sleeping one.

But today was full of surprises.

Rather than turn away, she buried her head in my chest; a deep, content sigh coming from her as she breathed me in. The rumble rolled over her, relaxing her tense muscles. She looked so at peace and perfect against my bulky frame. I was large for a Norseman, but even so close to Adrian, she just looked ... tiny.

There was a time when that superior height was supposed to help me in battle, before it had been used against me. I slid my shaking hand against her cheek, ignoring the scars that covered it. Now wasn't the time for these thoughts. There never would be a time if I had anything to do with it. She leaned into my touch, her body struggling to get closer than she already was. A growl slid up my throat with surprising ease, it's vibration echoing in the small chamber, all but shaking the metal. The girl stayed asleep as she listened to my beast's purr. At that moment, I knew I'd do anything to keep that contented expression on her face.

Fuck.

"I wonder what her name is." Adrian didn't mention the noises I made, didn't poke fun at me for it. Instead, he focused his attention solely on the girl in my arms, his hand reaching out to brush a stray piece of white hair off her face.

"Me too." An aching feeling settled in my chest at the content smile on her lips.

It was easier to see her now, really see her vibrant snow-white hair muddled with dirt and dried blood, misty eyelashes against high cheek-bones and alabaster skin. She looked like a goddess, fallen from grace. I ran my thumb across her chin, over a small white line that stood against it—the battle scar of a warrior still fighting her battles. No, goddess wasn't quite right.

She was a *Valkyrja*, steadfast, beautiful, and enchanting.

Tiny, my beast supplied, echoing my previous thoughts. The sound of his unused voice bounced around in my skull.

"We should remove the bindings on her wrists while she sleeps. I don't wish to harm her when she wakes." Osiris's voice echoed softly in the small space, and it surprised me how quiet it was. It was likely he was taking every precaution not to wake her. I glanced down at her face. For the moment, it was calm.

I could only imagine how that was going to change when she woke. She was going to come out swinging, and I was *ready* for it. I'd seen what she'd done to the Dragonkin, had scented his blood on her skin. She was a fighter, a fact that made my beast swell with a pride that I shared.

I brushed my thumb over her thin jaw, unable to keep from touching her. My beast settled under my skin, still staring through my eyes, rumbling softly for the girl we didn't know. I nodded to Osiris, realizing that everyone was looking at me to move. Fallon, the prick, even looked worried. Good, it would be good for him to learn to do something besides glare.

I motioned for Adrian to come closer, which he did near-instantly, unclipping his seatbelt and sliding toward me. I gently slid her head into his lap, and his hand immediately found purchase in her hair. She leaned into the touch, falling seamlessly into his gentle ministration. A growl forced its way out, my beast snarling in the cage of my mind. I damn near dragged her back to my lap.

I ground my teeth hard, berating myself for acting like such a pup.

Like a fucking idiot.

I gently pulled my jacket away from her sleeping body, revealing her bound hands and the vicious stains of red on her pale skin.

And the rest of her.

The white lace of the auction shirt emphasized her pale skin, hiding most of the scars that Darius likely didn't want bidders to see. Scars that would have turned most into trembling messes, but I'd seen the fire in her eyes. The will to live, to fight.

Like a Valkyrja.

When I saw her on the stage, I knew above everything else that we would help her. I didn't care about the bloodlust that still plagued me, or Sebek's petty anger. She had the heart of a warrior, and no warrior deserved to be caged. My free hand wandered up to my neck on instinct. I saw myself on that stage, gagged and beaten bloody. Not understanding where I was, as I was sold into the life that led me here. To my brothers. I'd decided long before the others agreed that she would not meet that same fate. I would have killed everyone in that room if it had come to it.

And it would have been a bloody, brilliant fight.

I reluctantly laid my hands on the ropes at her wrists, untying the knot with more care than I thought possible. I did my best to avoid looking at her scars. They littered her body, marking nearly every part of her skin.

"Eri." Panic laced Adrian's voice. "Look at her hand."

Glass shards that had escaped my first inspection, nasty jagged things, stuck out of her palm, and it was only now that I realized her wrists weren't the only things bleeding. The shards sliced deep, mangled, and mixed with the blood of another. The scent was harsh, and I leaned in, studying it. It was like a lit flame and volcanic sulfur—the Dragonkin.

"Curtis Hadfall." Osiris's words echoed above my snarl, his tone grave and satisfied, as I realized the scent matched the gore on his suit. I caught his gaze in the rearview mirror, and he didn't need to say anything else.

Osiris didn't use bloodshed as a fear tactic. He didn't need to when a glance was enough to make kings drop to their knees. Curtis got the side of Osiris that you wished never came out, the part of him that could ignore his distaste for touch. *Rex interfectorem.* If you were unfortunate enough to earn that privilege... Well...

Curtis got what was coming to him.

"We'll take care of it when we arrive. Remove the rope," Osiris said, turning to face the road.

My scarred hands shook as I pulled it away as delicately as I could manage, biting back a growl as it tugged at her tender skin. It was raw and bleeding, proof of her struggle. I ran my thumb over the abused flesh, brushing at the scars and the still-open wounds. Her scent hit me hard again. It was like her blood on my skin had relit the fuse that had ignited at the auction. The ruby-red liquid sang to me, and my finger warmed where the blood sat, causing minor shocks to spread throughout my body. Everything in me wanted me to bring it to my mouth to taste her, the need nearly all-consuming.

"That's a bad idea, Eri." Adrian's husky voice echoed in the car, and he stared at me with barely controlled bloodlust.

His eyes were hazed over as he did his best to stop his fangs from dropping. His hands were still buried in her hair, her face now contorted in pain that I hadn't realized I'd likely caused. That was the only thing that stopped me from licking her essence off my finger. I forced myself to bring my hand down to my jacket. I wiped the blood on the hem, doing my best not to touch her skin. Her hands rested on her stomach as I wrapped her up again, hiding her from us. I leaned back and looked away to stop the surge of bloodlust.

After a few seconds I spared a glance at Adrian. His eyes were closed tightly as his expression twisted into what I could only call a painful grimace. He had his fingers wrapped gently in the strands of the girl's dirty white hair. My hands clenched as I reached out and cupped her cheek, unable to resist the urge to touch her. I glided my thumb over her skin, settling on her chin.

"If you're finished." Fallon's voice was solemn when he spoke. The harsh Australian Aboriginal brogue of his native tongue mixed so heavily with the early Irish of his parents that it was nearly impossible to distinguish either of the accents. "We're home," he finished, his words clipped.

He scowled at the bundle in Adrian's and my arms, and though he tried to hide it, jealousy burned deep in the green depths. His face twisted, and he was out of the car so fast the glass of the window nearly shattered as he slammed the door behind him. A smirk came easy. Pissing off Fallon was often the best part of my day. It was nearly the only time we could get anything but indifference to spark in his eyes. I hated to see him so drawn into himself, lost in a past he couldn't change. He reminded me too much of myself as a pup. I couldn't let him fall for as long as I did. He needed guidance and family. He needed someone to knock him on his damn head.

But that had been Nero's job, and I hadn't been the best at picking it back up after his death.

"Bring her into the house. The *Charm* should last a few hours yet, so we have time to figure out what to do next," Osiris said on an exhale.

His commanding voice was steady, leaving no room for protest. My arms slid under the woman laid across my lap, pulling her to my chest securely. Adrian opened the car door for me, and all too soon we were in our home.

The quaint living room was nearly bare, much like the rest of the house. We'd never gotten around to decorating it more than it was. What little things were added had mostly come from Nero. His changes were subtle and easy to miss, contrasting the Gladiator's standoffish nature. He'd hung small trinkets along the walls, trophies from our feats, swords older than even I, fans, cards, carvings... They were so seamless that you couldn't really see them without looking, but they were there, painting our lives across our home.

The harsh stone I favored littered the walls that weren't taken up by Nero's small decorations. Osiris's gray color scheme was seen along the floors and the walls that weren't stone. Adrian's kitchen, designed meticulously by our youngest himself, boasted mixed marble counters and pristine black oak floors. Fallon, with his love of windows and everything comfortable. The latter hadn't been a problem. Each of the few pieces of furniture, a couch, and the dining chairs had been picked with care. Each matching the gray scheme. Even a few of his paintings had been included over the years, the color bringing warmth to the cold rooms. But the windows?

That had been a fight for the ages.

Fallon had held his own against Osiris at barely a hundred years old. Though, once a brawler, always a brawler. It was why he and Nero had meshed so well. Both liked to fight; wanted the thrill of blood being spilled through blows, not teeth. Then, after the dust had settled, the compromise had been the heavy metal shutters to protect us if we were ever to wake during the day.

Fallon leaned against the floor-to-ceiling window that sat just past the kitchen, near the family room. It overlooked our property and was his usual spot to enjoy the scenery.

"I still think this was a mistake." Fallon's nervous words pulled my attention from the woman in my arms.

His uncharacteristic fretting left an unsettling feeling in my stomach. He was probably right, and I knew in my soul, down to my bones, that this would get messy. We'd bought her, and we'd been ready to tear everyone in that room apart if it meant we got to her first. I still felt it, that craving. *The lust.* The strain I experienced was as mental as it was physical—something that happened in a blood frenzy—but that didn't make me feel any better about my reaction. It was easier to contain now but still very much there. It taunted me, tempting me with the things I could do.

The fire in her eyes. The softness of her skin. Yes. My beast's muddled, broken words echoed in my mind, and the strain in my pants grew a little tighter.

I cracked my neck, forcing the tension out.

"Too late for that, Fal," Adrian said with a click of his tongue. He walked over to the island in the middle of the kitchen, dragging out a few glasses that were tucked underneath it. With a shake of his head and a haughty smirk, he served up four glasses of pixie wine. "We already had this conversation. Do you really feel like losing your silver tongue twice today?"

Under normal circumstances, I would've been ecstatic about the rare treat, even more so when I knew drinking it would piss off Osiris. It was one of his older bottles, picked up some three hundred years ago when we were traveling in China. Instead, I was empty, almost numb at the thought of drinking it. Adrian drained his glass, his face contorting into a look of disgust. His mouth opened in a hiss, and I could see that his fangs were on display.

"I didn't lose. You're too stubborn to understand the gravity of the situation," Fallon seethed, once again steaming with rage.

His hands clenched and unclenched, prepping for a fight that Adrian couldn't give him. Fallon had *always* been a brawler. Unfortunately, none of us could match that seemingly endless need to fight that he and Nero had. It showed more and more in recent years how much he missed those brawls with our second eldest. Fallon bound up to Adrian, stealing a glass from his hands. Fallon didn't even try to hide his distaste for the wine, spitting it into the sink before dumping the rest.

"We fall to the sun in less than an hour, and Osiris's *Charm* won't last until tomorrow evening," Fallon said. "At the very least, she will try to escape."

I jolted at that word, nearly growling at it.

"At worst, she has access to us when we are weakest, unable to defend ourselves from her attacks." Fallon's glare jumped from Adrian to Osiris.

I knew what he would say before he said it, and I tried to get to him before he could destroy what little sanity Osiris seemed to hold on to.

"Fallon ..." He ignored me, his eyes burning with everything he obviously didn't want to feel.

"Are you going to stand by again, Osiris? Let us die like Nero?" Fallon's seethed words echoed before the room fell silent.

I couldn't have missed Osiris's shudder if I tried, his eyes snapping closed. Osiris grabbed at the cuff of his shirt, his throat bobbing. I clutched the bundle closer to me, my beast raging in me, filling me to the brim with irrational thoughts that I couldn't stop, thoughts that were only half my own.

He's going to take her away from us!

The deep, rumbling snarl started in my belly and quickly rose to my throat. It was the call of challenge, of war. My beast was ready to fight Fallon, to tear him apart. For a shocking moment, that same fear I'd seen in Fallon's eyes crept up my spine. *Because I would never hurt him, but my wolf sure as fuck wanted to.*

Osiris lifted his hand, still stained a fiery red, and the single motion silenced the rest of us.

"You speak out of anger, Fallon. Calm yourself," Osiris said, a deadly stillness showing as he looked at the dried trails of blood across his skin and the red stains on his dress shirt.

He moved across the room, stopping at the sink. He washed his hands, the movements meticulous and controlled, until the only hint of blood was in the shirt he wore. Fallon's mouth snapped shut, anger and regret keeping him from speaking further.

"It's already decided," Osiris said, Fallon's frustrated plea going unnoticed as Osiris turned toward me.

"Not you too, Osiris. You can't—"

Osiris shook his head, standing tall and *flitting* back to me. He paused briefly, hovering his hand over the woman's pale cheek. My beast snapped and snarled when he realized the other side of her face was marked purple like she'd been struck.

"*We* have already decided. You had your chance to dispute it.' Osiris placed his palm against her cheek with a sigh.

The sight had me jerking backward, the shock stilling even my beast. Yet, there was no tremble, no tension in Osiris's body.

"*What's* been decided?" Fallon raged, his hands clenched so tightly at his sides I half expected him to throw himself at Osiris. But he held steady, his furious eyes focused on where Osiris's hand pressed against her cheek. "We agreed to save her. There, she's saved. Now what? Do you intend to just give free rein of our home?" Fallon went on behind us.

"Oh, I know. Let's leave her the key to the shutters. I've been itching to remember what the sun feels like."

Osiris pulled away, turning his rigid gaze toward our seething brother. The tick of the clock and the slow breaths of the woman were the only things that broke the silence.

"She'll be fine until nightfall," Osiris said, jaw firming and hand clenching.

"What?" Fallon's confusion matched my own.

Osiris spared a glance at the stairs that lead up to our rooms, and my blood ran cold.

"No." Fallon seemed to pick up on it just as quickly. "No, you are *not* putting her there."

There was furious indignation in Fallon's tone, the kind that tore people apart from the inside, leaving their interiors bare. Osiris didn't even move, numbness sinking into his eyes.

"Osiris ..." I said, unable to manage anything else.

It burned to even think about, this would cross a boundary. It would open a floodgate of memories and pain we painstakingly kept buried.

She couldn't stay in Nero's room.

"It's the safest option for her *and* us. If you have any alternatives, say them now."

There weren't any. We didn't have any extra rooms. But that didn't make it feel any better. I stole another glance at her face, tracing the smooth skin. The calm of sleep replaced the panic of the auction, and it shook my resolve.

Could I let her stay in Nero's room? We hadn't even opened the door in years ... We'd left it exactly as it was, unfurnished but his bed.

"We get rid of her," Fallon seethed, but Osiris was done with the conversation.

Instead, he turned his attention toward Adrian, who was currently staring at an empty bottle of wine with a sick look on his face.

"We must call a vote." Osiris's commanding voice left no room for argument.

"No. Whatever the fuck you're planning, my answer is *no.*" Fallon's grated words slithered across the room, and I looked at the girl again.

I snarled low in my throat, my beast making it clear how he felt. She was *not* leaving his sight, and I couldn't say I didn't feel the same. For whatever fucking reason, I couldn't.

"She did something to us, something that I've never felt. Keeping that feeling unknown is dangerous, and if we don't figure out what it is and how to avoid it, we leave ourselves open to attack. Even you can't deny that, Fallon." Osiris's words were said with a chilling grace.

This was the Osiris of old, the one that always got what he wanted. It sent a jolt of trepidation through me to see the calculation in his eyes as he played at Fallon's own insecurity. Doubt crept into my thoughts, and even my wolf went silent. Osiris's off-color blue eyes found me, their numbness now blinding.

I wanted her to stay as much as the others did, but Osiris didn't snap. He hadn't looked like this for centuries ... and I had to admit, it scared the shit out of me to see it again.

"We figure out what she is and see if we can get her to stay long enough to understand the pull to her. See if there's a way to counteract it."

Osiris blinked once, twice. Then the numbness was gone, the weight of his age fading from his words. He dropped the calculating edge and became more focused.

Fallon was thrown off balance as he stuttered out his next words. "Better plan would be to get rid of her and never have to feel it again," he said, lacking conviction as Osiris adjusted the cuffs of his shirt.

"You know better than that, Fallon. You aren't one to hide behind weakness. Why start now?" Osiris turned away, silencing any other rebuttals. "I call the vote."

The vote was our way of keeping the peace through the centuries. Hesitation stopped me for only a second, my focus on her. On the stubborn tilt of her nose and the old scars across her skin. Was the *Smár Valkyrja* worth it? I wasn't sure, but my wolf wasn't going to let me disagree.

"I agree. We see if she'll stay," I rumbled out, the words morphing into the low growl I'd made in the car.

She sighed, her head turning as if seeking the noise.

"I agree. The house could use some feminine charm," Adrian chimed in.

"She'll never *choose* to stay with us," Fallon said. "We bought her."

"Then you have nothing to worry about. You only have to get through one more conversation with her, then never see her again." Osiris's head tilted as if goading Fallon to disagree.

Fallon's face twisted into a sharp grimace, and then he let out an angry sigh.

"You're all fools. The lot of you." There was no heat behind Fallon's words now. Only resignation.

"Maybe." Osiris reached out, pressing his hand to her cheek again, and it shocked me so badly that I didn't protest as he pulled her from my arms and placed her on the couch in our loft. His hands were unflinching. There was a reverence in his eyes that should've worried me, that should have made me question the consequences of our actions.

"I haven't wanted to touch someone in over two thousand years, Fallon," Osiris said with a shaky breath. "We're Vivas. Bound by blood, and brothers by choice."

The swirling blues of Osiris's eyes ignited a drive in me. A drive I hadn't had in nearly a hundred years. It was the want to fight, to conquer. To *win*.

"When one calls, the others follow," I chimed in, continuing our call to valor.

Our war cry, as Nero had called it.

Fallon said nothing for a moment, and I wondered if he even remembered the words. Over a hundred years had passed since they'd last been spoken.

"When one fights, we fight with them." Fallon let out a breath, his face contorting in anger before his mask of ice fell into place.

"I want to fight for this, Fallon, and I'm too selfish to lose this feeling. Not without at least speaking to her." A look of tenderness covered Osiris's face.

"Do what you will," Fallon said, defeated as he turned away from us. "I agree. Just don't come to me when this turns on its head."

He tried to hide the softness that grew behind his sharp indifference, but I'd known him too long for it to slip past me. He *flitted* up the stairs, his door clicking closed just moments later.

"Adrian, write her a note. Tell her we will meet with her at nightfall." Adrian only nodded, ambling off up the stairs at the far end of the room where Fallon had just disappeared, in the direction of the library. He looked to me next. "Eirik, the first aid kit, if you would. We should clean up her hand before the sun calls us."

I nodded and rushed off, gathering our rather old first aid kit, before *flitting* back to the living room, eager to see her again. Adrian was already there, his hands moving fluidly over a single sheet of paper. He flashed me a smile when he saw me.

"I'd say that went better than expected." Despite his confident words, there was doubt in Adrian's eyes.

"He'll come round," I huffed, still thinking about how Fallon had looked at her. I'd seen the longing, the curiosity. It was buried. Hidden behind fear and doubt.

"Are you so sure about that, Eri?" Adrian asked, finishing the letter with a scrawling signature.

"Yes," I said with a nod.

"Not going to expand on that one?" He asked, and I shook my head, ending the conversation and focusing back on the girl on the gray couch in the center of the room.

Adrian laughed, the sound subdued and quiet. "Didn't think so."

CHAPTER 9

AALIYAH

"What's on the agenda today, Natalia?" The cheerfully casual voice echoed throughout the room, almost disembodied.

I opened my eyes and was met with blinding white lights and the familiar smell of bleach. A man's face came into view over me, warping and shifting until I could make out his features. Thick brown eyebrows framed his hauntingly content green eyes, and his lips split into a chilling grin when he realized mine were open.

Monster.

There was shuffling to the side, and a woman responded with an agitated sigh, "How many times do I have to remind you, Doctor Castillion? My title is Doctor Nox. Use it," Nox scolded, and her indignation overwhelmed my other thoughts.

I wanted to express my anger as she had. I wanted to scream it until everyone in this building could feel it. But I didn't. Instead, I stayed silent, tracking Castillion with meticulous precision, mouth clenched closed.

Never make noise.

"And I told you to call me Marcus, Natalia," he said.

There was a cold Cheshire grin on Castillion's face, and bile rose in my throat, threatening to drown me. Whatever he saw in Nox's eyes caused him to sigh, his shoulders shrugging in defeat.

"What's on the agenda today, Doctor Nox?"

I screamed my mantra in my mind, drowning out the sickeningly sweet drawl of Castillion's voice.

Never make noise.

"Bone fracture stress testing. Let's focus on the shoulder blade and clavicle today. If we have time, I'd also like to test a few ribs," Nox said, her voice clinical.

She didn't care enough to look in my direction as Castillion smiled down at me, his expression sinking into my skin like poison. I forced my whimper down, choking on it as Castillion lifted his arms, turning to his box of horrors that appeared seemingly out of thin air. He ran his hand across its top, slowly tapping at the surface.

They get more violent if they hear noise.

"Sedative?" I could hear the slight clank of metal as Castillion searched for the right one.

My heart sped up, roaring in my ears. I focused on the blaring white lights above me, on the white walls, and the sterile smell of bleach. Anything but Castillion's soft hum and the way his eyes traced my face.

"Not this time. I'm curious to see how pain might affect how its bones mend," Nox said.

It. *I was an* it *to them.*

"You sure he's going to be okay with that?" Castillion didn't appear concerned.

"As long as we keep producing results with the blood and don't kill it, he doesn't care what we do." Nox's voice was like a whisper now, buried beneath my internal monologue.

Never make noise.

Castillion settled over me again with a metal mallet in one hand and a small metal tube in the other. My vision warped as he brought the cylinder down toward me, the metal seeming to flex.

It felt fake, wrong.

He ran the flat tip of the cylinder over my face, and I couldn't stop the trembles that came from it. His smile split sickeningly, showing his excitement. I swallowed hard, resisting the urge to spit in his face. If I hadn't still been healing from the last session I might have, but self-preservation won over my rage today.

"Recording started, Doctor Natalia Nox. August 16th, 2015. Regeneration study 143. Beginning with the clavicle fracture." Nox's voice sealed my fate.

She didn't look at me as she picked up her clipboard, clicking the accompanying pen's base a few times. The sound slid over my skin, frying my nerves. I bit back a cry as Castillion settled one end of the metal tube against my skin, onto my right collarbone. It was cold, and a shiver started there as he placed the mallet gently on top of the other end, almost lovingly. The tears flowed silently now.

Castillion brought the mallet up, the leer on his face too much to bear. I snapped my eyes closed, swallowing my terror. I didn't want to see it.

Never make noise.

The impact sent agony through my limbs, feeling wrong yet devastating at the same time. My bone cracked under Castillion's unrelenting swing, and I arched, trying to run from the pain as I barely kept the cry in.

"Shame, Glass. I was really hoping it would take more than one swing to break." His cruel words swept over me, mind-numbing agony tearing the breath from my lungs. I was thankful for it, for the inability to cry out.

Castillion gets more violent when I scream.

"Do one more. I want to get good data while we can. It will take a while to heal, and I don't want to wait." Nox's voice echoed in the room, and my head lolled to the side.

I couldn't stifle the whimper that slipped past my clenched teeth. I couldn't take another hit either. But that didn't matter to them. If it did, I wouldn't be chained to the table. The leader of Ascension Rising only wanted my blood, though I'd never found out for what. This test, and every other one they performed, was all them.

To Nox and Castillion, I was an it, an experiment. Nothing more.

Castillion lined up the metal bar again, and pain shot through me from the slight pressure. I watched him this time as he raised the mallet. Agony tore at my skin, and tears that refused to fall clouded my vision. He licked his lips as he brought the mallet down again with another sharp swing.

It hit with a resounding crack, and I choked on a sob as I threw my head against the table, straining against the restraints on my limbs.

I couldn't stop the scream this time.

I sucked in a hard breath, choking on the scream that fought its way up my throat as my lungs fought the intrusion.

Never make noise.

That damned mantra rang in my ears, reminding me of everything I wanted to forget as a tremor licked its way down my arms, unrelenting in its leisurely assault. The feel of tears, hot against my cheeks, slowly brought me back to the world of the living. Everything burned, and a stiff, achy feeling left me numb. Panic reduced me to a trembling mess, twisting at my insides as I ran my hands over my body. I pressed gingerly at my shoulder, expecting pain and a mending bone, but there was nothing.

A memory?

I couldn't move, too scared that Castillion was hiding in the shadows of the unfamiliar room. I was almost too shocked to register what had happened. I remembered something, a memory that didn't have a *Rend* before it. The *Rends* had been consistent, and I'd relied on that consistency—the pull, then the memory.

Only there was no pull this time, no *Rend*. I didn't have the familiar ache of dying. Instead, I breathed easily and not like I'd just spent the past several minutes with unmoving lungs. I was cold, frigidly so, but the chill I had came from the room's temperature, not death.

I dragged my hands against my face, too scrambled to process the information. Castillion's voice still echoed in my head, bouncing around, tearing at my insides like I had swallowed broken glass. I wanted to scream, cry, and let go of everything this latest memory brought me. But I couldn't, not now.

Not here, wherever here was.

I looked around the pitch-black room, my sight adapting quickly. It was something that had happened so many times before I almost didn't notice it. They liked to shut the lights off at the facility to save power. So I spent more days and nights in the dark than I did in the light, and just like those times, there was no natural light here. No light at all.

The plush blue sheets I laid on were not my own, and the room I was in was blindingly unfamiliar. Thoughts of the auction came back to me all at once, and I struggled to keep from falling farther into the bed.

Bought. I'd been *bought.*

I pushed the thought away, hiding it until I could deal with it. Until I was safe. A bitter sense of calm swallowed me, and numbness grounded me to the moment. It was a feeling I was quickly growing used to. With each memory of Doctor Castillion, with each scar I remembered, it always found me. It was my bane most days, but it would save me precious time today.

I took in the room's minimal design, and though I should focus on anything else, on how to get out or what I could use as a weapon, the first thing I truly noticed was that Prince wasn't in it. My steadfast knight hadn't returned after his departure at the auction house. I tried not to think about it, about him leaving me in this situation alone. He likely had a reason for it, one he would explain when he returned.

If he returned.

I shook, nausea making my head spin at the thought. I couldn't imagine a world without Prince. He'd become my everything twice now. The first time, when he'd found me at Ascension Rising—that was one of the first memories that'd come back to me. The second time was after I'd woken in my grave, unable to remember my name. I'd grown to love him twice, and I didn't want to think about doing this without him.

I ran a hand through my hair, grimacing at the knots as I pushed away the panic slowly rising in my chest. I turned, sliding my legs over the edge of the bed. The frosted wood flooring was like ice beneath my feet, sending a chill straight through me. I wrapped my arms around my torso instinctively as I approached the closest of the two doors in the room, dragging it open. It looked like a closet, though it was empty save for a few boxes. I closed it, an audible click sounding. The room was bland, almost blank by design, or like whoever inhabited it hadn't quite gotten to decorating it. Besides the bed in the middle, there was nothing, not even windows.

I surveyed the space, my eyes landing on the other door. I inched toward it, moving as slowly as I could force myself, keeping my steps measured to not make noise. Pinned on the coat rack, placed with care to make sure I would notice it, was a single piece of paper. I reached up and pulled it down. I skimmed over the page.

Our Dearest Guest,

Good morning! Or evening, I suppose. Either way, I hope you had a pleasant rest. We wanted to assure you of your safety and let you know we will be by in the evening, after we wake, to chat. Please don't mind the locked door. Fallon wouldn't let us go to our day rest with it open, the sourpuss. Talk to you soon.

Yours Truly, Adrian

Adrian. I fisted my empty hand, clenching my teeth at the name of one of my captors. I crumpled the note, tossing it onto the floor as I reached for the door handle. I expected to find it locked, as the letter had said it would be, but that didn't stop my stomach from dropping when the handle didn't turn.

I hated being trapped, *caged.* The entire thing felt far too familiar, and it was quickly escalating my panic into full-blown hysteria. I tried the handle again, my breathing spiraling out of control. I couldn't stop it, could barely see as I gasped for breath. Eliza's breathing exercise did nothing to help calm me now, not when the four walls surrounding me seemed to close in.

Trapped.

My hands went numb, and I fought the urge to slide to the floor. There was a noise on the other side of the door. It sounded distinctly deep, but it was so quiet I couldn't distinguish what it was.

It's Doctor Castillion humming, my subconscious whispered, the sinister tinge to my thoughts being my breaking point. *He's waiting for you to escape, so he has an excuse to put you on the table again.* I choked on my sob, leaning my weight into the door.

They get more violent when they hear noise.

I stayed that way for a few minutes until every inch of me was freezing, and that numbing clarity helped me pull away from the door. I clenched my hands, forcing the tremble to stop. I did the only thing I could think of to keep the living nightmares away and focused my panic into a rage. I hauled my weight back over to the bed, the chill of my body and the icy floor beneath me clashing with the heat of my anger until I couldn't distinguish between the two feelings.

The bed was one of the few things in the room that held any color, made of rich red wood. It stood out against the plain gray of the windowless walls. It was massive, meant for someone much larger than me. I searched it, looking for anything that could help me, and my mind focused on the four-bed posts at each corner. They were relatively tall, at least an inch above my head, with several ridges and bends carved into them.

And at the top, there was a crisp point.

I bit my lip, glancing at the door again, listening to that soft melody as it continued to creep its way into the room. I hesitated, once again frozen to the spot.

It's Doctor Castillion!

I couldn't fight the irrational thought, even as I looked at this room and knew it wasn't the kind found at the facility. Because what if *it was?* What if he found out I wasn't dead? What if the Vampires had bought me for *him?*

I felt sick as I flipped my head back to the bed, biting my tongue until the pain cleared the panic, and grabbing the post closest to me. I didn't hesitate again as I wrenched viciously, my entire body shaking at the force of my movements. The wood creaked and groaned, and I let out a frustrated cry when it did nothing further. I pulled again, putting as much strength into my movement as I could.

He's going to hear you.

Another sharp pull and another groan from the wood. My arms trembled and what strength I had wavered. I braced my feet against the floor, using all of my weight to my advantage.

Never make noise.

I sobbed, pushing back the encroaching sense of dread as the wood cracked. I could hear my mantra, burning my mind with its constant message until it was like someone was screaming it in my ear. Usually, I would listen to it. I would allow the habit of silence to overwhelm my need for anything else. But I couldn't do that. Not today, not when the freedom I'd finally found was in danger. Not when I had so much left to do, to see. I thought of Eliza. Her ability to burn water when she tried to cook and the beautiful smile she always had when we visited the sea. I could see Grigen, all mischief and joy, and the way he would grin with his entire face when he saw me coming. Even Dezen and Carter, with their kind words and endless patience.

The wooden post gave one more screeching groan before it snapped at the thinnest part near the bottom. I nearly fell back, stabilizing myself, using it as a kind of cane as the adrenaline flooding me made me dizzy. I sobbed, leaning into the wood, holding myself up with it.

I did it. *I* did it.

I didn't waste any time hobbling back over to the door, nearly falling as my limbs tried to catch up with my mind. I stopped, pressing my ear against it, listening for that consistent hum, letting out a breath of relief when I heard it still echoing in the halls on the other side.

I didn't have a plan, not one that made any sense. I ran on sheer adrenaline as I rammed the splintered edge of the wood into the round handle, bashing the wood against steel until the metal groaned. It gave way, the handle falling to the ground with a loud crash, and just as quickly, the door inched open. Again, I was left frozen, listening to the hinges creak as I fought the will to huddle against the wall.

Castillion left the door open again today to see if I would run. I couldn't. Not when I knew what he would do to me when he caught me.

I opened my mouth in a silent scream, unable to even grant myself the reprieve of sound.

It was a game he liked to play. A game I never won.

I gritted my teeth, gripping the bedpost so tightly that my knuckles went white. I wasted several precious seconds as I waited for them to fly through the open door.

But nothing happened.

I extended the wood out, pushing the door open the rest of the way. It swung into the hallway, not making so much as a sound.

"Such a good girl, Glass. I knew you wouldn't run."

I shook my head, pushing Castillion and his sickening voice from my mind. I was finally free of him, and I would fight for that freedom.

I would die for it.

The first step into the hallway was as liberating as it was terrifying. Dark gray walls were accented with geometric stone, and the gray-tinted wood floors gave the entire area a crisp look. The hallway opened up to a spiral staircase, and I looked down into the darkness it led to. I could hear it better now, a low distinct hum.

Like someone was singing.

I inched my way down the stairs with careful steps, ensuring no sound followed me. If whoever was making that noise had heard me break the door, he wasn't coming for me, which was more terrifying than if he had. Was he waiting for me? What if it was all a trick, so he could hunt me throughout the house?

Never make noise.

I clenched my jaw, gripping the post until my hands hurt. That deep song echoed now. The tune was in a language I didn't know, but the tone was noticeably melancholy. I inched my way to the corner of the wall at the bottom of the stairs. I couldn't see around the edge, not without giving myself away. The person on the other side could be facing me or turned around.

It was a game of luck, and I'd never been the lucky sort. I steeled my grip on the post, willing away the tremble in my hands and legs. I'd had little time to see the men that bought me while I was on the stage, though I distinctly remembered there being four at the table with the winning bid. So, which would it be? Which of the men was waiting just beyond the corner? Were they all there, deciding what they wanted to do now that they *owned* me? I could take one, *maybe,* as long as I got the slip on them first. Then I could knock him out and run. If I was lucky, it was still daylight, and I'd have some time before they could follow me.

I briefly thought about ending them, about killing whoever it was, but I knew I couldn't do that, especially if what Eliza had said was anything to go by. Even then, could I end someone's life? I steadied my breath, wishing on every star in the sky and praying to whatever God would listen that I could do what was needed.

I turned the corner, and in that instant, my breath caught, snagging in my lungs as I tried to keep it from morphing into a scream.

Huge, he was *huge*.

For a moment, I considered running back up the stairs, cowed by the sheer power the man seemed to hold by just *standing*. He was a goliath, and his broad frame matched that height, with thick cords of muscle that were exposed from the waist up. Dark, intricate tattoos trailed along his back and up his sides, the geometric patterns accenting his intimidating physique. He continued singing his foreign tune, his voice a deep timbre that was startlingly calming. He flexed as he moved, shuffling over the counters as if looking for something, and as the light shifted, I finally noticed them. Harsh streaks of white broke up the dark ink. *Scars.*

I couldn't look away, and my entire body froze as I watched him walk to one cupboard, his song stopping for only a moment as he said something. The tone was harsh, like a curse, and possibly in the same language as the song. His hair was wet and intricately braided over the top of his head, small strands falling over his neck. I hated the heat that rose to my cheeks. But Jesus ... How could someone be so devastatingly terrifying and roguishly handsome at the same time?

Was he a fucking *god*?

When he reached down and set something on the counter, I finally snapped out of my haze. It was a knife; I recognized the sharp steel and eerie gleam even in the dark. I shivered, the feeling turning into full body trembles, and I was unable to think of anything other than the auction. I recalled this man, blood-red eyes and fangs on display, and I rushed at him. I swung the wood hard, aiming for his head the best I could. Unfortunately, he stood well over a head taller than me, but I tried not to let that deter me. He must've heard me running, his head flipping toward me just as I reached him. The look of surprise on his face nearly stopped my swing in its tracks.

I was close, *so close* to connecting with his head, when his hand shot up faster than any human would have been able to. He grabbed the wood with a perplexed look on his face. Dark ink, matching the patterns on his back, wrapped around his left eye, surrounding the scar that stretched down his face in a jagged line from his brow to his jaw. The tattoo looked like a dragon guarding its hoard, curled around his shimmering blue eye as if it were a precious gem. Those eyes bored into my soul, ripping me apart and laying me bare. They were so blue they were nearly white, swirling and flexing like they were living seas. The man's mouth opened and closed as he glanced between me and what had been my weapon. I ran on instinct as I let go of the wood, my arms screaming now that the weight had been lifted. I grabbed the knife he'd set down, swinging it at him frantically as I backed away. The man jumped back at my swing, a chuff falling from his lips as he looked to his arm where the knife connected.

His surprise was taken over by what I could only describe as awe. I waited, ready to bolt at a moment's notice, for him to walk toward me and rip the knife from my hand, but he only stood and stared. I glanced at the intricate door just across the room, ignoring the thunder of my heart in my chest and the wobble of my legs as the adrenaline made my body ache.

The only thing keeping me from my road home was the giant in front of me. When he finally spoke, I held the knife high in front of me, desperately trying to look intimidating.

"I will not harm you, *smár Valkyrja*," he said, that deep rolling timber of his voice thick with an accent I couldn't place. "I swear it."

He raised his hands in a submissive pose, and I caught sight of more of those tiny white lines, this time tracing his arms and hands. Marks of damage and abuse. I knew them well, and it burned me when compassion rose in my chest.

He bought you.

He set the bedpost on the counter, never taking his eyes off me. It looked so small next to him, not even as thick as his arm. I swallowed hard, looking between him and the door again, struggling to find words. I'd tried to hit him with it, and now I wasn't even sure it would have done any damage had I managed to.

"Let me go," I faltered, unable to keep my voice even as trepidation strangled my vocal cords.

Never make noise.

"Would you like to sit down?" He ignored what I said, motioning toward the table with a grimace on his face.

He twitched, moving so deliberately slow that I relaxed against my rational mind's wishes. It wasn't a command, and everything about how he stood seemed subdued. He still hadn't rushed at me, and his eyes were a crystal-clear sky-blue, no red in sight. His mouth was closed, but I didn't see the imprint of fangs.

What game was he playing?

"I *want* to leave," I said firmly, keeping the man in my sight as he lowered his hands.

He nodded sharply, almost as if the action pained him.

"We don't intend to keep you here against your will, but I can't let you leave yet," he said, bowing his head and showing me his throat, his words soft but leaving no room for protest.

I clenched my teeth and searched him again, looking for some way past, when my eyes caught on the small silver chain on his neck. Though that wasn't the only thing I saw. A scar, nearly an inch wide and stretching across his entire neck, made me tremble. I couldn't stop looking at it, so reminded of my memory from earlier that I nearly dropped the knife. I ground my teeth, shaking my head and getting ready to charge at him again, knowing he outmatched me in size and, no doubt, strength. He raised his hand, shaking his head.

"We need to talk about what happened first, and we can't do that until everyone wakes for the night." There was no malice, no rage, no anything.

He was stiflingly calm in how he moved to the way he talked. Like he knew exactly what would put me on edge. I looked at his hands again, to his neck, his eye and his chest. All of them sported scars, and I found my defenses lowering a little more at the sight, even knowing I shouldn't. He motioned to the table again, only nodding when I backed away from him.

"Water?" he asked, his head tilting toward the sink.

All at once, I realized precisely how dry my mouth was and how terrible I felt. The adrenaline was fading, and I swayed on my feet. The man tensed but didn't move toward me, and I took it as a good sign but still shook my head at his offer. His jaw tightened, but he nodded regardless, once again giving me the feeling that he understood my weariness.

I glanced around the kitchen, taking in the modestly designed room. Marbled counters stood against white cabinets and a harsh black wood floor. The man stood by an island in the middle; just across from that was a table that could seat six. It was about the same color as the bedpost had been: a vibrant red. The walls were strange, patterned with what looked like metal sheets where the windows should be. It was a clean design, far more presentable than I'd expected during my walk down the stairs. Though I wasn't sure what I thought I'd find.

Coffins lining the living room? Bodies hanging from the ceiling?

A blood fountain?

I shook my head, almost ashamed of the thought, as I glanced again at the man. The knife was heavy in my hands, and I dropped my threatening stance just enough for my arms to stop aching. The man let loose a breath at this, and though he didn't move more than that, he continued to watch me closely. His eyes skimmed up and down my body in a way that felt scorching. We stood in awkward silence for a few more seconds before I couldn't take it anymore.

"Where am I?" The words were strangled in my throat, and I struggled to speak at all.

All over again, I was trapped and alone in a transparent cell. Waiting for the next session, for Castillion to come collect me again.

They get more violent when you make noise.

"You're at our home, *et in domum suam in solem.*" The deep lull of his voice on more foreign words was distracting, and I lowered my guard a touch more.

I bit my lip, clutching the knife as curiosity started building. He hadn't hurt me, and he didn't seem angry. Could this all be a big mistake? He'd said that they didn't intend to keep me here. Hope I shouldn't hold on to surged, and I struggled to keep it from showing on my face. Had they meant to save me? Eliza wouldn't have sent them ... but maybe?

I shook my head. "What does that mean?" I asked, unable to stop the question.

"Home of the sun," he said, throwing me off with his answer.

"That seems ironic," I said, focusing on the crow's feet that popped up at the corners of his eyes.

The rest of his face didn't move. Whether that was a good thing was still to be determined.

"That would be why Nero chose it." Another tick, this time at the corner of his mouth. His eyes lit up, and he crossed his arms over his broad chest. "Wanted to keep people on their toes."

I nearly smiled, shaking my head as I tried to sort through what this meant. This felt ... normal? Well, as normal as you could feel standing in an unfamiliar room with a complete Vampire stranger who bought you at an auction.

Maybe not normal, but not *terrible*.

"What's your name?" I asked, looking away from the man's steadfast stare, while still keeping him in view.

This time, the tilt to his lips was strikingly familiar. There was a curl to the corner, one that made him seem foolhardy.

"Eirik," he said, his curt response echoing in the room.

The name was harsh, with the first half sounding like a growl in his accented tone. It was intense, just like the man that held it.

"What's yours?" he asked.

"Aaliyah," I said, watching as his eyes slid closed for the first time since our altercation.

He seemed to soak in my name for a few moments before his searing blue eyes opened again, luminescent in the low light. His focus was just as sharp as before, making me shuffle in place as a dreaded silence wrapped around us. In my memories, it was always the silence that drove me mad, because it was rarely followed by anything pleasant. I waited, seeing if Eirik would say anything else.

He didn't.

So I waited some more. And more, and *more*, until I couldn't take it.

"You don't talk much, do you?" I asked, rocking back and forth between my feet.

Blood rushed to my face as I remembered where I was. That I was holding a knife toward the man, not discussing having a late lunch. It was addictively alluring, this aura that he carried. It was like my entire body knew he was safe, and even my mind felt the need to follow.

Was this the Vampire *Charm* Eliza had spoken about? I stiffened, narrowing my eyes. Eirik noticed, the tilt to his lips falling as his hand came up to trace his neck, tapping at the angry scar there. He didn't appear angry, not like Curtis had when I backed away from him. No, Eirik looked hurt. Like my distrust physically pained him. For a minute I didn't think he'd respond until that same familiar look lit up his face, and my heart once again thundered in my chest. It was more pronounced now, only further accented by the cross of his arms over his too-broad chest.

He reminded me of Prince, I realized with soul-wrenching clarity.

"Actually, I'm known for my *riveting* conversation." There was an almost comical tone in his words, and his head dipped in a mocking bow.

That combination, his Prince-like swagger, and the way he tried so hard to flourish his move was the last push I needed. The look on Eirik's face, like he was proud of himself, had me laughing. It was soft, barely there, but I couldn't stop the sound from coming up. His expression widened into a whole grin. The kind that made my stomach flip, and I loosened my grip on the knife as my tension eased.

Just as quickly as that expression took over, it fell, and Eirik's face shifted back to the blank expression I'd been greeted with initially. All the tiny hairs on the back of my neck rose, and every ounce of self-preservation in me told me I was being watched, that something dangerous was nearby. It wasn't dissimilar to the feeling of a ghost, like a cold creeping along my skin, and somewhere in the back of my mind, I remembered this feeling from the auction house. The whisper of earlier, when Curtis had thrown me against the wall for trying to run, his slap knocking me silly ...

Red eyes, wide with rage. Curtis's lifeless body hitting the ground. Power so ancient and thick in the air that it strangled me.

I flipped around, facing the new threat with the raised knife, just as Eirik spoke.

"Evening, Osiris."

That name rang in my ears, and the fear Eliza had burrowed under my skin with her story stole my words, blending with what I'd seen at the auction house. In that room, that had to be forever stained red. I tried to open my mouth to say something, but was entranced. *Osiris* was imposing, though not in a 'bigger than you' kind of way. In fact, he was several inches shorter than Eirik, though still managed to tower over me. His prowling eyes trapped me, making my nerves pop as fear buried the tentative peace that Eirik and I had crafted.

Predator. My mind whispered, and I took a step back, tensing.

"Aaliyah?" Eirik's voice was barely a whisper, one I was too lost to hear.

I glanced back just as Eirik tensed, eyes on me, not on the beast that had just entered the room. He hadn't seen what I had. The lifeless body of Curtis, the blood splattered across this monster's olive skin and pristine white dress shirt.

The numbness in his red eyes after he'd torn out a man's heart.

Or maybe Eirik had, and he didn't care. I was careless and had let my guard down when I knew I shouldn't have. I raised the knife, my focus back on Osiris as I pointed it in his direction.

Osiris's brow creased, though he didn't move. I kept searching for hints of blood and gore and found none. His back straightened, his crisp pinstripe suit out of place as he assessed me with the gaze of a king, of someone who knew their power. I looked up, trying to see if the black locks of his hair were hiding a crown. His eyes captured me as much as the power radiating off him, and I took another step back, suddenly startled by what I saw ... they were different blues. The left was a cool aqua, and the right a deep royal. I recovered, keeping them in my sight, waiting for the startling blues to turn red.

"Aaliyah." Osiris whispered my name like a prayer, sin grabbing every syllable.

It was dark, and the tone made my entire body heat against my will. That was all I could take.

"Stay the fuck away from me," I said in a cry, backing away from the two Vampires, unable to look away from Osiris.

He could kill me in an instant, without so much as a glance. He did it before, and though I wouldn't say that Curtis didn't deserve it, I didn't think he would've gone down so easily. He'd overpowered both Eliza and me. He'd been a Dragonkin.

And Osiris had torn out his heart like it was easy. Because for him it *had been.*

My breathing spiraled before I could catch it, and what had been calm breaths dragged into sharp pants. Each one burned like breathing in shards of glass, and I fought to keep the knife lifted as my arms wobbled, turned to jelly in my fright at the man who'd bought me.

A soft rumble sounded in the air, ringing like a song my heart knew. It thumped in my chest, reverberating through my entire body.

I closed my eyes, pressing them so tight that I could see white flashes behind them, but no matter how hard I focused, I couldn't get the panic to rein back in. I jolted back, stumbling on the cool hardwood, my bare feet suddenly aching at the icy feeling. I only vaguely heard the words 'panic attack' as I pulled the knife close to my chest, suddenly freezing.

The rumbled growl grew closer, slowly, like whatever was making it was wary of me. I didn't care what it was, only that it was helping me to focus.

"Aaliyah," a familiar voice whispered.

It was silent for one, then two heartbeats before a hand grabbed mine, and whatever I'd been holding toppled to the ground. The skin against my own was warm, heat sinking past the frigid chill that had built a home in my body, and I let out an unsteady breath. My legs all but gave out on me as I fell forward into an equally warm chest.

Vampires aren't warm. My mind assured me, and I sank further into the heat. Of course, this was a bad dream, and Eliza was waking me up. That was all.

That had to be it. Another bad memory I was going to wake up from.

The rumble morphed into a soft melody, the deep words serenading me. Slowly, my breathing evened out, and I opened my eyes. A pale chest, bare and littered with dark ink, was pressed against my cheek. It smelled like the sea mixed with heady undertones of coal and summer roses.

Not Eliza.

The rumbling didn't stop as a warm hand pressed against my back. It didn't move, it just held me secure like an anchor. I dared a glance up, meeting a startling blue gaze.

Eirik. He stared down at me, questions brimming in his expressive eyes. I froze, trying not to take in the addictive smell of him again, unable to move as I processed.

I was in his arms.

"You had a panic attack," he finally whispered, searching my face. "You okay?"

Was I? I'd just fallen into the arms of a Vampire, had taken comfort in his hold only hours after he *bought* me. I was terrified, beyond scared shitless. And the worst of it was that being in his arms wasn't what scared me. No ...

I was scared because I'd never been more comfortable.

Chapter 10

Osiris

Pain wrapped itself around my chest, aching like I'd been stabbed and left to rot in the sun.

I knew she was going to fear me. I'd expected it and had tried to prepare for it, but nothing would ever have made me ready for the way her eyes spiked wide or for the sour scent of fear that had covered that rich lavender. I was old, old enough to call for Challenge, old enough to get most Naturals to twist to my whims. Old enough to reek of power and rip out the heart of a Dragonkin.

Old enough to terrify, even when that wasn't my intent.

I wanted to take a step forward, to brush a hand across her hair and promise that I wasn't a monster, but that wouldn't be true. It had never been true.

So I stayed planted on the ground as Eirik pulled her out of her panic. They were pressed closely together, their sides facing me. The soft lull of one of his Norse folk songs echoed in the kitchen, and the familiar scent of harsh oak mixed with the rolling sea distracted me. I looked at Eirik, only half expecting the proud look on his face. His arm had a thin line of blood on it, the wound already closed.

I didn't have to ask, not when his expression told me everything.

"The *smár Valkyrja* packs a punch," he whispered against her hair, barely loud enough to hear, and she tensed. "Quiet too.'

My brow shot up, and I had to take a second to absorb what Eirik had said. Even with all the evidence, I still couldn't quite grasp that she had managed to not only sneak up on the *Úlfheðinn,* but she had *wounded* him. It was a feat that even skilled warriors struggled with. My curiosity expanded as I took a step toward her.

Her jump startled me, and the gurgled cry on her lips reminded me she didn't share in our current thoughts as she pressed harder into Eirik. Unfound jealousy threatened to crawl up my throat and slip out as a *Charm.* I wanted to comfort her, to tell her that Curtis's life was worth little more than the time it took his heart to hit the ground, but I kept my mouth shut. She didn't see me as something interesting or look at me with curiosity. I had bought her, killed a man in front of her, and she saw me as the monster I was. I found it difficult to move away from her, with everything in me telling me to close the rest of the gap, and the step I took away was dragging, almost painful. It was such a sharp contrast to how I usually felt that I struggled to keep my thoughts on the matter at hand.

"My apologies, Aaliyah." I lifted my hands placatingly, trying to portray a relaxed pose.

The move felt so wrong that I tensed, and my blood rushed as though preparing for a fight. My fangs burned, and I struggled to keep them at bay as the familiar feeling of the *Charm* surged up, like embers against my vocal cords, ready to grasp onto my words whether or not I wanted it to. The gift of the *Flame* sparked in my veins, amping up my need to move. And above that was the *gift* of my human years. The old magic surged, sluggish from decades of dormancy and my unwillingness to use that which had led to so much pain.

I slammed it all down, clenching my hands until they shook.

Aaliyah's button nose twisted up and her eyebrows furrowed. She glowed under the soft lights of the kitchen, her dirtied white hair framing her violet eyes and steadfast expression. I could see it now, the calling that Eirik had given her ringing true.

A Valkyrie. Brilliant, light-encompassed. I tried to remember, *again,* that she wasn't here of her own free will.

Not yet, anyway.

She peeled away from Eirik, looking confused as he held her steady. Her legs shook, and before she could protest, Eirik scooped her into his arms, walking her over to the table. He set her down, taking one more squeeze of her hand before he backed away, giving her the space she needed. She tensed further as her hands tightened, balled into fists over her lap, and I took notice of the bandage that was still there. There was no distinct scent of decay, and I couldn't smell fresh blood.

"Is it healing alright?" I whispered, forcing the heady *Charm* from my voice as I spoke.

Emotions raged in me, concern and worry. She looked confused for a second, her lips thinning before she nodded briskly. I didn't note any pain in her expression, and I calmed at the revelation. Her unrelenting scrutiny followed me as I stepped around the island, and she tensed as I reached down to the fridge there.

"I imagine you have some questions," I said, popping open the first bottle I found and pouring a drink into a spare glass.

She didn't speak, only continued her venomous stare. It burned me down to my soul, and even my skin felt raw after a few moments. I longed to hear the laugh that woke me from my day's sleep, the soft tumble of her voice that made it seem like even I deserved peace.

Eirik nodded toward the staircase, breaking our standstill to where a disheveled-looking Adrian stood, followed by a crisply dressed Fallon. They looked hesitant, as though gauging Aaliyah's reaction. Of course, she hadn't noticed them yet, with her attention still on me. Unfortunately, Adrian and Fallon weren't patient enough to wait. Adrian shoved his hands in his pants pockets, the loose jeans a staple of his home attire. He stepped toward us, measuring his weight to cause a creak in the floorboards.

Just as before, Aaliyah's attention flipped to the intruders. Again, my heart jumped in my chest and pain took its place there. I fought the urge to reach out and grab her hand. To pull her attention back to me, even if it was damning. Eirik began his rumbling growl again, and the tension left her shoulders.

"Good evening. I see you guys started the fun without us." Adrian winked at Aaliyah as he spoke, a charming smile gracing his lips.

"Though it smells distinctly like burnt toast, which I must say doesn't make for a splendid party."

I half expected her to snarl again, but when her cheeks lit to a vibrant red, hope flared in my chest. For what I wasn't sure yet, but hope nonetheless.

"Adrian, Fallon," I said their names slowly, giving them time to nod in our direction. "This is Aaliyah."

"Nice to meet you properly, Aaliyah." Adrian marched toward the table, extending his hand out.

Her eyebrows shot up just as her jaw dropped, and the blush on her cheeks extended down her neck. I caught the jolt in her heartbeat, and how it thundered caused my blood to surge. When she bit her lip, I nearly looked away. The flush of her skin made me want to see exactly how far down her blush went. I could trace it with my fingertips. I could follow them with my lips. Something inside of me snapped to attention, and I found I couldn't stop thinking about the way she extended her hand out hesitantly. She clutched at Eirik's suit coat, knuckles white as Adrian stole her free hand so quickly I doubted she even saw him move. He kissed her knuckles with reckless abandon, his lips lingering on the skin.

Adrian was naturally magnetic, his carefree smile and drawing personality helping to calm her. She looked at him like he was crazy, but didn't move when he pulled away. Nor when he and Fallon took their seats.

We sat in less-than-comfortable silence, and I found I didn't even mind. At that moment, with her eyes on me, even with the panic and fear buried in them, I was calm.

I took a deep breath.

"I believe we owe you an explanation."

CHAPTER 11

AALIYAH

Everything about the men at the table was a contradiction; their eyes, which had been so vividly red only hours ago, were now stricken with worry. Fangs that had been on display, gleaming under shining white lights, were now hidden behind tightly closed lips to stop even hints of them from showing. My emotions were in overdrive, and I couldn't distinguish between the stark feeling of terror from the auction and the small bubble of joy that had appeared when talking to Eirik.

How warm his arms were, how safe I felt there. He seemed less like destruction in that moment and more like ... a wall. Impervious. Resilient.

Whatever tactic they were playing at dragged on my already fried nerves. I'd learned this already at the compound, the finality of rage. They were planning on gaining my trust, only to rip it out from under me. That had to be their plan ... right? Eliza's tense words clashed with Prince's confident smile, and I wasn't sure what to do. Eliza knew Vampires ... but Prince wouldn't have left me alone with them if he didn't have faith in them. Trying to decide which one to trust was like being trapped in the ocean, with the only choices being to drown trying to swim to the surface or die to the monster that laid far below.

Because no matter how Prince had looked, they'd *bought* me. They each had held the same expression as everyone else in that room: want. They were monsters. Vampires. I could still hear the wet sound that followed Curtis's dying breath as his heart hit the ground. Osiris had shown me exactly how much stronger he was than the man who had easily overpowered Eliza and I. I wouldn't be able to defend myself if they used that strength on me.

Eliza's words echoed loudly in my ears, and the thought of trembling in her voice made me sick all over again. I stared longingly at the knife that I'd dropped in my panic.

They'll tear you apart if you give them a chance, Ali.

The insistent, gnawing pulse that had been the bane of my existence for the better part of six months built behind my eyes. The pressure caught me by surprise, and the sharp pain that came with it made me choke on the gasp that tried to fight its way up my throat.

Never make noise.

I gritted my teeth, digging blunt fingernails into my empty palm, willing away the *Rend* as best I could. I had to hold it back until I could figure out what these men wanted or if they were safe. Until I had the chance to talk to Eliza, confront Archon for setting us up, and figure out how to fix this mess. My eyes jerked frantically around the room, over the men that held me hostage and the crispness of the area. Gray walls, sharp stone and an eerie lack of natural light made everything seem cold. I didn't see what I wanted to see, *who* I wanted to see. I searched for Prince and his steadfast smile that always calmed my nerves. I needed him to tell me it was going to be okay.

Why hadn't he shown up yet?

Seconds went by, dragging into minutes as all sounds stopped, save for the consistent ticking from the clock above the table. The men, who hadn't so much as breathed over that time, continued to stare like I was a caged animal about to bolt. They were imposing in more than just stature. They *felt* powerful, and I knew instinctively that if they wanted to harm me, they could. Yet none of them moved, almost like *they* were the terrified ones.

They get more violent if they hear noise.

Eventually, during my manic scanning, I caught sight of a slightly mismatched pair of startlingly blue eyes, and I jumped back.

Osiris.

His face was sharp and perfectly angled, each point looking like it was specifically made that way. From my seat, I couldn't pick out a single imperfection on it. It was like someone had carved him from the finest of marble, taking care to make sure every detail was perfect. His tanned skin stood stark against his black pinstriped suit and crisp black hair, and if he hadn't been so intimidating, with his unwavering stare and otherworldly intensity, I would have called him beautiful. Darkly, sinfully, beautiful. For a moment, we just stared at each other. I couldn't read him, not like I could Eirik, and the last thing I needed right now was an enigma.

Prince's smile flashed again in my mind, and some of the tension faded away.

"We won't be harming you, Aaliyah," the man at the end of the table said, farthest from me.

I was so startled by the break in the silence that I flinched and flipped my attention away from Osiris, facing an entirely different beast.

Fallon, if I recalled correctly, was the last one I'd expected to speak. He sat with all the grace of a swordsman, and all the power of a bull, as he held me captive with a narrowed stare. The crisp white of his suit made him seem like an angel, with the make of a devil in his sharp green eyes. The look of them had me sinking further into my chair.

Blond hair framed his sharp jaw and narrow nose, and I quickly realized that Osiris seemed *warm* in comparison. Fallon was a picture of perfection, just as Osiris was, for entirely different reasons. Where Osiris was carefully carved marble, Fallon was crisply cut ice. He looked almost bored, his expression carefully lax and giving nothing away, just harsh lines accenting thin, sculpted lips. That perfection was daunting, and I clutched the jacket that was quickly becoming my haven. Because it wasn't just Fallon and Osiris that were perfect.

All four of them were.

They reminded me of Prince. They held the same robust bravado, even though it was mellower now than it had been when I first saw them. Of course, it helped that it now lacked the violence which accented it before. Prince had seemed confident in them, like they could help, or that they, at the very least, would do less damage than the others at that auction. Prince had been my rock for years, and even though he wasn't here, I knew he wouldn't do anything to hurt me. Not intentionally. I wanted to trust them because I trusted him, so I swallowed my fear, keeping my free arm cradled around me, protecting the soft spots on my body. Could I reason with them? Would they take me back home?

Maybe this was all a mistake? They had put me in my own room and hadn't hurt me. Eirik had pulled me out of a panic and hadn't retaliated when I cut him. I sucked my bottom lip between my teeth. Memories of these men at the auction crawled their way through me, planting seeds of distrust.

"Aaliyah, are you alright?" Eirik's distinct timbre bounced off the walls. It sounded familiar and unknown at the same time, his accent blending harsh vowels and hard 'l's.

No, no, I was not alright. This was all wrong, and I wanted to be at home. I wanted to see Eliza and to make sure she was safe. I wanted to hold Grigen and tickle him until he was on the verge of tears, laughing in that giddy way he did. I wanted to see Prince smile at me from across the shop, the easy tilt of his lips lighting up butterflies in my stomach.

I wanted to pretend like I wasn't dying, and I hadn't just lost any chance at figuring out *why* when Archon told Curtis we would be on Century Side.

I must've taken too long to respond, because Eirik's low rumbling growl started again, and Osiris cleared his throat. I tensed, cautiously watching the man I was most wary of. But, if my stare perturbed Osiris, he didn't show it.

"Fallon's right. We'll not harm you, Aaliyah. You have nothing to fear from us." There was a distinct lack of continuation in Osiris's sentence, one that made me nervous. It lingered in the air, drowning out my will to be silent.

We'll not harm you *yet*.

"You don't buy someone with good intentions,' I said, my voice barely above a whisper. I could feel the pulses behind my eyes now, dragging my attention in multiple directions. The stiffness in my muscles caused my words to shake. My next words were hissed. "Good men don't go to auctions."

I expected their bubble of kindness to burst and was ready for the rage to take over. I tensed in preparation, but there was only regret. It bled into the air, covering the room like a fog so thick I nearly choked on it.

"You're right," Osiris said with his face carefully blank of emotion, though his eyes were far away from our conversation. Familiar numbness lingered in them. "Good men don't go to auctions."

Osiris barely finished his sentence before Eirik was snarling out a response. "*We* don't go to auctions."

He scowled at Osiris, accusation burning in the way his lips twisted. The tender growl that had softened my fear and sparked warmth in my lungs morphed into a menacing rumble. It echoed in the room, bouncing off the walls. I sank away, once again glancing at the door. As if noticing that, Eirik's booming rumble stopped, and silence again settled over us. It was hard to stay still this time, hard not to bolt from my seat. Only fear kept me glued down, knowing that if I ran, it would be their instinct to chase. Eirik sighed across the table, running his hand along his bearded jaw as he looked at me. It was his eyes that calmed me down, the understanding in them making my heart beat against my ribs.

"We only agreed to go if we saved one, and look how much of a clusterfuck that's been," Eirik said as he rubbed at his torn neck, before looking away with a clenched jaw and shoulders tense, like he was holding the weight of lifetimes on them.

Saved one?

My mind buzzed, Darius and Curtis's conversation after the auction ringing in my ears. My nails sank into my thighs as I tried to stay calm.

She won't last the night.

The men didn't speak, as though they weren't sure how to respond. So when Osiris finally broke the silence, it made me jump. I didn't need to lift my head to confirm that it was him. I'd never forget his voice. The gentle caress of his words sang across my skin as he spoke, such direct contrast to the violence I'd seen him commit.

Useless. He'd whispered to Curtis. It had been so quiet I nearly didn't hear it. Sinful. Dark. *Bloodthirsty.*

"While I admit our intentions did not start out noble, we never intended to harm you." Osiris's voice teetered off, fading away as he sighed. "We were out of our minds when we placed that bid."

"Is that supposed to make me feel better about being *bought*? What's stopping you from going 'out of your minds' again?" I shot back against the cool wood of the chair, my own heated words making me flinch as they slipped out before I could hold them in.

Fear coiled in my stomach, and panic stopped my following sentence dead in my throat.

"You have no reason to trust us," Osiris said, finally turning away, giving me a reprieve from his stoic focus.

There was a heartbeat's worth of silence, before Adrian's sigh echoed in the room.

"Jesus. What Osiris *means* to say," Adrian cut in, "is that we aren't normally so ill-composed."

I couldn't stop the blush that came up at the sight of him. He'd taken me by surprise when he first showed up. His boyish charm matched his heart-shaped face and the seemingly innocent air around him. Slim, like a swimmer, and with hair like ruffled leaves in differing shades of copper and brown. He gave me a Cheshire grin, flashing bright white teeth.

With a distinct lack of fangs.

"In fact, I believe I speak for all of us when I say we acted out of character." Adrian stood from his seat.

His movement was sharp, and though he moved no more than that, it was enough to break our fragile peace, getting me out of the chair. I bolted to my feet, gripping the table with one hand and the jacket surrounding me with the other. Black spots danced in my vision until I was chasing unconsciousness. I gritted my teeth, powering through the feeling.

"Don't come any closer!" I screamed, keeping my focus on the amber-eyed man, who looked almost as startled as I did.

I wanted to snarl at the tremble in my voice, at the fear so apparent in my words. Adrian stopped, raising his hands placatingly. His lips curled into a frown, the emotion so deep it reached his eyes.

"Sorry. Wasn't my intention to startle you." His hands flexed, his arms flaring as they did.

My own muscles seized as I waited for him to move again. He didn't, only continued to stare as the others did. It all felt like a twisted game of cat and mouse.

And I sure as hell wasn't the cat.

"This is getting us nowhere," Osiris finally said, rolling the impatience out of his posture, his expression nothing more than a frustrated scowl.

His lack of patience seemed to startle the rest in the room, Eirik even raised an eyebrow, which seemed like a lot of emotion for the giant, based on what I'd seen so far.

"You know what we are, don't you, Aaliyah?" Osiris asked as his gaze turned to his hands, jolting when he realized I was looking at them, too.

He moved, gripping them tightly together as though my eyes burned him. I only managed a nod, not trusting the words I was about to speak.

"Of course I do." I let out a shaky breath, barely holding back tears. "You're Vampires."

Osiris flexed his hand, veins showing on his exposed skin. Then he seemed to fall away from reality, his eyes clouding. The familiar expression was one I often saw in Prince's eyes when his mind was on anything but the present.

"That's right," Osiris said wearily.

Just as quickly as his hands had taken up their stressed posture, he released them, before pressing his palm down onto the table hard enough for the wood to protest. I could see the tremble in them and the way he fought it.

"Though the actions you had to witness were deplorable," he swallowed, "I hope knowing what we are helps to explain at least some of the atrocities you saw. The reaction we had to you was something instinctual, and it was unlike anything I have experienced. Because of that reaction, we placed a bid on you."

I flinched at his words, but he didn't stop speaking. They were hard, resolute, and sure. Not to mention flooded with guilt. But he didn't shy away from them, didn't hide what he did behind a mask of sweetness.

He was honest, no matter how bad it sounded, and I could respect that over a lie.

"I realize how that must seem, and I would like to express my sincerest apology for it," he said, with a dip of his head, and I believed it against my better judgment, truth ringing in his words.

I focused on the clench of his jaw, my gaze shooting between that and his still-closed eyes.

"You're free to go, Aaliyah."

I would have sworn my heart stopped in my chest, as my lungs seized and I tried to force a breath. Did I hear him right?

"We never intended to take your freedom from you. Not like those at *The Devil's Details* had likely expected," he finished.

My mouth fell open, and I couldn't take my eyes off him. All at once, Prince's sure smile and calm demeanor made sense, and my stomach dropped knowing that I hadn't trusted him. There was sincerity in Osiris's tone, and none of the others disputed him.

I drew a deep breath and settled into the chair.

"Why?" I managed, choking on the word as it caught in my throat.

"Because denying you freedom goes against everything we value." He paused, again looking me in the eyes.

There was an ancient guilt there, one that told of centuries of living, and centuries of mistakes.

"We *are* Vampires, that much is certain ... but I like to think we're also more."

Eliza had made Vampires seem like the complete scum of the earth: murderers, rapists, *monsters*. These men didn't seem like that. I recalled Eirik in how he talked to me after I rushed him. After I *hurt* him. He didn't get angry or try to hurt me back. He spoke to me, calmed me down, and did everything he could to ensure I was in control of the situation. All of them had been strikingly kind when it was obvious they held the power.

Monsters didn't take your feelings into account, didn't hold you until your mind came back to you.

"We can return you to your home as soon as night has fully set if that is what you wish. *But,* I would ask something of you first."

I tensed, and Osiris shook his head, his hands raising softly. "We have no grounds to ask, and you have every right to say no ... but we have a proposition for you, if you'll hear it," Osiris said before sighing when Fallon flipped his rapidly growing scowl to him.

It was the first show of emotion I'd seen from the chilled man with vivid green eyes, if I could even call it that. Fallon spoke clipped words in a language that wasn't my own, and Osiris said something back in that same language. It hid their words from me. Panic built in my chest, and I glanced at the door, my heart thundering like a storm.

"Don't mind them, love. They slip between languages like Osi does whisky," Adrian said with a wink, stretching his arms into the air. There was a brotherly affection in his eyes as he shook his head at the two that were still arguing as though none of us were there. "They have always been the bickering sort. If it calms your nerves at all, they are arguing over the semantics of the deal. The language you're hearing is Gaelic. Fallon is a bit of a stickler, and though he *looks* like an icicle with a severe case of constipation, I promise he means the best."

That stopped the duo's conversation entirely, and Fallon rolled his eyes, glaring at Adrian with a heat that didn't feel angry. Adrian's sincere words did help, and he didn't have the look of someone who was lying. I swallowed hard.

"No tricks. Y-you'd let me leave?" Prince's surety filtered into my mind again. His confident smile, the adoration that he couldn't hide.

I rolled my shoulders, taking in how I felt, a habit of mine since I'd woke from my grave. I breathed easily, and the pain that had followed me down the stairs had faded. With a startled jerk, I realized the pressure that had been creeping in on me had dissipated.

Where had the *Rend* gone? I didn't have time to guess, as Osiris was already speaking again.

"Yes, it was our intention from the moment we entered *The Devil's Details*. We had always planned to set someone free," Osiris said, the words crisp and forced, but I could hear the truth behind them. "Had we had a choice, we wouldn't have been there to begin with."

That truth burned in Osiris's eyes, the differing blue hues shining defiantly as if that truth were seconds from consuming him. Above that, there was fear. *Fear.* I couldn't begin to understand what *he* was afraid of.

"What about the money you bought me for? You'll lose all of it," I said, trembling as I stared them down.

The men looked tense as they watched me with bated breath. Eirik even looked ... devastated? His eyes were closed tightly, his hands gripping the table with white knuckles. I could see his panic like it was my own.

"Money is inconsequential. Consider it a gift for allowing us to speak with you and as an apology for what you had to endure," Osiris said, his eyes never leaving mine.

For the first time since Curtis stole me from Century side, a true peace washed over me. They looked pained, but no one made a move to come closer to me.

"What—" My voice drew their attention, and each of them shuffled in their seats. It seemed so wrong. Why was I the only one not shaking? "What do you want?"

The men relaxed slightly, and my shoulders loosened as the adrenaline left me as well. My fingers stiffened, still gripping tightly onto the coat I wore. I pulled the jacket tighter, thankful for the sudden warmth as a chill swept through my body.

"I apologize for how we scared you, Aaliyah," Osiris started, fingers tapping against the table.

"Curiosity is the curse of immortality, and the way we reacted was anything but normal. Something about you drew on us in a way that I have never seen. We would like to know why." His head dipped, guilt in his gaze. "We would ask for you to stay here with us for a time. So this subject can be further detailed and avoided in the future. Of course, we will provide whatever you ask in return for your presence."

I couldn't help but consider that they might have the resources to help where no one else could. I stole a glance at Osiris, watching how he moved, like he knew everything there was to know about me. He felt powerful, but above that, he felt *old*. Like old blood, with the years to back it.

They might be able to tell me what I was or know someone who could. I took another deep breath, pushing down the idea for now. I couldn't just trust them, not so soon after being burned by Archon.

Eliza's list of Naturals to avoid, regardless of Prince, had been right so far. Archon had sold us out, and Vampires had bought me.

"What exactly do you think happened at the auction?" I asked.

Osiris's head shook, and his lips curled into a frown. For a moment, I didn't think he was going to answer me.

"You sparked our instincts into action." Osiris paused as though trying to decide what to say. "You threw us into a blood frenzy. That's not something that happens to Vampires as old as we are."

He hesitated as he finished the sentence, once again grabbing at his exposed wrist. But I couldn't focus on it, not when his words were exactly what I wanted to hear.

Vampires as old as we are.

Did he already know what I was? Was this just another play on words to get me to slip up? Everything froze again, and it took me a moment to verbalize my thoughts.

"How old *are* you?" I asked.

Osiris's lip twitched, something akin to a smile taking over his face, and I got the feeling that *old* didn't really cut it. Hope bubbled in my chest.

"Doubt he even remembers the exact number," Eirik answered, catching my eyes with his gaze. Sky-blue and unrelenting. "Once you live long enough, you stop counting ... but he's somewhere past twenty-five hundred," he finished.

I was expecting old, but ... *Damn.*

"And how do you feel now? Are you still ... out of your mind?" I asked, and Eirik swallowed hard.

"Not quite. Much the same feeling, though not as strong." He didn't need to finish the sentence.

He knew I wouldn't like the answer, not really. But he didn't lie. *They* didn't lie.

Again, Eirik told me regardless of what he thought my reaction would be, and I appreciated the truth more than I did my fear. They still had that pull to me, *but* it was weaker. They still felt the need to feed from me, *but* they hadn't lied about it.

Prince trusted them.

"I promise, we are no threat to you, Aaliyah," Osiris said, and the sincerity in his words kept me grounded. "Being in the presence of your blood has lessened the effect, and now that your wounds have been cared for we hardly feel it at all." There was a truthful panic in his eyes, the blues swirling with confusion and agitation.

I took a breath to center myself.

Prince trusts them.

I nodded. It wasn't a lot, but it was enough to get the men in front of me to lose some of the stress they still held.

"So I stay here until we find out why you reacted the way you did? That's what you want from me?" I took a shuddering breath.

"Yes, and as I stated, you will be compensated for your time. We may not have the gifting power of the Fae, but we can get nearly anything you might desire. Money, land, time," Osiris said.

It would be helpful enough if they found out what I was, but they didn't need to know that. What else could I want besides to live? I must have taken too much time to mull it over as words interrupted my thoughts.

"You don't have to decide now, mind you." Adrian's copper eyes lit up, hints of amber dancing in the depths, and the soft trill of his familiar accent drew my attention. "When you figure something out, let us know." There was a quick pause, followed by an almost comical panic. "If you agree to stay, of course, don't feel pressured into it." Another pause.

"We don't want you to think we are trying to force you into it—" As quickly as his rambling started, it was dragged to a screeching halt.

"Adrian." A tanned hand settled on Adrian's shoulder, and Fallon rolled his eyes. "Stop talking."

Relief lit up Adrian's face as he sighed, laughing off the anxious mumble. The sight of their interaction set a warm feeling in my stomach, and the pleasantness of it had me relaxing. These men offered me something invaluable, even if they didn't know it yet. The chance to figure out what I was and maybe fix myself while I still had the opportunity. I noted the absence of pressure behind my eyes again. I'd never held a *Rend* back this long, and the pressure *never* went away before the *Rend*.

Until today. When I remembered without a Rend to guide it, when it faded away without pulling me free from my body.

"So long as we can agree to a few things first," I paused. "I'll *consider* accepting your deal."

The relief that washed over Eirik's face further solidified my choice.

"By all means," Osiris said.

Black hair framed olive skin, and the tension he'd been holding onto seemed to be gone from every place but one, his hands still clenched tightly onto the table.

"I can leave whenever I want. I'm—" I released my clenched hands, loosening my grip on the coat. "I'm not a prisoner here?" I tried to force the question out of my voice, and the visible flinch that racked Eirik showed me I failed.

"You are no prisoner. Not here, not anywhere. I agree with your first stipulation," Osiris said, and I didn't respond.

"*We* agree," echoed the others at the table.

"I want to be there if we have to talk to someone. I will not be in the dark about any of this. Everything you know, *I* know." My words were more assertive now.

"You have every right to know. We agree." His melodic voice made me want to close my eyes.

"And I need to contact my family." Eliza had to be home by now, likely setting up a town-wide search for me. "They need to know I'm safe."

Their posture tightened as regret surged in the air. The answer was instant.

"Of course," Osiris said, as a brief silence washed over us.

"You never should've been taken from them." Eirik stared at me as he spoke, and I picked out the pain in his eyes; the understanding.

Was this the right choice? I glanced at the door again, trying to ignore how their gazes followed me. I closed my eyes, marveling at the absence of pressure in my head.

"Then ... I guess we have a deal."

Their collective sigh caused my heart to skip, and I sat back down in the chair. Osiris's face slowly, like it was unused to the motion, lit with the most stunning smile I'd ever seen, and I couldn't help the blush that worked its way over my face. It seemed so odd, the expression almost out of place on the stoic face he'd held most of the night. So different from the rage I'd seen at the auction house. It reached up, dancing in his eyes as the tension drained from his hands. When the others noticed Osiris's smile, they stared at him like he had pronounced himself a god and thrown himself at an altar, demanding sacrifice.

"Damn, Osi, don't think I've ever seen you smile like that," Adrian said, throwing his head back in a surprised laugh.

Osiris's smile fell, the expression that now seemed melancholy back in place. His eyes lost that glow, the kind that made him feel alive, and I was speaking before I realized it.

"I like your smile." My voice was soft, barely there.

It was a compulsive sentence, one that most people wouldn't have let slip. I spent so many years talking to myself that sometimes things still made their way out. From the shocked looks on their faces, I'd guess I did this whole social cue thing wrong again. Eliza would be disappointed in me for several reasons at this point.

Kidnapped? Check.

Vampires? Check.

Still unable to talk like a normal person? Check.

Did they think I was odd? I could see questions forming in their minds already. Heat flooded my cheeks as I snapped my attention to my hand that still clung to the coat on my shoulders, trying to find something interesting in the jacket's intricate tailoring.

"I mean, you're pretty when you smile."

More mortifying silence.

Was that the wrong thing, too? Did he not like being called pretty? I should have used handsome, right? Or should I just not have mentioned it?

I was going to stop talking now.

"I'll try to do so more, then." Osiris's voice sounded dazed, and I didn't have to look up to know that he was staring down at me, though I stole a glance at his face, regardless.

The slight smile pursed on his pink lips made my heart stutter, and blood rushed to my face. He still terrified me, to the point where I had to look away again, but something else danced in my stomach as well.

Blending until I could only feel a confusing mix of emotions. Adrian threw his head back in another deep laugh. The sound was full and sent a pleasant shiver down my spine. The rich tone reminded me of the songs that would sometimes filter into my cell. The deep lullabies would often help put me to sleep. Nilus, one of the night guards I'd remembered, had said it was Johnny Cash.

I searched the room out of habit, looking for a still-absent Prince.

"Are you okay?" The question slipped from Eirik's, the sound hoarse and strikingly masculine.

The deep rumble of it was surprising, the indistinct sound almost melancholic. Was *he* okay?

"Given everything that's happened in the last twenty-four hours, I'm fine," I said, as Adrian relaxed in his seat, his chair groaning beneath his weight. The sound of it pulled my attention to him, his head lifting up as he brought his eyes to mine. His lips held an easy-going smile.

"You're probably beat, then. What do you say to a shower while I make breakfast?" Adrian's eyes skimmed my face, and though I didn't see any criticism in them, his attention still made me self-conscious.

Those at Ascension Rising left my face mostly alone, as shown by the lack of scars, but a few had snuck through. A small nick at the tip of my nose, another over my lips. I looked down at myself and the filth I was coated in. I hadn't really noticed before, too caught up with everything to care. Now that I could see the grime, it felt heavy, and the need to get clean and out of these clothes outweighed any other thought.

"Yeah, that sounds nice," was all I managed, wobbling on my legs. Adrian tensed, forcing a smile without moving toward me.

"Wonderful. Fally, show her to the shower, will you? Any preference on food, Aaliyah?" Adrian carried a boyish charm, and I was thankful for it as Fallon grit his teeth, walking around the table to me.

He was slow, and though he obviously disliked being so close to me, that didn't stop him from extending his arm out for me to take, surprising me with the gesture. I hesitated for a second before accepting his offer, setting my hand on his cold forearm. If I thought I could make it up there myself I would have, but the adrenaline had left an icy feeling in my bones and even standing was arduous. Even the chill beneath my fingers was a shock, and I flinched.

I could feel Fallon's eyes on me through it all and smell the subtle scent of heat and warm rain. I couldn't fight the blush as it rose on my cheeks. Fallon's arm tensed under my fingers, though he said nothing.

Finally, after working up the courage, I shook my head at Adrian, doing my best to smile as I did. Adrian took it in stride, gifting me one of his own. I soaked it in, leaning into Fallon as we walked toward the stairs, the sound of idle conversation and pans clanging behind us. Maybe this wouldn't be bad after all. It could be worse.

After all, I hadn't even died yet.

Chapter 12

Adrian

There was something relaxing about working in the kitchen.

I walked my way across the cool black oak floors, tapping each of the cabinets as I went. I had always enjoyed preparing meals, as food had a tendency to make people happy, and I liked to see the smiles on my brothers' faces when I presented something new to them. One of these days, I'd have to recreate the clay kiln that my grandmother and I'd made in my backyard as a lad and really show them what food could be. I stopped my tapping, glancing over the countertops, listening to the near-silent hum of water falling from upstairs. I missed baking with someone else, missed the days when my grandmother and I would spend hour upon hour cooking up whatever we could think of.

Maybe Aaliyah would be interested? After all, her stay here didn't have to be entirely about figuring out our issue. If anything, I'd prefer to spend some time with her, to see if I could get her to make that soft peal of laughter again.

I shook my head and tapped the metal stove before turning on the convection top, holding my hand above it as I waited for the heat to seep into the air. Once it had, I placed a pan down on it, letting it warm up for the first meal of the day.

Pancakes.

I took a deep breath, basking in the smell of fresh herbs, vanilla, and the newly introduced spring lavender. I hummed, rubbing my palms together. The idea of feeding someone that wasn't a member of our family made me giddy, and I swayed around the empty kitchen, almost silly like. I wanted to impress, to wow, even with something as simple as pancakes. That wasn't a hard feat for the others in the Vivas household. Before my turn, Osiris had lived solely on blood, having spent *centuries* with no texture at all, and could frankly live without food even now. Eirik and Fallon had been appreciative but overall not affected by my introduction.

Nero, of course, had salivated over my eggs benedict. Though he'd always enjoyed my cooking, and he would even occasionally slip in and help me prepare a dish if it was something he was eager to have. I wished I could've done more of it for him. I'd only known our second eldest for a few years before we lost him, and though I didn't have centuries like the rest, I still felt his loss like an ache in my chest.

I milled about, still humming a vibrant tune while I pulled out the few remaining things I needed for the pancakes: some cinnamon, and my favorite whisk. Eirik sauntered down the stairs only a few seconds later. His hair, pulled tightly into his typical Viking braid, was nearly unmoving as he took his seat at our grand table against the now exposed windows, his back to the moonlight. The shutters over the glass had raised a few minutes ago, automatically sliding away to reveal our land after the sun had fully set. But Eirik wasn't paying much attention to me or our finely maintained moss yard that he'd *insisted* we put in. Instead, his head was tipped toward the staircase, his eyes pointed and focused.

"Well, glad to see you put a shirt on," I said, smiling as Eirik turned his head enough to raise an eyebrow at me.

The brute had been without one for most of the early evening, and during the entirety of our rather tense chat with Aaliyah. I doubted he even noticed until Osiris had pointed it out.

"Wasn't thinking of it," he said back, the harsh Norse drawl of his words sounding a touch softer than normal.

His eyes, stormy-blue, seemed to roll as the beast behind them assessed me. As always, I tensed under its watchful gaze. The two beings made up Eirik, and I understood that as a whole they were my brother, but the part that was *Úlfhéðinn* ... Well, I had a feeling it would always make me feel uneasy.

A bite from one was fatal, after all.

"Right. Right. You were far too preoccupied with destroying my non-stick pan trying to make ..." I paused, tapping at my chin as I set my bowl of pancake mix onto the marble counter to rest. "Eggs?"

The briefest hint of color appeared on Eirik's cheeks, though it didn't throw him off enough for an actual expression to sneak through. That color was something I always tried to get from our technically hot-blooded brother. Couldn't make Fallon or Osi blush, but I would damn well try to make Eirik.

"Didn't think they'd burn so fast," he confessed, with a cross of his arms.

"Oh, I have no doubt. Though I'm still trying to figure out why you needed the knife." I picked up my batter, tapping the bowl against the table to release some bubbles as Eirik spoke.

"She needed the comfort of it," he said with a noncommittal shrug. Like that alone would answer all my questions.

"You set it out for her?" I asked, and Eirik nodded.

"Heard her break the door," he said while rubbing at his neck, at the scar he refused to talk about. Just another of those things that were off-limits. Osiris and his issue with touch and his human magic, Eirik and his scars, Fallon and his Aislinn.

I sighed under my breath, trying to pull myself out of the melancholy mood we'd put ourselves in.

"So you knew she was coming downstairs, and you wanted to give her a reason to ... hurt you? Didn't think you were into that, Eri. I would've assumed you were the one who liked to dish out the pleasurable pain," I said, winking at Eirik, pleased to see him drop his hand from his neck as a scowl lit up his face.

"There are men who allow knives near their dicks, but I'm not one of them," he growled, rolling his eyes. "And I didn't hear her come down the stairs."

I flipped the pancake, barely catching it as I snapped my attention back to Eirik. A roguish grin took over his face.

"She surprised me."

I couldn't respond, too stunned by his words to do anything but stare. I set the pan down, almost laughing at the absurdity of them. Eirik? The *Úlfhéðinn* warrior with sharper senses than Osiris, the eldest of our Crypt, had been *surprised*?

"You're serious?" Fallon's familiar voice cut in, saying exactly what I was thinking. His words echoed down the stairs, his quiet entrance causing both Eirik and I to turn his way.

As expected, Eirik only nodded with a look of pride in his eyes. He tapped his hand against the red oak table, before looking back to the stairs, past where Fallon was standing. That quiet rumble I heard in the car started again in Eirik's chest, vibrating the wood of the chair he sat on. I called it a purr earlier and nearly ended up nursing a busted cheek from Eirik's right hook. But what *else* would you call it?

Fallon shook his head, inching his way down the steps, his hands flexing at his sides as he turned his head toward the bathroom door.

Aaliyah, with a voice almost too soft, was singing something. The otherwise quiet kitchen was brightened by it and the mood of the room picked up. As I started the sausage, I knew I'd made the right choice in keeping up with my cooking skills.

I rolled my shoulders, keeping my thoughts on food prep and off our guest. Though I wanted to think of her light eyes and stunning bravery, I couldn't. Not when I wasn't sure how I would react to the thoughts. I'd been careful up to that point to keep my emotions tightly under wraps, not wanting to spark a flare up. I flexed my hand, hunting for the feeling that I was dreading to find. When that creeping anxiety left me alone, I relaxed. I sighed and shook my head, looking down in dismay at the pan that held my latest pancake. Burned to a crisp. *Lovely.*

"Something wrong, Adrian?" Fallon said, sliding into his chair.

It gave a distinctive whine as he sat, the old wood creaking. Osiris refused to get rid of them, not when Nero had helped Fallon hand pick the set when the construction of our humble abode started. Fallon studied my expression, looking for what he didn't want to find there. The same thing he was probably trying to avoid.

The *Maker's Call.* Fear surged its way up my throat at the thought of Sebek's words crawling under my skin, making me do things I didn't want to do. It was easier to avoid now that it had been so many years, and I could deny the call if I fought it hard enough. But that didn't change the fact that it hadn't gone away. Not fully, at least, and it never would as long as Sebek still lived.

"I'm well, Fally," I said, smiling innocently at a slightly more relaxed looking Fallon.

"You have a flare up?" Fallon asked, using our term for the sickening action that it was. Someone else's will taking over, making you feel like, well, anything but you.

"No, I haven't felt the pull since the auction. Just trying to stay ahead of it."

Fallon nodded, dropping the conversation he didn't want to have. It was hard enough for him to think of his own *Call*, let alone mine on top of it, and his worry was endearing in a Fallon kind of way. It was a curse we shared, one that Eirik, Osiris and Nero couldn't relate to because Sebek had never used his *gift* as their Maker against them.

Fallon leaned into the chair, pressing his back against the gray wall. He'd changed into his more typical wear, of a light green dress shirt with the top button undone, and cuffs rolled neatly up to his elbows. He flexed his hands, his scarred knuckles on prominent display as he opened one of his candies. Not his prized Aldovin delicacy this time, but another chocolate I didn't recognize. Most noticeable were the uncharacteristic black slacks, a stark change from his usual white suits. They were loose enough to be considered casual but tight enough to hide any *reactions* he might have during breakfast.

"You, however, look like you could be better." I flipped a pancake, grinning when Fallon rolled his eyes and our game began anew. "Haven't seen those pants in a while. They look rather tight. Aren't you worried you might bust a seam?"

He didn't respond for a moment, only popped another candy into his mouth, though I caught the shake of his head.

"More worried you're going to set the house on fire," Fallon finally replied, pointing to the pan in my hand and the unfortunate pancake still in it. "And speaking of things we didn't expect ..."

Fallon focused on Eirik just as the Viking's eyes slid open, pointed and swirling blue. He regarded Fallon with a raised eyebrow.

"She got the jump on you? *The* Eirik Vivas. The Emperor's shadow?" Eirik huffed at Fallon's words, almost laughing, though the joy quickly fell away, and the haunted look that often came with the thought of Nero took its place.

"Nero would've beaten your ass for saying that. You know he hated being called Emperor," Eirik said back.

It was true. After all, he'd never actually taken the throne from his father. Just spit at his feet and won the title of Champion in the Colosseum. But close enough, right?

Fallon's head tipped back in an almost laugh before looking seriously at Eirik.

"You still think she's not dangerous?" Fallon asked, cracking his neck and rolling his shoulders.

Eirik gave Fallon a feral smile, the black ink around his eye tensing, making the dragon that twisted across his skin flex. It was the grin of a warrior, harsh and proud.

"She's a *Valkyrja*. Of course she's dangerous," Eirik said, glancing at the stairs again.

Fallon sighed, but he didn't fight the decision again like I expected him to, as though he'd come to terms with the predicament we found ourselves in. Though I knew better than that, Fallon was the tense sort, and he'd likely realized that his best option was to play lax until something pushed us to react.

I pulled the sausage off the burner and placed it on a plate before tossing the poor, obliterated pancake away. I made up five servings with mostly equal portions, giving Eirik more since he was 'eating for two,' so to speak, and Aaliyah more because she actually needed the sustenance that the food would provide. Osiris had found his way down during my musings, and it seemed we were only missing the newest addition to our table. I set the plates down on the red oak tabletop and reached for the blood wine. We kept a few bottles in a small fridge that was built into the kitchen's island. Most wines, mixed with a variety of blood, were best served cold. There was no point keeping them all in the little fridge, so we kept most in the cool cellar, the preservatives in them keeping them fresh, if you could call it that, for years.

I grabbed five glasses and picked a bottle that seemed like it would be best, Griffon mixed with a dry red. I suspected it would taste nothing short of dreadful, which was an unsettling thought. Sometime over the past ten years, blood from the bottle had stopped being as filling, and now with the sweet aroma of lavender in the air, the idea of drinking it was almost sickening. I'd have to talk to Osiris about it and see if we could find a donor sometime soon.

I poured out four glasses with practiced grace before filling the final one with water. Then I sat down, impatiently waiting for Aaliyah to walk down the spiral steps. We all seemed to think that same thing, as no one had made a move for anything on the table. The sound of water hitting the ground no longer sounded in the air, and the silence was almost deafening. How long had it been off? Was she okay? My body screamed at me to go check, and I nearly broke after a few more moments.

I was already standing when I heard the familiar click of a door sliding open. Aaliyah's bare feet hit the top of the stairs, showing luminescent skin and stark scars that were now too clear to ignore. She made no sound as she descended to the living room, her eyes tracing the walls. It was hard not to notice the fear in her stance, in how she moved, and my voice sank to my belly as I tried to find the right words to comfort her. She looked at us warily, like she wasn't sure if she'd made the right choice earlier.

"Thanks for letting me use the shower." Her voice didn't hold the hesitancy that her eyes portrayed.

Her strength, even surrounded by near strangers—Vampire strangers at that—was awe-inspiring. I put on my best smile, letting the practiced motion take over my face. I sat back in my seat, leaning in a relaxed manner, trying not to take her in. Her scent was clean and crisp, no longer muddied by that of *The Devil's Details*. It was a breath of fresh air, like spring lavender and black tea, and my gums burned, my teeth aching in my mouth. I tensed, waiting for the feeling of wrong that still hadn't come to me, and after a few seconds, I let the panic drain.

Still no *Call*. Hope radiated through me.

Aaliyah practically drowned in Osiris's black shirt, the hem coming to rest just above her knees, barely shorter than the shorts Osiris had found. It was adorable in a way I never would have expected.

"Why, of course! What's ours is yours while you're here with us."

She relaxed at the sound of my voice, before glancing at my upturned lips. She offered me a hesitant smile of her own, a calm taking her over as she walked toward us with unhurried steps. Her eyes were lighter, and part of me wondered how long she'd worried over this interaction. I hated the thought of her being unsure of us, though I understood it.

She stopped in front of Eirik, shuffling on her feet, and I now realized that his suit jacket was folded neatly in her arms. She ran a hand over the coarse fabric before extending it out toward the stunned Viking.

"Thank you for letting me borrow this." Her voice was like music to my ears.

I didn't care what she said as long as she kept talking. Her smile must have broken something in the giant because Eirik's own lips turned up in a slight grin as he clutched the jacket in his hands. His fingers tensed as he struggled not to lift it to his nose.

Same, mate.

She took her place next to me, nodding a greeting to the others at the table. I couldn't help but sigh as the stress I didn't realize I held flooded from my body. However, it was Aaliyah picking up her fork that finally pushed the rest of us into action. I didn't move to grab my drink, feeling unsurprisingly disgusted by the liquid in the glass, though I could feel the hunger in my veins as sure as I could the *Flame* in my blood. It wasn't quite the pull of the *Maker's Call*, so I couldn't blame it on that. Unfortunately, this feeling was all me, a craving I couldn't curb, for something that wasn't mine to take.

Disgusted with the thought, I picked up a bite, letting the pancake settle on my tongue and flood my mouth with its flavor before I grabbed the glass. I took one hard swallow like I used to do to swallow pills as a young lad. The liquid was precisely as foul as I was expecting, and my hunger barely ebbed. I knew it had gotten bad, our distaste for blood wines, but I didn't realize to what extent.

I focused my attention on Aaliyah and the way she savored each bite of food, her eyes sliding closed as she chewed. We all sipped our wine and watched. Watched her eat, watched her breathe. It was like an obsession that none of us could pull away from.

Bet we looked really normal right now.

Definitely not creepy at all.

"Excuse my lack of knowledge on the subject, but might I ask what you'll need to stay here? We rarely have guests, so I'm afraid we are rather unprepared," Osiris asked, his attention on his emptied glass of blood wine.

He twirled the delicate quartz flute once before looking at Aaliyah. Her face twisted, apprehension in her violet eyes as she bit her lip. It was hard not to notice her fear of Osiris, her hands shaking as she clutched them in front of her. It was even harder to see Osiris's expression fall as the numbness in his eyes spiraled into self-loathing.

"I guess that's pretty important. I haven't really thought about it," she said, then paused for a moment, shifting in her seat. "Well, clothes would be a good start. You have food covered, from the looks of it."

Osiris diligently nodded at each of her thoughts, his focus so piercing I nearly started talking just to take some of that pressure off Aaliyah. Osiris was many things, but subtle was not one of them.

"And, the room I woke up in should be fine to sleep in, if that's alright. Though, it might need a new door ..." she finished, either not noticing or ignoring how Fallon tensed across from her.

His jaw flexed tight enough for his teeth to grind, and he set his glass down to keep from crushing the delicate quartz.

"I believe we can make all of that work. We repaired the door while you were in the shower," Osiris finally said, shooting a glance at Fallon, who only glared in response. "Should you need anything else, don't hesitate to ask."

She nodded, her head dipping back down to her food. We ate in silence for a few minutes, and it wasn't hard to notice that the longer the quiet drew on, the more tense Aaliyah became.

"Thank you ..." Aaliyah said, just as I was going to speak. "For saving me from the auction, I mean, and for the food and for ... Well ..." she stumbled over her words, glancing between us and the windows in front of her.

"You're welcome, Aaliyah," Osiris said. "Think nothing of it."

Before the silence could reign again, I took action. Aaliyah was picking at her pancakes when I sighed, stretching hard enough to cause the wooden chair beneath me to creak. It caught her attention as I'd hoped it would, and she looked my way.

"So, tell us, Aaliyah," I said, and her vivid lavender eyes found mine. There was a hint of a question behind them. "What do you like to do for fun?"

Her expression scrunched like she'd never been asked that before. Then, softly, she said, "I like to read."

Something told me she was holding back. Maybe she liked to read with her family? I knew better than to ask when she was still so new to us. She was likely still feeling us out, ensuring we were safe before she even considered bringing them up again. It's what I would do in her situation. So I just grinned, leaning back in the chair, making sure her focus was on me. Her cheeks flushed a light pink when I winked.

"Well, I believe we can help with that. We have a full library that I'm sure you'd enjoy, and our property is about a mile square, so there are plenty of woods to admire a good book in, if that's something that would interest you," I said, glancing again out at our moonlit moss yard.

It sparkled as fireflies danced in the night air, the last of the year. Aaliyah let out a breath next to me, leaning on the table to stare out the window with me.

"That does sound nice," she said, a small smile teasing the corners of her mouth. Thin pink quartz colored lips shimmering. "What else is there to do here?"

"There are plenty of things. Of course, you know about Oakridge, but there is another small town another fifty miles out. It has a beautiful park. We could explore there?"

Her nose scrunched up, and the hint of apprehension in her lavender eyes had me stumbling over what to say next.

"That's not it, though! We have some pretty scenery around here. There is a waterfall nearby, and a natural hot spring that sits on our property."

Watching her peek at me as she heard my suggestions sent shudders down my spine, and I had to stop my mind from wandering as she pulled her lip between her teeth again.

"Can we walk to the hot springs from here?" she asked, curiosity overcoming her hesitance for a moment, and I loved it.

She turned toward me, her mouth tipped up in a small smile. Again, I found myself at a loss for words, completely stuck on the small display of beauty.

"That's an option for sure. But if you don't want to walk, I'd be happy to carry you." A laugh slipped from her lips at my wink. .

"There are other things to do in the house as well. One of us can give you a tour. That way, if you are awake before we rise, you have entertainment," Osiris cut in, and Aaliyah looked hesitant at the notion.

"If you think so." Her unsure tone mixed with a frown and sent a chill down my spine. I longed to see her smile again, I craved it. I wanted her to enjoy her time here, and to enjoy us.

"You live here now, too. What we have is yours to use. Besides, you're going to need a break from these three eventually. You and I need a place to hide away from them." Her smile at my words sent euphoria to every inch of me.

She glanced around the table for the first time since she'd sat down to eat. She was already halfway done with her plate, having eaten her serving so fast I barely even realized it. I was only a few bites in. Her eyes finally met mine, her cheeks still flushed that adorable pink. It was endearing, and I fought to keep her gaze.

But I couldn't, not when I felt *it* building.

What I could only describe as anxiety raced through my veins, and an artificial feeling of hunger expanded in my stomach. The ache that I'd grown to hate with such venom that it had consumed my younger years, swelled, and dread overwhelmed the joy I'd felt. It was the pull of the *Maker's Call*, a direct order from Sebek on the day of my turn, that still haunted me. Sebek's words radiated in my mind as clearly as they had that day.

You think you can refuse my gift?

Aaliyah's blood rushed, and red crept into my eyes. My control slipped as I flipped my head away. I vaguely heard the voices of my brothers behind me as I pressed my back in my chair, head pointed toward the door. In case ...

In case I needed to get away from her.

You do as I say, boy; you find any young lovely you can, and you drain them dry until these thoughts of the sun leave you.

I downed the glass of blood wine—the sick taste slithering over my tongue, helping to pull the feeling of pain away as I struggled to ignore the *Call*.

"Adrian?" Aaliyah's sweet voice echoed in the air, and I snapped my head down.

I kept my eyes closed, willing away the feeling of puppetry that Sebek's *Call* inflicted on me. I could feel her eyes on me, but I didn't dare open my own. I didn't want her to see them as they were, blood-red. I didn't want her to fear me. Just the thought sent my heart into haywire, and the feeling of need clashed with my panic. I scented the air with an unsteady breath, frowning as the arid stench of her fear settled in my mouth.

Too late.

I half expected her to run away, to bolt toward the door. I was only half waiting for a scream. The scent of her fear was killing me, burning me from the inside out, ripping my focus away until there was only the rapid beat of my heart in my ears.

Then, her hand, so warm and delicately soft, settled on my own.

A shock, not unlike the *Flame*, shot through my veins, tracing every inch of me until I was alive with energy. It made me tremble, and from the shake in her hand, I'd say she felt it too. It buried my fear in its ashes, and the *Maker's Call* faded from my mind as my eyes flipped open, searching for hers. The purple pools of her irises calmed my hunger like nothing else, and a warmth washed over me as she stared.

Not fear or panic, but worry was etched across Aaliyah's face. Clarity seeped into my conscience, and I took a deep breath, uninhibited by bloodlust.

"Are you okay?" Her question lulled my soul into a peaceful hum. The warmth of her hand spread up my arm, settling in my chest.

"Of course, love." The endearment slipped out before I could stop it, and I gave her a fangless smile, passing my joy into it.

She accepted my smile, giving me one of her own.

"Sorry, I'm afraid I have to take care of something." The words tumbled out haphazardly, and before I could stop myself, I turned my hand, threading my fingers through hers.

The warmth of that spark pulsed, moving until my entire body felt alive. Her hand was so small, pale, and warm. She didn't pull away, though her face flushed at the prolonged contact.

"Fallon, I might need your help, if you can."

Fallon nodded, a mix of understanding and stark resolve on his face. "Of course."

Standing, he brushed off his dress shirt, straightening it out until it met his perfect standards. When he nodded at me, I knew it was time to go.

That pulse built through Aaliyah and I's connected hands.

"Enjoy the rest of breakfast, and I'll see you after, okay?" I said, my heart losing its rhythm at the look she gave me.

Even after these years, the *Maker's Call* was still potent enough to pull me away from myself. I sighed and reluctantly let Aaliyah's hand slide out of mine. The heat left with it, and I found the lack of contact to be disturbingly cold.

"If you can get either of these old boys to laugh, I'll give you some of Fallon's chocolates." That got a smile, be it at Fallon's grumbling expense.

I turned toward him, ignoring the chill that now settled in my palm, before following him up the stairs, leaving that warmth behind me.

Chapter 13

Aaliyah

Stark silence met the now slightly emptier room, and I found the same twisting anxiety that had kept me upstairs creeping up my spine again. I hated silence. I'd spent years dealing with it, talking to empty walls and hoping they'd respond, or having one-sided conversations with Prince to fill the void. Unfortunately, the two left at the table weren't as chatty as Adrian had been and were only *slightly* more so than Prince. I shuffled my silverware around my empty plate, my full stomach sinking as I listened to the subtle sound of the clock that was placed just above the now open windows. Its consistent tick was the only thing that kept me from slipping into full-blown panic again. I glanced outside, forcing my focus onto the beautiful forest yard just beyond them.

Mossy greens alight with fireflies and the light of the full moon. It was meticulously maintained, all the flowers kept neatly in place, and the trees trimmed with care. I looked up, glancing at the other two left at the table. Had it been one of them that maintained it, or Adrian? I doubted it was anyone outside their family, as they seemed too reclusive for that.

Though, the idea of Fallon—the haughty man who had said maybe one word during the entire ordeal earlier—tending to flowers, was nearly enough to make me laugh.

I took a second to observe the two at the table again, hunting for what I was still worried might be in their gazes. Osiris was looking at his empty glass like it would hold the answer to every question he had, and he had a lot of them. I could tell because it was the same look I'd seen in the mirror every day for the last few months. Black ink twisted up his slightly exposed arms, his white dress sleeves rolled up just once, the light color contrasting the harsh pinstripe of the rest of his suit. The markings, like war paint, were dark, almost too harsh for his olive skin.

Eirik held much of the same, though his ink looked like it had been there since the day he was born. I fought the heat that crawled its way onto my cheeks, remembering exactly how well those crisp patterns blended with the muscles along his back. The rolling streaks were like flowing water along his skin, and the dragon at his eye was as intimidating as it was beautiful. He stared at me with the same intensity as earlier today, his eyes a deeper, more cloudy blue, almost like it wasn't *him* behind them. His head tilted, and a feeling akin to that of being hunted made me tense as the hairs on my arms stood to attention.

I swallowed hard and looked away.

"So ..." I started, not sure what to say but unable to continue dealing with their unending quiet and piercing stares.

This wasn't awkward at all.

"What do you need from me?" I asked finally, maybe with a little too much force. As soon as it slipped out, I tensed. "I mean ... How can I help figure out why your reaction at the auction happened?"

Ah, word vomit. I just couldn't manage to shut up for five. Freaking. Seconds. Was this a good idea? How much did I really want them to know? I struggled to keep my panic at bay as Osiris turned my way, a curious expression on his face. I could only hope they wouldn't probe too far. His eyes held his age, his power behind them, that mismatched blue showing exactly what I feared and what I hoped to gain from them.

Knowledge.

"Well, there are a few things that might lead us in the right direction," Osiris started, his head tipping toward me. He tapped his glass again. "What kind of Natural are you, Aaliyah? Knowing that might well hold the answers to our question."

I froze in my seat, and it only took Osiris a second to recognize my change in posture as his own back straightened, his eyes narrowing the barest margin. His head tipped and Eirik let out a disbelieving huff.

"You don't know." It wasn't a question. Eirik's voice was confident. Almost *too* confident.

That surety put me on edge, and made me feel like an animal in a zoo as they continued to inspect me. I clenched my hands, pressing my palms into the wood of the seat beneath me, grounding my feet into the cold, black oak floor.

"No," I said if only to confirm it to myself. "No, I don't."

"That's quite interesting," Osiris mused, leaning forward, excitement lighting up his face.

That trapped feeling only grew, and I dug my fingers into my thighs to stop from standing and bolting out of the room. My chest clenched, and the way that Eirik's eyes followed me told me that running was a terrible idea.

Something in his eyes told me he would take chase.

"No. It's a pain in the ass is what it is," I said finally. They didn't respond for a second, as though my words stunned them into silence.

Without warning, another huff came from Eirik. The sound morphed, falling into a deep rumble, then finally a low laugh.

"So, I take it you've been trying to figure that out yourself, then?" Eirik asked, shaking his head, as though he was shaking off the laugh.

Osiris didn't move, and for once his attention wasn't fully on me. Instead his calculating stare was on Eirik, watching how his face twisted from that soft smile to a narrowed scowl. The shift was so subtle I almost didn't see it, that moment the joy turned to pain. It made my chest ache with a longing familiarity. I glanced around the room, searching for Prince, and found him still missing.

"Yeah, we've talked to everyone possible. Besides you guys, I suppose. Eliza ... She isn't a fan of Vampires." I twiddled my thumbs, unsure how else to say it.

I rolled my shoulders, trying to lose the tension in them. I didn't hold the same reservations against Vampires that she did, but that didn't mean I knew who to trust. Was this really the best option, trusting these men, these strangers, with my secrets? Though it wasn't really a secret, we had talked to everyone that might know, and none of them had known what I was. I took in Osiris's inquisitive expression, lacking in malice and full of empathy.

"Eliza, she wouldn't happen to be a Siren, would she?" Osiris asked, grabbing his wrist in a tight hold until the already pale skin of his hand went stark white.

"You know who she is?" I asked.

Osiris shook his head, looking to the moonlit yard as I had.

"No, not her specifically. But Ilenia, her grandmother, is the Siren Eternal. She and our Maker have been at odds for centuries."

Hatred burned like hot coals in his words, shimmering behind the cool blues of his eyes, though the rest of his expression stayed carefully blank.

I knew better than to push, even though I was curious. Most Naturals had an innate dislike for Vampires, as they were often cruel to those that they viewed as below them. It shouldn't be a surprise that other Vampires felt the same way.

Even about their own Maker.

Eliza's hatred for them was seemingly unending, and I could only assume that her *baba* harbored the same hatred. From the look in Osiris's eyes, I knew his Maker was likely one of the main reasons for that.

"So, you and the Siren have been on a hunt for someone that might know what you are," Eirik said nonchalantly, betraying the tactical focus that filled his eyes. This time, I knew it was him looking at me, the sky-blue of his eyes piercing. In a way, it reminded me of Carter, one of Eliza's husbands. He was Dragonkin and I recalled Eliza mentioning his other half, the beast, that allowed him to shift. I wondered for a moment if Eirik was like that as well. "You must have talked to many people."

I nodded, knocked out of my musing by the deep rumble of Eirik's words.

"*Eliza* and I talked to everyone in Oakridge. We only had one person left to try. An old friend of Eliza's *baba*," I said, emphasizing Eliza's name, feeling uneasy about how level Eirik seemed.

I couldn't deny the safety that came in his words, the lack of question, the subtle worry. He ran a hand over his bearded chin before turning to Osiris. They spoke without words, their heads tipping as though conversing in their minds.

"Someone that hasn't already been here, someone that Ilenia would consider a reasonable ally?" Eirik tapped the scar on his neck before reaching into his shirt and grabbing the silver chain there.

I hadn't noticed the small emblem before, it having been tucked carefully into his shirt. The silver held the face of a wolf with crossed engravings that were like his tattoos. The Celtic designs were intricate, and his thumb passed over them, drawing me back to his contemplative face.

Then Eirik's face twisted, as though he'd finally figured out some big mystery, and the answer he found wasn't a good one. His eyes narrowed, flashing to Osiris again before coming back to me.

"You were going to talk to Archon Sewire," he said, once again more sure of it than I was.

Not to mention correct.

He crossed his arms over his broad chest, flexing against the too-small shirt he'd put on. At that moment, he looked like the most powerful person I had ever seen. It was the way he sat, his arms crossed and head tipped like he knew exactly who he was. He was confident in himself, his abilities, in anything else that he wanted to be, and for a second it terrified me.

"How did you know that?" I mumbled out, as I ground my teeth, fighting the need to fidget as best I could.

"Excuse Eirik. He spent many years captaining ships and he grew rather competent in deductive reasoning. However, he sometimes forgets how *intimidating* he can be." Osiris's emphasis on the word met Eirik with a narrowed glare, and Eirik just grunted. The sound was deep in his chest, and again the sky-blue eyes swirled and darkened.

"This is why Adrian is in charge of our information supply," Osiris said, shaking his head at Eirik's eye roll.

"And your redirection could use some work, Osiris," Eirik said, standing from his spot at the table. He paced by the open windows. "Archon Sewire was going to *help* you?" Eirik pushed, crossing his arms over his chest again.

Though he didn't give me the chance to say anything more; not that I could have. The continual tug of war of my conscience drowned all my thoughts out. Should I tell them? *What* should I tell them? The choices strangled my words as the muscles of Eirik's arms flexed, tensing as he leaned forward.

"What was his price?" His words, so soft compared to his stature, caused some of the tension to leave me.

Though he seemed agitated, he didn't move toward me, still keeping a respectful distance, and his hands where I could see them. It was so subtle a move that I nearly missed the feeling that had made him seem so familiar when I first saw him in the kitchen. Something had happened, something that made him know how to act around me.

It made my throat burn to even think about it.

"He didn't name one," I said finally, even knowing exactly what Archon wanted, and he likely got it. He gave us to Darius on a silver platter ... handed us to him in Vampire territory at night.

"He's a Djinn. They always want something," Osiris chimed in, his words snapping my attention to him. "What he wanted wasn't something you would be quick to offer, or he knew he could benefit from it. He likely sold your information to Darius for a cut of the profit."

Though he was right, it still hurt to hear it. Eliza's hopeful face came to mind, and it was all I could think of as I tried to find the words.

"He was the only choice we had," was all I managed, choking on the implications that only I knew.

He'd been my last chance, and he failed us in the worst way. I glanced again at the two left at the table, and some of the clenching around my chest dissipated. He'd been my last chance, *or so we had thought.* I had to stay hopeful that we were wrong.

That I had more time.

"Well, it was a shit choice. You walked into a Djinn's lair, in unfamiliar territory on the trust that he wanted nothing from you." Eirik's disappointed stare hurt almost as much as it enraged. "You could have gotten hurt."

I flinched at Eirik's bruising words as they threatened to burn me from the inside out. All I could think about was how Curtis's hands felt, the burn of his breath against my skin. About the feeling of a *Rend* against my conscience, the pain of being torn from my body. The agonized emotion on Prince's face every time it happened. It made me sick. Hurt, hurt, *hurt*. I *was* hurt. All I ever seemed to do was *hurt*. I was caught and bound and sold at a fucking auction they were at.

That thought fueled me as I stood, staring down at the man that was well over two foot taller than I was. Eirik's eyes widened, surprise clear on his face as I snarled at him with all the power I could muster.

"Don't you think I didn't know that? That everything about that walk was *wrong,* that I shouldn't have ignored my instincts? But you're right, I shouldn't have trusted Archon. I *didn't* trust him. I trusted Eliza, I trusted Prince, and nothing you say will ever make me regret that." I tapped my chest, pushing past the burning tension that caused my hand to shake.

Breathing became hard, and even as I panicked, I kept speaking. I wouldn't be silenced again, and I sure as hell wasn't about to back down.

"I still could get hurt. I'm sitting here on trust, aren't I? I am talking to you on trust." I pointed a finger at Eirik, ignoring the instinct to cower. "Don't forget that you *bought* me. From the same auction that Archon likely sold us to." Eirik jerked back, like I'd physically struck him. It nearly stuck the next words in my throat. "So don't kid yourself. I'm barely trusting you now."

The room went silent until only the clock above us could be heard.

A growl resounded throughout the small space. Eirik's eyes shone brightly back at me, shifting agitatedly between red and a deep blue. Again, I felt I wasn't looking at Eirik, his eyes wild and savage. I held his gaze, unwilling to be cowed.

"Eirik." The command in Osiris's voice sent my spine ramrod straight as he stood with palms pressed against the table, his eyes never leaving Eirik's irritable form.

Eirik's face contorted, the sharpness that had taken root across his cheekbones and high nose relaxing. The giant of a man clenched the table hard, claws dragging across the wood, though not hard enough to leave gouges. Finally, his eyes closed, and I could see him take a few settling breaths. By the time he opened his eyes again, they were back to their standard light ocean color.

"Your worry is warranted, though infuriating, *smár Valkyrja.*" Eirik ran his hand along his neck, finger tapping at the scar there. "You are a formidable warrior, Aaliyah, and I pity anyone that gets in your way. I see your fear of us, yet you stand against it. I look forward to winning your trust one day."

Determination brimmed his eyes, and it wasn't hard to tell that he meant it. It helped to dull the ache I still felt as I sank back into the chair. It creaked and groaned before going silent. Adrenaline left me, and a chill quickly replaced it.

"You look exhausted. We can discuss this more later," Osiris said with a sigh, brushing his hands over his suit as if removing dust that wasn't there.

His height hadn't really stuck with me, as he was seated when I came down. He wasn't as tall as Eirik and he held much less bulk; he was almost lithe. Just as I did him, Osiris studied me. Though it didn't feel intensive, it was a mutual curiosity, the same one I felt toward him. He tapped at his tattooed arms nervously, like my stare was scorching his skin so I looked away.

"Yeah, guess I am," I said, finally giving myself a second to assess how I felt.

I had been on edge for hours, even after we came to our *deal.* Though this had helped. Eliza's words still rang in my ears, but they were no longer loud enough to completely cloud my judgment. I couldn't think that these men were like that, the monsters that she described.

"Do any of your injuries need dressing?" Osiris asked, and I shook my head.

"No," I said.

I showed my hands, lacking the bandages I had on them when I went to shower. Just like with everything else, my body had healed itself, leaving small white scars in the wake of where the glass and rope had been. They visibly relaxed, which settled that comforted feeling in my chest.

Worry. Empathy. Those weren't the emotions of someone who

wanted to do wrong to you, but they were the emotions of Eirik and Osiris. I took a deep breath and smiled. Eirik smiled back without hesitation, the roguish grin once again bringing me back to the one person who I wished was here right now. Over Eliza, over everyone.

Prince.

Thoughts of him morphed the joy in my chest to lead, and it had me turning away.

"Good. Then do you need an escort?" Osiris asked.

"No, I think I'm okay," I said, tilting my head toward the stairs as I stood. I steadied myself on the table, hissing as my bare feet hit the cold wood floors. "Thank you, though," I mumbled, creeping toward the stairs.

They didn't say anything behind me.

I kept the tremble out of my step until I hit the door that led to the room I woke up in. They'd cleaned the splinters of wood up off the ground and put a new door in, just like Osiris had said. Though it wasn't a replica of the one that had been there before, with no delicate designs tracing the wood.

I walked in, taking only a second to close the door before I sank to the floor, my back pressed against the wood. I ran my hands over my face, stopping the residual trembles in their tracks. The longer I sat, the more stupid I felt.

"Damn it," I whispered to myself as I sank further against the door. "What a mess you've got yourself into, Aaliyah."

My habit of talking to myself continued, even though I tried to stop it. It helped to break up the silence, made me feel less alone. Vampires. I was in a house full of *Vampires*. I still couldn't quite seem to wrap my head around it or get over the fear it brought. Though it wasn't the same gnawing, creeping panic that I'd felt on the walk to Archon's. It wasn't my instincts telling me to run. It was my mind trying to convince me that trusting them was the right thing to do.

I wanted to believe it, and that almost scared me more than dying.

The room was still in relative disarray around me, though the bedpost had been reattached to the frame. I could barely tell which one I'd taken off; the wood pressed seamlessly together. The care that was taken with it didn't go unnoticed, none of it had. Their calm demeanors, the smiles, the damn *worry*.

I wasn't used to navigating people, let alone men. I'd barely spoken with Dezen and Carter blond daily pleasantries, and even then I'd always had Eliza as a barrier. Here, I was open, unable to stop my heart from pounding in my chest as I stumbled over words like a toddler just learning to speak.

What a fucking mess.

The first sob was quiet, and only the wet of my cheeks told me that there were tears. I forced my head to my knees, muffling the sound as I broke down, the realization that I'd nearly lost everything: my home, my life, my *family*, Eliza, Grigen, even Dezen and Carter.

Prince.

I sobbed again, unable to keep my thoughts from my knight any longer. It was his face that I needed right now, his sure smile and proud grin that had no right to make my heart skip.

"Please, Prince. I can't lose you too," I mumbled out, begging him to appear like he always did, with a tilted grin and a bow.

I wasn't ready to lose him, I was barely ready to be away from him for more than a few hours, and it had been *several*. I hadn't been without him for as long as I could remember, and almost none of the memories I'd gotten back were before him. He was my constant, and he'd simply disappeared after letting me loose to the men that bought me.

I winced at my thought. No matter how right it was, they deserved none of the anger that came with it. They set me free, agreed to help without knowing what I wanted, and had been nothing but patient with me as I more or less tried to stab them.

Scratch that, *did* stab one of them.

That seemed trustworthy enough, but I needed to make sure. I couldn't let the mistake with Archon happen again. I needed to be absolutely positive that they wouldn't turn around and hurt my family. It was the only thing keeping me from calling Eliza right now, from making sure she was okay and telling her where I was. I wouldn't put her in harm's way, not until I was sure they weren't a threat. Though, would that ever really be true? Osiris had pulled out the heart of the same Dragonkin that had overpowered us, and something told me that was *child's play* for him. They'd always be a threat.

Hopefully, just not to me or my family.

I sighed, taking a deep breath and forcing a calm I didn't feel.

I wasn't expecting the knock at the door, the vibration rattling down my spine. I tensed, freezing to my spot, instinctively reaching out to grab something, fingers gripping a spare piece of wood that must have been missed when they cleaned up while I was showering. It was small, barely larger than a quarter but it was enough to center me. I gripped it tightly as the tears on my cheeks went cold, and my breath came out in shallow pants. The shuffle of feet on the other side of the door was quiet, and I held my breath, unsure what I should do.

They knocked again, more insistently this time.

"Give me a second," I said, cringing at the croak in my voice.

I forced myself to stand, looking down at myself out of habit. I was a mess at best, in clothes that were several sizes too large for me. The scars that had been hidden under the white silk fabric of the auction now stood stark against the dark threads of my shirt.

I swallowed hard as the man on the other side shuffled again. I slid the door open, and it gave way with a creak, the hinges not quite used to the new weight yet.

My mouth dropped open at the sight of Fallon standing in the hallway. His blond hair was perfectly waved back, his head twisted away from me in what had to be an uncomfortable manner. He stood stiffly, his burly arms crossed over a broad chest, and his green eyes narrowed in on me as he looked me up and down. I hadn't realized how large he was considering how silently he moved, but he had to at least tie Eirik in sheer muscle mass, though he was a few inches shorter. Seeing him alone made me realize exactly how alluring Fallon was, how *intimidating* he was, with the crisp green dress shirt and pressed white slacks. He studied me, vibrant green eyes tracing my face and my hands before he looked past me into the room.

"Is everything okay, Fallon?" I finally asked, unnerved by his silence.

He didn't say anything for a moment, glancing over his shoulder at the staircase when he sighed. Fallon came off as the most reserved of the Vivas household. In fact, he blended so well into them I nearly forgot he was here. But I couldn't do that now, not with the sweeping way the sinful allure in his eyes held me captive.

They held worry, and I couldn't tell if it was for me or for himself.

He shuffled, sticking his hand into the breast pocket of his green dress shirt and pulling something out. He closed it in his hand so I couldn't see it before his head tilted, his brushed-back hair falling over his face. He put his hand out toward me, gesturing for me to do the same. Curiosity overcame me as I put my hand out, palm up, and déjà vu sank in as I recalled Grigen and his contagious smile. Just like I'd done with Grigen, Fallon placed a small item in my hand, closing my fingers around it. It was cold to the touch, and when I peeked at what it was I was met with something in a reflective wrapper. I brought it up to eye level and noted that the silver wrapping didn't have any marks on it.

"What is it?" I asked as I glanced back at Fallon.

His face scrunched just barely, and something told me that if he could blush he would have. The odd sight was endearing in a way, and it helped sweep away the ache of my breakdown.

"Aldovin Chocolate," he said the words so nonchalantly that I nearly thought nothing of it. Yet, when I watched the way his eyes softened at the sight of the treat, something told me this was more than just a regular gift.

"Why are you giving this to me?" I asked, trying not to flinch under his stony scrutiny.

He tensed as though trying to decide whether to respond. Glancing at the stairs again he sighed before he turned a serious gaze back on me, raising an eyebrow.

"Sounded like you could use it."

I cringed, gripping the piece of wood in my hand tighter. It ached against my palm, and I kept my voice down as I searched for what to say.

"You heard that?" I finally asked.

He nodded, because of course he did. They were Vampires. Damn, I would need to remember that.

"Why were you crying?" he asked back.

"Overwhelmed, I guess," I responded. "Not sure if you noticed, but you guys are kind of intimidating."

Fallon shook his head, keeping his arms crossed tightly over his chest.

"No, I hadn't." Though he said it with a straight face, there was a distinct dry humor in his words and I smiled at him.

"So, you like candy, then?"

Fallon shook his head. "Just chocolate."

I looked at him incredulously, and he barely moved, that bored look still on his face when he ushered me to open the wrapper. I did, keeping the piece of wood tucked in my palm as I unveiled the light chocolate with flecks of red. I popped it into my mouth, expecting a rich chocolate flavor, the kind that was bitter yet smooth like Eliza liked. Instead, the chocolate melted, tasting vaguely like strawberries and sugar. I looked up to where Fallon stood, gaping at him the same way he was staring at me, like I'd just grown an extra head.

Fallon liked *sweets*?

"Do you not like it?" he asked, looking affronted at the notion.

"No, I do. It's really tasty, I just wasn't really expecting it to be so ..." He didn't see the irony of the sweetness of his chocolate, or if he did, he didn't care. Fallon didn't seem like the kind of man that would keep treats in his suit pocket, let alone ones like this. I shook my head, blushing. "Sweet."

He raised an eyebrow, as if it would be anything else. Though he looked embarrassed, his head tipping up and his eyes narrowing.

Silence took over our conversation and I shuffled on my feet, still clutching my piece of wood like a lifeline. Should I say something? I wasn't sure. Of all the things I was still learning, conversation cues had been the hardest for me to pick up. Fallon didn't seem bothered by the silence, taking the time to look me over before he frowned.

It wasn't a deep expression or one that conveyed malice, but it felt raw. He was upset about something, and it was leaking through that bored look he'd kept up while talking.

"Why did you choose to stay with us?" he asked, that frigid tone once again coating his words.

It was distinctive, the change. Like he was putting on armor for a fight. I swallowed hard, trying to find the right thing to say. I wouldn't lie to them, not after they had been truthful. I could do the same ... with this, at least.

"Because ... my friend trusted you," I said finally.

And it was true. It was the final reason why I stayed. He didn't need to know anything else, not yet.

"Prince?" he asked, almost incredulously.

The question was so quiet I almost didn't hear it, and when I looked up, Fallon's expression was curious. My heart jumped, and at first, I wondered where he'd heard that name.

Until I remembered how he just found me, crying and talking to myself. He had to have heard me asking Prince to come back.

"That's him," I answered, relaxing into the quiet conversation we were having. "You look surprised. Trust me, I was too. But he'd never hurt me, and it looks like he's been right so far."

Fallon nodded and pried no more than that. It was nice, normal even, holding a conversation like we were. So even as fear I couldn't stomp down continued to force a tremble in my legs, I held steady, and tried to remember that we had a deal as I waited for Fallon to respond. He was silent for a breath more, before his mouth opened like he was going to speak.

But then he froze.

His nose flared and his eyes went wide as he searched me up and down. A cold panic followed as his gaze landed on my hand, the one that still held the piece of wood I'd picked up. I had loosened my grip on it, feeling less threatened. I must have cut myself.

I was scared to glance up.

"Fallon?" I whispered.

I waited. One second, two. Each one dragged on longer than the rest, and I tried to keep my heart from beating out of my chest.

And then I looked up.

As always, Fallon's face was a mask of ice and I was unable to see anything on it. No expression, no bloodlust, nothing. It was almost scarier than the alternative.

Until the red crept into his eyes.

It was strange to see outside of the auction house, and even stranger up close. The red swallowed everything from white to pupil, until it was a flowing mass of color. Instinct paralyzed me as Fallon's eyes widened with surprise. But I wasn't scared, not really. Not how I'd been just yesterday. The fear was there, but it was less oppressive.

More understanding.

Because for some reason, the shock that extended over Fallon's face, seeing that absolute panic in his red eyes, reminded me of my own. It reminded me of a *Rend*. So, rather than slamming the door in his face and curling into a ball and crying, I smiled. The kind that I hoped told him he wasn't alone, because whatever was going on ...

... it was hurting him.

Fallon jolted like he'd been shocked, the red flickering to a vibrant green before he flipped away from me and walked toward the stairs. His gait was even but hurried, and something told me he was doing his best not to run.

"Take care, Aaliyah," he said, a harsh growl in his words. They were pointed, meant to gouge. "Don't forget, you live with monsters now."

I smiled sadly at his retreating back, his words sinking into my skin. There was panic in them, some fear, and in some ways, they were a wake-up call. I turned away and forced myself to close the door softly, clicking the lock that was now on my side, into place. I gripped the foil wrapping paper, still tasting a hint of sweet chocolate.

They hadn't hurt me ... but something about my blood made them want to, and I needed to remember that. No matter how at ease I was with them, no matter how much I enjoyed their conversation and presence, I had to remember that they were dangerous, and it was best to keep them at a distance, at least for now.

My life depended on it.

CHAPTER 14

FALLON

Why? *Why* did she have to cry?

Her door closed, and I *flitted* down onto our ground level, fighting as the *Maker's Call* forced its way across my skin, settling in my stomach like acid.

You're mine, Fallon. She can't have you.

Sebek's words, still as clear in my mind as Aislinn's smile, made me sick. The nausea was so intense I nearly puked as I wretched the door to our mini fridge open, grabbing the first bottle I found. I tried to drown the pain with blood wine, but I was left with the same feeling I'd had at the auction.

Longing. Want. Fucking *lust*.

The wine tasted like ash and burned sand, something that filled me with rage, yet wasn't all too surprising. We'd been dealing with our lack of want for blood wine for years, as it slowly became clear it no longer sated us, and now even the flavor was degrading. I nearly screamed, as the panic that I'd fought down for years, *decades,* found its way into me again. I tossed the empty bottle into the sink, barely catching how it shattered as I flicked the water on and scrubbed my hands, rubbing them until they were raw. And even then, I couldn't focus on anything but the smell of her blood in the air.

On her smile when she realized what I'd given her.

I shouldn't have marched myself up to her door. I shouldn't have thought of bringing her comfort when I heard her cry. Mistake ... it was a mistake, and now the *Call* was making me pay for it.

"Fuck," I whispered, ripping my hands through my hair.

A rough *hum* sounded behind me, and I didn't need to turn to know that it was Eirik. He opened the fridge, and I turned to find him in his typical workout gear. His mind had also been elsewhere, based on the amount of sweat on him.

"You look like shit," he said, passing me another glass of the blood wine as he stood, looking with raised eyebrows at the mess I'd made in the sink.

He stared like he expected me to react, and I would have, had I been even slightly more focused on our conversation. I needed a fight now more than ever, but I couldn't even seem to give myself that.

Eirik scowled, downing his glass.

"What happened?" he asked, and I scoffed.

"Nothing," I said, following his example and downing the foul liquid. As before, it tasted of nothing but resentment. I snapped my teeth together, forcing a calm I didn't feel.

"Bullshit. What the fuck happened, Fallon?" The tap of Eirik's hand on the counter and the way his quickly darkening eyes followed my movements, told me there was no getting out of this.

Protector Eirik was in total control, and the *Úlfhéðinn* wouldn't be letting me leave until we'd had a conversation.

"What does it matter what happened, Eirik? Nothing I say is going to change it or get rid of the problem," I said, and Eirik glared, picking up the subtler tones in my words.

It was one of the many *perks* of being one of Sebek's Turned. It was easier to tell how the others were feeling when you all shared the same blood.

Literally.

"The *Call*?" he asked, pushing.

"Of course it's the fucking *Call*," I seethed. "She cut herself on a piece of the door that we missed."

"And that's why you're like this?" he asked.

"Of course it is," I shot back.

I flexed my hands just as Eirik rolled his eyes, setting the emptied glass down on the table. He crossed his arms, waiting for a response that I would not give.

"That's bullshit, Fallon, and you know it," Eirik growled, as his nose flared. "No, if this was just the *Call* getting the better of you would have already torn her apart. This is something else."

I froze, the gnawing feeling in my throat unfamiliar. It was the *Call* ... It had to be the *Call*.

"You don't want to admit you didn't mind her company. And when you realized it, your body tried to compensate. You scared her." Eirik's words cut like glass, and I laughed.

It sounded deranged even to me, sharp and pointed like a polished knife. He was wrong. He was *wrong*.

"She needs to know what she's getting into, Eirik. I only told her as much," I said back through clenched teeth.

"You scared her." The protective tone to his voice had me seething once again, and the pretense of calm exploded.

"She should be scared!" I screamed, surprising even myself.

That was the problem. She *should* be scared, but she wasn't. She shouldn't have agreed to our deal, but she *did*. She smiled so softly it made my heart clench, with understanding in her eyes telling me she knew I was being haunted. She made me think kindness was something I could afford. Eirik knew this, and he didn't give me the reprieve of letting it go.

"And you're mad that she's not?" Calm, so calm in how he spoke.

Always the warrior, the tactician. He knew how to tear down walls, even ones that weren't real.

Damned Viking.

"I'm mad that she's still here, that we didn't solve this problem how we should have," I said through clenched teeth, digging my nails into my palms.

"Bitching about it isn't going to change things, Fallon." Eirik took a step toward me, so close I could see the harsh lines of his scars against the black lines of his tattoos. "The only thing that can change is your attitude. So, are you going to keep being a little shit, or am I going to have to beat it out of you?"

There was no hesitancy in his voice, no regret in the storms of his icy blue eyes. His Viking was showing, his proud Norseman heritage rearing its head. The rush of blood that came from knowing a fight was near was exciting, riveting, and pride all wrapping into one emotion. Yet, even with the uncertainty I felt, the look on his face gave me a reason to keep talking. He was looking more like Eirik than he had in years. And even as I cursed it, I had Aaliyah to thank for that. Somehow, someway, over the *day* she'd been here, she'd bled more life into my brothers than the last hundred years combined.

"There's the Eirik I know," I said, not shrinking under his steadfast glare. Some of the tension left my shoulders, and I rubbed my hand over my jaw. "Stop trying to be Nero, brother. It doesn't suit you."

Poking at Eirik when he was in one of his moods was never a good idea. Pressing a still-sore wound was even worse. But I wanted it: the fight, the pain. I needed it. *He* needed it, and I knew as much the moment he launched himself at me. His first hit shook my entire body, the crunch of his fist against my jaw spurring me to move. We threw hits like it was a dance, and we fought like it was the last one we'd ever have. I could almost hear Nero now, egging us on from the sidelines.

I get the winner, he'd scream.

Blood sprayed, and before long the sound of hoarse laughs and snarls followed our brawl. I could see the anticipation in Eirik's eyes in the way he moved. Like he'd finally realized how bottled up he'd been. We were so lost in our fight that neither of us noticed the entrance of Adrian and Osiris.

"That's enough." The *Charm* in Osiris's voice was heady, and I could feel his power in the air as he walked toward us.

Eirik turned his steely glower to our eldest brother, but kept his hands raised, ready to begin again.

"We aren't savages. If you're going to fight, take it outside or to the training room," Osiris said, his distinctive glower following me as I glanced around us.

The room was still primarily intact. Maybe a few chairs were out of place, and the silverware that had been on the island was on the ground, but other than that we had remained mostly civil. Minus the blood on the ground, and even then, it wasn't very much. I recalled a time when the entire floor was covered in pig's blood thanks to one of Nero's many pranks.

"Because if you break anything in this room, you're going to be dealing with *me.*" The warning in Osiris's voice lacked force, though his disapproving stare wandered around the room.

The sight almost made me laugh. Osiris had always been one for organization, liking things to be in their proper place, nice and clean.

"I'll provide the popcorn and the shitty wine if you make that fight happen," laughed Adrian.

"You're still angry about our decision?" Osiris asked, reminding me of what had caused our little show to begin with.

"I think he's angrier about how he's reacting to it," Adrian chimed in. "Try looser pants. You'll thank me later."

He tugged at his jeans, winking in my direction. I rolled my eyes and reached down, lifting the button from my shirt off the ground, only now realizing that one of them had flown off. I promptly flicked it in Adrian's direction, scowling when he dodged the projectile.

"Someone's feisty today!" Adrian laughed it off again, skirting around the kitchen.

I was glad that he was back to his bubbly self after our meditation. The *Call* had him in a panic, and I hadn't seen fear that deep in his eyes since we'd found Nero's body.

"If you're so opposed to her presence, then why did you go to her door?" Osiris asked, tipping his head toward the stairs. He kept his words low, listening to the even sound of Aaliyah's heartbeat. She slept easily, snoring softly just upstairs.

"What does it matter why?" I asked, straightening my shirt and smoothing my hair back over my head.

My words lacked heat, and even Eirik huffed his approval. Bastard was right: I needed a fight. And damned if he didn't give me one. I ran a hand over my jaw, the mending bone aching under the press of my hand.

"Oh, stop your bullshitting, Fallon. I heard you, knocking on her door like a knight in shining armor while she was crying. Don't think I don't know you gave her a chocolate," Adrian said, his face lit with mock anger.

I rolled my eyes again but didn't comment. I wasn't sure why I gave her one, either. It didn't have to be the Aldovin, I had many other treats I could've shared ... but it came easy, handing her a piece of my soul when she didn't know how much it meant.

"She was crying?" Eirik mumbled, a look of anguish taking up his face.

That was a surprise itself, but then Eirik's eyes widened in a stark panic, shifting to a deep ocean blue as his hands shot up to his head. He'd been partially shifted before our bout, but the more subtle changes that came with his wolf were easier to see now that the confrontation had calmed. His nose pointed, while fangs poked over his lip. There was a sharpness to his face that looked painful.

We all shot back as the distinct sound of popping met our ears, and Eirik's bones shifted under the pull of his beast.

A beast that Eirik was currently losing control of.

"Fuck," Adrian said, jumping up onto the counter with lofted grace, and I wasn't much better as I scrambled back against the wall.

Wolves were a death sentence to Vampires, their bite nearly as sure as the sun. Though I trusted Eirik with my life, I couldn't stop the reaction to his energy as he shifted. My muscles tensed, prepping me to run before I even decided to, as just like that, we'd become prey.

Only Osiris didn't move away. He stalked forward, curiosity on his face as he flexed his hands before reaching out and pressing his palm against Eirik's throat. I could see the jolt, the strain that came with stopping himself from pulling back. I hadn't been around when he'd still worn gloves, and I didn't know the entire story behind why touch was so despised by Osiris. But from how he looked now, I didn't know if I ever wanted to know. He was haunted by a past we weren't privy to, always pretending like everything was okay, if only to keep the monsters at bay for a day longer.

Did Osiris expect this to work now that Aaliyah was here? Did he think this charade of stability could continue? Did Eirik think he could keep this beast at bay in her presence? Fuck, even Adrian and I were bombs waiting to go off. Our family was like broken glass. How long would it take her to cut herself on us?

Eirik snarled again, the sound so guttural that it sent a shiver down my spine and I hissed, slamming my head against the wall to keep from running. His heavy panting was the only thing any of us could focus on. Eirik's beast still paced behind his eyes, clawing at the proud Viking's sanity. Osiris kept a firm hold on Eirik's neck, unrelenting.

"You seem to have forgotten what I said about fucking up our home," Osiris said, brow raising as he turned to me, and the dent I'd made in the wall, as though this wasn't an unusual occurrence.

Like he wasn't dealing with Eirik in a blood frenzy. Something that hadn't happened in the entirety of my two hundred years alive.

"Calm yourself, Eirik," Osiris said, a snarl in his own words.

The hoarse, caged laugh that was expelled from Eirik had me recoiling. It wasn't *his* laugh. The walls were crumbling, and not just mine. I could see the madness in Eirik's eyes, the crazy I'd only heard about. This was the Eirik from tales gone by; those whispered over a quiet fireplace where none could hear ... before he, Osiris and Nero had abandoned Vampiric ideals.

When fear fed them as much as blood.

I never thought I'd see it, not when everything had already been in place when I was turned. They'd never exposed me or Adrian to their horrors, and from the fear on Eirik's face, he knew he was slipping. Maybe now he would finally understand why I fought so hard. Why I knew that keeping Aaliyah here would be our downfall.

My chest burned, and the thought of her leaving left a hole where my heart should be. I pushed it down, burying the feeling.

"Calm down? You want me to calm down?" Eirik whispered, but it wasn't him that was speaking.

I could see the fight burning in his eyes again as our Eirik tried to take back control.

"Yes, that would be preferable," Osiris said, his lips curling into a growl that rivaled that of Eirik's.

"*Muna langt fram.*" The old Norse words on Osiris's lips held a finality to them, and silence greeted us. *Remember from a time long lost.*

Osiris let up on Eirik's neck and pressed his hand from his chest to

Eirik's, and the giant let out a shaky breath before his eyes settled and his face fell into a mask of calm once again.

"*Dreyrugr, Vivas.*" The switch between Old Norse directly to Latin pulled me back to *us*. To what we were and what we stood for.

Bloodstained. What we were, what we were born from, and what we sought to pull away from.

To live. Osiris had handpicked our name after his turn, so we'd always have a family to rely on. It was unheard of for Vampires to stay with the other Turned of their Maker.

Still, Osiris had never been a typical Natural.

Finally, Eirik took a shaky breath and slid to the ground with a less than dignified thump.

"What the *fuck* just happened?" Adrian asked, still stationed on the marble countertop.

He was pressed against the cupboards, his head flicking between Osiris and Eirik. Eirik scowled, turning his head away, and the scent of regret and shame filtered into the room.

"I haven't seen you lose yourself to your wolf in centuries," Osiris said, with a shake of his head. "What happened, Eirik?"

Eirik could only shake his head, teeth clenching.

"He's agitated ..." he said, finally.

He ran a hand down his face, the tremble in his body removing the last traces of his looming shift.

"No shit, Sherlock," Adrian said, finally sliding to the ground. He brushed off his jeans, still eyeing Eirik warily.

"I think it's claimed Aaliyah as pack," Eirik said. "Her discomfort unsettles him, gives him the reins."

My eyebrows shot up, and even Osiris was left with his jaw dropped.

"When did you first notice this?" Osiris asked quietly.

Eirik didn't look like he was going to answer at first, or at the very least, not give an honest one. Then he sighed, rolling his neck.

"The auction. I felt it as early as in the parking lot, though ... It got worse the farther into the building we got," he admitted, freezing the blood in my veins. "The first solid hint of her blood was just before the curtain went up."

I remembered that moment, thinking he was catching the scent of the blood wine. I'd hoped that our issues with the bottled blood were finally over, only to be dragged headfirst into a frenzy by a lass who reached no higher than my shoulders. He'd been going mad since before we even knew she was there.

"This is exactly what I was worried about," I said, enraged knowing that my words would not sway them.

"This is nothing, Fallon. It's not the first time I've had to settle Eirik's beast. It won't be the last," Osiris said, tapping the counter. "But we can't very well leave it like this. We need a way to tie us all in, make sure we're safe for our guest."

Osiris looked around the room contemplatively before his eyes shaded over. Then he nodded to himself, resolution clear on his face. "I'll see if I have any of my tomes, and we can go from there."

Excuse me?

"Magic, Osiris?" I asked, unsure if I'd even heard him correctly. "You don't use magic anymore."

He hadn't in years, since making our wards for our home. Before that ... it had been centuries. Millenia. He hadn't used it to stop Nero from ...

And all at once, it hurt to breathe.

So I didn't.

"This is a good reason to start again," Osiris said, leaving no room for negotiation as he stalked away. Just dropped the words like they were simple, *easy*. Like they didn't shatter every expectation I had about our eldest brother.

What the fuck have we gotten ourselves into?

CHAPTER 15

AALIYAH

I tiptoed across the cool oak of the second floor of my new, temporary home, trying to keep the sound of my steps down. I'd slept for the better part of last night and well into today, my body desperately needing a reset after everything that'd happened. I wasn't sure what time it was now, though I had a feeling the sun was still up. That didn't matter much to me though. I just needed to get out of that room, even for a few minutes. Being stuck in there, alone with my thoughts, was starting to bring up memories I'd rather not relive.

I ached to see Prince, and every time I looked around to find him missing, another piece of me chipped off. I also desperately wanted to see Eliza and make sure she was okay. I was so worried about her it hurt to even think about what might have happened. I had to believe that she made it home, that she was safe. Every second I spent in that room I considered caving and telling the guys where to find Eliza's little herb shop, if they didn't know already. But I couldn't, not yet. I wouldn't risk Eliza's safety like that.

I took another step, pushing down my thoughts as I kept moving. If this was my house for now ... then I was going to explore it.

I felt more comfortable doing it now, less like an intruder in the Vivas household, and more like a tenant myself. They hadn't bothered me after I went to sleep. They'd been courteous, even downright friendly, and the calm that I felt around them was almost terrifying. So I wasn't going to look a gift horse in the mouth. Prince would be proud of how well I'd held up, or at least I hoped he would. I wanted to tell him about the Vivas Crypt, about this crazy experience. But he wasn't here, and I wasn't sure if I would ever get the chance.

I shook my head, clearing the thought. It was warmer in the house this evening, comfortable and not anywhere near as freezing as it had been the day I'd woken up here. It was like the heat had been raised, and I wondered if they'd done it on purpose or if I'd just been cold because of the stress.

I tried not to think too much about it as I turned down the narrow hallway, twisting the corner from my room, and right up to a glass door. It was a mosaic; vibrant colors showing a rising or setting sun. It stood out against the gray of the walls, and I'd first noticed it when I'd showered yesterday.

I couldn't see much through the glass, as the stain blended so well with the curves that it was basically impossible. I was almost positive that it wasn't a bedroom, but ...

Well, there was always the chance that I was about to stroll into one of their rooms. Hopefully, if it *was* a bedroom, they didn't sleep naked. Eirik hadn't been wearing a shirt when we first met, and I could still see his corded muscles, recalling with vivid detail the flex of them when he moved. The twists and turns of the dark ink of his tattoos, covered in a fine sheet of water or sweat. I couldn't stop the rise of heat to my cheeks, the mental image almost sinful as I chewed my bottom lip, trying to sort through the conflicting feelings.

Open the door? Leave it be? Risk catching one of them off guard? I shouldn't be thinking like this, shouldn't be letting my guard down around them just because they were beautiful.

They lure you in with their good looks and charm.

I shook my head, pushing away Eliza's voice and the instinctual panic that came with the unknown. I'd agreed to give them a chance and thinking like this wasn't doing that.

I pushed past the door, the creak of its hinges making me flinch. Past that mosaic was a game room of sorts, and I sighed in relief when I finally saw it.

It was a large room, fitted with a pool table and a piano as well as a few other choice pieces of furniture. As I expected, the metal shutters that covered the windows during the day were down, meaning that I had at least a little while before the others would come looking for me. The room was just as crisp as the rest of the home, with black oak floors and gray walls.

I took a step forward, taking in the comfortable red couch, one of the few blotches of color to be seen. I considered sinking into it to see if it was as plush as it looked, before something else caught my eye.

Walking past the couch, I went up to a door that practically called to me. The rich mahogany was stark against the walls, and I took a moment to admire it, taking in its intricate designs.

A man, wearing what I recognized as Egyptian clothing—thanks to the many history documentaries I'd seen courtesy of Dezen's obsession with them—stood holding a staff in the center of the door. His face, with a long, narrow and twisting beak, was facing the side. Curved lines and stark patterns surrounded him, and much like the mosaic, a sun was standing vibrantly in the background. It was carved with every detail in mind, down to the individual feathers gracing the man's body. Though, as I looked closer, I realized that some of the space seemed unintentionally blank.

Like it hadn't been finished.

I reached up, tracing the groves and rivets, the wood alive and coarse under my fingers.

"Beautiful, isn't it?" a voice echoed in the room. The deep timbre was smokey, and I jumped, flipping around to face the intruder.

I shouldn't have been surprised to see Osiris standing there with deadly grace, his attention on the door that was now at my back. Just like yesterday, he wore a pinstripe suit, this time with a dark blue button-up that made his contrasting blue eyes pop. He stared at me, assessing, his head tilting. It was almost unnerving how he stood, unmoving. Unblinking. *Unbreathing.* Like he was dead.

And he was, in a way.

"It's rude to sneak up on people, you know," I said, grinding my teeth and shifting on my feet.

He just continued to stare, his chest still and face void of emotion. It was so strange to see someone that looked so human, be so ... empty.

Was it common in Vampires? I knew that while their hearts beat, they didn't need to breathe or blink or do anything a human would need to, so why would they? I tried to reason that it was just how they lived, that they were used to it, and I wasn't yet.

But that didn't make it feel any less haunting.

"What are you doing here?" I asked, almost choking on the words that sounded more than accusing.

At least try to trust them. I sighed.

"Sorry, that was rude. You have every right to be here. This is your house," I mumbled the words, unable to keep looking at Osiris. Instead, I picked his shoes, the shiny black matching the floor. "I'm just ... I'm still ..."

For the love of fucking god, brain. Please, make a full sentence.

A sound caught my ears. It was low, like a breath but with more force. I glanced up and, as if Osiris had realized my panic, his shoulders relaxed and he blinked. Even his chest moved like he was breathing, though he didn't make a sound. My heart stuttered, and I tried not to show my fear as he took up a surprisingly human facade. If he, as a void, was terrifying, the way he could mimic a human was almost worse.

Then what was that noise?

I took a settling breath and kept myself planted to the ground even as I wanted to run.

Osiris hummed before he took a step forward, moving until he was next to me, eyes on the door. The heady smell of him, like a dark coffee with hints of mint, swirled around me until it was all I could focus on. He reached out, tracing the bewitching figure as I had.

"He is Thoth. The Egyptian god of magic, writing, wisdom, and the moon." Osiris supplied, eyes never leaving the decorated wood. "Most see him as the true origin of the Vampire."

Osiris pulled away, shaking his head, crossing his arms behind his back.

I should've turned away, walked back to my room and done my

exploring another day. Because Osiris was terrifying, in so many more ways than one, and I knew it would be in my best interest, emotionally and probably physically, to avoid him. But I couldn't look away from his eyes. The almost curious pain in them, a kind that I could sympathize with. It was like he was lost in his own home, an intruder even to those he called family. So, I couldn't leave him like this, not when he looked so open.

"You don't? See him as the origin then, I mean?" I asked.

Something flashed in his eyes, sparking like a light behind the differing blue canvases.

"No." Osiris looked at me, catching me in his gaze. It still made me tense as a surge of fear shot through me, though I didn't flinch away from him this time. "He was a God I worshiped in my human days, and though I no longer follow any religion, I've never lost my fondness for his message. For us, he has always represented family, the one we built, the one we chose."

Silence met us after Osiris's confession, and he gripped his hands together tightly.

"As for startling you, I apologize. I came to find you after waking, to discuss what we spoke of last night after you retired," he whispered, pressing his palm against the door, before he turned to me completely.

"What do you mean?" I asked, as his head tilted again.

What else could they have talked about?

"You wanted to be informed whenever anything happened, and I intend to stay true to that." Osiris nodded, sincerity clear in his eyes. It made my stomach flutter, and I was almost breathlessly surprised. "I won't go into the details, as they are not mine to tell, but Adrian and Fallon are afflicted with something."

The way he said it made it sound like they were sick. Could Vampires get sick?

"Are they okay?" I asked.

"In a physical sense, yes. They suffer from the *Maker's Call*. It means that our Maker *Charmed* them into doing something when they were turned. Every so often, it comes back up, and forces them to do things that they normally wouldn't." Osiris' words were measured, and his eyes traced every expression I made like he was cataloging them. "It's been years since it was placed on them, so they are better at dealing with it now and can ignore it most days."

Something felt inherently wrong with that. Their Maker brought them into the Natural world. They were supposed to care about those they created, right? So why did Osiris talk about it like he would rather gut himself than even say their Maker's name? It was the same yesterday when he talked about Eliza.

Our Maker has been at odds with Ilenia for centuries.

"What did he make them do?" I whispered, and he looked at me with a melancholic expression.

He sighed, and the breath froze in my lungs.

"Their *Calls* are violent in nature, ones that make them want to feed." There was no mistruth in his words, though there was an obvious inkling of worry. Over them or my reaction, I didn't know.

I swallowed, forcing myself to stay calm as I sucked in even breaths.

"Do they ..." I wasn't sure how to put it without asking outright if they were going to attack me. I didn't think they would, I hadn't gotten that from them in the few interactions that we had. Even though I didn't fully trust them yet, I wasn't worried that they would turn back on their deal.

"They feel compelled to, but it is not what they want to do. And they will not," Osiris supplied.

"How can you be so sure?" I asked, pushing.

Everything itched, and breathing suddenly became much harder. I flinched as Osiris flicked his head away, something akin to anger in the way his hands closed.

"Because they are my brothers, and their grit outweighs the words of a madman," Osiris snarled the word as much as one who seemed so calm could.

Madman.

"I promise you, they are no risk to you, Aaliyah. They see the signs, and they remove themselves."

For whatever reason, I think I trusted that. *Trusted the man that tore out a heart in front of me.*

"What about Eirik?" I asked, and a truly questioning expression slid over Osiris's face. "I've seen something in his eyes, something that doesn't feel ..."

"Like him?" Osiris asked before I could finish. "He doesn't suffer the same, and he is no threat to you either." He didn't say why Eirik was like that, and something told me I shouldn't push.

"Okay," I said, taking a second to breathe. Catching Osiris atten- tion, I whispered, "Okay, so you promise they won't hurt me?"

He nodded, completely, fully. There was no hesitation in his stance or in his rich blue eyes.

"On my life." The words held so much meaning, and he said them so easily.

"That's a little extreme, don't you think?" I asked.

"Maybe, but it shows conviction. What else is more valuable?'

My jaw dropped, and I was floored by exactly how *heavy* everything Osiris said was. Everything he did was done with purpose. He wasn't like Dezen or Carter. I couldn't use them as templates for what I should say or do around Osiris, or any of them.

He was startling, unique, and freaking *consuming*.

"Alright, then I ... I'll trust you on this," I said, finally. "And thank you. For telling me. Your honesty is a breath of fresh air."

Osiris tipped his head like I'd seen in movies, like a gentleman. He glanced back toward the door that had caught my attention, motioning to it so I would look as well.

"Would you like to see what's past him?" he asked, a soft richness to his voice making my legs wobble.

I couldn't help but nod. It was all I'd wanted since I'd seen the door. Something about Osiris's hand on the handle felt important, like he was doing more than just sharing his thoughts, like he was baring his soul.

There wasn't a lot that could have prepared me for what was behind it. I knew they had a library. I just wasn't expecting *this*. The room held a soft tone that the rest of the house lacked, its bronze oak floors not quite black, and the walls a warm tan instead of the expected gray. Books lined the walls and shelves, each meticulously in place. The ceiling boasted grand arching chandeliers, and what library was complete without a roaring fireplace and a cozy reading nook.

I let out a breath, suddenly in heaven.

"Why am I not surprised that this is your library?" I said breathlessly as I walked forward, pressing my palm to the back of a ruby-red couch that looked like the most comfortable thing I'd ever seen, a match to the one in the other room.

"Books are gateways to the past, a way to remember that which was lost," Osiris said, following me. "Though most of what you see here wasn't my accomplishment, I'm afraid," he paused, and I thought he would stop there, but he continued, his words so quiet I almost didn't hear them. "Nero had a fondness for collecting books."

There was pain in his words, the kind that I felt when I thought of my parents. The name rang with a kind of familiarity, and I couldn't help but recall Eirik's mention of him. Nero ... he'd named their home and had built their collection of books.

"Nero... I think Eirik mentioned him, too." I whispered, watching as Osiris's face twisted, his lips morphing into a resigned grimace.

I didn't expect him to say anything else, not when he looked like he was about to turn and leave. Then he sighed, eyes on mine.

"He was our brother," Osiris said, shaking his head. "We lost him a little over a hundred years ago now."

I ached for him at that, and I had no idea how to bring him the comfort that he desperately seemed to need. He looked choked, like he'd been stewing on the sentence, pretending it wasn't real. How long had he held onto it like that? Letting it burn him from the inside out.

"I'm so sorry, Osiris," I said, unable to stop the clench of pain as his eyes snapped closed and his hands balled.

I didn't think as I reached forward, grasping his clenched fist. He flinched so violently that I sucked in a breath and snapped my hand back. Recognition sank into my lungs and stopped me from speaking.

I looked up at Osiris's now wide, confused eyes. This time, I extended my hand out, giving him the choice. He glanced at my open palm before he reached out and slowly set his hand on mine. I gave him a second, watching as some of the tension drained from his shoulders before I moved.

I wrapped my arms around him, pulling him into a comforting hug, trying to channel my inner Eliza when she used to hold me after a *Rend*. He shuddered under the touch, and I held on. He needed a hug, needed to know that he wasn't alone. That feeling wasn't a bad thing.

It wasn't much longer before arms wrapped around me, and the chill of his body sank into my skin. The rich aroma of coffee lit up my senses, and I hummed as it lulled me into a calm.

You're trusting him.

"Thank you," he whispered, pulling back. He still kept me at arm's length, as if hesitant to lose all contact.

You barely know him. How can you trust him?

There was a cautious joy in his eyes that made me feel as sick as it did glad.

What if it's a trick?

"He would have been glad that you enjoy this place. None of us shared his exuberant love of books." A soft smile twisted at the corners of his mouth. "Please, don't let me keep you. Explore all you wish. Most of the tomes are in foreign languages, so if you require a translation, just let one of us know, and we'll acquire one. Come find one of us if you need anything."

His hand reached out, the barest hint of his fingertips skimming over my cheek. The chill was such a distinct contrast to the spark that lit up over my skin that I turned again, facing the books.

His hand slid off, and I found I missed the contact.

"Thank—" I said, turning back to face Osiris.

But he wasn't there. The space was now empty, and silent besides the subtle crack of burning wood that hadn't been lit when I entered.

"You," I finished to no one.

The room felt hollow with him gone, and even though I knew I shouldn't, I missed the security that having his arms around me brought. I shouldn't want to see the smile on his face that told me there was so much more behind his eyes than he was letting on.

"You know, you're not so bad, Osiris," I said to myself, walking to the first wall of books, leaning forward to decipher the titles. It was only when I turned back, attention on that stupidly comfortable looking couch, when one caught my eye. It was laid out on the red cushions, obviously placed where I would see it, and I knew it hadn't been there before.

I smiled, running my hand against the raised image of a ship against rolling waves. The title, in a twisting script that reminded me of Adrian's cursive, was *Home*.

I smiled, sinking into the couch and opening it to the first page.

"Tearing a heart out and scaring the living shit out of me aside ... you're kind of sweet," I mumbled, smiling at the thought, warmth again flooding me as I set off into a new adventure.

Trust.

I could get used to this.

Chapter 16

Eirik

The change came slowly, the shifting pull of my skin painful as the wolf fell away. I dug my claws into the ground, growling as the ache of it nipped at my lungs. It burned, and I relished it, the distraction it brought. It felt right, my muscles still flexing, trying to fit back into my human form. I heaved a heavy breath, standing straight before my legs had a chance to harden, and my bones popped and groaned as they fought to keep me steady.

Once I was finally whole again, I shrugged on the pants I'd stashed away under the roots of our weeping willow before I'd taken off into the woods that surrounded our property. The fit was loose as my body breathed life into the shifting muscle in my legs. I felt new, sharp and aware. Runs had always cleared my head and gave my beast a chance to stretch its legs. Now, with Aaliyah only a few doors away from me, I found I needed it now more than ever. My wolf was uneasy with her out of its sight, but it was almost worse when I was around her. His obsession was worrying. Not that I had given many fucks about it lately, too obsessed in my own way to care about the thrumming in my chest whenever she was near. My hands ached, and the need to find her and assure myself she was safe nearly overwhelmed me as I strolled across our moss yard.

I walked back through the front door to our home, breathing hard as I searched the loft. I expected to see Adrian meandering around the kitchen, fiddling with whatever new recipe caught his eye, but it was disturbingly empty. I listened intently, finding none of my brothers in the house.

I snarled, grinding my teeth as I honed in on the soft heartbeat that was just upstairs.

Did those fucks really leave her alone?

I bared my teeth, my wolf doing the same as it paced, and just like that, all the work I'd done to calm it down rushed away. The run was useless, and once more, I was tense with energy. I closed the door softly, the gentle lull of her breathing upstairs telling me she was asleep. Though I wanted to leave and chase down my *fífl* brothers, I wanted to see the *smár Valkyrja* even more. So, I began walking toward the stairs.

Dirt matted my hair and covered the rest of me. I'd never minded the mess, though Osiris was going to throw a fit when he saw the floor.

Good. The bastard deserves to squirm for leaving her without protection.

I let the smell of lavender mixed with the rolling sea calm me, as I *flitted* upstairs, past the leisure room and straight up to the door that had been Nero's passion project before he died. Thoth taunted me with unfinished lines and the cutting accuracy of Nero's woodwork. It hurt to look at, and I let out an angry breath as I pushed past him. He wouldn't keep me out, not today.

Aaliyah looked like a dream, curled tightly into a ball, a small smile on her smooth lips. There was a book in her hands, one that I recalled. The sprawling ship on the front was an exact replica of the one I'd captained in the early 1500s. *Home.* I huffed, not missing the distinctive smell of dark coffee and whisky that gave Osiris away. He'd picked the book, meaning he'd likely talked with her, and thank fuck for that.

I thought he was going to wither away, like a fucking coward. He hadn't been himself since Nero died. None of us really had. I didn't want to lose another brother, not so soon after Nero, and never fucking again if I had anything to say about it.

I looked at the book again. Aaliyah seemed to have enjoyed it, her hands still clutching the leather tome to her chest. It was so natural, seeing her here with a book in her hands and the calm of sleep on her face. As soon as she was in my sights, my beast paused. That manic pacing stopped and contentment filled me, almost like a drug. A low rumbling growl built in my chest as I walked toward her, kneeling next to her. I reached up to brush the hair away from her face.

"Smár Valkyrja," I whispered.

The push of my wolf had me going further, running a finger across the bridge of her nose, admiring the soft roll of her cheeks that were framed by blinding white lashes. The spark that came with her touch had me jolting back, like a flush of power and lust had lit in my blood, bleeding into me. I reared my head back as the wolf tried to take control, the shift of my face dragging me to my feet.

Was I losing control *right fucking now*?

My beast seemed to think so as he pressed at the forefront of my mind, tearing his claws across my willpower. I pressed toward the door, desperate to leave the house before she woke and saw me like this. A monster. *A beast.*

Until she whimpered.

I went rigid and even my wolf pulled back, his ears as trained on her as mine were.

Again, another whimper, smaller this time, like it was caught in her throat. It was the whisper of a name on a gurgled cry that set my rage on fire as I bit down on my snarl, bloodlust so all-consuming that I shook. I flipped around and faced her again, falling to my knees by her side.

Castillion.

I felt the fear in her voice so deeply it was like a stake had pierced my heart. I knew fear, had lived it, and in that moment, it didn't matter *who* this man that haunted her was. For the first time since the auction, my beast and I agreed on something.

He going to wish for death when we found him.

I pushed down the bloodlust, and tried to ignore everything else but her. She didn't need my rage right now, she needed comfort, someone to pull her out of the nightmare that no doubt felt real. I tried to focus on her button nose and the mischievous curve of her lips, but as always, my mind focused on the thing we shared.

Her scars.

I couldn't see many as most were covered by Osiris's shirt, but the ones I could only spurred on the anger.

"You're safe," I promised, setting my hand on her cheek.

The growl that had tapered off built again, and her whimper stopped. Though she didn't answer, only pushed her cheek into my hand, the warmth of her skin melding with my own. The heavy growl in my chest grew deep until there was nothing but it.

"Your demons can't hurt you now, *smár Valkyrja*, I vow it," I said, only taking a breath when the crease between her eyes softened. "They'd have to get through me first."

My beast wanted her protected, and I wanted it too, to an almost irrational degree. I wasn't the rash one. I strategized, used my beast to my advantage, and picked people apart slowly.

But I couldn't think that way. Not with her.

The closing of a door downstairs had my irritation welling, and the need to speak with Osiris clashed with my desire to be near Aaliyah.

I stood reluctantly, her sleeping face once again content. It nearly made me lay on the floor next to her, if only so my beast would settle with her. Instead, I covered her with a wool blanket, one that we kept on the small chair by the windows, my wolf finally settling as she curled into the fabric before I headed downstairs, where my brothers' voices bounced softly off the walls.

They better have had a good fucking reason for leaving.

"What have you found?" Osiris's commanding tone left no room for question, and Adrian was responding just as I took the last step downstairs.

"Well, Archon was definitely behind her capture. I spoke with one of his groundsmen, and he said he heard him talking to Curtis, telling him when the girls would arrive at his home."

I snarled at that, and each of them turned toward me.

"Evening, Eirik," Adrian said with a typical smile. It was easy on his face, and for once it lit his eyes as well.

I glared at him, snarling again when his smile turned sheepish.

"I take it you're angry then?" he asked, and I wanted to strangle him for his guilty shrug.

"Might I ask why you're in a fit?" Osiris asked, sipping his Branshi whisky that he'd gotten from Brewlin, a Gargoyle with a knack for distilling.

His eyebrow raised, and the sight made my teeth ache and my beast howl. He was settled in one of the dining chairs, peering out at the moss garden and the movement of fireflies. His attention only flipped to me when I snarled again, snapping my teeth together. He wasn't a wolf, but Osiris had been around me enough to know when the baser instincts were coming to the surface, which is why he stood, facing me fully.

I bared my teeth.

"Not that this isn't entertaining, but do you think you could explain? I don't understand wolfy speak, yet," Adrian said, lifting himself onto the marble countertop, pressing his elbows to his thighs before setting his chin on the palms of his hands.

"It appears that Eirik is irritated that we left Aaliyah alone," Osiris replied.

I nodded, scowling at the two.

"She was perfectly safe. Osi was searching the perimeter, and you were within earshot. Besides, I was *working*. I went to dig up dirt on our dear friend Archon," Adrian replied.

"One of you should have stayed," I said through clenched teeth, and Adrian nodded placatingly.

Osiris, the bastard, just continued to sip his whisky. He'd been distant from Aaliyah since her first night when her fear of him was visible. Something told me that changed tonight, and I could still scent him on the book that she'd held so close.

I glared at him as he sat back down.

"Where's Fallon?" I asked, walking until I was by the kitchen island, grabbing a glass and pouring myself a drink from the decanter that Osiris had dragged out.

"Running an errand," Osiris said. "He's been on edge and asked if he could take care of *The Devil's Details*."

I snorted, shaking my head. That meant the building was going to be gone by dawn, not that I was disappointed in that. I just wished I could have joined in. Fallon had a knack for violence, and though he preferred his fists, he was just as good with the *Flame*.

"Darius?" I asked, taking a sip of the whisky and snarling as Adrian reached for my glass.

He winked, trying to get a rise out of me, and my beast didn't let me back off like normal. I snapped at him, teeth bared like a damned dog, snarling like one too.

The fucker smirked.

"Gone. Adrian tracked him to the Midwest." Osiris's words were short and clipped, his arms crossed over his chest tightly as he glanced at the stairs.

"Then it's time to pay the Djinn a visit," I growled out.

"Soon, but not now. We need to lie low after our stunt at the auction," Osiris said, downing the rest of his drink.

"Speaking of," Adrian chimed in. "Archon's involvement explains how Aaliyah got to the auction." His words teetered off. "And the glass that was in her palm."

"But her other scars, they aren't new," I said, finishing his thought. I still scented her fear in the air, rage making it hard to speak as I continued, "She was having a nightmare when I got back from my runn... She mentioned someone. Castillion. Can you do anything with that?"

Adrian and Osiris stiffened, their expressions slipping toward anger. While I expected it from Adrian, with as open as he'd been about his affection for the little thing sleeping in our library, it was more of a shock to see hatred boil in Osiris's eyes.

It was deep-rooted, savage, *deadly.* His hands clenched, bones popping as the *Flame* skittered across the exposed skin of his wrist.

"Nightmare?" Adrian whispered. "I'll keep my ears open."

Adrian's tone had shifted so quickly that it was almost like whiplash.

It was cold, though he said it all with a cruel smile on his face. He was good at collecting favors and even better at finding weakness. It was an asset, one that even I couldn't deny. Hopefully, it would be useful to us now.

"Take care in your search, Adrian. Her trust in us is still being built. We *cannot* risk breaking it. She'll come to us when she wants us to know of her past. If we ever learn of it at all," Osiris said, his hands loosening as he reached up and adjusted his tie. Even though his intention was clear, that anger still crept into his stance, into his power that seeped into the air.

And as much as it irritated me, I understood. *She comes to us. Don't push her.*

"I know it's frustrating, Eirik. I want to know who did it as well, and we will in *due time*. But we have to act carefully."

I hated to admit that he was right. This wasn't the first time we'd played the long game with revenge, and it wouldn't be the last. I nodded begrudgingly, my wolf howling at the decision.

"Hey, that makes three of us that want to know." Adrian chimed in, his voice light again. "Four counting Fallon, even if the prick won't say it out loud."

The joking air to his tone cleared some of the tension in the room, even though the conversation still sat over us.

"Oh, I meant to ask. Do you think Archon knows what Aaliyah is?" Adrian questioned, changing the subject back toward another that deserved our ire.

"No. He may be old, but his record-keeping skills are abysmal," Osiris said as he set his hands on the table.

"Hmm," I mumbled, trying to think of our other options, when Adrian again poked at me.

"*Hmm* indeed, my dear Viking brother."

I shot him a glare, grinding my teeth.

"What are our choices, then?" Osiris asked.

Adrian brought his hand to his chin, tapping it contemplatively for a second.

"There are a few that might work for us. Xander. Though that flirty bastard's going to want something. We could also try Avedal. He did recently take over as Basilisk Eternal, didn't he?"

Osiris nodded once, and Adrian hummed.

"Well, I'll look around some more and get back to you," Adrian said, leaning against the cabinet and stretching his arms before he slid down to the floor, a soft thud echoing as he did.

He glanced at the staircase, a Cheshire grin lightening his face.

"Tomorrow!" Adrian clapped. "Today, I'm going to go see if Aaliyah wants to bake a cake."

His smile almost stopped me from growling at him.

Almost.

"No," I said, snagging his arm as he headed for the library.

He gasped indignantly, mockingly raising an eyebrow.

"Why not? Cake is good for the soul, you know," Adrian countered before his grin turned wicked. "Let me guess, you want to bake with me instead! Oh Eri, you should have just said so."

I rolled my eyes at his antics, letting him go. Adrian went to take another step toward the stairs when I growled low.

"She's sleeping in the library. Let her rest," I said.

He tilted his head back to look at me, realization dawning on his face, before his expression went soft.

"Ah, I see. Well, that must be a good sign, right? Shows that she's settling in with us," he whispered.

He looked longingly at the stairs again, before moving toward the cabinets, and picking out the items he needed to make the cake himself. I struggled not to head back toward the library as well, instead focusing on the soft heartbeat I knew I'd find. I recalled Aaliyah laying against the couch, sprawled across it with a book in her hands. Would that be our normal now? Her smile, her soft laugh, the comforting scent of lavender mixed with the rolling sea, and the ease at which she molded into our lives? My beast stopped his endless pacing, content with that idea.

Settling in with us.

I fucking hoped so.

Chapter 17

Adrian

Her voice, timid and low, echoed off the walls. It was such a different sound compared to when she first arrived a few days ago. More open, less afraid. I loved the change, loved to hear her fear slinking away. Eirik responded to her so quietly I struggled to hear it from inside, like he was trying to cover the words. They'd gone to eat under the stars tonight, as they'd done the night before, and if Osiris would hurry with his damn questions, we could join them. I wanted to be there too, to see the light in her eyes as she said my name.

She brought a unique kind of happiness to our home, a joy we'd been lacking since losing Nero, and I was quickly growing addicted to it.

"Are you listening?" Osiris asked, though there wasn't any real agitation in his voice.

I tilted my head at him and raised a mocking eyebrow. He stood with his arms crossed and black hair neatly brushed back. And God forbid he forget his pinstripe suit, that was once again *glaringly* gangster. I rolled my eyes jokingly and turned toward him fully.

"I was, just not to you," I said, and Osiris shook his head, though he didn't admonish me for it, as he also glanced toward the doorway. *Not so unaffected, are you, brother?* I grinned. "Now, what did you ask again?"

The tick of the clock broke the silence as Osiris's eyes closed.

"I asked where you were at in your search for an informant."

I tapped at my chin, trying and failing to keep myself on the matter at hand, before I nodded. "Ah, yes. I recall now."

A laugh echoed, followed by the soft sound of whispered words I wanted to be privy to. It sent a shiver of fear down my spine and set my nerves on fire. Oh, I *liked* that sound. I waited for it again, only for Osiris's sigh to meet me instead.

Like he hadn't also heard it. I groaned, shaking my head at the infallible male.

"We only just used Xander what, fifty-some years ago? If we use him so soon after our last request, who knows what he will ask for," I said, putting on the facade that so many called The Collector.

It wasn't wrong; I'd just never liked it much. I wasn't the cruel sort, and I did this solely for my family. But that wasn't how everyone saw it. To most I was a threat, a bundle of secrets that most didn't want out in the open.

Xander, though, was the *king* of information, and he knew it. He had collections hundreds of thousands of tomes long. His prices were never cheap, and I doubted Osiris wanted to be indebted to the Dryad so soon after our last encounter. But I wasn't sure he was going to like my other options any better.

"Axandre has always been known for ridiculous requests," Osiris said, sighing. Xander's true name didn't go unnoticed by me, though Osiris didn't seem to catch his slip up. "Anyone else?"

"Avedal is a no. He's currently in Japan with his husband for their 500th mating anniversary and will be indisposed until the Eternium," I mused. "We should consider sending them a gift."

The chirpy Basilisk had even shown his support for Osiris taking over as Vampire Eternal, but I wisely left that part out. He wasn't the only one, from the sound of it. Sebek drew on people's nerves, and there were more than a few Eternals that were ready for his reign to end.

No one had ever been so close to making it happen. No other Vampire had lived long enough to call for Challenge.

I bit my tongue and considered my next words carefully.

"There's also Magelav," I said tentatively.

I flexed my hands, crossing my arms over my chest as I leaned into the counter. I was hesitant to even bring them up, as they'd always found our bloodline abhorrent. Not that Osiris was much better around them. His hatred bordered on obsessiveness, and that he even let me finish saying their name was a testament to his distraction.

I didn't really know why Osiris avoided them so vehemently; he hadn't told me ... but I knew why they hated us. Sebek had made a game out of killing their lovers a couple centuries back, and Magelav had never really forgiven him, or *us* by association. But they would be a powerful ally to have, if we could sway their opinion by association of us and convince Osiris to make a deal with them. A Chronomancer Sorceri that could look into the future ... It was hard to find a better informant.

"*The Bog Sorceri*? They're still alive?" Osiris asked, his spine straightening, eyes narrowed and sharp like polished steel.

"Alive, yes. Though, getting them to help might be even harder than getting Xander," I said, snickering.

Osiris paused for a moment, pinching the bridge of his nose, before he looked toward the yard. His jaw clenched, before he sighed.

"I could force their hand, they owe me a debt ... but I have no wish to deal with a Rourovic," Osiris mumbled, a seething hostility in his eyes.

I lifted my hands placatingly, crossing them off my list. *Don't bring up Magelav again, heard loud and fucking clear.*

I was happy to see at least some form of tension in our eldest brother at the mention of our Maker. And, apparently, also a Sorceri. There was emotion in his eyes, worry, rage, tenderness ... which was all better than the cold blankness that had taken up residence.

I'd count it as progress.

"Which do you think is the best bet?" he asked, a hand on his jaw as he looked at the door again, his attention wandering.

Fallon said something, and Aaliyah laughed at it.

He'd made a joke, and I wasn't even there to hear it; oh, I was going to *kill* Osi. I tapped at the table.

"In all honesty, I have no idea. This is unfamiliar territory. *You* don't know what she is, Osiris. That limits our options by leaps and bounds. The only other person I could think of would be Sebek, and I'd rather rip out my own eyes than ask him," I said with a sigh. "So, I'd say Xander is probably our best. They don't call him *The Keeper* for nothing, you know?"

Osiris sighed, but didn't disagree.

"I was worried you might say that," he said finally. "I'll write to him, see what his terms are, and we can go from there." Osiris shrugged his shoulders, glancing one more time longingly at the door outside, before he turned toward the stairs.

"Maybe use the phone, Osi," I quipped, jokingly elbowing Osiris's arm as I passed him.

I'd spent enough time here. It was time to soak up some of Aaliyah's laugh that the other two were hoarding. Osiris tensed as I passed, and even with two layers of cloth between us, and a hundred years of bonding, he still shuddered at the touch.

"No, a letter will suffice," he said. "Have a good evening, Adrian."

Oh no, he wasn't getting off that easily.

"You're not going to join us on the lawn?" I asked, making sure it was loud enough for Fallon and Eirik to catch. Eirik's growl echoed over the mossy garden. "Even Fallon's out there."

"No," Osiris said, his tone clipped.

"You know, that's not going to help her get used to us," I said, hand on the door handle.

"I believe you're all doing just fine."

Bullshit. I spun around, glaring as Osiris moped over a choice that *he* was making.

"Oh come off it, you ancient bastard. Don't act like you didn't show her the library." He raised an eyebrow, mouth opening to protest when I cut him off with a swiping hand. "Oh, my mistake, you just *happened* to wake an hour before sunset and just *happened* to be there to show her." I rolled my eyes. "Well, it's fine. Don't join us tonight, because I have the perfect way to show her a bit about us later this week. And your attendance *will* be required."

"Getting quite demanding, Adrian. You seem to be forgetting that I out-age you."

Though the words were sharp, they held a humor that I'd come to know from Osiris.

I shook my head.

"Well, I deserve to be demanding sometimes, having to keep you lot in check." Osiris shook his head as I gave him a hard look. "The sixth is approaching, and we can't very well ignore our tradition. So let's make her a part of it," I said, cringing as the sound of Fallon and Eirik mumbling along to Aaliyah went silent.

This may not have been the best idea.

"It's November already?" Osiris whispered.

"Yeah, sneaks up on us every year. But I think this could be good ... for all of us," I said, and I meant it.

We'd spent the last hundred years, most of my existence as a Vampire, mourning our brother. Unable to move on, unable to heal. Not that Nero wasn't worth the pain of it, if anything he was worth all of it. I loved him just as they did, and I'd only had a few meager years to know him. I just didn't think he would like to see us like this, so broken down at his loss so long after he was gone. Hell, he would've started throwing punches hours after we pulled him off that spike, charred to a crisp.

The thought made me sick.

"Let's remember Nero how he'd want to be remembered. And help Aaliyah realize we aren't the bad guys along the way." I wanted to remember him as the proud gladiator, a man with a heart of gold and a smile that lit up rooms. I wanted to remember his life. I was so tired of always focusing on his death.

"I'll think on it. Talk with the others," Osiris said, his jaw clenching as he turned away.

"Thanks. And Osi?"

"Hmm." He didn't face me again.

"Did you just *Eirik* me?" I asked incredulously, hoping to get something out of Osiris. But he didn't react, and my chest pinched. "That's cruel, brother, even for you."

I was met with more silence. I hated it. Hated every sour touch of guilt that I tasted in the air.

"He wouldn't like to see you like this," I said. "You were close, closer than any of us have the privilege of knowing."

Osiris tensed, his entire body going so rigid that I almost regretted saying anything. He turned and faced me for only a second, looking like he was going to speak, or explain why it was so hard on him. The hurt on his face, still as raw as it had been that day, burned me. He blamed himself and I wasn't sure he'd ever find the courage to heal.

God knew he wasn't the only one that struggled with the loss, but he felt it in his soul. In a way I doubted I'd ever understand.

"That's enough, Adrian." He didn't say anything else, turning and stalking up the stairs.

He didn't have to. The tears spoke for him.

I took a few more minutes to compose myself before I found my way outside, bare feet against the soft moss of our yard. The moon, a waxing crescent, lit up the garden, and those in it, beautifully.

Aaliyah smiled when she noticed me, and though it still held apprehension, it was genuine, and my heartbeat faltered at the sight.

"Evening, love," I said, not catching the slip of the tongue before it tumbled out of my mouth. It came so easily that I barely even thought of it until Aaliyah's face lit up a brilliant red. The blush extended over her high cheeks and down her neck, the sight leaving me breathless.

Jesus, she was beautiful.

I cleared my throat, trying to stare at anything but her. The way she looked at me, full violet eyes and pursed lips, had me straining, and a sweeping spark of pleasure lit up my spine. I smiled through it, trying not to show that I'd just gotten worked up over a smile.

"I've come to help you escape these two foul-mannered ruffians," I said, plopping in front of her, two plates in hand that she just now noticed.

Her eyebrows rose, and she leaned forward.

"I think they might just be that way to you, Adrian. We've been having a wonderful conversation," she said, her singsong voice tinged with mischief.

"Truer words have never been said. They're cruel to me for *no* reason. Savages, I tell you." I winked, passing her a plate as she struggled to keep from laughing. I leaned in close to whisper the next bit, shivering as she did the same. "Fallon won't even share his chocolate with me, can you believe that?"

Said icicle man glared at me, an eyebrow raised in question. But that look didn't last long, as a beautiful laugh finally slipped past Aaliyah's lips, as I was hoping one might. I doubted I could have grinned harder. Even Eirik quieted, a tilt to his lips.

"What do you say to a treat? Cupcakes, from the other night," I said after a moment, motioning to the plate I handed her.

Though I would've appreciated the chance to make them with her, the smile on her face made it worth the effort of doing it alone.

"Did you make these?" She asked.

She pulled back the aluminum foil, placing it softly on the ground next to her, her face glowing as she picked up the small cupcake. It was chocolate with a blue buttercream frosting and enough rainbow sprinkles to cover a city.

"Sure did," I said, grinning like a madman when she beamed up at me. "Got magic hands, love. They can do anything."

She didn't catch the dirty joke, and I was too smitten with how she grinned at me to make another one.

"Thank you, Adrian. I can't remember the last time I had a cupcake." She hummed before reaching down to break off two pieces.

How she said it like it was so common had my entire body tensing, and before I could stop, my eyes trained on the scars that ran up her arms, across her neck, even nicking her nose and lip.

Don't think about it.

She happily handed one piece to Eirik, who took it with a dazed look on his face. He focused on her arms too, and I could see his question on the tip of his tongue, though he held back while shoving his bite into his mouth. Fallon was looking away, his face a mask of boredom that clashed with the fire in his eyes. When he didn't immediately take the piece, Aaliyah laughed.

"Come on, Fallon. I know you like chocolate," she said.

His head swiveled to her slowly, like he was moving through water. She didn't see the conflict he was having, the glancing he made at the same scars that were grinding at my heart.

Let her come to you. Don't think about it.

His jaw was clenched tightly, and his tight lips looked even thinner with the pressure he was putting on them to keep them closed. Though that didn't last long as Aaliyah reached out, a piece of cupcake in hand. It took Fallon nearly an entire five seconds to realize what was going on, then his eyes went wide.

But dutifully he leaned forward, opened his mouth and took the bite. Aaliyah smiled so widely that even Fallon looked surprised.

Well I'll be damned, Fallon had emotions.

Be calm, my bleeding heart.

We sat under the light of the moon, sharing stories and laughing at bad jokes. The Vivas household felt complete for the first time in years. I knew Osiris would come around eventually, and I was sure Nero was looking down on us, happy to see we'd finally found something to smile about. I leaned back, basking in a sense of peace I'd thought we'd never find again, watching as Aaliyah's eyes lit up at the tale my brothers weaved. With Eirik chiming in and Fallon poking fun, well ...

I knew we'd made the right choice.

CHAPTER 18

AALIYAH

"I promise you'll love it," Adrian assured, laughing as I scowled, all while moving around the kitchen with all the grace of a bat out of hell.

It was hard to believe that what had led us to this moment was an auction. I'd called them *monsters* when they'd won my bid, so sure that they'd intended the worst that I'd been ready to die for my freedom. But now, I couldn't even fathom how I ever saw the man in front of me as anything but kind. Adrian was loading a small bag full of treats and drinks, all while putting the finishing touches on his latest meal that was just getting ready to be pulled off the stove. I wasn't exactly sure what it was, something in a big cast iron dish that smelled like butter and greatness.

This wasn't the man I'd seen at the auction. This was a man who smiled more than anyone I'd ever seen. This was a man who always seemed to know how to make me smile back, and I might not know what the plan for tonight was, but I had a feeling he was right. I *was* going to like it. How could I not when that much butter was involved?

I shook my head, unable not to smile as Adrian flashed me his Cheshire grin. His copper eyes with hints of deep amber twinkled, glowing sharply against the black of his shirt. He looked dazzling in the soft kitchen light, and the sight made my chest pinch, made me want to smile back with reckless abandon. It was a feeling that I'd already grown used to once before.

With Prince.

"Maybe not. You still haven't told me what it is," I said, shaking my head, still perched on the chair at the dining table.

Everyone had been hush-hush since we sat under the stars and had dinner a few nights ago. Though that didn't scare me, whatever they had planned didn't seem nefarious and if I was being honest with myself, I *trusted* them. More than I really wanted to, more than I knew I should. It was probably why, when Adrian's head fell back in a laugh, smooth and rich, it made my heart skip and heat flush to my face.

"Well, I guess we'll just have to see. But, I *promise*," he pressed his hands together, his grin only growing wider, "you'll love it."

He reached over, pulling the cast iron pan off the stove. I went to speak just as he cursed and dropped the skillet back down. I jumped at the noise of it slamming like the cracking of glass, and because of the look of pain that lit up on Adrian's face.

"Damn bastard," he hissed, holding his hand close to his chest.

His face contorted into a familiar grimace and my stomach sank as I hopped to my feet, stumbling over to where he stood.

"Are you okay?" I asked, fidgeting under the distinctive smell of burned skin, though some of the tension left me when he held his hand out to me without fuss.

There was nothing that hurt quite like the scorching of skin, and that thought had me reaching out to cradle his wrist so I could get a better look. As soon as I made contact, a familiar spark lit up my nerves, shimmering across me, fluttering in the pit of my stomach and tightening every muscle it went across. That heat settled pleasantly before slowly creeping away until I just felt a pleasurable contentment. My hands tightened, and I compulsively tried to seek the feeling again.

Adrian trembled and I grimaced, freezing in place before shaking my head and pulling back my hands. He was in pain, and I was making it worse. The apology was on the tip of my tongue when Adrian lifted my head, his strong fingers under my chin. That spark lit up again, and I was left wordless as Adrian stared down at me, adoration sparkling in his eyes.

"I'm good, love," he whispered with a breathless tone to his words. I shivered at his affectionate term, the sound of it turning my legs to jelly.

I looked down at his still-extended hand, and it showed no outward signs of a burn. The smooth skin stood stark against his black shirt, almost begging me to reach out and touch it again.

I shook my head and glanced up at Adrian's face, masking my guilt with a smile. His heated gaze traveled along my skin, and it was like that spark was trying to find me again. This time I sank into the feeling, the pleasurable pulse burying in me. Adrian beamed, his joy now sinfully balanced with the heat in his eyes.

"I'm going to have to get hurt more often if it means you'll keep looking at me like that," Adrian whispered, his words seeking to destroy my ability to stand. "You could kill a man with that smile."

What on earth was happening to me?

Then he winked before turning around, plucking out whatever was in the cast iron and placing it into the glass dish he had ready on the counter. He'd left me breathless, confused and pent up all in one motion. He reached down and grabbed the bag on the ground, just as I tried to shake off the feeling.

He came back to me with that vibrant smile still on his face, the hint of mischief in his expression making my heart thunder in my ears. The bounce of his hair, the way his copper eyes crinkled at the corners. That softness of his touch, and the devilish twist to his perfect lips. In that moment, he was the most handsome man I'd ever seen. From his skin to his soul.

Gods, I was in trouble.

He extended his hand, bowing in a flourish, dragging me right out of my thoughts. The move itself was abrupt, and I flinched, the action so habitual that it took my breath away. I flushed, noting Adrian's worried frown as I took his hand. That shock from before built low this time, like an ember rather than a roaring fire, and the comfort it brought made my skin sizzle with energy. Adrian didn't ask, though I knew he was curious. They'd all stayed away from the topic of my scars; of the things I did that weren't quite normal. I wasn't sure if it was more for my sanity or theirs.

I recalled Osiris's eyes again from the auction, the rage that was in them, the blood on his suit. The memory made me shudder.

We left the house and meandered into the woods, down a well-used trail. I wasn't sure how far we walked, but as we drew away from the house, I heard the murmur of familiar voices. There was a glow in front of us, one that flicked and moved.

Sure enough, a few minutes later, we were in front of the largest fire that I'd ever seen. Eirik was throwing logs on, tending to the flames as we walked through the tree line.

"Took you long enough," Eirik said, before *flitting* over to us.

He was wearing a black T-shirt and jeans. The fabric clung to him, and I couldn't look away from the flex of his arms as he ushered us over to a few stumps in the ground. I noted someone had purposefully cut them to resemble chairs, and I sank into the makeshift seat, focusing on the roaring fire and the crackle of burning wood.

"Had to get the goods. Couldn't very well leave home without them," Adrian said with a wink, not letting go of my hand as he took the stump next to mine.

"A bonfire then?" I whispered, looking at Adrian.

He smiled again, a smile that was quickly shredding my resolve to make sure he was trustworthy enough to let him near my family. Though I couldn't say he was the only one. Each of them had been the same in their own way, though none was as outright about it as Adrian.

"Not just any bonfire, love," he said, bringing my hand to his lips before letting it go. He leaned away, pulling some glasses from his bag and a drink I hadn't seen before. "This is a special day for us, and we wanted to share it with you."

He reached down to the bag again and shuffled through it, searching for something.

"Special?" I asked. "Why would you want to share something special with me? I haven't known you for that long."

"Maybe not, but it sure feels like it's been centuries," Adrian said with a wink, before his smile dropped a touch. "This is ... well."

A weight sat in the air, and for a moment none of them spoke, just watched the fire burn, their anguished expressions speaking for them. Until finally, Fallon took a harsh breath, his head falling back.

"It's the anniversary of our brother's death," Fallon supplied, his tone so darkly poised that I nearly jumped out of my skin at the sound of it.

Emotion swallowed the conversation, and sympathy grew in my chest.

Another reason to trust them.

"Nero?" I asked.

What if they're tricking you?

I bit my lip to force the thoughts away, keeping my heart from beating out of my chest as the others shifted, staring at anything but me for the first time since I'd walked down their staircase.

"He had a fondness for bonfires, and we've made it a habit to have a big one every year after we started building the home. Since he passed, we've done it in his honor," Osiris said, and Eirik nodded in agreement.

Eirik and I shared a glance, and like most times, something swirled in his eyes. It was so close to the surface that it almost seemed like someone else entirely was staring at me.

I swallowed hard, tearing my gaze away. That was a question for another time.

"What was he like?" I asked, genuinely curious.

Adrian's face fell, even as he fought to keep the smile in place.

I had overstepped, I realized, and I turned away.

"Sorry, I shouldn't have asked," I started, but Adrian shook his head.

"No, please. Allow me. Nero would be *ecstatic* at the chance to talk about himself," he said, a laugh slipping through his tight lips.

He took a few seconds, clearing his throat as he sank against the tree stump, his eyes tracing the dancing flames before a small smile lit up his face. It was the kind that held melancholy and made my heart twist in my chest. There was so much love in his gaze, so much hurt, that I nearly reached out to him.

But I stopped myself, fear holding me hostage as I tried to keep calm. I had to be sure they were safe first, and when I touched him, I couldn't think clearly. My chest tightened at the thought, and I knew I was already past that. They weren't going to hurt me, not in the way

I was expecting. But I still didn't understand why I couldn't get enough of Adrian's glowing smile, or the way Eirik's sure eyes followed me promising protection. Why Fallon sneaking me chocolates when he knew I was feeling down made me blush, or why Osiris's steady presence always kept me grounded. All of them held me closer than I was ready for, in a way that made my chest ache for more.

It scared me.

"He was proud, a gladiator. And damn if he wasn't the best god damn swordsman I'd ever seen," Adrian laughed, as if remembering something. "But he was also kind. He helped me and Fallon come to terms with our *Calls* and was always there to pull us back."

Love laced Adrian's words as he smiled at me, and I didn't have any time to respond before Fallon was adding to Adrian's thoughts.

"Nero was sharp as a whip and had a silver tongue to match it. Few rivaled him. He fought like an avenging angel, and he was practically a god in the art of war." Fallon wasn't one I would describe as emotional, but the words he spoke now held as much tragedy as they did love. "There's no one else I trusted more to have at my back."

"He wasn't just good at fighting. You brought it out of him, Fallon. He was a master of many other things," Osiris said, and rather than frown like I was expecting, Fallon's face lit up with a rogue grin.

The kind that had my entire focus snapping at him. He was dazzling under the light of the fire, looking so blindingly familiar that it shocked me silent, and burned me down to my core. I nearly looked down to see if the flames had made their way to me and snuck up my legs and right into my chest.

"He and Osi used to play beautiful duets on that rickety old piano in the game room. Like personal shows," Adrian gushed, sinking into his seat and sipping at a drink that I hadn't seen him pull out. "God, they would go for hours. Sometimes they could even get Eirik to join in and sing one of his folk melodies."

Eirik grunted an affirmation from across the fire, his lip tilting up before the motion was lost. He stared into the fire, like it would tell him what to say. He didn't speak, even as the conversation carried on around us. Eirik wasn't one to speak to begin with, but it almost felt wrong that he wasn't chiming in. He hurt. It showed in the tension in his arms, in the unblinking eyes.

"He sounds amazing," I whispered, again searching the fire and finding it lacking in the worst possible way.

Adrian was right: I loved this. The warmth that I got surrounded by them, the happiness that came with their dashing smiles and other-worldly grace. But it was missing someone I couldn't ignore, couldn't look past.

Prince wasn't here, and none of their stories could mask that. He already knew them at the auction, and I'd been expecting him to be by my side as I made my way through this new adventure. Him not being here sucked the joy out of me, and made it hard to focus as Adrian's soft voice echoed around the fire, still telling stories I wanted to hear, but couldn't seem to get a grasp on.

"I know someone a lot like him, I think," I finally mumbled, and silence met me as I spoke.

Something felt raw about the words, like I was sharing my deepest secret by telling them about Prince. In a way, he was exactly that. He was my best friend and had been my *only* friend for years. By telling them about Prince, I was laying myself bare.

"Who?" Eirik asked, moving around the fire so quickly I didn't even notice him next to me.

Those startling blue eyes caught mine as he took a seat on the ground, no other free tree stumps near me. Eirik had a calm energy about him, one that helped me relax.

"My best friend," I whispered, and Eirik nodded in understanding, without even needing to know anything else.

Empathy burned in his eyes, swirling, telling me without words that he knew what haunted me in more ways than one. It was exhilarating, freeing, and terrifying all at once.

"Prince?" Fallon asked, thankfully pulling my attention away from the tattooed man that so easily threw my emotions into overdrive.

"Yeah, that's him," I said.

"What happened to him?" Eirik asked, and I froze.

Indecision nipped at my heels. I could shrug it off, tell a half-truth. But I didn't want to. I wanted them to know about the person who got me through the worst times in my life. They had shared Nero, and I wanted to share Prince.

Because he deserved to be known. I didn't know him in his life, or how he got to the compound, and I hated to think that he'd been another prisoner in that damned building. But I knew him in death, and what I'd learned then was a gift I held close to my heart. It was going to come out eventually, anyway. Might as well be on my terms. Hopefully, they didn't think I was crazy. It wouldn't be the first time I'd gotten a strange look.

"I don't actually know ..." I mumbled, trying to find the words. "He's ... well ..."

How did I say it?

"Dead?" Fallon supplied, so brutally upfront that I laughed.

That got a few raised eyebrows, but I shrugged them off.

"Yes, you could say that. But I never knew him when he was alive, so that's not exactly new." My words tumbled out, and the others froze.

This was it, the moment their stares would turn questioning and accusing. I tensed in anticipation for it and was met only with a soft rumble that echoed in the clearing. Eirik, I realized, the deep sounds coming from his chest so soothing that I sighed.

"What do you mean?" he asked, and I was stunned.

I took a deep breath and, before I could talk myself out of it, spoke.

"I can see the dead. I act as a bridge, I think ... between this world and whatever comes after," I said, feeling like a weight was lifted when Eirik only nodded, curiosity and awe clear on his face. But he didn't look at me with damning eyes or accusation. Heat rose to my cheeks. "When he found me, he didn't try to leave or pass through me. He stayed with me, and he's been by my side ever since." The thought burned me, and I had to turn away from Eirik as tears clouded my vision.

"Well, he was. I haven't seen him since the auction," I whispered, grabbing one trembling hand in the other. I could still see his face, that rogue grin and sharp jawline. The way he would smile. It made me laugh, the sound wet and strangled. "You have him to thank for me being so calm."

"If that was calm, God help the poor soul that makes you angry, *smár Valkyrja,"* Eirik mumbled next to me, a short laugh startling the breath out of my lungs.

"Thank you for telling us, Aaliyah," Osiris said carefully. "That could help us in finding out what you are."

I nodded at Osiris's careful words, leaning into the stump I sat on. Peace washed over me, and I breathed out a sigh of relief.

"I hope so," I said back, pulling in the tumultuous emotions, and forcing a smile when Adrian's worried look met me.

"To Nero." Eirik broke the silence, lifting his drink before snagging my attention with his eyes. "And to Prince."

My lips trembled as I smiled through tears. The others echoed the words, and I did too.

"May their souls find peace in the afterlife, and if not peace, then at least a good fight," Fallon said, finishing his drink and standing.

Taking that as my cue I stood, ready to be back in the house where I could lick my wounds in private. This had been an engaging night, and I needed some time to reset and get my head in the right space again. I was getting ready to help Adrian pack up when Osiris stopped me.

"There's something else we wanted to do tonight, Aaliyah," he said, directly behind me. I flipped around, startled by his closeness. I bit my lip.

"What is it?" I asked, and Osiris fiddled with the pocket of his suit coat before pulling out a necklace.

It was made up of a slim golden chain with a small *lavender* gemstone at the bottom. It was simple and beautiful, and I looked at Osiris, unable to formulate a question as he smiled slightly at me. His lips curled at the corners, the devious tilt making my insides twist and heat creep into my cheeks all over again.

"You got me a necklace?" I asked, softly.

"Yes." Osiris looked embarrassed for a second, looking away from me. "It's a protection spell. One that will make sure none of us take fang to you without your consent."

Do you trust them?

"You did this for me?" I was breathless as I stared at the simple pendant that felt like old magic.

How had he managed this so quickly? Only those blessed with the power of magic, Sorceri, could make charms like this, and I knew it often took days to get in touch with them. When Eliza was getting her protection spell for the shop renewed, it had taken two weeks just to get the Forgemancer, a Sorceri with the ability to produce magic items, to respond.

"We didn't want you feeling at odds in your home," Osiris said, motioning me to turn.

I did and he reached around, clipping the necklace in place for me. His fingertips skimmed the skin there, the barest touch against my neck. A sharp jolt followed it, much like it had when I'd touched Adrian earlier. It sent shivers down my spine, and I caught the gasp behind my teeth. The touch was gone in the next instant, and the weight of a spell from the pendant hit immediately. Osiris whispered a few words in a language I didn't recognize, and the metal heated for a second then settled against me.

"How?" I asked, still frazzled by the touch.

Osiris paused, and I glanced back at him. He peered down at me, again unblinking. He didn't breathe, and his human mask wasn't on right now as he seemed to contemplate his words.

"I studied as an Echomancer in my human years, and though I use different magic now, I still have some basic concepts memorized. A protection charm was easy enough," Osiris said, as if saying the words were the easiest thing in the world.

But the looks in the others' eyes told me that this was much more significant than he made it seem. An Echomancer. I tried to remember what Eliza had said about their magic but came up blank. Osiris's hands flexed before they moved behind him. It was a tension that reminded me of myself whenever I heard Castillion coming down the long hallway to bring me to the lab.

Osiris knew I was still wary of them. He hadn't pointed it out or prodded to know why. He just knew and took steps to make me feel better. I choked on the words that fought their way up my throat; the guilt at my reaction to them felt oppressive.

"You didn't want me scared," I whispered, a tear trailing down my cheek.

Osiris reached up, like he was going to wipe it away, but stopped at the last moment. His eyes clouded over, a numbness to them that ached in my soul.

"My dear, the last thing we want is you scared."

Heat flared in my chest, and I reached up, gripping the charm at my neck, unable to look away from the tender expression on Osiris's face.

And I knew then my trust in them was sealed.

CHAPTER 19

PRINCE

Now, I was no stranger to the sight of blood. I'd seen every way there was to kill a man and had done more than my fair share when I was still alive, even danced in it once upon a century ago. But this?

This was a slaughter.

It had taken me the better part of the last week getting here, to the facility that haunted my every waking moment, the one that had the gall to experiment on my girl under the guise of study. I didn't want to leave her, even knowing that the Vivas Crypt would take care of her just fine, but I had to. I needed to make sure that it was all behind us, that *he* wasn't aware she'd made it out. Thanks to the dead having less than ideal means of travel, it had taken me far more time that I would have liked to get here.

Meaning I had to fucking *walk*—excuse me, *float*—all the way here. I'd forgotten exactly how far away it was. When Aaliyah first woke we hiked for nearly five days before finally stumbling into Oakridge. It was a trek for *me* to make, and my chest still burned when I thought of her doing so. By the fifth day, she stumbled more than she walked, and I'd never in my life wished I could hold her more than that moment. Carry her, take the burden off her shoulders like she so rightly deserved. But I couldn't, not physically anyway.

So *here* I was, standing in the middle of a room painted a horrendous shade of brownish red, doing the only thing I could.

Making sure she's safe.

The normally crisp white walls were cracked and shattered, and it looked like a tornado had rolled through and decimated the place.

I sighed breathlessly and began the tedious job of searching the room the best I could. I couldn't move the bodies or the debris, so hopefully I could get what I needed from the surface. It was just more time that I was away from Aaliyah, and every second burned me. I needed her smile, needed her with everything that I was. I would move heaven and hell to stay by her side, even if I wouldn't get the chance to hold her myself. And I would do what I could to make sure her demons stayed far fucking away from her. I needed to make sure they hadn't found out she was alive, hadn't checked the *grave.*

The thought made me sick all over again. I could still see her crawling out of the ground, her spirit snapping back from that first *Rend.* She hadn't remembered me then, not at first, and that alone nearly broke me.

I shook my head, glaring at the bloodied room around me again, tracing what was left of the bodies. I didn't care for anyone here. In fact, I wanted to be the one to slit their throats and parade their bodies in the street.

But this was brutal even for me, even for *him.*

Castillion's lifeless corpse was caught in an endless scream, his jaw completely dislocated and hanging crudely from his face. His arms were missing from his body, and I couldn't seem to find them in the sticky mess of limbs, though he had his innards strewn around him like a sick altar. His eyes had been gouged out, and from the lacerations on his face, I would say that he was made to do it himself.

His blood mixed with the likes of Nox and the guards, each body seeming more broken than the last. But I couldn't see anything to suggest that Aaliyah's survival had been discovered.

So I moved on, sliding through the wall and down the familiar hallways. Past the glass cage that had been Aaliyah's hell for years. Each of the following cells was empty as well, some as bloody as the rest, others just *empty*. I wanted to believe that some had gotten out, but I wasn't holding my breath.

Had I had a heart, it would have ached for the others that had been trapped here. The ones that had been test subjects for when Aaliyah was unable to go back to the table.

I shook the thoughts off and moved quickly throughout the rest of the compound, checking each room, and was happy to find that *he* wasn't still here.

Sir Amoun—what a fucking joke.

When there was nothing left to see and no more bodies left to gloat at, I turned. I was hoping to find something, even another spirit, if only to beat one of the bastards into the ground. But fate wasn't smiling at that idea today.

I walked through walls, taking back the measured steps until I met the forest that surrounded the compound. Then I walked toward the one thing I didn't want to see again, that I would have given anything to avoid. I could only hope that he hadn't made it here, that he'd left in a rage and didn't think to check if she was still in her *grave*. Because if he had?

Then we'd have a much bigger problem on our hands than her dying.

Fuck, fuck, fuck, *fuck*.

I paced around the grave, the disturbed dirt making me numb. I couldn't very well be nauseous without a stomach, but my soul really tried to fake it.

I snarled soundlessly, glaring at the obvious signs of disturbed earth. Long gouges were dug into the ground, and trees were torn up at their roots, scattered around the forest. There was even more blood and a few more body parts to be found.

I didn't want it to be him. *He* hadn't found it. She was safe. *She was safe.*

But that was a fucking lie. She wouldn't be safe until he was dead in the ground, and his undead heart stopped beating. This just proved it.

I ground my teeth, feeling nothing but needing to get rid of my rage. So, I screamed so hard that my body shook.

Still, no sound.

I hated it, hated feeling so useless. Aaliyah needed me, and all I could do was tell her she wasn't safe. That *he* knew she was alive. I shuddered, the defeat sizzling in my chest as I moved away from the grave and toward the consistent pull that had always dragged me forward.

It was time to go home.

Chapter 20

Aaliyah

The soft glow of the fireplace lit up the library, and I sank into the small chair that sat in the corner, my eyes on the forest outside. Osiris had gotten it for me after he noticed my interest in their yard and the windows that overlooked it. It had been such a thoughtful gift that I nearly cried, and only managed to stop when Osiris looked like he was going to keel over at the sight.

I ran my hand over the ornate arm rest, smiling at the memory.

The others had each taken up an activity around me, saying that it was what they would do anyway, even if I didn't believe them. Eirik was dutifully cataloging the library's many books on Naturals, hoping to find one that Osiris had missed that might give us a hint as to what I was. Though that wasn't his only reason. I saw him sneaking books off shelves; books I'd already asked Osiris about, ones with knights and castles. After I'd told them about Prince, Eirik had been intent on giving him back to me, however he could. It was endearing how he wandered around the library, humming in that deep tone of his, shaking his head at books that didn't fit his idea.

Adrian was perched under me, laying on the floor and whispering stories. I couldn't look away from the smile on his smooth lips, the way his eyes danced in the firelight.

"And that was the day that Fallon got stuck running through town square in his birthday suit, covered in Zinnia jelly, so he couldn't *flit*." Adrian finished telling me the story of the first prank he'd pulled on Fallon after his turn. "Thought he was going to kill me. Heaven knows he tried." The laugh he gave betrayed the dark subject of which he spoke.

Eirik smirked from his place against the wall, his hand still tracing the tomes.

"You're lucky Nero had a soft spot and hid you from Fallon," he said, shaking his head.

"No, he liked to tease Fallon as much as I do. Fallon was lucky Nero didn't *join in*."

That made me smile. Their banter always did.

My chest tightened and I tried to ignore the missing two. Fallon and Osiris hadn't made it; Fallon was taking care of something in town, and Osiris was probably off making sure that their territory was secure. At least that's what he would say. Something told me he didn't really like being around me, and while that hurt, I tried to understand it. I'd thrown a wrench into their lives as much as they had mine.

Hell, just over a week ago I pretty much considered him to be the vessel of all evil. I thought after our time in the library, and by the bonfire, that we'd come to an understanding, but it seemed I was wrong.

I twirled my finger against the wooden window frame drawing small circles, before I reached up and grabbed the charm at my neck. I played with the lavender gem until it warmed under my touch.

"I have something for you." Osiris appeared so suddenly that I jumped, catching a glimpse of him just as I tumbled off the chair.

I hit the ground with a thump, landing next to Adrian, who laughed haughtily. Osiris was at my side before I could even register the fall, helping me to my feet. I groaned, holding back the urge to reach back and rub my poor behind.

"I thought we agreed it was rude to sneak up on people," I grumbled, unable to stop my pout.

He raised an eyebrow, his gaze skimming me before landing on my hands, which were firmly on my hips.

"Yeah, Osi. Sneaking is *rude*," Adrian mocked, standing on his own and brushing off his pants, before he looked me over as well.

He still had that smile on his face, and when he realized the only thing I'd hurt was my pride, his grin grew even wider. Osiris's lip twitched, something akin to amusement in his eyes as he brushed Adrian off and extended a hand to me. In it was a book, bound thickly in dark leather, with an intricate helmet shown on the front, the bold design sporting harsh arches where the eyes were, and a curved piece of metal fixed proudly on top.

It was beautiful.

I looked at Osiris with a raised eyebrow of my own and smiled when he bowed. It had been easier to see him now after the bonfire. That had solidified it, the trust I held in them. I reached out, grabbing the book and bringing it to my chest.

"It's a tome that you brought out to the living room that first day. I translated it for you," Osiris finally said.

I didn't miss Eirik's huff, looking almost deflated that Osiris had handed me the book, mumbling something about getting it to me first. I let out a breath, a warmth filling my chest, my finger tingling as I opened the book.

"Thank you, Osiris," I said, breathless as I flipped to the first page, running a finger against the scrawling script. It was clean and so beautifully written that it almost felt like a crime to touch it. "You did this?"

"Yes. I'm fluent in several languages, though I am particularly well-versed in Latin," he whispered.

His hands were tensed, gripped tightly at his sides as they always were. At least, whenever he was near anyone. It was an instinctual response, and I knew I wouldn't like whatever had caused it.

"You have a good eye. This was one of Nero's favorites," Eirik butted in, easily flipping to the cover again, tracing the ornate helmet that was dug into the leather. "Aeneid, an epic poem. It's about the fall of Troy and the ancestors of the Romans."

I liked the sound of an *epic* poem.

"I'm sure I'll love it," I said.

"Ah, while you're here, Osi, why don't we tell Aaliyah about what we found?" Adrian asked, sitting up and crossing his legs.

I looked back at him in question.

"That was part of the reason I came up," Osiris said, before turning his attention to me again. "We have narrowed down someone that may know what you are; he's a Dryad. I've penned him a letter, so he should get back to me soon. He's nothing if not punctual."

I smiled at that, unable to hide the joy that came through me. He'd kept his word. They'd told me everything and had kept me in the loop. They'd been kind, joyful, and even fun to be around. The only thing they hadn't done yet was tell Eliza I was here and that was because I wasn't ready for it.

Or I *hadn't* been. I'd wanted to make sure they were trustworthy, and as I continued to rub circles around the spine of the book and smiled at the men who'd done everything they could to make me feel at home, I knew they were.

"Thank you for telling me," I said, and I meant it.

"He's a known record keeper of Naturals. If anyone knows what you are, it will be him," Osiris said easily, and I tried not to get too hopeful. Eliza had said the same thing, and each time we had been left with nothing but guesses.

I clutched the book tighter, biting my lip.

"I won't intrude anymore on your evening," Osiris said, and that expression on his face, one that I was slowly realizing was doubt, made my stomach twist.

Then he turned away, and I moved, grabbing his hand in mine on instinct, not liking the pain that had taken up residence where stress had resided. My mouth went dry, and I tried to find words.

"Wait, Osiris," I mumbled out, still holding his stiff hand.

The room went silent, and the other two didn't stop me, though I could feel their panic in the air. Osiris didn't move, didn't breathe.

"Stay. Please," I said, and Osiris peeked over his shoulder.

I was expecting to see many things in his eyes, but vulnerability was not one of them.

He turned toward me, easily lacing our hands together. The spark that came with touching any of the Vivas brothers sent shivers down my spine, and he seemed to sigh into the touch, as if waiting for something to happen. He met my gaze again, and what I saw had butterflies dancing in my stomach. He looked alive. Not like he had these last few days. His eyes burned with emotion, and as his hand squeezed mine, even Adrian gasped.

"I'm not very good company," he whispered, doubt clouding his gaze.

What had caused him to hurt like this?

"I think you're discounting yourself, Osiris. I love your company," I said carefully, unable to not notice how Eirik's breath stuttered and Adrian tensed.

Osiris swallowed hard, glancing at our joined hands. There was a warmth there, the familiar spark of pleasure pulsing like a beat.

"Of course, *lux mea*." His breathless words nearly stole my response, and I couldn't even find the will to ask what that meant.

Lux mea.

He reached out, pulling his hand from mine and pressing it to my cheek with inquisitive admiration.

"Osiris." Fallon's crisp voice bounced off the walls, much like the echo of the library door as it bounced off the wall.

It snapped me out of whatever spell I'd been under and Osiris let his hand slide away as he turned to face Fallon. Even though his hand had been chilled, I felt even colder now without it.

"What is it?" he asked.

Fallon ground his teeth, and looked at me with a worried glower.

"*He's* been spotted in the states." Fallon hissed with his entire body tensing, and just like that, Osiris's entire expression changed.

He sneered, his face morphing into a dark expression that felt like the start of war. Then he and Fallon were gone, like they had never been there to begin with.

"Well, that's a way to ruin the mood." Adrian hummed from his spot against the wall.

He looked tense, the emotion in his eyes a sharp, dreary contrast to the chipper tone of his voice.

"Who are they talking about?" I asked, my chest almost seizing when Adrian's expression turned haunted.

It was a look I knew all too well.

"A fucking bastard," Eirik chimed in, walking over to us.

He leaned in close, not quite touching, and ran his nose over my temple. The huff of his breath was warm.

"For once, I agree with your course language, Eri." Adrian looked lost, almost *scared*. "Sounds like our Maker might be coming to pay us a visit."

Adrian and Eirik had left me in silence a while after Osiris and Fallon, and for the moment, I didn't mind. They'd been on edge ever since Fallon came by to tell them the news, and each second they worried only added more tension on my shoulders.

I didn't ask anything about their Maker, though that didn't stop me from thinking about him after they'd left me alone. What kind of monster could he really be for his own *Turned* to hate him this fervently?

Was he the reason for the haunted looks in their eyes?

I took a deep breath, and sank into the couch. Stressing over it wasn't going to help the situation, and I had to trust that the guys knew what they were doing with this. I *did* trust them. That thought helped to ease my worries as I looked over the book that Osiris had translated for me. I ran my hand over the cover, taking a settling breath as I traced the stunning picture of a helmet on it, the glowing trails of gold making the book appear hardy. It had been so thoughtful of him, though I wasn't sure when he'd found the time. Osiris's thick scrawling script was nice to look at too, so cleanly developed that it felt like a crime to not note every detail.

It made me smile thinking of how different he seemed. He was the one I was still most wary of, the one that stayed away. But I couldn't force myself to see him as the same man that had killed Curtis. That was an Osiris avenging, and Curtis had deserved it. This was the real Osiris, showing that he was here, how he seemed to know best.

I ran a hand along the page, smiling as a chill slid across up the room. I shivered, pulling the blanket closer to my chest as I picked up where I was in the book.

I read for a few minutes, trapped in the story, when the cold became too overbearing to ignore and I stiffened as I realized it wasn't *just* cold. The chill in the air caused me to shiver again and I strained to focus on the words that no longer held my attention. I knew the distinctive feeling of a ghost, the ice lingering across my skin.

I wasn't alone here.

I took a heavy breath, fogging the air in front of me and bracing myself for the touch, for the feel of them moving through me.

But it never did. Even as I waited, even as I knew the pull would tell them to reach out to me. It was only a few seconds later when I breathed a sigh of relief, tears falling involuntarily as the familiarity of the cold finally sank past the initial chill. I looked to the side, and I was on my feet before my brain could process it, searching for *him.*

My valiant Prince.

And sure enough there he was, braced against the far wall, looking like he was exactly where he belonged. I choked on a sob, so desperate to touch him I had to sit back down, holding the book close to my chest like it was him I was hugging.

"Took you long enough," I whispered to an ecstatic-looking Prince.

His signature crooked grin was in place, his entire face calm and open. I couldn't tell if I wanted to scream or cry. Everything came down on my head, and the sight of Prince had me falling into hysterics.

Prince had come back. He didn't leave me.

Crying it turned out, vetoed screaming, and before the first sob was finished Prince was in front of me.

I looked at him on instinct, *always* searching for the comfort of his presence.

The capture, the auction, all of it was nothing compared to how it felt at this moment. I'd tried to come to terms with the fact that Prince was gone, that he wasn't coming back. His disappearance had rolled in my stomach like a lead weight. Seeing him now, in all his glory, made me realize exactly how much I needed him. How much his presence helped to settle me. He was my best friend, my confidant, my *everything.*

Now he was back, and I couldn't seem to stop crying.

Prince's expression morphed, his eyes squinting together; a look of regret rippling over his face. He dragged his hands together, clasping them within each other before bringing them to his lips. *Sorry* was what he wanted to say. I could feel his apology in the air, taste his regret, and it only caused me to sob harder, even as I smiled through the tears.

"I missed you so much, Prince," I said and he smiled, bringing his pointer finger to his nose with a nod.

You okay? he asked.

"A lot better now," I managed, wiping my eyes until I could see him clearly. "You were right about these guys. They weren't what I was expecting."

Prince's face lit up with a knowing smile, like that was precisely what he'd expected. I guessed it was, considering how he'd acted at the auction.

"What happened, Prince? Where did you go?" I couldn't stop the question from coming. Prince looked at me with a tender expression before he crossed his arms in an 'X' in front of him, in our signal for *danger*. Just as quickly he slid two fingers over his eyes, closing them.

He was taking care of danger?

Our language was bare, and sometimes things didn't translate as well as we would have liked. Maybe now that I had access to different books and items, we could develop a better system.

"Am I still in danger?"

Prince's face went taut, reluctance warring with deep-seated pain in his expression before he nodded once. That told me more than any words could have. A familiar numbness stopped the hysteria that fought to build in my mind, keeping me calm enough to speak.

Never make noise.

"Is it them?" I whispered, trembling so hard that the book nearly slipped from my hands.

A pause before he nodded again.

I couldn't respond. I could barely breathe. All at once, the peace of my new home came crashing down around me. I sank further into the couch, staring past Prince, my focus waning.

"Do they know I'm alive?" I choked out, that damned mantra ringing in my ears.

They get more violent when they hear noise.

I nearly started crying again when he nodded sharply, almost like he was guilty. His face tipped down, and my chest began to ache for a whole other reason. Did he want to leave now? Had I finally done what he wanted by finding these men? Was this him saying goodbye?

Could I live without him?

Prince almost immediately shot up, taking a step back. His face set into a look of pure determination, and that proud grin of his finally returned to his face. He gave a violent shake of his head.

His hand shot over his heart, his pinky and ring finger down. *Forever.* Just like he'd said in the forest months ago, when I didn't remember him as I crawled out of the ground. The *same* symbol had been the first thing I'd remembered, the night we had come up with our sign.

I felt terrible that the weight on my shoulders lifted. Prince didn't want to leave, but he should. He would find peace in the Void, and he wouldn't have to deal with the mess that was my life and my *death*. I was selfish in wanting to keep him here, and I couldn't find the will to let him go. He was my everything ... I couldn't lose him too.

"I love you, Prince." It was the first time I'd said it out loud, the first time I'd even thought of it, but I did. I loved Prince with everything that I was. He was my forever too, and I wanted to make sure he knew that.

His face morphed into an expression of awe, his whole body trembling as his eyes slid closed. I wished I could pull him to me. I wanted now more than ever to hold him close. I needed that comfort, for him to whisper to me that it was all going to be okay ...

But he was dead, and the ache in my chest to hold him wouldn't change that.

CHAPTER 21

ADRIAN

Fallon glanced over the small table that usually held our quartz chessboard. Though that wasn't what was currently atop the clear glass surface, as scattered across it was a rather hectic looking game of Bones. The wooden domino pieces, made from some rare aspen, if I remembered Nero right, were laid out meticulously on the makeshift board, and the Boneyard was nearing empty. The cross pattern of the pieces stretched to each edge of the table, as what was likely to be our last match neared its end.

It was a simple enough game. Each of the dominos had two numbers shown as dots, one on each side of a dash. The goal of the game was to win with the most points, and after this play, that winner would be me.

I smirked, laying down my piece, the six of the domino facing inward, with a seven facing out. The other three arms of the cross being three, one and four.

"That's fifteen, Fally," I said, counting up the points on the edge of the x-shaped pattern. "Looks like I may be winning *The Lisa* back yet." I winked, and Fallon's eyebrow rose in challenge.

He'd won our game of chess in a rather startling fashion before I even had a chance to marvel at the painted beauty. Damned show off. I doubted he'd give me another chance to win it back again so soon.

Though I could dream.

Fallon glanced between my face and the board with his narrowed green eyes, calculating and sharp, trying to intimidate me. I nearly laughed. It might work on others—scratch that it *did* work on others—but I knew Fallon as well as I knew myself. I wasn't scared of him, and none of his angry grumbling was going to change that. He rolled his eyes when I blew him a kiss, before they landed on the flower that I'd carefully tucked away in my suit coat pocket. It was a wildflower that often bloomed in the forests around our home, a stunning lavender color, and the moment I found it I knew I needed to have it. I wanted to give it to Aaliyah, to see the joy in her eyes when she realized it was for her.

The thought made it hard to breathe, and something akin to warmth spread through me. That heat was unfamiliar, exciting and as addicting as the soft way she smiled at me.

God, her smile.

"Don't count on it, Adrian. You're only four sets ahead," Fallon smirked.

The points total, or sets, was how the score was kept. If the tile point count at the end of your turn was a division of five, then you got one set for every division. Meaning, that he had to get at least twenty points to tie me, and thirty-five was the max he could get in a single turn. So, he was right. It wasn't hard to turn the tides of a game that was this close.

He sorted through his tiles and plucked one from the graveyard, before reaching out and placing that same tile down. "My apologies. That makes you two sets behind."

"Spoil sport," I mumbled with a smile. "You know, I don't get why you wouldn't bet your chocolate. You *gave* Aaliyah a piece," I goaded, wanting to laugh when Fallon's face twisted into an unconcerned glower.

He'd been slipping away from his *cold bastard* facade from the moment we walked her through our door, and he sure as hell didn't want to admit it. But I wanted him to, *needed* him to tell me I wasn't the only one that was feeling the inferno in my chest, this adoration for someone that I'd known for mere days. Because she didn't feel like that, it was like she'd always been a fixture in my soul. The others wouldn't tell me if I tortured it out of them, too scared of their own responses to even think about what they meant.

So Fallon, cold, unreadable, grouchy *Fallon*, was my best choice.

"Maybe I like to watch you squirm. It's not like this is the first time I've told you no," Fallon quipped back, motioning for me to take my turn.

I laid down another tile, no points to be had on this one as the count of the Bones was only seventeen.

"No, I suppose not," I said, measuring my next words carefully. "You two seem to get along better now. Well, after she hand-fed you a cupcake and all."

I waited, too focused to breathe and needing to see even a touch of what he was feeling on his stupid, stony face. And I got my wish as his lip twitched, and his hand came up to touch his mouth before he could stop it.

Then he scowled and tossed his attention back down to the table.

"I tolerate her," he said, the thick hint of a *Charm* blending with the heated brush of our *Flame,* and suddenly the air tasted like fire and ice.

I smiled again.

"You don't give people that you just *tolerate,* your prized Aldovin chocolate, Fally," I pushed again, keeping my words teasing but mellow.

Fallon was on edge. We were *all* on edge and I needed to pull him back. This was the only way I knew how, with Nero not around to beat the fight out of him. That would be the preferred method, but I for one wasn't a fan of having my nose rearranged.

And God knows it would be if I tried to fight Fallon.

"Come on, just admit that you like having her around," I said, skimming my finger across the last tile in the Boneyard.

The wooden texture was harsh and I picked it up, frowning at the double sevens.

That would be a problem.

"She's a physical response, one I can't stop," Fallon said, his head turning away from me. "I don't enjoy having her around, I *tolerate* her for the sake of our Crypt." He ground his teeth, emphasizing the word again, as if trying to convince himself more than me.

At that moment, Fallon looked as vulnerable as I felt. We made it a point to be there for each other. We shared the same type of turn after all, the *Maker's Call* destroying our free will for most of our earlier days. Leaving us with a lasting *Call* and all the poor memories to go along with it.

I swallowed down the sight of the bodies, like I did every time I thought of them, hiding away from lifeless eyes with a broken smile as I set down one of my last few pieces.

So I wouldn't let him sink, not like this.

"You know, it's not weak to feel, Fallon. I don't know why you think it is," I whispered, the sound nearly drowned out by Fallon's tapping at the wooden dominos.

He didn't respond for a second, reaching out and placing a tile that again held no score. He kept his head low, the tension in his neck showing how hard he strained.

"I disagree," he finally said, meeting my gaze head on. Fear raged past the anger, and the distaste for our agreement. "I would say losing Nero made us the weakest we've ever been. Our Crypt wouldn't have even been at the auction if he were around."

"Now that's not fair, and you don't know that," I said, pushing my hair back. "Sebek is a problem, and he would've been a problem even if Nero was still alive."

He would continue to be a problem until we found a way to get rid of him. Which was hard, considering the bastard was older than literally everyone but the Hallowed Three.

They were odd and flaky at best, the Three, being the ones that originally came up with the idea of Eternals, the ones that lorded above to take care of anything that the leaders couldn't agree on. They didn't have a race, at least not one that any of us *simple subjects* were privy enough to know. So I doubted *they* would take care of Sebek anytime soon. They hadn't even been seen since before Osiris was turned.

"I think Nero would have loved Aaliyah," I said, placing down another blank piece, leaving thirty-two points on the board.

Fallon didn't hesitate, placing his piece down and calling the game.

"That's thirty-five. Bones," he said, crossing his arms and raising an eyebrow with a haughty look.

It was so level and raw that I sighed, and just like that we were back to pretending everything was okay, and I knew I wouldn't be getting anything else out of this. I relented and forced a smile, swallowing the need to keep pushing.

"Damn ... Fally," I said, stretching my arms. "Well, out with it. What do you want?" I asked, as per our arrangement.

Normally, we picked our prizes before the games started, but today we were more interested in getting away from ourselves than the goodies that would follow.

"A dozen German chocolate cupcakes." He rolled his head from side to side, and I smirked, nodding my agreement.

Fallon and his damn sweet tooth.

The sound of the mosaic door opening, the creak of the old hinges echoing in the air, told me we weren't alone. Our brothers knew how to move around our home without making a sound, which meant there was only one person that could be interrupting our game. I took in the fresh breath of lavender, melting into the strange peace that it brought me.

"Ah, good evening love," I said, turning toward Aaliyah as she closed the door behind her.

She smiled softly, waving toward the both of us. It made my chest tighten, and when blood rushed to her face it lit up her cheeks in a stunning red color, and I had to wonder ...

How far down did it go?

I was going mad, stark raving mad, but I couldn't stop staring at the way her lips lifted, at the stubborn tilt of her nose. She was wearing my shirt today and what looked to be Eirik's boxers. The fabric dwarfed her, making her seem comically small. I wanted to see her laugh again or poke fun at Eirik or *anything*.

"Doing some more exploring?" I asked, hiding the breathlessness in my tone with a twisting smile.

"No. I think I left my book in the library. I was going to finish it today," she said, stepping toward the intricate door.

"*The Fall of Troy*?" Fallon asked, his arms crossed over his chest.

"That's right," she said, reaching over and caressing her arm with her other hand.

While she'd obviously grown more used to us, there were still strange habits that she had. Ones that I was realizing weren't necessarily because of us. She twitched when I tried to get her attention, her head turning to the side as she tried to shrink away from it. Not to mention the scars, the ones that we were supposed to just ignore until she was ready to tell us about them. Which I understood, *I did*. But that didn't stop them from tearing at my soul.

Just as suddenly as it had happened, she frowned and focused on the space beside her. Her body lost its tension, softening in a way that had me leaning forward.

"Well, could I interest you in a game of Bones instead?" I asked, wanting to enjoy her company and have her nearby.

And force Fallon to realize that she belonged here.

Fallon glared at me, but I paid him no mind as I leaned over our table. Aaliyah looked between the two of us and at the small table we were at. There were only two chairs, but we could make do.

"I don't want to impose," she said finally, shuffling on her feet.

I opened my mouth to speak, to tell her it wouldn't be a problem, when Fallon spoke up.

"You wouldn't be," Fallon supplied, and I nearly laughed.

He looked just as irritated with his own words, glancing back at the table that still held our last game.

"Like Fally said, we'd be happy to have you. And maybe you can teach this posh brat a thing or two about humility." I winked again.

She turned away, staring into space before looking back at us and nodding. We quickly moved the table, setting it so Aaliyah could comfortably sit on the couch while we played. We had to resort to putting the Boneyard in the box, but we made do.

"So what's Bones?" she asked, looking over the now cleared table.

"Well, most people just call it dominos. Nero first learned it in China, when the game was still played on ivory pieces. It's a game of luck and skill," I said, grinning.

It was nice to talk of Nero, of his joyful moments. We'd spent so long pretending that he hadn't existed to escape the sadness of his death that I was worried I would forget him.

"I've never played before," Aaliyah said, as I showed her the drawing Boneyard, and she picked out her seven pieces, laying them face down on the table so we couldn't see them.

"It's pretty easy to pick up," I said, winking at her as Fallon and I did the same.

"What are we betting this time?" I asked, watching as Fallon dragged his gaze up from the table where his eyes had been firmly planted.

The deep green swirled, not unlike Eirik's did when his wolf was at the surface, as he followed her blush the same way I had, his jaw clenching.

No doubt thinking exactly what I had. *How far down did it go?*

"I don't have anything to bet," Aaliyah said, chewing on her bottom lip.

She looked at me, before a shy smile slid onto her face again. It softened the look in her eyes and made the dimples of her cheeks flare, pushing out pouty lips. It would only be a few inches, and my lips could be on hers. Would she mind? Or would she sink into it? I could imagine the breathless sounds, the taste of lavender like a drug.

"How about your time?" I finally asked, unable to mask the lust that had crept in. "Hard to find time to do anything fun with these jokers around. If I win, spend a night with me? We could bake or watch movies?" I finished, watching the way her eyebrows scrunched together with rapt fascination.

We could sit under the stars, and I could see if your lips were as silken as they looked. See how softly you would whisper my name.

I shook my head, clearing the thought before I could lean forward and make a fool out of myself. Aaliyah looked between me and Fallon, and something like endearment lit up her eyes. Fallon froze at her stare, his hands clenching his thighs under the table. I could hear the crinkle of his perfectly pressed white suit pants.

"Does that work for you, Fally?" I asked, and he shot his erratic gaze at me.

His narrowed glare told me I wasn't helping, and I winked at him, all too aware of his *problem.*

"You can pick something else?" Aaliyah supplied gently, easily picking up on Fallon's agitation.

Though, it was surprising. Even with him being ill-composed, he was still perfectly presented. His face was lax, his shoulders back, and *not a strand of hair was out of place.* But she noticed, like I did, the small things that gave away how Fallon felt. It was like she'd known him forever, and her smile danced along the seams of his shattering control.

"No," Fallon said, releasing his death grip on his legs. "Your time is fine."

I nearly cheered. Baby steps.

"And if I win, you owe me a piece of chocolate," I said, trying to catch him off guard.

Of course, he didn't give me the time of day as he raised an eyebrow, crossing his arms with a teasing intensity.

"No," he responded, and I grumbled as Aaliyah's laugh skittered across the table.

I smiled, even as I tossed back my response.

"You're a terse bastard." I grinned like a madman as Fallon's lip twitched, and he *laughed.*

Okay, perhaps laughed wasn't the best word. He breathed air out slightly faster than normal, through his nose. His lip looked like it had seen a smile once and was trying to imitate it. But *still.* When was the last time he laughed? Smiled? When was the last time *I* did without care? Aaliyah's smile lit up my consciousness, making it hard to do anything but grin. Somehow she'd managed to sneak joy into what had been a dragging existence. She made Eirik sing his foreign melodies again, gracing the halls of *et in domum suam in solem:* our home under the sun. Osiris held life in his eyes.

And Fallon laughed. *Laughed.*

"Fine, we'll go for *The Lisa* again," I said, my disbelieving laugh making Fallon stare oddly at me. "The regular?" I said, ignoring it as I leaned back in my chair.

"What does Fallon get if he wins?" Aaliyah asked, glancing between us while she fiddled with one of her tiles.

She stood it up on its short end, so she could see the marks.

"Same thing he always wants. Man and his damn sweet tooth ..." I mumbled, and Fallon barely reacted, too busy matching Aaliyah's moves as she stood more and more tiles up.

When she noticed he was matching her, standing his tiles up, a mischievous smile lit up her face and I almost forgot how to speak.

"I'll have to bake him a sweet of his choice, in whatever quantity he chooses," I said. "Last time he got enough cookies to feed a country, I swear." Fallon's lip twitched again, and one of his pieces came tumbling down.

Aaliyah laughed as her own crashed down.

"Stop whining," Fallon said, not even looking at me.

"What do you want if you win?" he asked, motioning to Aaliyah, and she paused for a second before a blush lit up her cheeks.

And then she bit that damned lip, and my cock had something to say about that, pressing against my jeans like it was a fucking jack-in-the-box.

"Could ... Could *I* have a piece of chocolate?" she asked finally, and Fallon looked taken aback. "If that's alright, I mean. I don't think I've ever had something so tasty before."

She blushed, touching the tips of her fingers to her lips as she looked down at the makeshift Bones table. Fallon sat silent, but he didn't refuse, just swallowed hard, his face unmoving.

"You *bastard*," I gasped, head thrown back as Fallon turned a twisting glare in my direction. "What's your secret? The man hoards that damn chocolate like it's his lifeline."

"He didn't say yes, though," she said, shrugging her shoulders like she hadn't just basically made the pope swear his fealty to Satan.

"Oh, he did. That was a bona fide yes. I hope you win just so I can get some second-hand enjoyment from watching you eat it."

The sound of the wooden tile tapping against the glass was enough to make me glance back at Fallon's scathing glare.

"Let's play," Fallon said icily.

"Alright, no need to get your panties in a twist."

We picked away at the game, placing tiles. It only took Aaliyah a turn to understand the rules as she constantly peered between Fallon, me, and over her shoulder.

She was a natural, picking up points like she'd been playing for centuries, and always seemingly seven steps ahead. Twenty-five, thirty, twenty. Before Fallon or I even had a set of ten, she called Bones.

Fallon stared, disbelieving, and I nearly broke down into tears, I was laughing so hard.

"Pay up, Fallon! I'm looking forward to this," I said, wiping my eyes as Fallon continued to stare, less than dignified and jaw-dropped as Aaliyah blushed crimson.

She glanced over her shoulder again, trying to escape Fallon's unrelenting gaze.

"You don't have to if you don't want. I can pick something else," Aaliyah said nervously. "I'd understand. They seem important to you."

Fallon finally slammed his mouth closed and sighed as he reached into his pocket, pulling out a crisp chocolate. One good thing about not having a body that heated for you, was that his chocolates never melted. Even though Fallon was giving up what he considered more precious than gold, he didn't seem upset. More pleased as Aaliyah's grin lit up again, and she slowly snagged the treasure from his hands. Fallon shivered as her skin brushed his, his eyes only half open as she popped the chocolate into her mouth.

"You look mighty pleased with yourself. Were you a Bones shark in disguise? Tricking us into believing that you'd never played?" I teased, and she blushed again, licking her lips in what hadn't meant to be a sensual action.

A sneaky smile slid over her face, and she held back a laugh as she glanced over her shoulder at the air. Like she'd been doing during the match. Like she was *talking* to someone.

My stomach dropped a bit, a realization coming to me.

"No. I've never played." She bit her lip, all but cackling as she helped us flip the tiles to put back in the Boneyard. "But I think Prince might have."

Ah, and the glances suddenly made sense. There was a contagious delight in the way her eyes twinkled that made me jealous. I hadn't realized that kind of joy was possible.

And I'd never seen that much love on someone's face.

The way she said his name and looked at the man we couldn't see, made me wonder if she would ever look at me like that. I shook my head, pushing down the thought and giving her an easy smile.

"Ah, he's back, isn't he? Sneaky." I wagged my finger at her, causing her to laugh. "Well, if he's a man of Bones, then he's alright in my book. Though we'll have to remember that you have an advantage on your side. Otherwise I'll never win my night."

I only meant it jokingly, but I knew when Fallon flipped his head toward me I'd missed something. Then he smirked.

"You never told Adrian what you wanted if you won," Fallon said to Aaliyah, tipping his head toward me, and her eyes widened.

I'd forgotten too, and part of me wondered what she would ask for. Her face flushed again, the delectable red taunting me.

Definitely not to fuck her against the stacks of the library. Not that, definitely not *that.*

"Right, I wasn't thinking about it," she said finally, glancing at us then behind her.

Suddenly she smiled, like she had all the answers she needed.

"What do you think, Fallon?" she asked softly, and I swear he would've blushed if he could have.

"German chocolate cupcakes," he replied smoothly, turning away from her, even as she beamed at him.

"I'll get them made up this evening then," I said with a wink. "You could join me in making them, if you want."

"I'd like that," she said with a nod, as we pushed all the pieces back together so we could start another game.

The door creaked open again, and Osiris and Eirik ambled in.

"Good evening," Osiris said, eyes snapping to Aaliyah as she smiled in greeting, just as a low tumble of a growl started in Eirik's chest.

"Osi, Eri. You just missed Aaliyah and her dear Prince stomping Fally and I at Bones. Join us for a game?"

They nodded and we made room for everyone to sit around the increasingly small table, though none of us seemed to mind.

One game turned into two, and laughter and mock taunts lit up the game room. The light airy sounds reminded me of the home that I'd thought was lost. We played until the sun was rising, and the pull of sleep became too much to bear. Even then, none of us could stop smiling. Aaliyah won all night, and I'd lose to her every day to keep that smile on her face.

For the first time in a century, the house felt like home.

CHAPTER 22

AALIYAH

It was odd how easily we fell into a routine. One day into the next, a smile, another laugh, and before I knew it, it had been two weeks. *Two weeks* since my life had taken yet another turn into territory I hadn't been expecting.

The *Rends* had been less frequent here. In fact, since that first night —which I wasn't even sure *was* a *Rend*—I hadn't had a single one. It was freeing, if not terrifying. I wanted to let my guard down, to give myself a chance to breathe with this new reprieve. Yet something continued to poke at me, tearing down this veil of peace.

How long would it last?

I wasn't sure of the answer, but what I knew was that I liked this more than I'd expected, this peace. It wasn't a constant war between the others and me, not like I expected it to be. Instead, it felt natural and comforting.

Like home.

"You're ridiculous, Osi." Adrian's soothing voice pulled me from my musings.

We were seated in the living room, a small fire lit in the fireplace in front of me. It was dim, but even with the minuscule amount of lighting, I could see the irritation on Adrian's face.

What were we talking about again?

"No. *You're* ridiculous if you think we will get anything but high-quality, tailored clothing." Osiris's quip back was stern, and he almost sounded indignant.

He pulled at his suit coat, tugging at the cuff before straightening out the pinstripe until he looked utterly perfect. Right, we were talking about clothes. Because while I enjoyed wearing theirs, as their shirts smelled *terrific,* I'd suggested that getting new clothes was something I wouldn't mind. Osiris took that as, 'buy everything in the store and have it here yesterday.' I hadn't asked for anything besides that since we'd made our deal, so he jumped at the opportunity to get it when I asked.

"You called seven different tailors over twenty minutes demanding they be here for fear of losing our *business.*" I caught Adrian's sideways glance and his harsh swallow at the word business. "Audric even canceled his orders for the week to accommodate—"

A deep growl interrupted Adrian's words. It took me a moment to realize that it had come from Eirik, who was planted firmly to my left. His leg brushed up against my own, and his long arm was stretched across the back of the couch. He all but encircled me. That typical faint smile caught his lips when he realized I was staring. I blushed red, turning away from the rumbling man.

"The tailor doesn't have to be a man, you jealous brute," Adrian scoffed, rolling his eyes. "Besides, Osiris probably already thought of that."

Adrian brought his hand up and pinched his nose between his thumb and forefinger. The room fell into an uncomfortable silence. The kind that ate your nerves and threatened to pull out your hair one strand at a time. I leaned harder into Eirik, my hand finding his shirt.

"You're both spending a lot of time arguing over what should be Aaliyah's decision." Fallon's words held a smooth tone that managed to calm my erratic thoughts.

Finally, a look of realization slid over Osiris and Adrian's faces. Eirik's hand cupped my cheek, the warmth of his skin seeping into my own. I found myself drawn to his heat, a heat that the others lacked. He pulled my face toward him, my eyes landing on his own.

"What do *you* want?" His question echoed around the now silent room.

All eyes were on me and struggled not to fidget under the scrutiny. I swallowed hard, panic welling in my chest even as I fought to stop it. I glanced around the room on instinct to find Prince, always my silent guardian, standing next to the couch.

His smile worked wonders on my frayed nerves. His arms were crossed loosely, the epitome of relaxed, and the expression on his face gave me the reprieve I needed. I couldn't think with them staring at me, their eyes burning holes into my skin. None of them went to say anything else, they just focused on me.

I both loved and hated it.

What *did* I want? My gaze drifted, falling to the hard planes of Eirik's face and how his lips pouted. I wanted to reach up and tuck the strand of stray hair that had fallen from his braid back behind his ear. That feeling was something else, another bit of unfamiliar territory, the warmth that built in my chest whenever one of them was near. The way my heart seemed to skip at the sight of them.

His lips were so close, I was just inches from ...

I was getting off track.

"Stop overthinking it." Eirik's tone was sincere but brisk, the sound bouncing around the room.

His thumb brushed against my cheek, the calloused feeling sending a shiver down my spine. He could see it on my face then. He knew I was panicking. My focus fell to the thin white lines on his hands; stark against the tan of his skin.

"Why don't we call Eliza?" I swallowed hard, the words struggling up my throat. I'd been putting it off, calling her.

They told me she was safe a few days ago, having heard it through the grapevine. That had taken a weight off my shoulders, and I'd nearly broken then and told them to call her. But I'd been a coward. At first, it was because I didn't want her to get hurt, but now that I knew these men ... it was because I was too terrified of her reaction when she realized who they were.

What they were.

But I had to see her. It burned me to think that she was probably looking for me, and yet I hadn't done the same.

"She has all my clothes, and I'm sure she wouldn't mind bringing them here. Not to mention she's probably worried about me." I pulled my bottom lip between my teeth.

"If that's what you want," Fallon said, sipping at his drink. "If you're ready to see her, we can arrange it."

That surety in Fallon's voice that I'd come to crave, helped to settle my nerves.

"Right ..." I clenched my hands.

"Something wrong?" Fallon asked, setting down his drink and looking at me with a curious expression.

What was wrong? Only that Eliza hated Vampires, and they happened to *be* Vampires. It felt sour to say after so much had changed. I'd thought the same, *hated* all the same, before them.

"I can assure you. While they may growl and posture, they only want you to be happy here. However that may be," Fallon continued, obviously trying to calm me, and for the most part it worked.

His expression was completely closed off, though I could see the worry in his eyes. I'd learned quickly that Fallon expressed things differently from how a normal person would, or even a non-normal one. He wasn't the type to say what was on his mind. Instead, he did things to show it. I still had the wrapper to the chocolate I'd found on top of my book this evening, and I knew it was him who continued to sneak them into the library. He always placed them in spots where he knew I would find them. I smiled softly.

"It's not that. I want to see Eliza, to make sure she's okay. I just need to warn you first."

That got everyone's attention. Fallon leaned forward, and Osiris stopped his obsessive dusting of the bookshelves that had taken his interest. Eirik leaned in close, once again reminding me how warm he was. Adrian took his spot next to me, sitting on the couch's arm with a mischievous smile.

"What about?" he asked, reaching out and brushing a hair out of my face.

He moved so slowly and with such purpose that I didn't flinch, and I was once again reminded exactly how much I wanted to stay here.

"Like I said that first night ... Eliza doesn't like Vampires. I don't think she's going to take me being here well," I finally said, fiddling with the hem of my shirt. It was large, reaching down past my knees, one of Eirik's. I could tell because of the heady aroma of the sea, and the hard oaky scent. "You need to be ready for her to do something ... drastic."

I expected rebuttal, but only got reassurance as Eirik's hand squeezed my shoulder lightly, and Osiris nodded in contemplation.

"Don't let that haze your decision. Whatever she has to say about us doesn't change her relation to you. If you want to see her, then we will do everything in our power to make it happen," Osiris said, tapping the shelf he still stood by.

As always, they surprised me. Osiris didn't ask that I didn't see Eliza or that I meet her elsewhere. He adapted, putting my need to see Eliza above whatever she would have to say about them. It made me warm and I beamed, letting go of the hem of my shirt. Osiris's eyes widened like he was seeing it for the first time, before they softened, and though he didn't smile I knew he was happy.

"Thank you, Osiris," I said, leaning back once again.

I took comfort in the shirt again, playing with the soft hem.

"But ... I do have another request if it's not too much of a bother?" I asked, my cheeks lit up at the words. I couldn't believe I was about to say this.

Eirik hummed next to me, as if sensing the embarrassment. He pulled me closer, laying his arm on my shoulder in a move that would have frightened me two weeks ago. Now, I just sank into his warmth.

"Can I keep wearing your guys' shirts for pajamas?" I felt embarrassed even saying it. I pulled my focus away from Eirik's, barely catching as his eyes went wide at my words. "They're very comfy."

I mumbled out the last bit in an attempt to make myself sound at least somewhat less crazy. How could I explain that I'd slept better these last few weeks than I had my entire time at Eliza's? Nightmares hadn't haunted me nearly as much, and I didn't want to jinx that by changing up my sleeping routine.

"That won't be a problem at all, love." The adoration in Adrian's voice lessened the tense feeling that had taken over my muscles.

"See, problem solved, Osi." I could hear the teasing edge to Adrian's words.

It lessened the tension in the room another degree, and sighed at the lighthearted banter. Osiris grumbled something about calling the tailors back and getting my measurements anyway. Eirik brushed his thumb against my cheek once again before pulling back and resuming his previous position with his arm extending out behind me.

I could practically see the irritation on Osiris's face as he stared down at Adrian, who didn't falter as Osiris all but glared a hole into his skull. It was only a moment later when a sigh fell from Osiris's lips. His head turned and his eyes locked with my own. I tensed up, and my fingers dug into the fabric of the couch beneath me.

"We can call Eliza after our meal. Hopefully, she will be available sometime this evening." The softness in his voice was comforting as he stood and walked toward me.

I melted as he reached a hand toward me. I slid my fingers between his on instinct, standing with him. The action was so normal that I barely noticed it, too busy enjoying the feeling to be confused by it.

When had I grown so used to their touch?

"Come, Aaliyah. I believe it's time to break our fast." I followed him. His steps slowed for me so I wouldn't struggle to keep up, and a giddy excitement mixed with unfound dread.

Come hell or high water, I was going to see Eliza.

The sound of the clock rang throughout the room, the soft click of its hands echoing as the seconds counted down. It was driving me crazy, poking at my already frayed nerves, a constant reminder of *who* was coming.

Eliza had been in hysterics when we called her. Well ... hysterics didn't quite cut it. I could still hear her choked sobs when I told her it was me. I'd done that, hurt my friend, my family, and that was *before* she found out I was with a Crypt.

That was when the screaming had started.

"I still think we should have gone with a tailor." Osiris's voice sounded tired.

He had his hair brushed back just slightly off from normal, like he'd rushed in doing it. He wasn't sitting at the dining table like I was, instead he leaned against the window, staring out at the yard. His pinstripe suit, normally pressed, was lacking in its usual sharp pleats. He looked disheveled. It was moments like this that had me regretting my decision. Osiris only swayed because of me, and it was eating at him. Even though he didn't say it, I knew I wasn't the only one worried about meeting Eliza.

I knew Eliza, knew how she acted and how fiercely she protected those she loved. She would understand why I was here, and she would come to realize that these men weren't like the Vampires she'd encountered before.

I wouldn't stop until she did.

"It is going to be fine, Osiris. You're overreacting," Adrian chided. "Besides, Audric said he'd still take her measurements in case we wanted to order something later. Not to mention, this was one of Aaliyah's stipulations. Two birds with one stone, as they say."

The screech of chair legs against the ground echoed as Adrian took a seat next to me at the kitchen table. I flinched at the sound just as he laid his hand down, palm up. My nerves were strung tight, and I struggled to keep from fidgeting in my seat. I glimpsed Adrian's worried expression before I reached for him, putting my fingers through his own as though it was instinctual. I wasn't sure why I did it, or why it felt so natural to place my hand in his. All I really knew was that it calmed the thunderous roar of my heart enough for me to breathe. Adrian's lips split into a hesitant grin, the smile stretching all the way to his copper eyes, and my hand gripped his a little tighter.

A knock at the door cleared the silence of the room; along with any will I'd mustered up over the last hour, it seemed. Yet, it felt like time slowed as the door opened and Fallon allowed Eliza into the house.

And by that, I meant Eliza forced her way past a disgruntled Fallon with all the grace of a bull in a china shop, and immediately sought me out.

"Thank fucking *Himal*," she said, pulling me out of my chair, ripping my hand from Adrian's as her arms wrapped around me in the tightest hug I'd ever received. I held her back just as tightly, tears burning the corners of my eyes.

"You're okay, you're okay, you're okay," she said on repeat as she pulled back, checking me for injuries she wouldn't find. She was thorough in her examination, making me laugh with her enthusiasm.

"I'm sorry. I am so sorry, Ali." Eliza was choking on her tears. "You have no idea how glad I am that you're okay."

"I think I do. I was so worried they would have had someone else waiting when you ran," I said through sobbing laughter.

I glanced between Dezen and Carter, noting the absence of my favorite little dragon. Though I wasn't surprised that Eliza hadn't brought him to the home of a Crypt, it still hurt not to see him. "Where's Grigen at? I hope you haven't been slacking on chocolate duty."

"He's with my *baba*. And trust me, she's taking great care to make sure he's getting a *proper* sugar rush." She shook her head, her smile shifting into a frown. "What happened, Ali?" she finally asked.

"The guy drugged me." Even thinking about saying it made me sick. I heard the jolt of something hitting the table, and a low growl that likely came from Eirik. "He took me to a bar or something and put me up for auction."

A deadly tension sparked in the air at my words, and even my skin tingled at the sheer force of it against my senses. I looked toward the guys, who were currently in a stand off with Dezen and Carter.

Well, at least they hadn't started throwing punches yet.

"It was rough ... but it would have been a lot worse if not for the guys. They saved me, Liz," I said, trying to show her that the men at her back didn't mean me any harm. Didn't mean any of us harm.

But Eliza's eyes just narrowed in a savage kind of hatred as she turned to stare at the men that stood rigidly at my back. Cold, vicious tension wafted off her, as she pulled me behind her.

"Right. They *saved* you." There was question and doubt mixed in her voice.

I nodded, and the look in her eyes told me she didn't believe that, not for a second. I shouldn't have expected it to be that easy. Eliza was nothing if not stubborn, and that trait was going to be the hardest to overcome with her.

"Well, I hope you'll excuse us for a moment. I'm sure Ali has a lot more to talk about in *private,*" Eliza said, abruptly gripping my hand as she looked around the home.

I'd warned them this might happen, that Eliza would want to talk to me alone, so the guys stayed seated, though I didn't miss the worried glances. I gave them all a small smile, hoping to settle their nerves.

"Dezen and Carter can keep you guys company in the meantime. Come on." She grabbed my hand, all but dragging me upstairs. When I pointed out my room, she pulled us into it.

Eliza didn't move for a moment, just took in the space, admiring it. She had her hands pressed tightly onto her hips, her weight leaning heavily onto her left leg as she did a once-over of the room. After a few seconds she nodded, turning back to face me. She lifted her hand and drew out a symbol in the air.

It was circular, flowing like water around breaks in an endless stream.

"There." Eliza's aqua eyes met my own. "The mute spell is in place. I had Dezen make it for me before we came here." The stress drained from her shoulders in that instant. Her hand slid into her coat pocket, and she pulled out a small metal sphere. At my confused look, she smiled.

"And this is a transportation spell." Her thumb ran over the metal, and a spark ignited on the surface. The sphere glowed red hot, hovering in the air.

"I got it from my *baba,* after the incident." Eliza's lips thinned, and she looked like she was going to cry again. "It's long-range, with a short charge time. I can't even imagine how she got a hold of it." She shook her head, reaching out to me, waiting for me to grab her hand again. "Come on. We don't have a lot of time. We have to get you out of here while Dezen and Carter keep them distracted."

Confusion spread through me before quickly turning to dread.

I knew the determined look in her eyes well. It was the same one she'd had when she knew what she wanted and was planning on getting it however she could.

"What do you mean, get out of here, Liz? Did you not bring the clothes?" Eliza swallowed hard, glancing at the door that was behind her. I could only stare at her, unsure of what else to say.

"No, Aaliyah. The plan was never to bring you clothes. This is a rescue mission," she said, pausing to look around the room again, her scrutiny making me jump. "Those fangs must have *Charmed* you into staying. If we can get you out of their area of effect, then it will wear off."

She flexed her extended hand out toward me expectantly. Her manicured nails, usually pristine with fresh paint and dazzling little gems, were chipped down. The once vibrant pink was now faded and broken, like she'd been biting them. I glanced at her face, taking in the dark circles under her eyes and her ruby-red hair in disarray. Guilt bit at me and I once again found myself at odds. She'd gone through all of this for me. She'd worried for me, *mourned* for me. She thought I'd died there, or worse. Then I repaid her by waiting weeks before contacting her, even after I knew the guys weren't a threat to her or the others. I let my fear of her reaction cloud my judgment, and I'd hurt Eliza because of it.

My gaze flicked around the room, landing on Prince, who was pressed against the far wall. There was a hollow fury in his eyes as he forced a smile, trying not to show that rage, that pain. He lifted his hands, hesitating before pressing his right hand over his chest, pinky and ring finger down. As always, that sign made my chest clench, and I felt on the edge of tears again.

Forever.

"I'm here by choice, Eliza," I said, holding my hand close to my chest in the same way that Prince had. "They didn't *Charm* me."

"Ali, I know you think that, but—"

I cut her off. "No, Eliza. I *do* know that. They have been kind, and they offered to help me figure out what I am." I barely got the words out before Eliza gasped.

"They *know*?" Eliza stiffened, her eyes narrowing. I sighed.

"Not about everything. I haven't told them about the *Rends*," I mumbled, regret about that fact taking hold.

It was something I'd been struggling to bring up to them for days now, since the bonfire really. I felt terrible that I was keeping it from them. I trusted them with my life, and that meant that I needed to trust them with my death. But how did you start a conversation about something like that? *Hey, sorry to drop this on you, but I'm dying. No one knows why, and the only way we might be able to fix me is by figuring out what I am. No pressure or anything.*

Eliza relaxed at my admission, and her relief left a sour feeling in my stomach.

"They can't help you, Ali. I know you think they've been nice, but they're Vampires." The prejudice in her voice had me shaking my head.

I knew her reason for it now, and I knew it wasn't going to be easy to convince her they *were* kind. That they were so much more than that.

"You said that about Djinn too, Eliza."

She jumped, indignation spreading to her eyes.

"And I stand by both statements, Ali! I never should've pushed going to Archon's. It was a mistake I've regretted every second of the last two weeks. We'll find another option. There has to be someone else. As soon as we get home, we can start looking again. We still have time before the ball, I'm sure we can—"

I shook my head, cutting her off again as I took another step away.

"The men downstairs *are* another option, Eliza."

She laughed, her tone busted and wrong. The panic in her eyes was nothing like I was used to seeing. Eliza was trembling, her entire body shaking with the effort to stay standing. Guilt swallowed me again.

"How can you say that, Aaliyah? Vampires are—"

I shook my head at her, refusing to hear anything else about the men downstairs. I had no doubt that there were terrible Vampires, just like evil Djinn, cruel Dragonkin and monstrous Sirens. There was wickedness in every race. I'd learned that at the auction and in the memories I didn't ask for.

But one thing I knew for sure, the men downstairs did *not* deserve that title: Monster. It made me sick to even think about it, and I'd been the same as her. Called them the same before I'd even given them a chance to explain themselves. I'd learned from that moment, and I wasn't going to let Eliza drag them through the dirt as if they deserved it.

"They aren't like that," I said firmly, unwilling to let her degrade the men who'd saved me.

"Did they also agree to not touch you?" Her words confused me before a blush lit up my face. Accusation laced her tone.

"What do you mean?"

"I saw you holding one of their hands, Aaliyah. You're close to them, closer than you've gotten to Dezen or Carter. Hell, I'd say closer than you are with me."

I jolted back. "That's not true, and you know it!" I said, clutching my chest. Her words stung and the hollow feeling in the pit of my stomach spread up my arms, leaving me numb in its wake. "They may be helping me, they may be important to me, but you are my *family*. You saved me too, took me in when anyone else would have run."

The words choked me, and the thought that she really believed I'd chosen them over her like that. That I would conspire with them like this was some grand evil plan.

It made me sick.

"Ali," she said, but I shook my head, backing up again.

"You're my family by choice, Liz. So please, *please* listen to me," I begged, forcing the tears down so I could try to speak. "I'm not sure why I'm so comfortable around them, Eliza. They just feel—" I didn't have a word to describe it, this mesh that I felt with them.

"Let me guess, safe?" Eliza asked, and I hesitated.

They felt like home.

"It's what they *do*, Ali. They draw you in. Why can't you see that?"

I groaned in frustration.

"They wouldn't do that—"

Eliza just kept pressing until she was right on top of me. The pain on her face outweighed her frustration. "How do you know? You've known them for what, two weeks? You don't know what they'll do."

Something in the way she looked from me to the door told me she thought she did.

"Yeah. Well, neither do you!" My outburst caused her to stumble backward. "I can't explain it, Eliza, but I trust them." I sought out Prince. He was staring like he had at the compound, his thoughts far away, devastation pulsing from him in waves. "Prince trusts them."

I watched him until he finally found the will to look at me. Appreciation shone in his hollow smile.

"And you would trust a ghost over me?"

Rage ignited in my belly, and I wanted to scream: *Yes! I would*. I trusted Prince over everyone, even myself. But I bit my tongue, holding in my harsh words to try and bring reason to Eliza.

"I'm not trusting anyone over you. I am taking everything you're saying seriously." My eyes watered, and I struggled to find what to say. "I'm scared, Eliza, terrified that my time is running out. They've given me hope. I don't feel like I'm going crazy here. I haven't *Rended* here." I settled my resolve, crossing my arms. I was against the wall now, but I'd never felt stronger. "This is my choice to make, and I choose to trust them."

And I did. For whatever reason, I did. I wasn't sure if I would regret it, but I would face that when I got there.

Because it was my choice to make.

Because I wanted to sit with Adrian and hear his mystical laugh as I missed another shot at pool. I wanted to see him smile, really smile, the kind that lit up his entire face and brought dimples to his cheeks. I wanted to talk to Eirik, figure out what was going on in his head, and learn more about what went on behind his soulful sky-blue eyes. I wanted to see if I could get Fallon to smile, if only for a moment, sneaking chocolates when we didn't think the others were watching. I wanted to read with Osiris and watch his face soften when he spoke of his family.

I didn't want to lose this feeling.

"Dammit, why do you have to be so stubborn!" Eliza groaned out, as she ran her hands through the longer fiery red hair on the left side of her head, a disbelieving laugh on her lips.

"I learned from the best," I said, motioning to her.

This was getting us nowhere.

"Why don't we make a deal, Liz," I finally said, glancing at Prince, watching as he narrowed his eyes, curiosity in his expression. "I'll go with you, prove it's not *Charm*, and show you that this is what *I* want. Will you believe me then?" I stood tall, and pride lit up Eliza's face even as she grumbled.

Then, she sighed and smiled, an honest one that took years of stress off of her.

"You've grown a lot, Ali," she whispered. "I'm proud of you, you know?"

It meant more than I could say to hear that from her, and my grin wobbled. She nodded, and my chest stopped hurting.

"If we get out of their range, *and* you still stick to this ridiculous story, then yes. I'll believe you." She reached her hand out to me, that smile still on her face.

"Good. I'll go let everyone know—"

"No. I won't take that risk, Ali. *If* it turns out this isn't a *Charm*, then I'll bring you back." There was no room for argument in her eyes, and I knew I had to give her this if I was going to get her to trust the guys.

So I nodded, sighing.

"I'm not going to change your mind, am I?" I asked.

"Absolutely not." She responded with a full grin, and I found I didn't mind.

I glanced over to Prince, giving him an easy smile that I hoped settled his nerves. He looked nervous, hand pressed against his semi-transparent jaw. When he noticed I was looking at him he smiled back, standing straighter before he pressed his hand to his chest in that all too familiar way.

Forever.

"I missed you, Liz," I said, slipping my hand into hers, just as I turned my head toward her. "See you soon, Prince."

Light burst around us, making the room glow. It was a heavy kind of magic, *old magic.* The teleportation charm singed across my skin like a live wire, and pressure built in my chest.

"Missed you too, Ali," Eliza whispered with a smile.

Then we were gone.

As soon as it started, it was over. We were in the forest behind Eliza's home; the wooded area familiar. The humid air smelled distinctly like salt and timber, and the new moon made the forest nearly pitch-black. But I knew this place like the back of my hand. I recalled playing tag with Grigen here a few times, noticing our little stick men strewn about the ground.

Eliza tugged at my arm, turning me until I was looking into her shining aqua eyes. They glowed so brightly that they were all I could see.

"How do you feel?" she asked, and I took a deep breath, so much so that my head pounded.

I felt as I had before leaving the house. Though, now my skin was icy in the chill of fall, and a creeping feeling of sadness settled in me.

"Normal, if not extremely dizzy," I said, pressing a palm to my forehead.

My head ached, burning so sharply that my vision blotted when I strained to look around.

"Take me back, Eliza." I didn't have to see Eliza's face to know she was surprised.

"Their *Charm* range is outrageous," she said, disbelief clear in her voice, like I couldn't *possibly* choose their help.

"Come on, I'll have Dezen look at you when they get back from the house. You just haven't had time to adjust." Her words echoed like they had been screamed at me as we marched forward.

"It's not a *Charm*, Eliza." I tried to sound soothing as the pain spread through the rest of my body. "I trust them. They can help."

My mouth went dry and nausea set in. I kept telling myself that it was just the spell, that it was giving me a headache, that this was normal, that *I* was normal. That the pressure dragging down my spine was *normal.*

God dammit, why now?

"*Himal,* I can't believe this," Eliza said, cursing her god just as a frigid chill fought its way up my throat. "Alright. Alright. I'll take you back."

I choked on a response, and I dreaded the realization of what was happening as Eliza came to a stop.

"Ali?" she asked, but I couldn't answer.

She flipped around to face me, likely to ask why I'd stopped walking. But when she saw my face, she froze.

And suddenly I couldn't breathe.

I choked, coughing on a viscous liquid. Eliza's scream reverberated around me as I ran my hands along my face. It was wet, and I couldn't *stop* coughing. When I finally pulled my hands away, horror swallowed my cry.

"Ali!"

It was blood.

The pull was vicious, tearing me apart as a scream died on my lips. Everything went black in an instant, and when I could finally see again, I was *somewhere*.

The ground was a sheet of sterling silver, and it wobbled as I stood. There was nothing else, no sound, no smell, no color.

Where was I?

There was nothing for miles. Not a tree, not a building, no Eliza. This was wrong. Just endless silver and an obsidian sky, blank of even stars.

Where had I *Rended* to? Where was my body?

I could move, yet when I looked at my hands they were still semi-transparent. My breathing picked up, though no air flowed past my lips. I choked on a silent sob, falling to my knees as I searched desperately for the thread that had held my soul to my body before. I almost wished that I couldn't move, that I was being forced to watch myself fall. Nothing greeted me. Nothing held onto me, because *it* had finally happened.

I was dead.

CHAPTER 23

EIRIK

Strength was a quality I'd always held in high regard. Someone able to remain steadfast against insurmountable odds would always have my respect. It was why Nero and I had been so close. We fought together. We drank together. Then fought some more after that. So, as much as it made my blood boil and my wolf snarl behind my eyes, I had to admit that these men, who were busy sipping my favorite mead like they owned the bottle, held strength.

Their magic swirled in the air, and even though they smiled kindly as they spoke, I knew they could do damage. It would be a tough fight, even two versus four. Sorceri and Dragonkin were like that, dangerous, and with Dezen being a Hemomancer he was particularly useful against us. Thanks to Osiris starting life as an Echomancer, over the years I'd dealt with my fair share of people who could control blood; far more than anyone should. Now, ever since Aaliyah had gone upstairs with Eliza, I'd been preparing for another fight.

"I've always wondered who lived in this place. Carter and I saw it several years back on a hike." Another smile.

And a lie.

All the Naturals in the area knew this territory was under the protection of the Vivas Crypt. The man, Dezen, didn't back down from the glare Osiris gave him, choosing instead to smirk at him. The look on Osiris's face was familiar and volatile, the same one he'd held regularly before introducing Aaliyah to our home. The fury in his eyes masked with disgust, his back straight and *Charm* practically pulsing off of him.

Osiris wasn't feeling particularly in control of the situation. A normal man would see the crumbling sanity in his eyes and know to back off. They'd know that they were teetering on a high-wire, and bloodshed was the least of their problems.

Seemed these men forgot who they were dealing with, or they were stupid. Really fucking stupid.

"We honestly thought it was abandoned. Glad to see we were wrong." The lie slithered past Dezen's all too fake smile, and he assessed the room.

"We have other estates we visit from time to time. Though we always find our way back here." Osiris didn't hide the distaste in his voice as he downed his glass, his eyes darting between the two intruders.

This was why we didn't allow strangers into our home without a vote. They were a threat, a disruption to our peace. Uncomfortable silence sat in the room, drowning out the oxygen until the only thing left to breathe was tension. The only noise came from the clock ticking above the windows.

"While the girls are talking, why don't we bring in the clothes?" Adrian, always the peacekeeper, chimed in.

He had his arms crossed behind his back, and brown curls covered the copper of his eyes, while enthusiasm hid the sharpness of his words.

"That's a great idea." It was the first time Carter spoke. He downed his glass and stood, taking us in as we all followed suit. I had to give it to him for not cowering. Another strength. I ground my teeth at the realization. "There's only one problem."

My back stiffened, and my *Úlfheðinn* snarled. Then, as if taking stock of the beast hidden in my mind, Dezen smiled.

"What problem?" Fallon asked, now next to Dezen.

He'd *flitted* so fast I hadn't seen it. An icy rage clashed with the searing heat of the *Flame* as it crawled its way up his arms.

"We didn't bring her clothes." Carter's voice held a deeper tone, and his eyes didn't show distress like they should. Instead, I saw his dragon, twisting behind the light greens, mocking, testing our limits. Didn't they know whose home they were in, who they were speaking so carelessly to?

"Don't act like you didn't expect this." That ever-present burning smile didn't leave Dezen's face as he spoke. I wanted to tear it off. My jaw seized, and pressure built where my skin fought to give way to the wolf. "Eliza has already gotten Aaliyah out of the house. Now that she's out of your *Charm* range, she'll understand what happened."

The accusation in his tone forced a snarl from my chest. I already had my hand around his throat when he spoke again.

"She'll realize the monsters you are, and she'll understand why we don't trust fangs." The vicious thud of Dezen hitting the wall had him laughing; as if he had the upper hand in this situation. Like I couldn't tear out his throat. "Look at you, proving my point."

His words meant little to the wolf behind my eyes, and flashes of a past that felt all too recent, strangled me. All I could think about, all I could feel, was being dragged out of my room. Being tossed into a caravan and stripped down.

Was Aaliyah panicking? Did Eliza force her to leave? Or worse.

Did she want to?

"Where the fuck is she?" My snarl drowned out my words, masking them in rage and desperation.

"Like we would tell you. You held her against her will—" Carter's words came to an abrupt stop, his throat clenching as power flooded the room. It was sharp, brittle, and it caused the hair on my arms to stand.

It wasn't the power of the *Flame,* or the seductive drag of a *Charm.* No, this was old magic, dark magic. The magic of Osiris's youth. Echomancers were the mimics of Sorceri, able to use bits and pieces of each magic type, and Osiris's magic had been potent before his turn.

Though he rarely used it, Osiris held the key to one of the most devastating magic reserves in the new world, and as lightning skittered across my skin, I shivered at the sheer power of it.

My beast cowered, and I struggled to move.

"Aaliyah wasn't here against her will. We agreed to help her find out what she is." It was the deadly calm of Osiris's voice that caused my grip to loosen. The clinking sound of a glass settling against the table drew my attention.

"So, when she comes back here of her own free will..." Osiris paused, tugging against the cuffs of his dress shirt to expose the tattooed skin of his forearms. Harsh black markings gained before his turn.

Bloodbath. There was going to be a bloodbath.

"... I'll be expecting a full apology."

Like a switch flipped in their minds, the men in our kitchen finally realized what they'd done.

Osiris was a beast, hidden behind crisp suits and chilling magnetism; a beast kept locked up, so no one else would have to suffer its wrath. He may have been tamer since Nero's death, but he'd always been this man. *Had always been Wrath. Rex interfectorem.*

The Kingslayer.

More magic swirled in the air, this time unfamiliar and cold, as a searing feeling started on my arm. The hand attached to Dezen's neck boiled, skin bubbling as the blood in it seized. It was a technique I was dreadfully familiar with, one that tore apart the cells and vessels in my hand ... Fucking Hemomancers. I didn't let go. Instead, I leaned in, and finally. *Finally,* Dezen dropped the smirk as fear bled into his expression. Every strength had a tipping point, and even though Dezen was intent on 'saving' Aaliyah, he'd met his. I appreciated their valor as much as I hated it. They cared about her. It showed in their willingness to face our wrath to get her out of here unseen.

"Now. You're going to stop burning Eirik." The pain instantly ceased, and my skin began knitting closed where the welts had appeared. The harsh pull of Osiris's magic felt foreign as it worked to mend the wound. He used it so seldomly that it didn't even feel like him. "Eirik, Fallon. Release them."

The *Charm* was so heavy in Osiris's voice that after Dezen hit the ground, I took nearly ten steps back. That wasn't a command, but the *Charm* from his previous sentence had bled into it.

I hadn't realized Fallon had subdued Carter. He was clutching a sword, one he pulled off the wall. The shining Damascus steel gleamed with a single trail of red. Fallon kept it raised, running his finger across the steel, the edge digging into his skin. His attention never left Carter, the snarling beast unable to look Fallon in the eyes, and for a moment I wondered what Fallon had said to him. What had transpired to place fear that deep?

Now Dezen and Carter were on their knees.

"Tell me where she is, so we can hear from her whether she would like to leave."

A single word escaped them, forced from their mouths by the heady command of Osiris's words.

"Home." It was enough. I was already walking toward the door.

"Eirik, Fallon. Find her." Osiris leaned in, his eyes dragging over Dezen's.

His face twisted into a scowl and made my stomach tense. This had been normal, an expression that never left Osiris's face before two weeks ago. So why was it such a surprise to see it back?

"Bring her back here. We will hear Aaliyah's desire from her own lips."

I forced a nod before he continued, "Adrian and I will keep these two company until you return."

Fallon was by my side, his calm sort of rage keeping his indifferent mask in place.

"Osiris," I said, and he glanced at me, fire bleeding into his gaze. "She'll be upset if you kill them."

It must be a cold day in hell for *me* to err on the side of peace. Nero would have laughed had he been present, and I'd be glad to be the center of his joke if it meant he was around to see this change in his brothers.

Fallon and I were gone before another word could be uttered, Osiris's silent confirmation following us out the door.

CHAPTER 24

OSIRIS

Old magic and the stench of blood settled in the air. It was a scent that would typically incite the need to hunt, to feed. But that wasn't what was on my mind now. No, everything was buried by the smoldering rage that scalded my throat and forced my *Charm* to the surface, dragging the *Flame* along my skin.

It was a rage that made the magic I'd sworn off build in my blood.

"I'll admit you have valor. Few would have been temerarious enough to do what you did today," I said as I tapped at the table, watching the way Dezen and Carter paled from their spots on the ground. The *Charm* in my voice kept them immobile as I stepped toward them, reining in my temper with a threadbare leash.

They had taken Aaliyah from *our* home. It was an egregious insult, but above even that it was maddening ... because they had succeeded. We had invited them into our home, had shared drinks and bit our tongues when they sneered and judged. And they betrayed that hospitality by stealing someone that was under our protection. The very thought of their deception forced my magic forward. The lights above us flickered, shaking as I glared down at the men that dared to threaten our peace.

Uneasy tension radiated off them. They couldn't move, likely could barely breathe, and I was glad to let them suffer a while longer.

"Osiris," Adrian said, sipping at his drink. His auburn hair was ruffled, and his typically mischievous eyes were honed on our guests. It wasn't often he looked so scornful, even if he continued to smile. "You promised to play nice."

I clenched my fist until the spark died down, and I nodded begrudgingly.

"My apologies, gentlemen," I seethed, unable to keep the contempt from my tone. Fortunately for them, the *Charm* still faded from the air, like the sizzling of dying embers. It allowed the men that were kneeled in front of me to fall forward. "We haven't been the best hosts. Please, allow me to rectify that."

They gasped for breath, trembling under the force of what had been an intentional *Charm*. That they were still conscious was a feat.

I poured us all another drink, motioning to the table for them to see, but not bothering to look if they actually took my offer. Adrian tipped his glass at me from where he stood, keeping his eyes on our guests.

"Now, why did you take such drastic measures to get Aaliyah from our company?" I asked.

Carter growled in response, smoke coming from his nose and extending around his snarl. That dark, ashy smell tainted the air. It blocked out the soft aroma of lavender that I'd grown accustomed to, further souring my mood. I grabbed the cuff of my shirt, trying to find control in the coarse fabric that strained under my fingers.

"Is that a *joke*? We got her away from you because you're *monsters*." Carter didn't hesitate, his words cutting in every way they shouldn't.

Because he was right, and I knew Aaliyah deserved better than what we had to offer. But we had come to an agreement, and I was far too selfish to push her away unless she wanted to go. Until I heard from her own lips that our deal was off, she was under my protection. Even then ... I lifted my chin, raising an eyebrow as I savored a drink from my glass. It pushed down the words I wanted to say, the insults I wanted to throw.

"What, no response to that?" Carter asked while standing, shaking off Dezen's hand and regarding me with a bloodthirsty rage.

Dezen grimaced, cursing under his breath.

"Not one that you would appreciate," I said, ignoring Adrian's indignant sigh.

There was a beat of silence, before Dezen met my gaze. He flinched as he did, quickly looking away when he noticed the odd coloring of my eyes.

"We did what we needed to do to free Aaliyah from your *Charm*, *Challe* Vivas ... I hope you understand. Aaliyah means a lot to us, and we protect our own. And if you didn't *Charm* her, then we saved her the pain of being connected to the Turned of Sebek Ra," he said carefully.

Even hearing his name made me sick, and heat swelled in my hands. The control that kept me from gutting them where they stood nearly snapped as the *Flame* seared my skin against the now heated glass. I set it down, glaring at the orange glow until it faded.

Someone inhaled sharply, just as Carter began speaking again, his ignorance of the dangers around him only fueling his hate. "So feel free to crawl back into whatever shithole you came from, and leave Aaliyah alone. She's suffered enough, and she doesn't need a house of fucked up fangs to deal with too."

There was barely a breath before Dezen grabbed Carter by the arm, dragging him back before he could say any more.

"Carter, for fuck's sake," Dezen hissed, as though he'd finally come to realize who they had insulted. Who they *continued* to insult. His tone had changed, and he no longer paraded like he was the apex predator in the house. "Please excuse him, he's an idiot."

Another day, another time, I might have handled it differently. I would have used their blood to paint my skin red before I hunted down their families. But I couldn't harm them, these men that I knew Aaliyah held dear. I wouldn't risk her not forgiving me if I damaged them. So, as much as I craved to put them in their place, I held back.

Only because of her were they still breathing.

"No, Dezen. They deserve to hear it." Carter had every brash aspect I expected with a Dragonkin. Unquenchable rage, the inability to stop once started.

Power.

It glowed around him. His green eyes were so familiar it was nause-ating. They were quite the combination: the third-born son of the Drag-onkin Eternal, Teviticus Halsen. The protégé of the most powerful Hemomancer in the world, Edwin DelMer. The blood granddaughter of none other than Eternal Ilenia, the Siren Queen. Powerful, yet so young in their ways.

A match made in my own nightmares.

"Did you forget what *just* happened?" Dezen hissed through clenched teeth, tugging on Carter's arm. " I get that you're pissed, but the Vivas Crypt is being very *generous* in allowing us to stay with them until Eliza and Aaliyah can get back. Just hold your tongue for ten fucking minutes, then we can go home."

At least one of them had the sense to understand the predicament they were in.

Tension continued to build in the air, until Adrian began to whistle.

"Exactly. The girls will be back soon with Eri and Fally. So, there's no reason we can't get along in the meantime. I'd say we got off on the wrong foot," he said, breaking up their hysterics before it could escalate into full-blown panic. He walked to the table, grabbing the drinks I'd poured and handing the now standing Naturals each a glass before he finished. "Come on then, drink. Let's talk this out."

The two men stared at Adrian wearily but accepted his offering.

"I'm Adrian, the youngest of the Vivas Crypt." Adrian bowed, smiling sharply.

That false intrigue and joy he portrayed were almost sickening. So cold compared to who Adrian was.

"The Collector," Dezen whispered.

He likely hadn't expected Adrian to be our information liaison. Most didn't. It was a dirty job, one that Adrian excelled at with his quick wit and charm. Adrian's smile didn't fall as he winked at Dezen, leaning back on the table.

"Sometimes. Only when Osiris asks nicely, mind you. He's not particularly good with his people skills, if you didn't notice," Adrian snickered, downing the contents of his glass before he set it on the counter.

He slapped his hands together then, a small spark wrapping around them before dying in an ember. Carter's gaze followed it, narrowing at the use of fire. The gift of the *Flame* didn't end there, as Adrian's eyes glowed in the low light.

"Now. What can we do to convince you we mean Aaliyah no harm?" Adrian asked, hopping up to sit on the counter.

The way he sat with lax shoulders and an easy smile, made him seem open to attack. Like he was trusting them not to take advantage of his kindness. But that was anything but the truth, as cruel intention still lit up his eyes, clashing with the smile that twisted his lips.

"Don't take this the wrong way, but there isn't a single word that could come out of your mouth that we would trust." Dezen was honest to a fault, even when he was held at a knife's edge.

Admirable, but infuriating.

"Well, that's quite rude," Adrian said, shrugging his shoulders nonchalantly. "You're telling me you don't think cake is better than pie? I don't think we can be friends anymore, Dezen."

Dezen was too stunned to speak, shocked by Adrian's cavalier attitude. But Carter took offense to Adrian's calm disposition, his nose flaring as steam once again spilled out in front of his face. Before Dezen could stop his hotheaded pack mate, Carter stepped forward.

"Is this a fucking game to you?" he asked, fuming.

Adrian snorted and opened his mouth to snark back. Likely to tell the Dragonkin that was *exactly* what he thought this was, if only to twist him up more. It was Adrian's interrogation tactic, his way to destroy someone without needing blows. I'd normally be inclined to let him continue, but I grew tired of hearing the cocky Dragonkin speak.

"This is a waste of time," I said, debating the consequences of tearing out the growling man's heart.

Aaliyah had gotten over it once, and she didn't look at me with quite as much distaste anymore. But that had been Curtis, the man who had kidnapped her, taken a hand to her. Carter was her sister's mate. And though they held some of the same blood, they were obviously not interchangeable.

I ground my teeth.

"Now Osi, we have to at least try to make nice. Aaliyah wouldn't want us to be at odds." Adrian, always the peacekeeper. He didn't fool me today; as I again glimpsed the fury in his eyes, as he calculated every way possible to make their deaths look like an accident.

"You agreed to this plan because you wanted to keep Aaliyah safe, right?" Adrian asked, flashing a smile when Dezen and Carter reluctantly nodded. "Well, then we want the same thing!"

"And why do *you* want her safe?" Carter asked through clenched teeth, his mistrust easy enough to spot. "Do you pine for her, Vampire?"

Adrian hid his wince well, not answering even as Carter laughed and Dezen did his best to rein him in.

"But it's not just you, is it? *Adrian.* Couldn't get a woman to like you the normal way. Had to *Charm* your way there. No wonder Aaliyah was holding your hand."

Adrian's smile finally fell, his temper coming to the surface as his eyes flashed red.

"Now, you have it wrong, gentlemen," I said, raising my hand, stopping Adrian's advancing form. He grimaced but didn't move.

"You can lie to yourself, but you can't lie to me, *fang,*" Carter hissed again, unfazed by Adrian's rage. Or my own. "Have your little lackies get the girls. It doesn't matter. You'll see soon enough that we were right."

I scoffed, not at the insult of calling the rest of my Crypt *lackies*, but Carter's use of the word *little*. Of all things, that wasn't a word used to describe Eirik, and it seems his absence made them forget the altercation they'd had.

"Settle in, it's going to be an entertaining evening," I said, leaning back, focusing on the forest past our windows, and waiting for the familiar scent of lavender to reach me again. Carter snarled just as I flexed my hands. He looked at Adrian like he might attack him, his body tensing for a fight. I was still unable to cool the rage in my blood when I finished. "If you wish to keep your heads for the reunion I suggest you calm yourselves."

Cold. Deadly. Numb. I'd killed more men seeking revenge for my Maker's misdeeds than either of the two in front of me could dream. I only had so much patience.

My hands began to ache, and I covered the skin at my wrist, holding my hand over the brand that still burned.

"I'm not fucking scared of you, *Kingslayer.*" Carter hissed the title out like he understood what it meant. Like he'd seen the bodies that I'd stacked to earn that cursed name. Death had been at my doorstep since the moment I'd said goodbye to the sun for the last time. Still, I held back, hand tapping against the counter, my thoughts on Aaliyah's bright eyes ... I had to hold back, needed her to look at me in that soft way she did.

"I'll kill every single one of you, I swear it." Carter snarled it like it was the first death threat I had gotten, like I hadn't spent over two thousand years living as a Turned of Sebek Ra. But it wasn't the threat to me that snapped the thin leash on my control. *I* could withstand it.

But he broke a cardinal rule in going after my brothers.

I had Carter pinned to the wall before anyone in the room could breathe, a deadly calm replacing the rage as disgust skittered across my nerves at the feeling of his skin on mine.

"No?" I asked, my head tilting as the Dragonkin struggled under my palm. Sparks of power jumped from my hand to his exposed skin, burning him. "You aren't the first that has wanted me dead, son of Teviticus. And you won't be the last." There was a commotion behind me, Dezen struggling with Adrian as the Hemomancer tried to free his friend from my grasp. I reached my hand out, using his own magic against him as I pinned him to the wall using his blood. It was sluggish, the power feeling sickeningly wrong. I turned back to the Dragonkin, seeing the understanding in his gaze when he realized I was more than just a Vampire. I was an Echomancer, a wielder of magic. Death if he continued his foolish thought. "But I can promise you this. Should you threaten my family again, I will not be the one dying."

I leaned in, snarling in the face of the man that had drawn on my last ounce of patience.

"You are alive because Aaliyah cares for you, that is the *only* reason. So accept my kind hospitality. Before I see if she'll forgive me for killing another Dragonkin."

I dropped him to the ground, my control on Dezen slipping as well. As soon as the Hemomancer's feet hit the wood floor he ran to Carter's side. He said something, asking if the man was alright like I'd done more than scare him.

I rolled my eyes and poured myself another drink, just as Adrian began to laugh, snickering to himself as he sat at the table. He winked at me, then turned his Cheshire grin to the two stunned Naturals still plastered to my floor. "What did I say? *Terrible* people skills."

CHAPTER 25

FALLON

716 North Halden Street.

The home of Eliza Barlow, Carter Halsen, Dezen Lal and their son Grigen. We'd found their address the first day after rescuing Aaliyah from the auction house, when she first laid down the requirements for accepting our agreement. We'd known she wasn't ready to reach out, that she was worried about trusting us, and I didn't blame her for that.

And now we were going to take her from said house.

I considered stopping Eirik, telling him we should head back, that this wasn't our place because it was her choice to make. A choice she made when she left with Eliza.

My heart burned in my chest, and agony kept me moving. Why would she leave? Did she not enjoy our company? Even I found her enjoyable to be around at times, and though I didn't want to admit it, I wouldn't mind her staying in our home. I'd grown accustomed to her presence like she'd always been there—a member of our family for centuries, not days.

The house came into view and Eirik's shoulders lost some of their tension. Something had triggered him earlier, causing him to be reckless. He'd slammed Dezen against the wall and nearly shifted on the spot.

Which was why his actions were so *unnerving*. He had nearly torn the man's throat out and had endured a magical burn just to drag fear into the man's eyes. Adrian and I weren't privy to the pasts of our elder brothers, a fact that I grew more and more tired with every day. *Their horrors were their own to rot with*, as they said. I hated it. If we were the family we tried to be, shouldn't we be there when the demons came to play?

I just knew it was going to catch up with us, one day. A past we weren't ready to fight was going to knock on our door, and I could only hope we would be strong enough to overcome it without losing another one of us.

"Aaliyah?" Eirik's harsh voice was clouded with worry. *'Smár Valkyrja*, are you there?"

The knock of his hand against the door went unanswered. She didn't want to speak with us, not that I blamed her. All of her words and smiles had been a ruse to gain safe passage from our home, a tactic that I couldn't fault her for. She was smart, and she'd played her cards perfectly. It was so easy to see now that I thought about it; the way she flinched when we got too close, the fear that always sat in her eyes. She saw us exactly as we were, and we were too smitten by her presence to realize it.

We were the monsters that *bought* her. Fucking *monsters*.

"Come on, Eirik." The Viking looked at me with narrowed eyes, confusion muddling their depths. "She obviously doesn't want to come with us. She's made her choice."

I ran my hand across my face. This was for the best. We didn't need the weakness she'd bring, not so close to the ball, not when Sebek was practically at our throats. Allowing something that provides you happiness to exist in your life gives your enemies something to target.

Something to tear away from you.

"You don't know that. Eliza could've taken her against her will."

I scoffed at Eirik's words, shaking my head as he continued to pound on the door.

"Are you hearing yourself?" I asked him.

Eirik's face contorted in pain and his hand went to his neck. The jagged scar bobbed as he swallowed.

"She wanted to leave with her family. She'd been too scared to tell us otherwise."

Monsters. Blood against an ashen ground and Aislinn's eyes haunted me. This outcome had been destined from the start. Why would she choose to stay with us when her family was made clear? Her kindness was better used somewhere harm wouldn't befall her.

"She wouldn't leave without telling us. She agreed to stay," Eirik said.

I shook my head. "Four unfamiliar men surrounded her. She probably agreed to get us off her back until she could get back home." My heart twisted at that word. Home.

"You're wrong." Eirik pulled away from the door, stubborn determination on his face.

There was more emotion in his eyes now than I'd seen in over a hundred years. Fire, depth, worry. I wanted to hate her for this, hate Aaliyah for breathing life back into my brothers, only to rip it away. But I couldn't. I couldn't fault her for choosing safety.

"Am I?" I lowered my head before turning and stepping off the porch.

Eirik flipped around, cold fury on his face as he stalked up to me. I expected him to start a fight and to have to catch a blow with the way that he raged.

But instead, he spoke.

"Don't run from this, Fallon," he said, a sharp snarl clinging to my name. His face sharpened, his nose flaring as his wolf shot to the surface. "You can't decide on something like this just because you don't like how it makes you feel."

"It makes me *feel* sour. It makes me *hurt*."

Eirik went to speak, indignation burning in his eyes, but I cut him off.

"It makes me realize how alone we are. That there is no happiness for the spawn of Sebek, Eirik."

He jolted like I had struck him, a firm snarl on his lips.

"You know that."

Eirik's chest-deep growl echoed in the air, his fury masking his understanding. My jaw clenched. I went to speak again, to say some bullshit about moving forward, when he froze. The sharpness on his face honed in, and his head flipped around, landing on the forest just past the house. I narrowed in on the spot and found nothing.

"What is it?" I asked, and Eirik didn't respond, instead he breathed heavily, like he was looking for something.

The red bled into his eyes, and the pop of bones echoed in the air. The shift didn't finish, but the panic was so clear in Eirik's expression that braced for an attack.

"*What is it,* Eirik?" I asked again, taking a step toward the forest. I listened, trying to hear or smell whatever he was sensing. But there was nothing.

"Something's wrong." The words slid past clenched teeth, and Eirik's eyes narrowed.

Another deep breath, then a panicked noise that had no right coming from someone as imposing as Eirik. He breathed a word, the sound so guttural that I knew it came from the beast inside and not the man. A name that shot ice down my spine and had me moving.

"Aaliyah."

Eirik bolted toward the thick woods, moving so quickly that I nearly lost him as I chased behind. Each step brought a little of what he'd sensed, and the closer we got, the more I realized what was happening— that the scent of iron was in the air. It was like a nightmare, tumbling through the underbrush. There was no moon in the sky, only the thick scent of blood and a familiar body plastered against the ground. Aaliyah —like a fallen angel, with white hair sprawled across wet earth, shining like a halo soaked in blood—was strewn across a familiar set of arms. The strangled cries of Eliza suddenly breached my mind, and sharp lavender blended seamlessly with a rich chocolate, the scent so heavy that my fangs dropped.

It was the same at the auction, that same searing bloodlust in my ears telling me that blood had been spilled. A lot of it.

Eliza was crying, sobs so loud that they roared in my ears, mimicking a heartbeat. It rocked my frame and stole whatever will I had left as I truly caught sight of her.

Of Aaliyah on the ground.

Tears streamed down Eliza's face as she desperately held Aaliyah to her. I strained for a heartbeat but found none.

Because Aaliyah's heart wasn't beating.

You're mine, Fallon. She can't have you. Sebek's cruel words, the same ones he spoke right before ... right before he made me kill Aislinn.

Now Aaliyah stared at me with the same blank eyes, blood spilling out around her, painting her skin and the ground around her red. Dead. *Dead. Dead. Dead.*

Unholy rage seized every muscle I had, and I ripped Eliza off of Aaliyah, slamming her into the nearest tree. She looked shocked, recognition sparking as she realized we were here. Eirik screamed something in his native tongue behind me, the sound so brutally raw and unhinged that I felt it in my soul. It destroyed part of me, tore me down to my foundation and left me to rot as I *begged* this to be a dream. I could only feel the stutter of a pulse against my hand as I strained again to hear a heart that no longer beat, praying to gods that had long since abandoned me that I'd misheard, that Aaliyah was *still alive.* But there was nothing.

You'll feel better when she's gone. The bloodlust will purge her from you.

"What the fuck did you do to her?" I screamed, but Eliza didn't respond. She was still sobbing. "What did you do?"

The flick of my *Charm* in the air jolted through her, and her head slammed against the tree as she tried to fight the words. Hatred boiled in her eyes, and I felt the same as she finally let out a breath.

"I don't know. Something's wrong." The words were grated and soft, choked out past my hand at her neck. "This is wrong."

Blood against an ashen ground.

I wanted to vomit, the sickening feeling crawling through my nerves. I could smell it in the air, the sweet tang of sunlight and the sound of Aislinn's laugh. It blended so seamlessly with Aaliyah, with her sweet smile. It happened again. I'd *told* them this would happen. I trusted, I grew close, and now Aaliyah was dead, too.

I was a fool. A *fool* that couldn't stop the wrenching agony in my chest.

I pulled away from Eliza, piercing her with a glare as she slid to the ground, landing with a huff. I should kill her, tear her heart out and make her bleed. An ache built in my chest and I looked back to Eirik. He was whispering to her, holding her body close with trembling arms as he desperately searched for a heartbeat that wasn't there. Salt muddled the smell of blood, as tears slid down his face. Her eyes had slid closed, and the chill of her death sat in the air.

I *should* kill Eliza, and as I turned back to her, noting the worry in her gaze that had no right to be there, I nearly did. But I couldn't do it ... not to the family that Aaliyah held so high.

Family that had gotten her killed.

"You killed her. She loved you, and you killed her," I ground out, the snap of emotion jerking my head to the side, and I couldn't tell if those words were for her or for me. "How could you do this?"

"I didn't do anything!" Eliza finally screamed, choking on the words as she grabbed her fiery red hair. "It doesn't normally last this long."

Even after Aaliyah was dead on the ground, she didn't want to tell us.

"It sure as fuck looks like you did something!" I was barely keeping myself from tearing out her throat and dragging her body back to our home for Osiris to string up. "Aaliyah wouldn't be dead on the ground if you hadn't fucking done something!"

She hesitated, sitting as she glanced between me and the *body*. Her teeth chattered, and she stared like she expected Aaliyah to gasp; to sit up like nothing happened. It enraged me, soured my thoughts as I fucking spiraled.

"*Say something!*" I screamed, unable to hide the anguish anymore, as a *Charm* slid through, clinging to my words.

"This happens to her sometimes," Eliza said instantly, as regret flooded her eyes. But she'd already started. I leaned in, focusing on her words. "*Rends.* She calls them *Rends.*" Another sob. "She's dead."

I nearly screamed at her again, rage boiling over into the deadly tone of my voice.

"I'm aware. I would like to know why before you join her." There was no mistake, no room for argument in my words. Defiant aqua eyes met mine.

"Her soul is pulled from her body for a time, and when it snaps back, she remembers."

I froze, glancing again at Aaliyah. She was dead ... but it didn't sound like this was the first time it had happened. Eliza shook her head, rubbing her neck as she glared at me.

I gave her the same back.

"Remembers?" I asked.

"She has acute memory loss." Eliza took a shuddering breath, wrapping her arms around herself. "She believes she died before, and six months ago she woke up in the ground. Didn't remember how she got there, or even her own name."

I was too stunned to speak. Woke up in the ground? *Died before?*

"She thinks that these *Rends* are like her soul catching up with her body. They force memories to come back, but lately they've been getting longer."

Panic was quick to swallow me. So, there was a chance she could come back to us?

"Thirty seconds, a minute, two minutes. Each time she *Rends*, her body shuts down, and she's been worried that she won't snap back one of these times."

"How come we've never seen them?" I asked, and Eliza shook her head.

"She said she hadn't had any at your home. She was getting better, and I took her away." She ran her hands over her face, and the scent of shame filled the air. "I think the trip stressed her body out. I think I did this."

Guilt swallowed her, but I turned away, leaving the woman to cry as I took the few steps back over to Aaliyah. She may not have meant to do this, that much was becoming clear as the initial panic ebbed, but she'd still done it.

And I couldn't forgive her for that.

Eirik was cupping Aaliyah's cheek, his head on her chest, ear over her heart. He was humming one of his old folk tunes, one I recalled. He used to sing them around the house, a few glasses of whisky, and he and Nero could sing the house down. The low grumble of his words backed his devastation.

I leaned down, listening, straining to hear a subtle thump in her chest. I pressed my hand to the cooling skin above her heart and begged that she would listen, that she wouldn't leave like this. I turned away, facing the silent woods, my mask cracking under the strain of agony. I fought the tears that sprang to my eyes as my hand began to tremble.

We waited, praying for a miracle because we didn't have a choice ... and if Eliza was lying, and Aaliyah didn't come back? Then everything be damned, our lives, our hopes, the Eternium and this *fucking* Siren that took Aaliyah from us.

If she didn't wake, then I would make true to the reputation of the Turned of Sebek Ra.

Chapter 26

Aaliyah

Nothing. There was nothing.

I had no idea how long I'd wandered, how long I ran through an endless sea of morphing silver, searching for a connection to my body that was no longer there before I finally fell to my knees. Disbelief weighed me down, and I closed my eyes, begging for this world to fade away and for the forest to come back into view. Because this couldn't be real, *none* of this could be real.

I couldn't be dead.

There was a faint pressure that poked and prodded at my skin, like it was testing the give of my soul. I knew innately that it was the Void plucking at me, my gift working to send me past this existence. The same gift I'd used to help countless spirits pass on was now going to be my downfall.

I grabbed at my chest, feeling nothing but empty, caught between acceptance and horror. I'd been so close to finding out how to fix this. I *had* to have been.

Because I couldn't stomach the idea that this had all been in vain. That death was always going to win. I sobbed, clutching my sides as tightly as I could, feeling nothing. I'd failed ... I'd failed myself. I'd failed Eliza. I'd failed Prince. I'd failed *them*.

Adrian, Fallon, Osiris, Eirik.

I'd failed them, and they didn't even know. They were probably still at the house, talking to Dezen and Carter, waiting for us to come back downstairs. I ... I never got to say goodbye. I choked on my anguish, wailing silently into the silver abyss. Everything shook, and I *screamed* until I couldn't even manage that, sliding the rest of the way to the ground, curling into a ball around myself. I wanted to see them again, I *needed* to. Their company had brought me peace, and it took me dying to realize that I didn't want to lose that. I hadn't expected to feel this way, not after what little time I'd spent with them, but I did. They felt natural, like my Prince. My whole body ached at the thought of him, going numb where there should be feeling. I could see his face, the panicked horror when he saw my body but no soul.

I was taking his only way to be free with me. I *was* the path to the Void, and now he was stuck in the normal world. *Alone.* That was my snapping point, my sanity tumbling over the edge until what was left of me was only broken bits.

I should have fought harder against Eliza, I should have explained more. I should have told them about my curse sooner.

I should have, I should have, *I should have.* I could only repeat that phrase like a broken record of my mistakes.

I strained again, searching for a connection that was no longer there, praying for the tie to my body to snap me back. I waited and hoped, as seconds passed by, that I would feel it. I pressed my hand against my chest and forced myself to hold on, to not give up. My other hand pressed to my face, and as heat bled into my skin where my hands were, I *cried.* No tears flowed, and no noise fell from my lips.

It was ironic that I'd spent so much time struggling to stay silent when I'd been alive, and now all I wanted to do was *scream.* Scream until someone heard me, or I woke up from this nightmare that couldn't be happening. But it was pointless, and I knew in my soul that this was it. There would be no waking up, and no one was going to hear me.

Because the dead couldn't interact with the living.

Because the dead couldn't *speak.*

I curled tighter, using my hands as an anchor to keep me searching as another press on my soul made me lurch. I didn't *feel* it, not in the sense that I would have had I been alive. But it was there, and the Void was growing frustrated that I wouldn't let go. I shoved it away, because I needed to keep fighting for as long as I could, until there was nothing left of me to fight for.

I had to get back to them ... I had to get back to ...

Who?

Dread covered me like a cold sweat as I searched for the names of my family, of my friends. Those who *loved* me. I knew they did, knew that they were waiting for me to come back.

So why couldn't I remember them?

I wracked my brain, desperate to remember the names that refused to come to me. Another push from the Void had me crying out, and I pressed my head to the ground. My only comfort was that the warmth didn't fade from where my hands were. I rocked back and forth as every second fought to steal another memory from me.

Every second making the heat burn a little hotter.

I lifted my head, glancing around, facing the same stilled silver expanse. I clutched my cheek, using that warmth as a crutch to keep my mind stable. *Why* was I warm?

The heat became a raging inferno that cut through the chill. It hurt, searing me in a way I never thought I'd be happy to experience ... because it hurt, and I *felt* it.

A soft melody crept over my ears, so deeply melancholic it nearly lulled me to sleep. The sound sank into my skin, making my entire body buzz with energy. Although I couldn't understand the words, the meaning came through. Grief and anguish mixed into a serene song, and the grave tone wooed me, dragging me back to my feet. I tried to place the voice. Who could sing so beautifully?

I strained to hear it more, stretching onto my tiptoes.

"Please, *Elskan.*" A hoarse whisper.

The familiarity of that voice was buried in my subconscious and the thought of it made me smile. Who? That soft, haunting melody resumed, and for a second I thought it was my mind finally giving up. Who? Another voice chimed into the tune. Smooth met jagged as the words combined, and the perfect combination echoed in the empty space.

Who?

I let out a haggard sigh, the answer finding me like a tidal wave. I stretched my hand into the air, desperation overwhelming me as I began to shake.

I couldn't die yet.

I couldn't leave *them* yet.

I had so much left to do, so much more that I needed to know.

Eirik and Fallon's voices blended together, and that warmth I felt turned into a searing agony. The connection I'd been lacking locked into place, and with a tug that was equally vicious and euphoric, I slammed into my body.

The snap felt like it was ripping me apart from the inside, and I screamed, arching to escape the pain. My thrashing forced the hands from my skin as I choked on the breath that bubbled up from my lungs, past the screeching I couldn't stop. I grabbed my throat, feeling the crusted blood just as voices echoed around me. They were frantic, as desperate as I was to stop the white-hot agony that gripped my muscles as they flared to life. It felt exactly like it had six months ago, when I'd just crawled out of the ground. I barely got a glimpse of a shell-shocked Fallon and an enraptured Eirik, before my eyes slid closed and the memory took over.

My useless body didn't flinch as it toppled unceremoniously into what would be my unmarked grave. Nilus and Donavan weren't gentle with me. They barely glanced in my direction as my body bounced into the newly dug hole before falling still.

But why would they be gentle? Being alive hadn't stopped them and their cruel habits. So why would I assume that being dead would change that? I was nothing more than a failed experiment. A nuisance that had finally reached the end of its usefulness.

I wondered what I'd done to seal my fate. What had been the final straw? Or had they made a mistake and killed me by accident?

Or had the elusive Sir Amoun finally sentenced me, pulling the trigger that he always seemed to have his finger on. There to reap the rewards of my torture without ever having to face his captive.

Donavan worked to cover me with a thin layer of dirt, enough to keep me from being discovered for a while, at least. I doubted someone would ever reach wherever the hell we were. A dense, eerie forest surrounded me, so clustered that even dead I could feel the weight of it bearing down. A fiery pit of anger settled in my stomach as I realized I ached for the small comfort of my cell. At least its glass walls gave the impression of wide-open spaces.

Or maybe I just wanted the convenience of the familiar. A forlorn glower settled on my face as I squatted next to my body.

So, this was to be my afterlife? Watching over my decaying bones until the end of time, trapped in yet another cage. For the first time in years, I wanted to cry, or scream, and it burned me to the core to know I could do neither. The people of Ascension Rising spent decades coaxing the twisted sounds out of me. One gash at a time. With each bone Doctor Nox broke, and with each scar that Doctor Castillion had seen fit to give me. Now, there was nothing, no sound, no sign of my existence or my pain. Now, I couldn't even scream. They took that from me, too.

Rage licked at my skin, doing nothing to stop the constant numbness of death.

"Hard to believe they killed it," Nilus whispered, his words holding the same harsh, twisting accent that had haunted me since they had posted him as one of my guards.

It dragged me back to the present, bringing me out of my stupor. His voice was a deep rumble. Russian, I remembered him saying. It matched his unruly frame. He was the largest of the guards that kept watch over my cell. He'd always leered at me, and I found it hardest to sleep when I knew he was outside of the glass walls.

I took a deep breath in, though no air flowed through my lungs. That hurt the most, knowing that after all those years, I wouldn't get to experience the things that had kept me from slipping away from myself. I'd dreamed of my mother's butter cookies, fresh from the oven. I wanted to relish in the songs of the blue jays that used to sit outside in the small birdhouse my father and I'd built.

Most of all, I wanted to feel the brush of the crisp fall breeze against my skin mixed with the subtle heat of the sun. I'd imagined it burning away these last years.

I wanted to remember what freedom felt like.

"I heard it was an accident. Doctor Castillion wasn't paying attention to its blood loss or something, and they ended up pushing its body too far. It must have been bad if not even Doctor Nox could bring it back." Donavan's answer sent a chill through me, and if I could have warmed myself, I would have.

Yet, his words didn't hold remorse. He barely looked phased. I wasn't even a person to them. I was an it. Monsters. Every single one of them. They didn't care about what had happened. They didn't care that they'd ended a life, my life. If I could even call it that.

"Wonder what will happen now. Our job was to watch it." The first emotion that wasn't indifference finally lit up Donavan's face. His lips twisted into a devastated glower. "Do you think they'll let us go? I really don't want to have to go job searching again."

And that was the last nail in my coffin. Or would have been, had I had one. How could I call my captivity a life when everything else mattered more than it? Donavan was more worried about losing his job than he'd ever been about my well-being. Maybe I deserved it: this complete disregard. Was I the monster that Doctor Castillion continually told me I was? How could a sane person do this to anything but a monster?

I barely even remembered a time before it all. It seemed like so long ago—my life before my world came crashing down, and they destroyed everything I'd held dear.

"I guess the question was finally answered. Even it isn't immune to death." Nilus's sickening voice, twisting with his harsh Russian accent, pulled me back to the present again.

The grave was complete or close to it from the look of it. Donavan gave a joking smile. One filled to the brim with the kindness I'd practically begged for. I hated that they were so calm. I wanted to make them understand what they'd done. What they were taking so lightly.

They killed me.

They took my chance at happiness away when they killed my parents. When they strapped me down and broke me for no other reason than *morbid curiosity, treating me like I was anything but a living being. They took my life away from me with every scar they gave me.*

The soundless scream that slipped from me went unnoticed. I should've expected the feeling of emptiness that threatened to consume me. I'd seen it all before in their other failed experiments. Ghosts were nothing new to me, but to be one. I understood why they sought me out, why they were desperate to touch me. They wanted to be free, and I gave that to them.

I curled in on myself, my resolve crumbling as Donavan piled more dirt over me. I looked around the clearing, begging that Prince would find me soon. Then at least I wouldn't have to see this alone. But he wasn't here, and likely wouldn't go looking for me for a few hours yet. He hadn't come into the experiment room today like he normally did.

Donavan gave one last pat to the pile of dirt that housed my body, looking down with a smile. Like it was a job well done. He stood in one movement, and his tall, bulky frame towered over me. His shaggy brown hair settled over his thick eyebrows and sky-blue eyes. He brushed his hands over his dirtied pants, turning to Nilus with a wily grin. He hit the other man in the back with a swift strike, as I'd seen them do before.

It was a friendly interaction I'd found out. But that fact didn't stop my reaction.

I swung my arms up above me. Trying to protect my head from the blow that wouldn't come. Instead, hatred like acid raced through me, savagely tearing me apart. I despised that I couldn't stop the response I had to them. Even when I was dead in the ground, the people of Ascension Rising controlled me.

"We should get back. Don't want to lose dinner." Nilus brushed his black hair back.

He didn't react to the smack he'd received. He didn't take another glance at my grave, likely forgetting I was even there. As if I wasn't dead next to them.

As if I wasn't rotting.

They walked away. Not a care in the world. I could hear their jabs at each other as they walked. Small quips between two friends. Donavan saying he'd done most of the work, Nilus returning a snide reply. I was nothing to them, not worth a tear, barely worth a grave. I sank to my knees, desperate to feel the grass under my fingers, to dig my hands into the ground, but that wasn't what greeted me. Instead, the empty feeling of my fingers running over the cold, void earth sent shudders through my body. My life couldn't have ended like this.

I needed to live.

I curled up, wrapping my arms around my transparent legs. I held myself, staring at the mound of dirt on the ground with contempt as I waited for Prince to find me, like I knew he would. What else could I do?

I never expected death to be like this.

I shot straight up, gasping for breath as the memory faded. I blinked away the darkness that covered my sight, my eyes roaming the dark forest as soon as I was able to see; *forest*. Not emptiness. Not silver.

I let out a broken laugh that ended on a sob as I sagged into a cold body, and I shivered as I wrapped my arms around them. Everything hurt, and I struggled to keep from crying out as I held whoever it was tight. They smelled like heat and rain on a warm summer day, a combination that soothed the weariness in my bones and helped me take steady breaths. They trembled, their exhale skimming my cheek before they hesitantly pulled me closer. I couldn't find the will to care that I flinched as they moved, too overjoyed that I could *feel* their chill, hear their heartbeat under my ear.

I was alive.

The Void hadn't claimed me. I was *alive*.

"How?" A grating voice met my ears like the person behind it had torn their vocal cords.

I lifted my head from the firm chest I laid against, noting the crisp white suit that was now stained brown and red. Green eyes stared down at me, boring into my soul.

Fallon.

His shaking hand came to rest on my cheek as he looked me up and down. There was a gentleness to his expression that I hadn't seen before, one that made my heart clench when I saw how firmly it mixed with grief.

"*How*? How are you alive?" he whispered, the shock on his face almost making me miss the tears still in his eyes. I swallowed hard at the sight; broken by the anguish he couldn't hide. Everything I'd wanted to say to him caught in my throat. He didn't know what'd happened. He didn't know that it was he and Eirik who'd saved me. "Is this real?"

"It is," I said back, my chest clenching as his eyes closed and he let out a haggard breath. "I'm here ... and I'm so sorry, Fallon."

The stray tear in his eye slid over his cheek, dripping off his chin as he leaned forward pressing his forehead to mine. The intimacy of the moment shocked me, shattering what was left of my will. I knew I couldn't imagine how badly this had hurt him, how much grief still ate at him.

When he pulled back, he'd schooled his features, and the cold mask he always kept on had slid over his face. He nodded at me, acting like he'd wiped away his hurt, but I still felt the shake of his hand, still saw the raw agony in his eyes. It was something I'd never forget.

Something I wished I'd never have to see again.

"*Never* do that again, Ali," Fallon whispered, looking over my shoulder as he pulled his hand away.

A low growl went off behind me, cutting off any response I would have had, and a quick tug had me landing in a completely separate set of arms. Heat warmed the chill of death, and I hummed as I looked up at Eirik. His face held a delicate hope as his thumb ran over the pulse point at my wrist, stopping every few swipes to feel the beat of my heart against him. That low curling growl only grew as he brought my hand to his face. He dragged his nose over my knuckles, his brows coming together as he whispered words I couldn't hear against my skin.

Eirik was a giant, his body engulfing me in a cocoon of security. It'd be so easy for him to use that strength against me, but instead, he moved with careful consideration, treating me with a gentleness that betrayed his power. He brushed the hair out of my face, his fingers reverently trailing the contours of my face, before he leaned forward, this time skimming his nose over my temple.

"*Smár Valkyrja*," he whispered, like a prayer against my skin, the tremble in his voice weary. His eyes were a stormy-blue that nearly matched the darkness of the night. "We thought we'd lost you."

Guilt made it hard to breathe. While this wasn't a typical *Rend*, they'd still been completely unprepared for something like this. They'd thought I died, and I wasn't sure I would ever be able to make up for their pain.

"I know ... I'll explain everything when we get home," I started, flinching at the hoarse burn on my vocal cords. "Just know that I'm sorry. That I never meant for you to find out like this, that if I'd known this was going to happen I would have told you sooner."

Confusion and curiosity helped to melt away some of Eirik's tension, as his eyes shifted a shade lighter.

A strangled gurgle sounded behind me, and I turned toward the broken cry. Eliza was on her hands and knees, trembling. She pressed her hand firmly over her mouth, to cover any more distress. Her guilt, her worry and her strain bled into her sobs.

"I'm okay, Liz." My voice caused her to jump, her eyes bolting to my own before her head dropped again.

"I did this," she said on a choked breath, her cries still rattling her body. "I took you from their home, and the stress must have caused you to *Rend*."

"Eliza—" I tried, but her breathing spiraled, her sobs swallowing my attempt at comfort.

"I killed you, Ali. I killed you," she screamed, sliding the rest of the way to the ground. "I killed you ..."

How she laid, pressed to the cold earth, reminded me of my own hopelessness in the Void, and I knew I couldn't leave her like that. She *hadn't* killed me, she couldn't have known what would happen.

I'd agreed to go with her, this was on me. My death was on me.

I wiggled out of Eirik's steadfast arms, ignoring his grumble as I crawled over to Eliza.

"No," I said softly, as I slid onto the ground next to her, and pulled her into a makeshift hug. I held her as she continued to shake from the weight of her sobs. "You did nothing that hadn't been happening already."

She continued to bawl as pain slowly began sinking past the effects of the *Rend*. My head began to pound, and my muscles threatened to give.

"You were trying to do what was best for me." I held her tighter as my arms began to tremble. "Don't put this on yourself, Eliza. You're my friend, my sister. I can't stand seeing you cry."

I kept her close like that until her tears slowed. Until she could pull back and wipe her eyes, looking cracked, but whole. I could only smile through the ache, hoping that it was enough. I pulled myself up, hissing as my muscles protested.

"How long?" My question was soft, and Eliza's face fell again.

"Five minutes, give or take," Eliza croaked out, looking like she was going to be sick. Or throw herself on the ground again. "But it was different, Ali. You started bleeding ..."

I could feel the truth in her words, and the crusted blood on my skin.

"I thought this was it. This was where I finally lost you." She looked at Fallon and Eirik. "They showed up after you ... *died*. They came to find you, to make sure you were alright. They were *worried* about you."

She sounded regretful for even saying the words, but respect burned in her eyes. Respect for the Vampires that had now saved me twice.

"Do you know what happened?" she asked.

I wasn't sure she *wanted* to know. I still wasn't sure what to think. I couldn't *Rend* again. I doubted I'd survive. I'd gotten out on sheer luck, and my body was at a tipping point.

"I was pulled somewhere else this time. Somewhere dark ... there was nothing for as far as I could see. Only a black sky and a silver floor." Eirik and Fallon moved closer to us, Eirik taking up my right hand again. The warmth helped me speak, gave me strength.

"I wasn't connected to my body, and I think I was in the last stage of the Void." I clenched my hand over my chest. "My gift was trying to send me on, past death. I could *feel* it. I didn't think I'd be coming back." The hand gripping mine tightened.

I stole a glimpse at Eirik. His eyes were closed, his free hand at the scar on his neck, trembling.

"I'm not entirely sure what did it, or what reconnected the string to my body," I whispered, gripping my chest as I turned to face Fallon next. Green eyes refused to leave me, and I struggled under the weight of them as I remembered the song, and the touch. "But I felt again." I reached out and brushed my fingertips against his cool cheek, and he leaned into the contact as if compelled to. I glanced at my and Eirik's connected hands before I continued. "I heard the most beautiful song, and then I was back."

Eliza looked at me in disbelief, her body shaking as she struggled to find any words. Her mouth opened and closed, tears building in her eyes again. I almost didn't say what I was thinking, what I knew to be real... But I had to tell her. She, of all people, deserved to know.

My sister by choice.

"I don't think I'll be able to *Rend* again, Eliza. My body can't handle it anymore."

She let out a sharp cry then, her hands going to her vibrant red hair. "You don't know that. It could have just been—"

I cut off her words with a shake of my head.

"No, Eliza." I smiled even as I shook, hiding the fear that rolled in my veins. "I could feel it. My time's up. If I *Rend*, I'll die, and I won't be coming back."

"No. No!" Eliza flew into hysterics again, and Eirik pulled me to his chest. A deep rumble started in his chest, vibrating down my spine, and warmth washed over me.

"I didn't say I was giving up," I choked out the words as I coughed. Everything ached, and my eyes started to drift open and closed as I sank into the heady warmth of Eirik's chest.

Eliza shook her head, disbelieving.

"You just said you can't *Rend* again, Ali. You don't have a choice. You can't control them!"

I clutched Eirik's shirt, taking a deep breath. The slow rumble of his familiar purr, for lack of a better word, helped to dull the ache in my head. I looked up at him, giving him a small smile that I hoped showed my apology.

"I've always had a choice," I said, looking back at her. Devastation shone in her eyes as she crumbled. "The same choice I made before."

Eliza appeared terrified by my words. Like she was disbelieving, like I couldn't mean what she thought I did. I *had* to be *Charmed*. They *had* to have held me against my will.

She didn't want to believe that I was choosing this.

"I stopped having *Rends* at the Vivas home. I went days without any.

Two weeks." Her disbelief egged me on. "I don't know if it will work, but maybe staying there will keep them away."

"Do you really want to give up your lost memories? You can't even piece together a solid year!" Eliza was grasping at straws. Fear held her hostage as she looked between the two men surrounding me.

"Are they really worth remembering? Ascension Rising wasn't a childhood, Eliza. I think I can live without knowing if it means I get to live." That caused the men to jump, and Eirik's growl turned hostile. There would be a lot of explaining to do when we got back home.

Home. I liked the sound of that.

"What if it doesn't work, and you die anyway?" she asked, sinking further into the ground.

She looked tired, frazzled. I struggled to find the words to make this better.

"What if it does, and I get to live a long, happy life?" I asked softly, after a moment.

Eirik's hands tightened around me, his purr falling back into place, skipping slightly before it resumed.

"That's a short-term solution, Ali. It won't be a good quality of life."

Eliza, always stubborn to a fault, but I loved her, and I knew how much she cared for me. We would need to work past this hatred of Vampires, but that was for another time, when we had the chance to be alone.

"That's where we disagree, Eliza," I paused. "Please trust me."

"I—" she was obviously conflicted. "I do." There was a sincerity in her words, backed by the guilt she shouldn't be shouldering. "I've always trusted you ... I should have trusted you before. I was just so scared, Ali."

I smiled and tapped Eirik's chest. He huffed but stood with me in his arms. I was thankful that he continued to hold me, as I was unsure if I could walk on my own.

"I forgive you, Eliza." Her shoulders slumped and her hands rubbed her face. The resignation took over, and for a second I wondered if she would object again. "And I can't fault you for trying to save me. You're a good sister."

She exhaled, wrapping her arms around herself, before she lifted her gaze to mine again.

"You'll visit?" Her words were soft, echoing in the woods.

I wanted to pull her close, to tell her I would never abandon them. They were my family, even if my path was taking a new direction.

"Of course," I replied, "who else is going to sneak Grigen chocolate?"

She sniffled, then laughed quietly, the airy sound bouncing around the forest. It was clear and crisp.

A hand found its way to my face, and I was suddenly turned toward a startled-looking Fallon. His eyes searched mine, the deep green exposing the rawness of his emotion. The sharp angles of his face were gentled by his inquisitive look of disbelief.

"You're going to stay with us?" he asked like he hadn t been expecting that answer.

"I think you're stuck with me," I said as I reached up, clasping the hand that was settled on my cheek. A spark lit where our skin touched, and he swallowed hard before his lip tilted into a barely there grin that made my heart thunder against my ribcage. They'd saved me, given me hope, and brought me a sense of peace I'd been missing. They were an enigma, and something drew me to them like a moth to a flame. I was tired of running from it.

Eirik began to rumble in earnest, and I sank into his arms as he leaned in and whispered, "Then let's get you home."

Chapter 27

Eirik

I shook with tension, every muscle, every atom in me still screaming over what had happened. The heavy scent of blood in the air, sharp against the muddied earth and cold sea, the lack of breath and an unbeating heart ...

My arms tightened around Aaliyah, pressing her closer to my chest. She didn't seem to mind, leaning into me with a contented sigh, her eyes falling closed. She was exhausted, her body still shaking as she got over the post effects of her *Rend*.

I still couldn't believe that I was holding her, that she was alive in my arms. Her heart had stopped. I'd *heard* it. She was dead.

Until she wasn't.

I rolled my neck; the stress refused to fade even as I heard her heartbeat now, felt its rhythm against my chest, and soaked in the soft heat from her skin. My beast still thrashing violently in my mind hadn't settled either, but at least his focus was back on Aaliyah, and not on tearing apart the Siren that took her from us. His gaze was prominent as we assessed Aaliyah's bloodied skin. She was pale, even more so than normal, likely from the blood loss. Other than that, there were no indications of what had happened. No wounds to mend, or bones to set.

Just dried blood and haunted eyes.

I ran my nose across her hair, taking in her scent and letting it calm me. It was instinctual and something that I would normally be able to stop, but it was too raw right now, and the wolf in me wasn't about to give full control back. Some of its tension crept out, as Aaliyah's laugh echoed around me, vibrating my chest. I pulled away and looked at her.

"That tickled," she said, smiling lazily up at me as her eyes slid open.

They drooped like she was just coming out of a long nap, her breathing slow and labored. Dark circles under her eyes had me leaning in closer as I memorized that smile, the curve of her lips, and the way her nose tilted up. I wanted to engrave it in my mind, into my soul, so I'd never forget it. It was everything I didn't deserve, and I was selfish in my need to bask in it. The small hint of dimples at the corners of her mouth only grew when I huffed.

I did it again, running my nose across her hair, soaking in her scent —a unique mix of lavender and the rolling sea—startling another gasp from her.

"You're smiling," she whispered, soft and breathless, and I paused at the words.

She reached her hand up slowly, giving me time to pull away, like I would even consider straying from her freely given touch. When her finger traced my lips, I leaned in. A rumble started in my chest, building up to a soft growl that I had to convince myself *wasn't* a purr. My beast finally stopped his manic pacing within my mind, curling into a ball as Aaliyah continued her leisurely exploration of my face. We watched her with rapt anticipation, soaking in every move she made, following her retreating hand when she went to pull away.

She laughed again, pressing her palm to my cheek.

A grumble went off behind us, and I was reminded that it wasn't just Aaliyah and me on this trek back to our home. Fallon walked with a stoic expression, his arms crossed tightly over his chest, bending the fabric of his suit in a way he would normally avoid. He didn't notice though, his eyes following the Siren like she was a war criminal on the way to the gallows, and he was to be her executioner. The Siren, *Eliza*, wasn't looking much kinder, her narrowed glare speaking for her.

She didn't fall under Fallon's steadfast glower, which was impressive in its own right. Seemed she shared that trait with her husbands.

"You know, we already established that I'm not going to take Aaliyah away again. I just want to get Dezen and Carter and make sure she gets home okay." Eliza turned toward Aaliyah and I, ignoring the shift in my beast's growl at her stare.

She rolled her eyes, looking every bit like Siren Eternal Ilenia. They held the same unrelenting grit, the same wicked silver tongue.

"That means you can let up on the death glare," she finished, brushing back her fiery red hair as she stepped past Fallon, moving to be closer to Aaliyah.

Jaw clenched hard like he was barely holding back a snarl, Fallon glanced sharply at Aaliyah, then back to Eliza. His face was a mirror of calm, but it was the seething fire in his eyes that was anything but normal. The brittle expression barely looked real, his facade crumbling like rotten wood.

Something had snapped in him, seeing Aaliyah like that. Something he'd been worried about since the beginning: getting attached. But it was too late for that. The moment Aaliyah's lavender scent had hit my nose, and the twinkle in her eyes that screamed warrior had floored me, I knew we were already lost. I vowed to protect her then, from the auction, from my brothers, even from myself. With everything I was.

Now I made that vow again. She wouldn't die. I couldn't handle it, and from the look of it ... neither could Fallon.

I could only imagine how Osiris and Adrian were going to take it. Adrian would be fine, mostly. He'd always been the optimistic one, ready to turn a sour mood sweet. But Osiris, well ...

I just hoped he didn't kill anyone.

"I'll stop my *death glare* when you're out of my fucking sight, Siren." Fallon's cold words echoed around us, his arms crossed and his gait harsh as the tension wreaked havoc on his mindset.

He was going to need a fight after this, one I was happy to give him.

"Now you're just being a dick. My name's Eliza, Vampire," Eliza spat out, grinding her teeth but not backing down.

She swatted as she moved over a patch of undergrowth, looking agitated at the spider web she ran into. But she didn't complain, didn't call her husbands to come get her, instead she insisted on walking with us. She wanted to protect Aaliyah, was willing to risk her life to do so, and I could admire that.

I glanced back down at the woman in my arms, noticing her worry as she glanced between Eliza and Fallon. The rumble in my chest turned hostile just as she spoke.

"Can we not fight?" Aaliyah whispered the question, pressing a hand to my chest, holding it there until the rumble died back down.

Her painful grimace was enough to shut my wolf up entirely. Her hand dropped, and she rubbed the space between her eyes.

Damn bastards.

Fallon continued to glare, grinding his teeth. Another step, and his mouth opened to speak again.

"Fallon," I said, shooting a pointed glower over my shoulder at him.

The Fallon that I knew would've fought this, would've thrown himself at me or anyone else close enough that would prove a challenge, ready to duel to decide who was right. But he didn't, he just stared at Aaliyah and her grimace. His eyes mellowed, and he swallowed hard before jerking his gaze away.

"Fine, I'll be pleasant to our guest," he said, shaking his head.

We walked in silence after that, besides the occasional mutter of something from Aaliyah, or a quip between Eliza and Fallon. Before long, we were walking up to our home. It was a sight I'd never found more comforting. That feeling quickly fell to the ground, as it only took a few seconds before Osiris was *flitting* out of the front door, tracing the red and brown streaks across Aaliyah's face.

Genuine panic took root on his face, and a tremble worked its way down his body as his eyes flashed red. That scared expression was familiar, and I tightened my arms around Aaliyah, instinctually trying to keep her safe; to make sure she was still there.

"What happened?" he whispered, his hands clenched so tightly I heard the bones popping under his skin.

Manic eyes stared back at me. It was a look that I never thought I'd see again, one that had been slipping into Osiris's gaze ever since the auction. Power. Control that was just out of reach.

Aaliyah's touch pulled me away as she patted my chest, and I looked down at her. She smiled and motioned for me to set her down. I grumbled again, leaning in and running my nose across her temple before reluctantly doing as she wished.

She shivered as her bare feet hit the frost-laden ground, wobbling, and I nearly had her back in my arms. But she moved forward before I could, approaching Osiris like one would a wounded beast. He looked the part right now, the expressive glint in his eyes holding his pain. The sharp pressure of his *Charm* slid over the yard, and tension continued to seep into him the closer that she got.

Even my beast tensed. Knowing Osiris didn't stop the drag of fear that came with how he looked. That was what his power was, what it had grown into. Yet, Aaliyah didn't stop, didn't cower. Where kings had fallen to his feet begging for mercy, she stood unafraid.

"I'm okay, Osiris," Aaliyah said softly, inching toward him with even steps, until she was right in front of him.

"Why are you covered in blood?" Osiris's words were choked, thick with tension and twisting with a smooth, old Egyptian accent. "Your blood, Aaliyah."

He reached out, his hand stopping mid-air like he'd hit a wall. His head slowly tilted, looking past Aaliyah, and at Fallon ...and the Siren.

Osiris didn't move, didn't try to appear human-like he had since Aaliyah started staying with us. The reigning silence and tension in his form that lacked fake breaths. Osiris's eyes went fully red, and a rage I'd thought lost to time, flooded them. His hand snapped down, and he took a jagged step forwards. I moved, intent on stopping him from killing someone that Aaliyah considered family, or at the very least trying to make my intervention look genuine, when she again proved she deserved the title I gave her. My *smár Valkyrja*, didn't pull away from Osiris like a sane person would do when faced with his wrath. Instead, she only gave him a second to protest before taking the last step, wrapping her arms around him.

Tiny ... but fierce. My beast whispered, silent behind my eyes as I let out a breath, marveling as the red bled from Osiris's eye, and confusion blended with affection in their mixed blue depths. Only a second of hesitation met him before he returned the gesture, holding her so tightly that it looked like they had molded together. Osiris didn't hug; he didn't touch. Hell, I could count the times that he'd touched me on one hand. But something about Aaliyah made him feel safe enough to.

Something about her felt like home.

They pulled back from each other, and for a few tense seconds I wondered if Aaliyah's touch hadn't been enough to stave off a bloodlust that was decades in the making. A shiver shot down her spine, goosebumps now clear on her arms. Osiris must have seen them as well, his eyes going wide before he flipped around. He gave us his back and his arm to Aaliyah as he led us inside where a panicked Adrian and a stunned Dragonkin and Sorceri sat, balking at us. Osiris didn't pay them any heed, leading Aaliyah to sit, before *flitting* away and returning with a wet towel and a heavy blanket. He wrapped her tightly in the blanket, watching for signs of distress before he cleaned the blood off her face with care while he checked to see if she had any open wounds.

The unhinged look in his eyes, and the way he kept glancing at the intruders in our home, told me he was barely seconds away from breaking, and that if I were to take Aaliyah away from him like my beast was screaming at me to do ... then the Siren and her husbands wouldn't be the only ones facing Osiris's ill temper this evening.

"What the fuck did you do to Carter and Dezen?" Eliza hissed from behind us, rushing past Fallon and toward her husbands, who softened at her worry.

They sat at the table, looking wary but overall unharmed. I expected worse, given Osiris's current state.

"We merely had a conversation. They have no lasting damage," Osiris said, still carefully cleaning Aaliyah, not looking at the raging Siren.

"You fucking monsters—" She didn't finish, Osiris flicking his hand toward her, pinky and ring finger bent, in a position that I hadn't seen since he'd made my and Nero's protection charms around the time of my turn. It was how he cast spells, and now as his fingers shook, I wondered if we might be surprised again today. Rage simmered beneath his skin as he looked between the Siren and the blood on Aaliyah's face.

A snap of red in his eyes, and the pressure in the room became suffocating.

"Mrs. Barlow. I would like to remind you that you stole someone from our home, and your husbands threatened us. In. *Our*. Home," Osiris's words were smooth, almost clean, betraying the way his hand still shook.

The Dragonkin, Carter, stood in front of Eliza like that would save either of them. The tick of the clock above the table seemed to count down the time they had left, and I watched Osiris's carefully controlled power spiral in his hands. It started as a spark, our *Flame* igniting on the tips of his fingers and down his arm, lit with the stench of sulfur and dark magic.

Aaliyah reached out, and as if she'd been doing so for centuries, she pressed her hand to Osiris's cheek, softly pulling his attention to her. She was careful in how she moved, making sure he saw her approach, saw her hand and had the time to pull away if he wanted to. But no sane man would turn her away, not even Osiris in his panicked state. The *Flame* died, and though rage made his jaw clench, he nodded, going back to tending her face.

"Eliza wanted to make sure that I was safe with you guys," she whispered, pulling her hand back to her chest. "She's my family. Please don't fight."

Osiris's jaw clenched for one, two beats, the grinding of his teeth audible before it softened and he nodded again.

"We're fine, Eliza," Dezen finally said, laughing nervously and never taking his eyes off Osiris. "We came to an understanding. From the look of it, so did you."

Dezen nodded toward Aaliyah, who smiled softly at the Sorceri. I ground my teeth, gripping the island hard to stop myself from walking in front of her, to shield her from his stare.

"Glad to see you're safe, Aaliyah," he added, looking genuine enough.

The snarl still built in my chest, his swallow telling me he saw the wolf behind my eyes tracking him.

"Had us for a loop, love. What happened?" Adrian asked, finally moving from his spot at the table, looking torn.

He was surprisingly quiet as he looked her up and down. It seemed even Adrian couldn't find the words to calm the situation.

She sighed before biting her lip.

"I was going to tell you all of this after Eliza brought my clothes. I just ... I want you guys to know that I'm not saying this because of what happened in the woods. I trust you guys with my secret. I trust you guys with *me*."

Pride swelled in my chest and a weight lifted in my stomach, even as I knew whatever she had to say would sink like lead. She rubbed her arm, the exposed skin drawing attention to the scars there.

"I died."

Aaliyah didn't cut corners or sugar coat it.

Straightforward and honest, she looked uncomfortable as she searched us, landing on the place next to me. Her lips tilted into a melancholy smile and I tensed, not wanting to acknowledge the empty space I knew would always be occupied.

Prince was keeping her calm.

I ground my teeth, wishing I was doing that for her.

"What do you mean, you *died*?" Adrian asked, mouth agape as he walked up next to her. He reached out just shy of touching her cheek, before he pulled back, anguish filling his features.

"It's not as serious as you think. It happens all the time, really," she said, like her heart hadn't stopped beating. "The first time, though, was about six months ago now," she finished, holding up the fingers at the same time.

Six months? She'd been *dying* for six months?

What the *fuck?*

"I woke up under a foot of dirt, buried in a shallow grave. I didn't know who I was, where I was, or how I got there. I didn't even know my name." Her head tipped down and she shot a sad smile at Osiris when he jolted. Guilt spread in the air, tainting the taste of lavender. "It didn't stay that way for long," she whispered, finally.

She shuffled in her seat, only stilling so Osiris could continue his soft assessment, making sure nothing else was wrong with her now that most of the blood was gone from her face.

"Something is wrong with me, some kind of disconnect between my soul and my body, I think," she said, shuddering. "Every time I start to remember something, pressure builds in my head, and just when it seems like it's going to overwhelm me, I snap."

She clenched her chest like it physically hurt, and I swallowed hard.

"My soul gets pulled from my body, and while it's outside, I'm dead." My heart skipped and panic made bile rise in my throat, my wolf snarling at the thought. "That's what you and Fallon saw, Eirik," she explained softly.

Silence; cold, blistering silence filled the room, before Aaliyah let out a haggard sigh. Her eyes were clouded with the ache of a past she couldn't outrun, and my hands jerked at my side as I fought the will to go to her. Osiris was still next to her, now holding both of her hands, his gaze firmly on the ground. I could still feel the snap of his magic in the air as he tried to hold it at bay.

"Eventually, something pulls me back to my body, and I remember whatever had been poking at me. Normally, it's related to whatever triggered the pull to begin with. I remember a lot about Prince." She smiled into the empty space beside me, her lip beginning to tremble. The shakes moved to the rest of her body, and her breathing hitched sharply. "These *Rends* last longer each time I'm pulled away, and this most recent one seemed to be my breaking point. I—"

Her sentence died off, and the salty scent of tears hit the air. It felt wrong, smelled wrong, and I stepped forward, brushing my nose against her temple as my wolf guided me to, Osiris be damned, as my instincts ran high. She sighed, as comforted by my presence as I was hers.

"When Eliza and I teleported to the forest, it happened again. Pressure built in my head, and then what I can only assume was my soul was pulled out of me. Normally I'm stuck like that, watching, unable to move as the outside world moves along without me ..." She bit her lip, tensing as she recollected the moment. "But I wasn't tethered to my body this time."

Stunned silence, and then a choked sound from Adrian.

"I don't understand. It hasn't happened while you've been here," he said, his face twisted in concern.

"It happened once, that first night. At least, I think it did. But other than that, you're right. I've had more peace these last two weeks than I've had in months," she said, looking almost guilty as she glanced at Eliza.

Had she been dealing with this so continually that she didn't even get a spare moment of peace? My jaw clenched tight, my focus on the tension in her shoulders and the way she still shook. She was always so strong, holding this on her own. It broke something inside of me, to know how much she suffered, likely under our own roof.

Should've done better. My wolf snarled, snapping and raging in my mind. I didn't disagree.

"I think something about you guys is keeping me stable, and when I was away from you, it all came crashing back. The *Rend* took me somewhere else, somewhere dark, somewhere where being dead didn't feel fleeting. I didn't think I was coming back."

She looked up, glancing between Fallon and I with a smile that caught in my chest. I had never been the emotional type; I was a Norseman. I fought, I fucked, and I stormed my way through the last several decades however I saw fit at the time.

But nothing had ever caught my attention like the way Aaliyah spoke now. Her head held high even as she trembled, and the strain of today and every days prior, stacked on her shoulders. She faced Osiris when any man I knew would have fallen to their knees. She died and still came out of it smiling.

I was in awe of her, of her strength. It pained me as much as it filled me with pride. Fallon had been right, that first night. She *was* dangerous. But she was also kind, loving. A *Valkyrja.*

Beautiful. My beast added, huffing. *Tiny. Fierce. Beautiful.* He repeated, before he paused, and the rumble began in my chest. *Mine.*

That word shocked me, lighting my nerves on fire with the rightness of it.

"But then I heard something, felt something." She pressed her hand to her cheek, like I had.

I could hear the thump of her heart where I stood. I focused on it, unable not to.

"It's been out of control lately, and we were worried something like this might happen. It was why Aaliyah was meeting with Archon," Eliza chimed in, from her spot next to Dezen and Carter.

She was still examining them, making sure that they weren't harmed. It was much the same as Osiris was doing to Aaliyah.

"Still can't believe you trusted a Djinn," I mumbled.

"Yeah, well, we're trusting you too, Vampire," Eliza snarked back, and I snarled before I could stop it.

"What do you think is causing these *Rends*, love?" Adrian asked softly, and Aaliyah sighed, dropping her head to her hands in frustration.

"Wish I had an answer, even a guess ... but I don't even know what I *am* and I don't remember enough to try and figure it out. No one we've talked to has been able to help."

That made sense. If Osiris didn't know, there were few others in the country that might. Xander may very well be our last chance. I looked at her again, to the soft arches of her smooth face and the way her eyes lit up when she caught my smile.

To the scar that slid down her neck into her shirt.

And every semblance of warmth crept from my body. I ached and burned like I had when I first saw her against the ground. The ground she'd crawled out of only a few months prior.

Because it wasn't the first time she'd died. But how did she die to begin with?

I tried to hold it in, to keep from pushing when I myself couldn't bear the demons on my own back. But I had to know, needed to understand ...

Why she fucking died.

"You said you woke up in a grave. How did you end up there?" I asked, the snarl clinging to the words.

The beat of war roared in my chest and my beast snarled, raged and rattled against the chains in my mind. It begged for blood; blood I would give it. Because someone had hurt Aaliyah, and I was going to return the favor tenfold.

"Eirik," Aaliyah started quietly, reaching out to me as she had before.

"*How*, Aaliyah?" I asked, stepping back, not allowing myself the comfort of her touch.

I didn't deserve it, not after what happened to her. I'd deserve it after her tormentors were rotting on spikes. Even then ...

"I don't know a lot about my past, like I said, I haven't remembered a lot ... but I do know I wasn't somewhere pleasant," she said while standing and inching toward me.

I wanted to pull away, to stop her, but she reached out. Pressing her shaking palm to my chest again, and like before my wolf settled, dragging the rage out of me one breath at a time.

"Deep breath. I'm okay," she said, but even her soft words didn't stop the sound of a whip cracking in my ears.

"Where were you?" The words came out as a snarl, and she smiled. *Smiled.* It was soft and dripping with sadness as she tried to comfort *me.* "Who did this to you?"

I didn't deserve that comfort. She did. She needed it, and instead she was doing her best to make sure that I wasn't falling apart. My wolf snarled and raged in my mind, breaking down, shattering like glass as she pulled away.

"I was at a research facility, or at least I think that's what it was. Doctor Nox called it the Ascension Rising Project," she said, never looking away from me, even as Adrian sucked in a hollow breath behind her.

"Research. What do you mean?" He stumbled over the words, looking at her.

I looked to the scars that had caught my attention at the auction, the same ones that I knew hadn't come easily. The snarl built again.

"Someone wanted my blood. I don't know for what," she said, letting out a haggard breath as she closed her eyes. "I only remember hearing whispers of it when they thought I was still unconscious."

She took a shuddering breath as her hand wandered to her shoulder. To a phantom pain that still ached in her bones. What I had left of my calm demeanor snapped, and the crack of the whip finally morphed into words, *his* words.

You'll break, boy.

"I'll kill them," I bit out, the words more gnarled than whole, and I could feel the shift coming on as I slammed back, unable to hear anything but the beat of my heart roaring in my ears.

"Eirik," a voice whispered, sweet and feminine, everything that I felt in my soul I needed.

I grabbed at my neck, the old wound burning as I struggled to breathe air that was no longer of use to me.

"They'll regret the day they were born, I swear on it." The words weren't my own, but it felt like they could be.

The shift of my face cracked, and a rumbling growl tumbled from my chest. Someone protested, spoke of a monster, spoke of me. But it wasn't them my wolf focused on, as Aaliyah's vibrant violet eyes took up my field of vision. The soft scent of lavender tickled at my senses, burying the hurt.

Her hands pressed to my cheeks, and she took a deep breath. The voices in the background grew sharp and worried, begging her to back away from me. But I would never hurt her, my beast would never hurt her, and we snarled at their audacity.

"Breathe for me," Aaliyah whispered. "I'm okay."

But she wasn't. Having to say what happened to her was only making it worse. Her hands shook against my skin, and her lip trembled as she fought to make *me* feel better when the torment was tearing her apart. She was a fighter, a *Valkyrja*, but she held the same scars I did, the same pain.

But where she stood defiant, I crumbled. And it destroyed me.

"Continue, love. Please," Adrian asked, and she shook her head.

"It doesn't matter now, Adrian. Me saying it won't change it." She twisted toward him, lips tilting in that damn smile.

Why wasn't she screaming? Why wasn't she crying? How was she so calm?

"Tell me," I said, holding back the shift enough to press my forehead to her head.

"Eirik—" she started, but I shook, desperate to know ...

To know how I'd failed her.

"Please, *Elskan*," I begged, my wolf howling in my mind, watching her with me.

"They needed my blood. It didn't matter what they did to get it, Eirik."

I choked, unable to keep the change back anymore as I stumbled back, all but running toward the door, Aaliyah's words following me as I fell away.

And the wolf took over.

CHAPTER 28

AALIYAH

Agony.

It had stretched across Eirik's face and lit up in his eyes like a fire that couldn't be stomped out. Something about how he'd looked at me felt so raw that I couldn't continue speaking. Even as the door closed and silence filled the room. I couldn't get another word out, each one sticking to my throat, choking me. I should've expected this, should've proceeded with caution before I just jumped right in and told them about what I'd been dealing with. Because I'd seen the same pain I'd felt in them as well.

Instead, I'd laid it all out and pulled their own demons to the surface.

I looked around the room, searching for Prince. He was pressed against the far wall by the front door that Eirik had just stormed out of. Surprisingly, he wasn't looking at me, his eyes on the swaying door that hadn't fully closed.

A crack rang out in the room, surprising me enough to make me flinch. Talking about everything made it worse, and the tics that I could generally handle came to the surface.

"I'll go make sure he doesn't destroy anything," Fallon said, a lost

311

look on his face as he moved silently out the door, following the sound of Eirik's snarls.

Then another was gone, and I stayed planted in my spot on the chair. I understood their need to get some space, but it stung none-theless to see them go. I just hoped this wouldn't be too much, that they wouldn't send me away when it was all over.

I pushed the thought down, because I knew it was just that; a thought. I knew these men, maybe not like I knew Eliza, or to the extent that I knew Prince ... but I knew their character, and their eyes had never lied to me.

They wouldn't do something like that.

"Jesus Christ, are you okay?" It was Eliza's words that pulled me back.

She stared from across the room, her eyes full of morbid curiosity. I turned to see what had caught her attention. Osiris stared at the counter, clutching the shards of the glass that had been in his hand. I jolted, a strangled gasp caught behind my teeth, frozen as he didn't let up, continuing to apply pressure like he couldn't feel the glass.

That must have been the cracking sound.

I jumped to my feet, rushing at Osiris. He didn't notice me until I was right on him, when I grabbed his hand, trying to ease it up without thinking. He flinched, not softly like he was surprised, but jerking it away. His entire body seized, and when I finally caught his shaken gaze, it wasn't Osiris I was looking at. There was a scared young man in his eyes, someone who had dealt with horrors, and hidden them behind the mask that had become him.

I pulled my hands back like I'd been burned, guilt flooding me. He looked right through me, even though his eyes were on mine.

"Osiris?"

His teeth ground as I called his name, and the numbness in his eyes wavered, but he didn't let up on his grip.

"I need you to open your hand, Osiris," I whispered, reaching out my hands to him, leaving the choice up to him.

I strained for several tense seconds, questioning if he was going to give me his hand. Blood continued to pool from the open wounds, and

I began to tremble when his face twisted in pain that I doubted was all physical.

Then, his jaw clenched and unclenched before he reached his hand out, setting it in mine. A spark of heat left my skin tingling as I urged him to move further. Slowly, like he wasn't sure, Osiris unfurled his fingers. The glass had shredded his skin, and I hissed at the look of it. It was already stitching closed around the shards.

"Adrian, I need you to get the first aid kit," I said in a panic.

But Adrian didn't move, as he peered out on the dark garden, and the fluttering of fall leaves outside. Far away from here, buried in his mind.

"I understand that this is a shock, but I need some help," I cried out, tears welling.

I gritted my teeth when he finally looked at me, his eyes wide and skin paling. He looked slowly from me to Osiris's bloodied hand, like he was unsure of what he was seeing. I choked on my frustration as I grabbed one shard, pulling it out as carefully as I could, startling as blood flooded the wound. Osiris didn't move, just continued to stare at me.

"Who did this to you?" Osiris whispered, a dark, dangerous edge clinging to his words.

There was pressure in the air, a kind that reminded me of being in a space too small for my body. I swallowed hard, choking on my words as I continued to pull shards out, his skin stitching closed as quickly as it had been split apart.

"So, it wasn't just Eirik that wasn't in the right mind to hear this," I said, chewing my bottom lip, continuing with the glass.

Each shard fell to the table with a defined clank and blood slipped over my hands—it was harsh; a deeper red than any human's and far more viscous. It slid down my arms, and the sight made me sick.

The hint of a memory without pressure came as a surprise, and I sucked in a ragged breath as the click of glass against the table suddenly sounded like steel.

What fun will we have today, Glass?

"I'll never be in the right mind to know, *lux mea*. It doesn't matter if you tell me now or wait until the sun has stopped burning in the sky."

I jerked at Osiris's sudden words, the richness of his voice voiding out Castillion's. His conviction leached into them as he clenched his hands tightly, even as I tried to get him to release his grip.

Blood pooled again, and a feral expression unfolded on his face. He was unflinching, even as his fingers dug into the open wounds. His mind turned off to the pain in an all too familiar way. Eyes narrowed and hollow, like he was staring at someone that was no longer there. Eirik often looked the same. So did Fallon, even Adrian. I bit my lip, clenching Osiris's hand in my own, trying to offer comfort it seemed he'd never had.

How long had they been holding onto this? Years? Decades?

"I won't be in the right mind until the ones that did this have been strung up by their entrails and destroyed in every way I know," he snarled the words, and the drowning feeling of a *Charm* burned in the air. It felt like fire, a burning power that was unrelenting and uncaring in its assault.

Eliza sucked in a breath behind me, and I heard her shift to get to me. Osiris didn't notice, or he didn't care as he leaned in, stark rage seizing his voice as he asked again...

"*Who?*"

"Breathe, Osiris," I said, not pulling away as Osiris's attention snapped toward me again, staring through me, not at me.

"I—" he started, and I cut him off, bringing his hands under my chin.

He smelled like coffee, dark and rich. His blood dripped down my arms, landing on the ground like rain.

"I said *breathe.*" I mimicked it, taking an exaggerated breath in and then out like Eliza had taught me.

Tense silence met the room as Eliza, Dezen and Carter tried to decide whether to intervene. Adrian was uncharacteristically quiet, not even focusing on me as he continued to stare out the open windows, lost like the rest of them.

"You can't let this consume you," I said, hoping the words would reach him. Hoping somehow even Eirik and Fallon would hear me wherever they'd gone.

Had it been the right choice? Telling them something that so clearly brought them pain. Because right now, it didn't feel like it.

"I'm not saying it because they don't deserve it. Because they do. They deserve whatever hell you have in your mind, *but,*" I said, emphasizing the word when Osiris's eyes lit up like an open flame, the distinctly different blues swirling like sapphire lava, "*you* don't deserve this torment, Osiris. It's not your fault I was there. It's not anyone's fault but theirs." I whispered the words, still holding his hands as a tremor worked its way through his body.

Slowly, like he was waking up, Osiris came back to me. His eyes, devastated and drowning in a fear I couldn't process, were his again.

Eliza hesitated behind me, before grabbing onto my arm, and I looked at her over my shoulder, giving her a small smile. She gave one back, though still stared at Osiris with apprehension.

"I think they need some time to process, Ali," she cautiously said, like I would disagree.

"Yeah, I think so too," I said, turning back to Osiris and giving him a small smile as I let go of his hands.

The shock that came from touching him faded, as it had every time I lost touch with one of them. It left a warm feeling in my chest, one that clashed with the anxiety of the conversation. I sought Prince, only calming completely when his tense smile slid into my view.

Though he didn't appear much better than the rest of them. He looked like he'd aged, his gaze dipping to the ground, his hands flexing like he wanted nothing more than to hold me.

I took a deep breath and pushed down the want I shared. I smiled back because it was all I could do. The only comfort I could give to the man that had been my rock, my only friend.

My best friend.

"They worry about you," Eliza said in a grumble, and I reluctantly turned away from Prince to look at her. "In a weird, 'kill everything' kind of way."

"I know," I replied as she pulled me into a sideways hug. She tried to avoid the blood and sighed when she didn't manage to. "I care about them, too."

"I can see that." Eliza glanced at Osiris again, hesitance still keeping the fear locked inside her. "You sure you're going to be safe here?"

I nodded, holding her tightly for a few more seconds.

"And you'll let me know if you want me to kill them, right? And you'll make sure to visit—"

I laughed, the brittle sound ringing in my ears. I was all too happy to hold her a little closer. She pulled back, and though tears were in her eyes, she looked proud.

"It's going to be okay, Liz. Go get Dezen and Carter some ice. And give Grigen a hug for me." It was her turn to laugh.

But she also nodded, looking at Dezen and Carter, who didn't appear too worse for wear. They each gave me a nod and a smile, and I returned the favor. I'd never been close to either of them, but they'd been willing to risk harming themselves to save me, even if I didn't need saving.

And I will never forget that.

"See you soon, Ali. Love you," Eliza whispered while turning, walking out the door.

"Love you too, Liz," I said back, waving until they reached their car.

I turned to face the others, hoping to comfort them and only found Adrian and Prince. Adrian looked as shaken up as I felt, his hand over his mouth like he was going to be sick. When he realized I was looking at him, he straightened, and a shaky smile curved on his lips. Whatever had been tormenting him before was still there, but at least he responded. He struggled to keep it in place as I spoke.

"Are you okay?" I tried to ask it softly to keep his attention on me, and not on the scars that I could feel his eyes tracing.

"Dandy, love," he said in a shaky breath. "Why don't you go hop in the shower? I think I'm going to go try to find the others, make sure they're all right in the head, then start dinner. You look famished."

Then he was gone, and I was alone. Well, alone with Prince.

Adrian was right, I was famished. And exhausted, drained, and terrified. But I didn't say that, just took a deep breath as I gave my valiant knight a smile, the kind that I hoped made me seem less broken than I felt. Like always he smiled back, a softness in his eyes that burned as much as it healed. He pressed his hand over his heart, ring and pinky finger tucked away.

Forever.

This was the decision I'd look back on as either my saving grace, or the moment I died and didn't realize it.

"Forever," I whispered back, mirroring Prince's pose. And even though the ache still lingered, and I questioned if I was doing this right ... I felt hope.

Hope that something more than death awaited me.

CHAPTER 29

FALLON

I slid out the door, the wispy sound of Aaliyah's words still replaying in my mind, cutting into what little calm I'd held onto as I chased down a rather temperamental Eirik.

Brisk winter air that I still hadn't quite grown used to flicked against my face. It did little more than annoy, but it was sharp, biting.

Experiment.

She'd said it with a melancholy smile, still trying to make us feel better even as she talked about it. Even as she clutched at her arms, trembling. Even as she was forced to remember things that had stamped marks onto her soul and into her flesh just minutes after she'd *died*.

Eirik was right. She was a warrior, a Valkyrie. She'd shown her scars and proven that you could live with them. That you could accept them for what they were. While all we ever did was bury them deeper, pretend they didn't exist until something like this happened, until we couldn't hold the facade anymore.

I followed the haphazard tracks that had been carved into the snow. First of human feet, a fall, then the marks of paws. An irrational anger burned inside me at the sight. Of course, he'd shifted. I had all but heard it, but that didn't make the fact that there wasn't a fair fight waiting for me any more pleasant. My knuckles ached and I rolled my shoulders as I walked the trail that Eirik made into the thick woods. But even if I hadn't had the path to guide me, I would have known exactly where he was going.

I slid into the small clearing where I knew Eirik to be. It was his favorite place, one his wolf would find comfort in. White wildflowers, peeking up from under the snow, resilient to the cold, covered the space. They never seemed to wilt, something that I hadn't really taken notice of until now, as I glanced from them to Eirik. He stood on all fours, volatile deep blue eyes that spoke nothing of the man I knew, keeping me frozen to the spot. The wolf snapped its jaws, staring and raging, with the hair on his back on edge. I again tried to find Eirik in the beast's gaze.

"Eirik?" I asked, trying to mimic how Nero would speak to our brother when he lost it.

It had only happened once, just after my turn. Something someone had said and the sound of scraping metal had sent Eirik into a fit.

Calm down, brother. We're here.

"We're here for you, Eirik." I tried to mimic Nero's soft tone.

Even to me, it sounded stilted and cold. I couldn't force warmth into it, all the heat in my body was too focused on rage to gravitate toward any other feeling. Rage was safe, familiar, and it *burned*.

The wolf snarled again, jolting to the side and circling me. His tan fur glowed, shimmering even with the lack of moonlight, and slowly red swallowed his eyes until any hint of my brother was gone. I was left with only the beast. It made my instincts flare to life. Vampires were predators, and becoming prey was unnatural. The red sheen of bloodlust in Eirik's eyes fought to take up my own, threatening to swallow my will.

Eirik bent down low, his snarl echoing in the clearing.

"Eirik, *don't*," I said again, steadily raising my hands in a submissive position.

Eirik snarled, rushing forward, and I cursed as I jumped out of the way. His teeth snapped where I'd been, the sound bouncing around in my head.

"For fuck's sake, Eirik. Stop!" I screamed, finding my footing as I put the agitated wolf shifter in my line of sight again. "You're helping no one with your fucking tantrum!"

The bastard snarled, fucking *snarled*.

We circled each other like that, and even as I searched, I found nothing in those red eyes that I recognized. I warned them this would happen, warned my fucking self, and look where it had gotten us.

Rage burned until my stomach was ash, and I nearly puked.

I'd always heard that the Vivas's name was cursed. That being the spawn of Sebek was enough to turn even the best luck against us, and right now I believed it.

"Eirik, if you would." The frigid chill of Osiris's voice was even more pointed than the winter air, and it had my insides curling.

Every cell in my body wanted to flee, and even the wolf trembled. It only took a few moments before that tremble morphed and Eirik lay naked on the ground, panting. The thick feel of Osiris's *Charm* was still heavy in the air, one that hadn't been pulled back, instead pressed down with full force. Eirik groaned, the sound a mix of agony and horror as it morphed into a snarl.

"Don't talk to me of temper, Fallon," Eirik snarled, his beasts influence still clinging to his words in the form of a growl. He shook, his teeth gritting as sea-blue eyes pierced me. The thickness of his words laced with the heaviness of his old Norse accent came through, as he continued to pop and huff at the forced shift.

I raised an eyebrow.

"You just lost your shit. I think that warrants a few questions about your fucking sanity, Eirik. You can't very well hunt someone down when all you have is a vague name. You're smarter than that."

Eirik snarled again, his wolf still dangerously close to the surface. It flashed in his eyes, and I wanted to scream when my legs tensed to run.

"I can't sit and do nothing," he said, a tortured grimace on his face as his hand gripped his neck like he was choking.

The familiar scar under his fingers glowed.

"I'm not saying do nothing. I'm saying use your head," I said.

"Mighty talk for you, Fallon. You've wanted her gone since she got here. You hold no attachment to her." His fierce anger didn't wane, and I clenched my jaw at his words.

Because he wasn't wrong. I'd wanted her gone, *still* wanted her gone. I didn't want to deal with the thought of growing close to anyone else. It fucking terrified me, and what I'd seen tonight only made it clearer that I couldn't handle it. None of us could.

"Fuck. Do you even hold any love for us?" he asked, cruelty clinging to his words as he pulled himself to his feet.

Dirt and grime covered him, and he glared at me like I was to blame for the ache in his chest. Like I hadn't *tried* to get us out of this unscathed.

Like Aaliyah's story didn't burn me too.

I flung myself at him before Osiris could *Charm* me not to, and the satisfying feeling of battle roared in my ears. Eirik's eyes widened as he looked at me, surprise taking root in the blue depths just seconds before I had him on the ground, fist connecting with the right side of his face. I wondered if he saw what I wasn't able to hide, the ache in my chest that wouldn't abate.

"Fallon—" he started, and I swung again.

His head jolted to the side, my knuckles skimming his cheek before hitting the unrelenting ground. Pain shot up my arm, sinking to the bone.

"No. You don't get to fucking say that," I snarled out through clenched teeth. Using the ache to ground me, I pulled back. "You are my brother, and I love you. I love every fucking one of you. You are my family, my *mob,* so don't you dare say I don't care for you!"

I screamed the words, uncaring of who would hear them. Uncaring that the cold mask I'd made my home slid away, I snarled. Eirik's eyes, still wide, blinked once, the remaining red slipping from the blue depths.

"Now isn't the time for fighting," Osiris said from somewhere behind me.

That cold calculation in his tone only served to piss me off more, and I turned to glare at him.

"Now is exactly the fucking time for fighting," I said, standing again.

Mud and dead leaves stuck to the white of my suit, staining it, blending with blood that smelled of lavender. I hated how out of place it was, the break of color like a jab.

"Calm down." Osiris's words, so starkly cold, made my skin tighten.

It was wrong, even compared to the Osiris that I knew.

"God, Osiris. Get that high and mighty look out of your eyes. It doesn't suit you," I said finally, looking down at Eirik.

Silence met us, and again I was forced to focus on the only other thing on my mind.

They needed my blood ... It didn't matter how they got it.

"We can't keep on like this. We're tearing ourselves apart."

I hadn't heard Adrian slip into the clearing, but it was his words that whispered over us, fading much like the brush of wind.

"What's that supposed to mean?" Eirik asked, huffing as he stood. He rolled his shoulders, wincing. Part of me felt bad for attacking him so soon after a shift. I knew it hurt, coming back to his more human form, but damn if I didn't feel a little better knowing that the bruise on his cheek was from me.

"Don't be fucking daft. Aaliyah's story may have been the final straw, but this has been a long time coming." Adrian shook his head, sighing when Osiris's eyes narrowed. "We can't keep living in the past. Not if we want to do right by the little love, by Nero ... by ourselves."

Like an ice bath, Adrian's words froze me to the ground.

"It's not that easy, Adrian," Eirik started, but Adrian only rolled his eyes.

"Oh, piss off. It's exactly that easy. I'm not saying we spill our guts, and all is right and rainbows. I'm saying that we acknowledge what happened to us. That life, or *death* in this case, dealt us a shit hand." He glanced between us before his eyes landed on me. "And move on."

He sighed when none of us spoke.

"Look, I'm not telling any of you to do the same, though I hope you do. I can't stand to see you hurting anymore." Adrian laughed as he spoke, the sound brittle and bitter. "And for the record, I'm not letting her go."

"She already agreed to stay, Adrian," I said, trying to understand where our youngest was taking this.

"You know that's not what I mean," Adrian said, smiling back in the direction of the home.

He'd always been soft for her, but there was something else in him now, something more substantial. Something that made my blood go molten and freeze at the same time.

"You intend to court her?" I asked, and Eirik tensed beside me, the rumbling growl in his chest so vicious that it shook the ground.

Osiris only stared, blinking slowly like he was trying to appear unbothered. Then his head dipped, just enough to notice. Adrian shot me a grin.

"That's right. I fancy her, have for days now. Finding out we nearly lost her was just the last push I needed." His eyes closed, likely trying to forget how she looked with dried blood covering her skin.

He didn't have to see her looking like a corpse. Didn't strain to hear a heartbeat that wasn't there. But he knew enough, and I saw the tremble work its way through his body as his eyes opened with a burning determination.

"Not sure she'd take a bastard like me, but I need to try. I've regretted many things in my life. I won't let this be one of them," Adrian said, ignoring Osiris's flaring *Charm* as it lit up the air.

"This isn't how we do things," Osiris said, his teeth clenched tightly.

Adrian looked disbelieving in Osiris's direction, huffing a short laugh.

"You really want to call a vote on this?" Adrian's eyebrow raised and Osiris tensed.

They stared for a moment unmoving, before Adrian laughed again. It wasn't the joyful one I'd grown used to these last few weeks; it was harsh and accusing.

"Fine." Adrian shook his head but stayed firm in his spot. "I call a vote. I want us to be happy."

"That's not a vote, and not what we're talking about, Adrian," Osiris responded, and Adrian shook his head, crossing his arms.

"Isn't it?" Adrian asked. "I want to be happy, and I see that with her. I see it in her smile, and in the way she dances around the kitchen when we bake."

I see it in giving her chocolate, when she laughs like it's our little secret.

"I see it in the way she reads, the way she smiles and gets lost in the world of words. She makes me want to keep living. And if that's not happy, I don't know what is." Adrian's eyes lit up, his lips tilting into a genuine smile as he crossed his arms. "This is exactly what we're talking about, Osiris. I'm voting for our happiness, one that you're all too stubborn to see."

"I vote yes," I said, nodding toward Adrian. "You should be able to be happy, Adrian."

But he just shook his head.

"You aren't getting it, Fallon. I want us *all* to be happy," he said, pointing to each of us like we were all pieces of the same puzzle.

Like he wanted us *all* to win her favor.

"She'd never agree to something like that," I said, even as the words wreaked havoc on my mind, on what it could mean for us.

"Why not? Her friend has two husbands. It's not like she's not used to it. It might even be something she'd like as well. We won't know unless we ask." The foolhardy grin that I'd seen so many times before lit up his face. Joy sparked in his eyes, and it seemed like life bled back into him.

"You're truly suggesting we share?" I choked out.

Adrian shrugged but didn't disagree. He brushed his hair back before he hummed softly. "If she wants it, everything from here out is at her pace, as it has been. So yeah, I'd take having part of her heart over having none of it ... and don't think I don't know how you look at her, too."

His goading words held more truth than I wanted. They poked and prodded at emotions that they had no right to.

No one spoke, and only Eirik's growl was clear in the air when Adrian sighed.

"Look, I'm suggesting we pull our heads out of our asses and do this right. I'm happy to just spend time around her, but if she wants more then I'd be a damned fool to tell her no," Adrian finished, obviously done with the conversation. "You would be, too."

I settled my resolve, drowning out the thought that maybe, just maybe, we could make that work; her violet eyes shining up at me, the soft caress of her lips against mine, and the gasp of my name on her breath.

Until she ends up dead in my arms again.

"So, I call the vote again," Adrian said, looking between each of us. "I want us to be happy."

She wasn't meant to be mine. My happy ending died with Aislinn, but Adrian's didn't have to. So I held my tongue while Eirik snarled and Osiris covered his mouth like he was going to puke.

Not a breath was released between the four of us, before the silence broke.

"Yes." The rumbled response came from Eirik, his head tipping in agreement.

No surprise there. He'd been smitten with her from the start. Though I was surprised that he hadn't put up more of a fight at the thought of sharing her.

Could I share?

I shook off the thought.

"Osiris?" Adrian asked.

Multi-colored blue eyes bore into Adrian's, our eldest looking more numb than I'd seen in days. He gave a sharp nod, looking lost.

"Find your happiness, Adrian," was his short reply.

"I think you'd find yours too, if you tried, Osi," Adrian said, and Osiris didn't move.

He just nodded, giving his affirmative, calling his vote as he shook off his coat. "Yes."

Adrian didn't say anything else, his eyes speaking enough. He worried for Osiris, we all did. I could only hope this didn't break him. I couldn't handle losing Nero. Losing Osiris too would shatter us all.

"Fallon? Need a final vote." I was the last one, again the one that would determine the outcome.

But this was different. It wasn't inviting someone into our home for a brief stay. It wasn't a stranger that I didn't know. This time, I was bartering with my soul, and with the impending consequences that would come with it. But could I say no? Was it fair to Adrian to deny him *happiness* because I didn't think I was capable of it?

"Yes," I said, the words like ashes in my throat.

I wouldn't court her because I knew it would do more damage than good ... but Adrian would make her happy, would make her smile. And that would be enough.

It had to be enough.

"It's settled then. I'm going to go start dinner and see if I can get a smile out of *our* girl. She's had a long day." Adrian nodded toward us, before he turned away and the crunch of leaves followed him into the woods, leaving us in silence as the soft whistle of a tune echoed around us.

Could I share? The ache in my chest almost seemed to tell me I couldn't afford not to.

CHAPTER 30

OSIRIS

I slid my hand over the rich mahogany in front of me, the texture coarse against my skin and stark against the gray walls of our leisure room. Thoth's intricate design watched me, his likeness carved into the delicate wood, his resemblance exact to how I remembered him as a boy. The door had been handmade, a gift from Nero when the construction of our manor first began. He had a knack for crafting things, one of the many hobbies that he had picked up over the years, much like Fallon and his paintings.

But the door ... he had never finished it.

I sighed, the numbing pain of regret burning my throat like a bitter drink. He should have been here, spending his days lounging just past Thoth's watchful gaze, sipping whisky over words with me. Or sparring with Fallon in the dojo, trading blows until the sun called them to sleep. Trying out one of Adrian's new meals that our youngest brother had been dying to make. Trading war stories with Eirik, both of them singing folk melodies from their human years, laughing over times long past.

Making Aaliyah smile ...

Instead he was lost to us, and would always be lost to us. Dead because of my lack of proper judgment. The thought of his body,

327

charred to ash on that silver pyre in the Russian winter, made me physically ill. Even after so many years had passed, the pain had yet to dull.

Would it ever?

Did I deserve it to?

I ground my teeth, swallowing the emotion, forcing it down. I moved my focus on what had brought me here in the first place, to the little slip of our home that I called my own. The scent of lavender wafted through the closed door, telling me exactly who was just beyond the aged wood. I shouldn't be here, but I couldn't seem to force myself to stay away. I cracked it open just enough to peer through, watching as Aaliyah walked along the stacks at the back of the room on the right of the fireplace. Rows upon rows of books greeted me, the sight grandeur, bright even under the soft glow of the fire. She tapped at the spines as she hummed, like she was looking for the right one. She fit in so easily, blending into the room like she had been born for it. This had always been my favorite room in the house, though not *exactly* for the books.

Rather, for the whisky cabinet in the back, *paired* with the books. Would Aaliyah like whisky? I couldn't help but scoff at the absurd notion, knowing she had the same sweet tooth as Fallon. However, I could picture her here with a glass of wine, and a book in her lap, completely entrapped by the story.

She seemed to realize I was there without prompt, turning to me with a smile that made the pain dull in my chest. Not gone by any means, but a peace settled over me, a serenity that only she seemed to be able to invoke. Her eyes, lit like violet stars in the night sky, shined with a joy that I hadn't had the pleasure of seeing for years. Her head tilted away, and she skimmed the rows of books again, all older than her by decades. Bibliosmia lingered in the air, giving off a feeling of comfort.

The room was dimly lit by the lights that hung above us and the fireplace burning in the corner. Adrian must have just lit it. The air smelled distinctly of our *Flame*, sharper than a match with more acidity.

"Osiris?" Aaliyah asked.

I hadn't realized how close she had gotten, now standing just feet away. Her lips pulled up into a beautiful smile and watching them curve as she said my name was a euphoric experience. I fought the spark of pleasure that lit up my nerves, ignoring the ache in my gums and the sudden strain of my pants. It was such a strange reaction to something as simple as her saying my name. I ached to step forward and pull her into my arms, but the last thing I wanted to do was scare her.

No, I never wanted to see fear in those expressive eyes of hers again. I wanted them wide with heated tension, a sweet whisper of my name on her lips as I fucked her against the stacks. I wanted to touch, to feel, to *feed*.

Aaliyah tilted her head in question when I didn't respond. So innocent in how she stepped toward me, trust carved into her smile. That trust was like ice against my skin, and I felt like a damn fledgling, with no control of my emotions or my reactions. I had felt it before, at the auction house, and every day since, whenever she was around. But I hadn't ever thought to act on it. She didn't deserve that. She didn't deserve to deal with the rot inside of me.

Adrian had stirred this feeling in me, in *us,* with his declaration to court her. The conviction in his words *almost* made me believe it would work, that her being in my future with more than just an occasional smile wasn't so unattainable.

Almost.

Anything she felt for me would be based on the lies she saw, the fake calm I had played so well these last years. I couldn't hurt her like that, and I couldn't very well lay myself and all that I had done bare to her either. Couldn't tell her *I* was the reason she never met Nero.

"Looking for a specific read?" I finally asked, as I tried to keep hoarse emotion from my words. She didn't seem to notice, her face still twisted with worry before she nodded slowly, turning her head toward the stacks again. I thanked and cursed every god I could think to name that she wasn't focused on me anymore.

"Yeah. I finished the Epic, and I was looking for something similar. Maybe something about knights or princes? I know Eirik had a pile somewhere ..." Aaliyah said, glancing over my shoulder, the twinkle in her eye telling me she was looking at Prince.

She seemed lost to me at that moment, and for a selfish second, I bristled. I wanted Aaliyah's attention on me. Her bright eyes on *me.*

"I'm not sure where Eirik would have stowed his finds, but I know a few he likely missed. Come, I'll show you where they should be."

Her attention was back on me, her eyes lighting up as she realized I was smiling softly down at her. She seemed to enjoy the emotion, and it came naturally enough when she was around. I walked past her, keeping my pace even and slow so she didn't have to hurry to keep up with my long strides.

We walked through the room toward the far end of the stacks, and I stopped just shy of the wall, reaching up, and pulling at *The Art of War*. It didn't come down from the shelf. Instead, a soft click echoed in the air, and the small picture of Alexandria that was above the fireplace slid forward.

Aaliyah looked at me with gleeful excitement, hurrying over to the painting. It was a few inches above her head, and she waited for me as I followed.

"Why am I not surprised that you have a secret room?" she whispered, and I smiled, barely stopping myself from reaching out and pressing a hand to her heated cheeks, a small dimple at the corners of her mouth.

"Not quite a secret room. Just a nook for older books." I moved the painting, sliding it out of the way and exposing our oldest collection. There were six books, each a varying degree of 'knightly'. They had all been written when such topics were more commonplace. As always, I hesitated on a particular read. Hidden away in the corner, pressed to the side of the small compartment, was the book that I never thought I would read again. Gifted to me by the monster Sebek himself. I pulled it from the shelf, being careful not to hold it too hard. The book was ancient, and even the magic binding was fading after being transcribed for my five hundredth year, just before Nero had been turned. The original tome was stashed away in a vault in Paris, along with the rest of Sebek's many treasures.

In my hands, the two thousand-year-old tome was a dusty yellow, the cracked leather casing holding in the aged paper. Though it held no official title, I knew it to be the saving of Iris Imperial, by Sebek and Arvand Ra. It was the most accurate representation of knightly one could get. The story itself was a marvel, written by an Echomancer after the rescue. It portrayed the brothers as kings among kings. Surely it would be what she desired.

Even if the thought of portraying Sebek as anything other than the narcissistic sociopath he was made my blood boil. Sebek's name in old Coptic was etched onto the top left corner.

ⲀⲘⲞⲨⲚ Ⲣⲁ.

It wasn't a name he used often. Sebek's own maker had culled it out of him long before he turned me. For whatever reason, when he had given me this *generous* gift, he had etched that name like a reminder of his past. Or it was some strange, sick way for him to relate to me: the Turned he had abandoned after his whim wasn't recognized, just like the three before me. After no one could live up to his expectations of his lost brother. I spent decades wondering if Sebek was a decent man before his brother's second death, the time when he lost his twin forever. I wondered if he went crazy afterward, haunted and desperate for the companionship he lost. I wanted to believe he wasn't always that way, he wasn't always a man who seemed to be seconds from a psychotic break.

I wanted to believe he wasn't always crazy.

"That book must have stolen your favorite whisky for you to be glaring at it like that," Aaliyah joked next to me, pressing a hand to my clothed arm.

I read the tension in her words, the way she stood frozen by my side, staring at the tome with a look of confusion and apprehension. Her body was tense, and her hand trembled against me.

I had startled her.

Heat burned in my chest, and guilt ran through me. This was precisely what I hadn't wanted to happen. I wanted Aaliyah to enjoy my presence and for her to spend some nights here with me. I could bask in her company while she read and possibly delve into that mind of hers. I needed to speak to her, to have her company in any way she would allow.

Instead, I had upset her.

The warmth of her skin reminded me she was here with me and I clenched the book tightly in my hand, having to put considerable effort into not just throwing it into the fire.

"I don't think this translation is in English." I knew it wasn't in English, but rather Latin. "But this is the story that would best suit your needs. If you would like, I could start translating it tomorrow."

She paused for a moment, focusing on my face before she blushed. The soft red crept up her cheeks, and confusion muddled my senses.

"Would you read it to me, at least until you get a translation done?" Her soft question gave me the opening that I needed.

"I would be honored," I said.

Somehow, her words were exactly what I wished to hear. My hand slipped into hers, our fingers locking together. My eyes slid closed. She didn't move, and I wasn't even sure if she had breathed. I was too addicted to the touch of her skin against my own to let go. Her hand, so much smaller than mine, fit perfectly.

Pull away, pull away while you still can.

When my eyes slid back open, they landed on her. Her own eyes were wide as she stared at me, though she didn't move to pull her hand away. Her gaze traveled down to our joined hands. She seemed to study every detail like she was committing it to memory—her pale skin against the olive of my own. It was still mind-boggling that the familiar sickening feeling of dread didn't sneak up my spine.

I walked her over to the couch that sat by the fireplace. The dark red of the fabric was warm to the touch, and we sank into it, the cushions benefiting me as the depression of my body pulled her to me. She was settled snugly to my side, her warmth sending shivers down my spine. She fidgeted beside me and her cheeks lit up a fetching shade of pink as she leaned into my shoulder, her attention fixated on the tome in my hands. Though the blush didn't leave her cheeks.

I wanted to reach out to her, and press my fingers against the flushed skin. Instead, I kept my hands firmly pressed on the tome. My fingers ran across the intricate design on the front, the depiction of the sun god, Ra.

"This is the story of how Anovic and Servine Restire saved a young princess by the name of Bellona." I changed the names on the fly, unwilling to even say them out loud.

Arvand and Sebek had been curses in our home for as long as we had been Vivas, since I had crawled my way out of Darius's harem and made a promise that I would never fall like they had.

Arvand Ra. Sebek's twin brother, both in life and in death. Even having never met the man, I resented him. It was because of him I was here now. That I had the *joy* of being turned. All for sharing a namesake, because Arvand was Usire before he was turned, the Coptic translation of Osiris. Sebek simply couldn't resist the temptation to turn me after hearing of my likeness to his brother. It was unfortunate for us both that the resemblance ended with a name.

I settled my thoughts, looking at Aaliyah again as she traced the twisting symbols on the first page while she waited for me to start.

It didn't take long for me to fall into the story, the act of reading nearly as soothing as Aaliyah's presence by my side. She was silent but I could feel her eyes on me, her focus making my skin tingle. Page after page fell from my lips slowly as I got used to the old script again, and like a dance never forgotten, I spoke to her of a tale she didn't know was real. She entranced me with her reactions as much as the story gripped her, her gasps at the grand sword fights, the way she would twitch closer when the storytelling grew suspenseful. It seemed like far too soon I was flipping to the last page, hours having gone by in seconds. The creeping feeling of the sun had begun to set into my bones, an hour away at best. I hated to admit that I enjoyed the read; it was as beautifully crafted as I remembered.

I wasn't ready for her to leave my side, even after the hours we had spent together. She had leaned her head on my shoulder, studying the foreign words as I read. Her warmth was seeping into my soul.

"Was that story enjoyable?" My question had her glancing lazily up at me, her eyes ever so slightly clouded.

Her lip slid between her teeth, and her hesitance to answer gnawed at me. It felt like an eternity as I waited for her response. Was the story not up to her standards? Or did she simply not enjoy my company? The acid ate at me at the thought. I may not pursue her as Adrian intended to, but I wanted her to enjoy being around me, as I did her. Especially if she stayed ... if she chose Adrian.

I ignored the clenching in my chest at the thought.

When she finally nodded I released a breath, the stress falling from my shoulders.

"I think I may have heard that story before." Her admission had me turning toward her, and I focused on her eyes, their vibrant color shining in the dimly lit room.

The story was centuries old, and nearly all copies were in the posses-
sion of Sebek. With the sole exceptions being the one in my hands and
the one that Xander had coerced out of Sebek several years back. The
story itself wasn't astonishing I supposed, some princes saving a
princess. Perhaps she had just heard something similar?

"Where did you hear this story?" I pulled my fingers through her
hair, gently untangling the knots.

"I think ... my dad."

I focused on her lips again and the way they trembled.

"I don't know. It's not a memory that I have, but I *know* I've heard it
before."

"What happened to him?" I asked.

She jolted and pulled her body away from mine. Agony tore
through me at the scent of her pain. Her soft voice, barely above a whisper, made my soul ache.

"He and my mom died when I was little." Her hands were clenched
together in her lap, as she stared into the fireplace. I swallowed, suddenly
lost for words.

"I am sorry for your loss." I grabbed one of her hands in my own, the
heat of her skin calming my feelings of uncertainty. The slight contact
soothed both my nerves and my rage.

"Thank you," she said, and I rubbed my thumb along the back of
her wrist. Soothing the stressed skin, which was pulled taut as she
squeezed on my hand.

"Who took you in after your parents' passing?" The question was
quiet.

Aaliyah's flinch was the only thing that told me she even heard it.
The scent of tears flooded my senses, and I froze; unable to move as I
worked out what was happening. She was crying. I wasn't sure what I
had said to cause such a reaction. A hatred like no other washed over
me, a loathing for myself—anger for both my stupidity and my inability
to leave well enough alone.

She was crying because of *me*.

But why? What had happened to her that had caused so much grief?
It was the pain that fake smiles couldn't hide. The kind that is brought
on without reason, without warning.

"It was them, Ascension Rising," I whispered, the evidence clear as she nodded, the movement sharp.

That feeling from before, when she first returned covered in dried blood, threatened to swallow me again. The need to hunt, to bleed dry those who dared harm her beat against my chest.

Aaliyah choked on her tears, gasping as she tried to force them down. There was something eerily wrong with how silent she was. Even as she fell apart in my arms, she barely made a noise.

"Sorry. Not sure why I'm crying right now." She trembled and tried to cover the break in her words with a broken laugh. "I remembered it recently ... how they died, I mean. It's still fresh in my mind, I guess. Sorry." She choked out the words, wiping at her eyes, trying to hide her tears like they hadn't happened.

I wanted to let her be, to leave it at that so I could go figure out exactly who those at Ascension Rising were. It was almost second nature to let her deal with her own demons, because that was what *I* would want to do. But I stopped myself, because I didn't want that same feeling for her, the desolation that came from being unable to let the pain go. I clenched my hands and something snapped as the peace we had constructed broke down. Her hands went to her hair, and I saw her need to run before she even started moving. I opened my arms, hesitating for only a moment before I pulled her against me as she had done for me before, holding her as tightly as I could at the awkward angle from our spot on the couch. She flinched hard at first, her body tensing in a way that made me sick, before she relaxed against my chest.

She let out a thankful sigh as she shook against me, holding onto me like I was the only thing keeping her anchored to the ground. Her eyes bared her soul, affection so clear in them I jolted. I moved one hand, pressing it against her warm, wet cheek, marveling when she leaned into the touch. A spark of pleasure erupted, one that was unfound, and I couldn't stop it from devolving into white-hot euphoria when she sighed. I traced her face, eyes landing on the pursed pink lips that had taken up my thoughts. I was so close, until she was only centimeters away, and I ached to feel the press of her against me; her skin heating my own.

She trusted me, held me close to her, not knowing the lives I had taken with the same hands that comforted her. That thought ripped apart the feeling of her in my arms, and I jerked away, choking on the thoughts that I shouldn't be having.

Disgusted with myself.

"Osiris?" she asked, as I pulled myself from her arms.

Hurt was clear in her eyes, and guilt kept me from speaking as I turned away, *flitting* from the room without so much as a backward glance. Leaving to fight my own demons.

As Eirik would say ... like a coward.

CHAPTER 31

AALIYAH

I wallowed in the library for what seemed like hours, staring at where Osiris had been, trying to decide if the tingle in my lips was from our near kiss or from the nerves that came with thinking about it.

He looked so disgusted.

I bit my lip, unable to move from my spot. I knew that whatever caused that look wasn't me. His other actions proved that ... but that didn't stop it from stinging.

I sighed, dropping my head into my hands. Why were these men so hard to read? It was like one second I could see everything that was happening in their minds, and the next it was like I was trapped on an island where the only salvation was to know ...

And I was drowning.

A flash of light and a lingering cold in the air told me Prince was trying to get my attention. Tension seeped from my body, and I looked at him, always more than happy to meet his gaze. He was relatively close to the couch, though not quite against the wall. His eyes were closed, face twisted into an expression of disbelief as he swirled his finger around his ear, over and over.

Idiot. Idiot. Idiot.

I laughed, unable not to at Prince's silent exasperation, the absurdity of it making my chest burn. I shouldn't be disappointed that Osiris didn't kiss me. I shouldn't be disappointed about anything. We had shared a wonderful moment in the library. He read to me and smiled so kindly that it made ...

Well, it made my heart skip.

Gods, what was happening to me? Osiris and the others took me in. They were good people, good friends. Thinking that they would be anything more was a heartache waiting to happen. I groaned, rubbing the space between my eyes and wiping away the tears that had slid past my defenses. I shouldn't have told him about my parents, not so soon after hearing about Ascension. But I felt safe with him, knew he could be trusted with my secrets, so they just spilled out around me.

Like toxic sludge, or glitter you could never really get rid of.

I stood, my joints stiff and achy. I stretched before I turned, walking out of the library, intent on getting my mind off Osiris and his twister-like emotions. Prince was still making motions to my side, his hands moving in a fashion that I didn't recognize, irritation clear on his face. He had me so distracted that when I stepped through the door that had Thoth carved intricately into the surface, I barely had time to register that something was in my way. Rather than hitting nothing, I ran right into a wall.

A cold, hard, unmoving wall that smelled like sin and heat.

I steadied myself, a hand against a cold chest. The body under it shivered, but didn't move as I looked up, peering into Fallon's sharp green eyes as his face twisted into a barely there scowl. Had I pissed him off, too? I sighed, about to ask him what was wrong when he lifted my chin, leaning in close.

I tried to stop it, the flinch that followed. Fallon looked sick, his thumb running over my jaw, against the gritty dried tears that hadn't quite been brushed away. Against the scar over my lip. That intense gaze traveled across my skin, from my eyes to my nose and across my now burning cheeks. The sharp turn of his jaw showed me a slight stubble on display. The fierceness in his green eyes, the tilt to his eyebrows ... God, the man was hauntingly beautiful.

"Crying again?" he asked, grinding his teeth as he let me go, pulling his arms tensely to his chest, his familiar white suit tensing over what had to be corded muscle beneath.

That cold chill that lived in his eyes and had terrified the life out of me my first night here had grown on me. So, even as he grumbled, looking uncomfortable as he reached into his suit pocket, I couldn't help but smile.

He mumbled something about running out before he pulled out a familiar foil. The chocolate I'd grown used to seeing strewn about the library was on his open palm. Normally, he was much more subtle about how he gave them to me. I'd find one on the book I was reading, or in my favorite chair. One of the few times he'd given me one in person was the last time I was crying. My heart ached in my chest with a feeling I couldn't name, making me smile.

But I also knew they meant something to him. He treasured them, and I didn't want to be the reason he ran out.

"I can't keep taking these, Fallon. I know they're important to you," I said, pushing away his hand.

He rolled his eyes, and with more care than I thought he was capable of, he placed the candy into my palm. He folded my fingers around it as he had before. The familiar shock that came from touching any of the Vivas brothers crawled up my skin, and I shivered.

"Just take it, eat it in front of Adrian if you can." He raised an eyebrow as if daring me to argue. "And stop crying," he said that bit with a grind of his teeth, like the tears I shed pained him.

It helped to ease some of the ache that had been left from my moment with Osiris, and I smiled at him. He looked away with his jaw still clenched tight and I caught sight of a small scar just along the bottom of it. It wasn't harsh like Eirik's, more smooth, almost accidental. I shoved down the need to ask how he'd gotten it.

"I'll be sure to, though I can't promise that I won't share it this time. He's very convincing," I said, and Fallon shook his head, hiding his amusement well.

"He pouts, is what you meant to say," he responded.

"Maybe, but he does it well."

Fallon's lip twitched, and his shoulders dropped just a touch. He shook his head, tapping at the pocket he'd just pulled my chocolate from before he glanced behind him.

"Don't take Osiris to heart. He's still adjusting," Fallon said after a few seconds, a quiet, almost mournful tone to his words. "We all are."

I nodded, the heat in my chest turning to lead. I took a step back, pulling myself away from Fallon as guilt tried to steal my voice.

"I know. I'm sorry I laid all that on you guys." I wished I'd more to say. A better way to apologize for the deep-rooted agony that I'd seen in their eyes.

I hated knowing that I'd caused it.

Fallon, in an uncharacteristic move, sighed. He took a step toward me, erasing the space that I'd put between us. He didn't reach out to me like he had before, hands clenched at his sides.

"Don't ever be sorry for confiding in us, Ali." His hoarse words sank into my bones, and my stomach twisted at his demanding tone and the sweetness of the nickname. "And it's not you, it's him. Years of bad memories find a way to trap you."

A whisper, one that had his eyes closing as he turned away. His hands clenched and unclenched several times before finally going lax. When he opened his eyes again, the chilling cold was back in full force, and any hint of emotion that had slid by was now buried. He twisted away fully, walking away without as much as another word. I bit my lip.

"Well, maybe we can all figure out how to get past this," I whispered to his retreating back. I couldn't stand by and watch him hurt like this. He didn't need to tell me, but he needed to know. That I was here for him, like he was for me. "Together."

He froze, his entire body tensing as I finished my thought. I expected him to continue walking, so when he spoke, so quietly that I almost didn't hear it, it made me jump.

"Maybe."

He looked back over his shoulder, the closest thing to a laugh that I'd heard from him slipping out. He shook his head, entire body taut as he extended out his hand for me to take. "Come on, Adrian's got dinner going."

I smiled, moving up to stand next to Fallon, taking his hand in mine. I flinched, nasty thoughts still close to the surface. He didn't mention it, just held my hand a little tighter, and the shock of contact wiped away the rest of the sour taste in my mouth.

The chill of his skin, the slow pace he walked to make sure that I didn't drag behind him ... I didn't want to admit it, but something was building in my chest, something more than admiration for the men that had saved me.

I just wasn't sure how to deal with it.

CHAPTER 32

EIRIK

"**F**allon, if you eat that cupcake, I swear to *God.*" Adrian's voice lacked any real threat, though his heated stare was trained on Fallon, who at least had the decency to raise an eyebrow.

Adrian had made the sweet treats a few hours ago, him and Aaliyah likely trying out a new recipe. She'd taken to cooking with him these last few days, and even now she watched the two bicker with a soft smile, eyes bright with affection when she didn't think anyone was watching.

I liked that look; it made my beast settle. Made *me* settle.

But the recipe hadn't gone as planned, and the cupcake in question was one of only a few that had survived. Not that Fallon really cared about that, far too pleased to have the chance to ruffle Adrian's feathers. It was a game they'd played since Adrian's turn, one that I doubted would ever end.

As if proving that point, Adrian gasped when Fallon lifted the cupcake and stole a bite, all without losing eye contact. Aaliyah covered her mouth next to me, choking on the laugh as Adrian let out a disgruntled noise.

"That was mine, you bastard!" Adrian rolled his eyes and crossed his arms, but didn't go for a blow, as Fallon finished the cupcake knowing he would win in a fight.

Fallon's grin was the one of victory.

I shook my head and looked at Aaliyah again, only to find her peering up at me. There were smudges of white against her dark clothes, one of Fallon's black shirts knotted in the back to shorten its length, blots of flour and sugar. It added to the sweetness of her scent, and I breathed her in while I had a second to do so. I doubted I would have the chance again tonight, since I had to patrol the territory.

As if noticing, Aaliyah smiled up at me with a questioning look.

"What do you have planned tonight, Eirik?" she asked.

"Patrol," I said back, turning away. "Need to check our wards."

They were strong, ones that Osiris had crafted centuries ago during his human years, ones that had now been repurposed to protect our home. But that didn't mean they couldn't fail or be tampered with. I liked to check; it calmed my beast and helped to stomp down the obsessive protectiveness that I often felt about my family.

"Mind if I come along?" Her quiet question zipped across my skin.

I narrowed my eyes on her exposed arms, huffing when she ran her hands against them.

"It's cold," I mumbled, and she laughed.

"And I have a jacket," she responded as she stood straight, stretching her arms above her head, a sliver of skin showing as her black shirt rode up her stomach. "Though, if you don't want me to, I can stay back."

I shook my head, reaching out and tucking a piece of that white hair of hers behind her ear. The flush of her skin was warm against the tips of my fingers.

When I pulled away, she smiled again, and bound off toward the closet by the front door. I followed her movements, shaking my head, amused by the way she swayed about. Adrian leaned over the counter, watching as she fiddled with the coats.

"Have fun, love! We'll have dinner ready when you get back," he said, jabbing Fallon in the side when he didn't immediately move. "It's the least you could do, Fally. Helping me with dinner after you so rudely stole my treat."

Fallon rolled his eyes but stood.

"Well, since you asked so nicely." Thick with sarcasm, Fallon smirked when Adrian glared at him.

He turned to me, giving me a look and a shallow nod. It wasn't much. A bob of his head before he glanced at Aaliyah, who had fished out a winter coat, one of Adrian's older ones, and one that looked like it might fit me if I was half my size. I raised an eyebrow as she bit her lip, looking from me to the coat, before she went back to her search.

Fallon tapped at the counter, his gaze far away as something new dredged in those green depths. Curiosity, maybe even want. It was hard to tell, as he swallowed hard, then turned back to Adrian. But it was new, raw, and different. Adrian's words hit me again, his want to court. It had struck me dead in the chest when he first said it, like I'd lost my chance for her smile to be mine. *But could we share?*

And it seemed Fallon was having the same thought.

Aaliyah walked up to me, lip still bitten between her teeth. I reached out, pressing my thumb against it, her eyes flying wide, mouth sliding open in surprise. My beast hummed, appeased.

"I don't need a coat," I said, lip tilting when she frowned.

Her worry was endearing, and my beast rumbled in my mind, the noise sliding down until my chest vibrated with it. I walked past her to the closet. I opened it, ducking under the frame, and looking up into the caged section at the top. I dragged out a shabby jacket, the only one I had, and pulled it on. Though she still looked at me like it wouldn't be enough, she nodded with a smile. I gave Fallon and Adrian one more look before we turned toward the door and walked out.

The brisk fall air carried a hint of the sea, even so far from the shore. It was that familiar salty chill that had eventually convinced me to build our home here. I took it in, letting it settle me and wash away what had been a more-than-eventful three weeks.

We walked in silence, comforted by the soft sounds of the surrounding woods. I glanced up, searching the sky like they had when I'd been a boy. I let out a breath, rolling my head, loosening the tension in my shoulders. My other half lurched just behind my eyes, marveling at the sky with me. The acuteness of his presence was something I still wasn't used to. He'd never been this close to the surface for so long, like he was always waiting for a moment to steal my skin.

It'd been over two centuries since my last accidental shift, yet in the previous three weeks, I'd lost myself several times. I couldn't seem to keep myself from flailing like a pup, my wolf so eager to run out and greet Aaliyah in the flesh that he nearly took the reins every time she looked my way. It had only gotten worse since Adrian's words.

His damned intention to court.

I took a second to note how she watched each step she took, focusing on where she was walking. I pulled my pace down, keeping it slow so she wouldn't have any issues keeping up. She breathed normally, and I nodded in relief that she wasn't tiring. After her *Rend,* I'd been more worried about her straining herself, but our walk wasn't affecting her adversely.

My beast didn't seem to think that, impatiently pushing me to pull her into my arms, to ensure she didn't fall.

Her hair hung in a long ponytail that stretched down to her lower back, and I couldn't help but wonder how she would look with it braided. Or imagine her pale skin adorned with striking war paint, her face sporting a victorious grin. She had a delicate beauty that mixed with the strength in her eyes.

She's stunning. A good Valkyrja. My beast whispered.

"Do you like the stars?" Her voice, always melodic and soothing to my ears, echoed in the air. I loved hearing her speak. But for it to be centered on me?

It was heaven.

"I do," I growled out past increasingly thin lips.

Even after just having shifted earlier today, I found it hard to hold back. My wolf wanted to come and play, to bask in her presence as I was. If she noticed, she didn't care. She moved a little closer, coming to a stop as she tried to follow my gaze through the thinning tree canopy.

"Tell me about them?" she whispered, taking in the sky above us.

"Not much to tell." The hoarseness of my voice caused her to jump, and the rumble started in my chest almost immediately.

I still wasn't sure why my wolf felt the need, but she smiled at me, and that was all that mattered. She sank further into my side, the brush of her arm against mine making me regret putting on the jacket. Her laugh caught me off guard, and I grabbed her attention with a turned head.

"I think there's plenty to tell." She smiled widely, tracing the stars with a naked reverence. "What happened to your riveting conversation?"

The softly spoken prod was enough to keep me talking, if only to hear her make another one.

"Alright, *smár Valkyrja*." Her eyebrow rose at my old Icelandic, as it always did. "I will tell you of the stars."

She leaned in close; close enough that I could hear the steady beat of her heart. She searched the sky with a dreamy kind of wonder, as she waited for me to begin. The skin of my palm warmed, and I hesitated a second before reaching out to her.

I waited for her to deny it, to turn away with one of those soft smiles of hers. I would have accepted it, knowing how touch can trigger unwanted memories. When she slid her hand into mine, my skin jumped. The partial shift caused me to shudder, and my eyes widened at the lack of control.

I shook my head, tightening my hand around hers, threading our fingers together so I could point to where I wanted.

"Where I came from, we believed stars were living embers, placed in the sky by the Old Gods."

She leaned in, her head just shy of my chest. The press of her heated skin burned me, tearing across my nerves in the best way. She made my blood roar, my heart thunder in my chest, and I realized in no uncertain terms how close she was. Her soft skin beckoned me, called for touch. Her eyes held a kind of curiosity to them, and I could tell just from the look on her face that she wouldn't stop me if I reached out to her. She would allow the touch because she trusted me.

That was why I turned away, loosening my grip on her hand. She shouldn't trust, not a bastard like me. Not when I had enough innocent blood on my hands to stain me for centuries more. As much as I hated to admit it, I shared more with Osiris than most could see. I spent too many years killing, for someone to look at me like that.

Soft, like she knew I wouldn't hurt her.

"If you look there, you can see the twisting of *Nidhogg*. He was said to have been a serpent that spent his days eating at the roots of the world's tree, *Yggdrasill*." Her fascination with my story was my saving grace. Her eyes flicked between my face and the sky, a comforting smile keeping me grounded.

"There, the brightest star you see is *Lokabrenna*. Loki's Torch. It glows the brightest during fall, and on nights like this my entire clan would gather outside. Torches would be extinguished, and we would show our devotion to the Old Gods by dancing under their starlight." I could still recall the old sway, warmed by the heat of a roaring fire and the bodies of those around me.

She shivered, and my beast thrummed in my mind, so with her hand still in mine, I moved us. We took a step and began walking again.

"You danced?" Aaliyah asked, her eyes still on those same stars I danced beneath all those years ago, even as she walked.

"Yes, though I was never very good at it," I said, tracing her lax expression and twisting smile.

"You're joking. I would have guessed you were the best," she said, turning toward me.

Her face lit up crimson when she caught me staring, and my beast purred at the sight.

"Sorry to disappoint," I said, entranced by her laugh that followed. "My sisters were the dancers, even my father. But I basically had two left feet."

"Oh, it couldn't have been that bad. You'll have to show me sometime ... I do love to dance," she said with a wispy sigh. There was a purity in her voice, a wonder that made my heart ache. "Your home sounds beautiful."

"It was," I whispered.

I recalled a similar interaction so long ago now that it almost felt like a dream. Explaining the stars to my youngest sister, Tove; with her laugh on the wind, her quiet questions and her soaring curiosity.

"Do you miss it?" Aaliyah asked, as if reading my mind.

"Every day." A rumble built in my chest, the deep melancholy of my beast matching the mood that had taken us. It was a call of pain, one I couldn't stop.

We walked in silence for a few more moments gazing at the stars, before Aaliyah turned toward me again. Violet eyes told me everything. I didn't want to see that I was worthy of the joy that was buried in them, that I was allowed to be at peace.

How would Nero deal with this? Would he be able to let go of his past long enough to accept Aaliyah's kindness? It seemed like my mind always took me here, questioning what my lost brother would do, how he would react.

I wanted to know more than anything, and at this moment, I could use his advice.

"Can I ask you something, Eirik?" She bit her lip, glancing away from me when I raised an eyebrow and nodded.

"What are you?" she asked, squeezing my hand. "Besides Vampire, I mean."

I took a moment to consider her question, only now realizing that she didn't know of my heritage, didn't know of my wolf. He stood at attention behind my eyes, tracing her even now.

"I am many things, *smár Valkyrja*." Her nose tilted up again, as her lips slid between her teeth, biting into the flesh. "I am a Norseman, or as Adrian likes to call it, a Viking," I started, tracing the back of her hand with my thumb.

Aaliyah took a second to look at me, and I felt small under her curious gaze. Then she smiled up like she'd just realized something.

"Viking ... that makes sense," she said with a laugh. The sound gripped me, and I wanted to hear it again. "What does it mean, '*smár Valkyrja*'?"

"It means small Valkyrie or tiny warrior."

She brushed next to me, and I couldn't stop the smile that built at her indignation. She was adorable in the way she shuffled.

"Everything is tiny to you," she grumbled.

"Can't disagree." The smile I'd been chasing lit up her face again, an amused glint in her eyes. She said nothing else, her stare burning me in the best way, so I continued. "The Valkyrie were revered and known for their spirits, which shone brightly through their eyes."

Her breath caught on a gasp. I could see that same light shining now, leaking through her smile. "And their strength, their ability to know when to harm and when to help. I called you that because, even in fear, you sought your freedom. You saw me and didn't cower. You fought valiantly." That caused me to smile, the kind that Nero would have called 'brash'. "You even struck me."

She shuddered.

"I'm sorry for that, you know ... I wasn't exactly in the best state of mind when I woke up." Her head tipped, and her smile dropped as she turned away from me.

Guilt wasn't an emotion that suited her, not when she had every right to fear me. Only inches from me, completely trusting in my presence. I could kill her before she had time to blink, before she could even breathe a scream. My tongue caught, and my wolf snarled in my mind, his agitation at my thought shaking my body with a deep resounding growl.

Aaliyah flinched at the sound, turning toward me with a questioning glance. She couldn't see the monster that sat by her side. She didn't know to stay away.

And I knew I couldn't either.

"You acted as any warrior would. I could never fault you for that," I said before she could question my shift of mood. "Besides, you did something that day that few can say they have. You surprised me, then you followed that surprise by landing a strike."

I could recall that moment with perfect clarity, the wisp of her white eyelashes against luminescent skin. The tilt of her nose and the fire in her eyes that screamed her will to fight even as she trembled. At that moment, she was the most beautiful thing I'd ever seen, a true fighter.

A Valkyrie.

"You're happy I hit you?"

I shook my head. "Proud," I said, looking toward the sky again.

Aaliyah didn't quite seem to understand why. She didn't know that most people only *dreamed* of hitting me. Half the time they only managed to because I wanted to see the fear in their eyes when they realized how sorely outmatched they were. But those days were long past now, buried in a Roman crypt with the other half of my soul. How a slip like her, someone barely up to my chest, in a home unfamiliar to her, had hit me, still stole my thoughts at night.

"I am also a warrior of Odin, a *Úlfheðinn*. Hitting me is a feat that few can claim." The rumble of my wolf's agreement broke out across us.

"What does being *Úlfhéðinn* have to do with it?" she asked in a whisper, unable to tear her eyes away from me.

"It's a term meaning 'warriors of the wolf', or 'wearers of wolf skin.'"

Her eyes widened, and she leaned a little closer. Her scent spiked in the air, and I was once again reminded of her closeness. I battled for control over my base instincts.

So close, so soft, so warm.

Innocent, *tiny*.

I clenched my jaw tightly, shaking my head.

"It got a little lost in translation. I'm a wolf shifter, a Lycan."

Confusion marred her features, and moonlight lit up the white streak across her eyebrow. My throat clenched at the sight.

"So, you're not a Vampire?"

I shook my head, holding back my wolf's push as he again fought for control.

"I'm that, too," I growled out through clenched teeth.

"How can you be both? I thought Vampires could only turn humans."

I reached toward my neck, tracing the scar there.

"Worthless mutt, not even worth the price I paid," Brazen hissed, dragging me across the ground by my hair. The silver chains bit into my skin, stopping me from changing when the pain became overwhelming.

I still recalled Brazen's heavy hand. The feeling of his whip against my back, screaming until even my voice had given up on me.

Fitting punishment for an unruly slave.

She'd been through something traumatic. It was shown on her skin, in her eyes, in the way she moved. In her words. How did you tell someone who had been through hell themselves that pain kept you alive through the turn? That it was nothing compared to the feeling of steel cutting through bone.

"We're Vivas. Nothing is impossible," I said finally, unable to turn away from her.

She frowned as though she could see that pain, her hand tight against mine. I ran my thumb over her wrist, clenching my jaw at the feel of raised skin.

One strike, two, then Brazen dropped the whip.

"Tell me more?" she asked, distracting me, pulling me away from the unrelenting swings that still haunted me. "About your home?"

"Always." So I did. I told her of the stars, of dancing, and anything else I could think to add, until we approached the small structure that held our wards.

Or rather, *had* held them.

The small wooden box was in shambles, shards strewn around the ground like it had been shattered. The familiar twist of Osiris's old magic no longer swirled in the air.

I snarled, the shudder of my skin nearly shifting me on the spot; only Aaliyah's trembling hand on my arm stopped it. I looked around, pulling Aaliyah behind me, shielding her as I searched the area. She pressed into my back, going rigid as I painstakingly searched.

But no one was here.

Whoever had destroyed our wards was long gone. They had to have come sometime today, between now and my last scout. I couldn't scent anything on the air, so they obviously knew what they were doing. Tension like a bowstring kept my back rod-straight, and my wolf thrashed and tore at my mind.

I turned, picking up Aaliyah bridal style. I ran my nose over her temple, my wolf only calming when he was sure she was safe in our arms. Even then, his agitation threatened to drown me. She gasped but didn't protest. Not when she saw the look on my face.

Someone had been here. Someone had targeted our wards, leaving us vulnerable. Someone thought to intimidate the Vivas Crypt.

My arms tightened around Aaliyah, with only one thought on my mind. I wanted bloodshed, had so since Aaliyah told us of her story, and I couldn't get it, not yet. But I could get whoever dared to threaten her now.

I hoped they knew who they were dealing with; I hoped they feared death. And if they didn't, then they would soon.

It was about damned time for a hunt.

CHAPTER 33

AALIYAH

Shards of wood were scattered over the snow dusted ground, bathed in the same subtle moonlight that had guided our peaceful walk. The sight of them made my skin numb, bitten by a false chill as panic swallowed my voice and I trembled even in Eirik's tight grip. My eyes jerked around the small clearing, searching for a phantom threat that I could feel in my bones was no longer here, just as another more familiar chill shot down my spine. Prince stalked through the tree line like a man possessed.

The sight of him made me jump, my nerves like live wires bouncing against concrete, not recognizing Prince as *Prince* for the barest moment. I shouldn't have been surprised to see him. He'd always been in tune with me, and though I hadn't seen him on the walk here, I knew he'd been close.

He looked around the clearing, only glancing over his shoulder at me to make sure I was safe, the slow trace of his gaze helping to banish some of the numbness before he inspected the shattered remains of what had likely been the ward house. The hard lines of his face sharpened as rage took over. He lifted his head and turned toward us completely. His hands lifted, like he was going to signal something to me, before frustration sank into his eyes and both arms fell to his sides. He did the same again, only to drop his hands once more, his mouth opening in what I could only assume was a silent curse.

He had something to say, and no way to say it. That thought burned in my chest, and only served to make the growing feeling of *wrongness* sink into my bones. I remembered this feeling well; it was the one that had been constant at Ascension Rising, always pressing against my thoughts and reminding me that monsters were never far away. It was the one that had told me Curtis was following us through the streets of Century Side before he'd made himself known. I hadn't listened to it before; I'd ignored it.

I wasn't going to make the same mistake now.

"We need to go tell the others," I said, resolute even with the shake in my voice.

I clutched Eirik's shirt a little tighter, and he huffed, the sound muddled with a growl as he ran his nose against my temple again. He took a steadying breath, and I didn't miss the way he scanned the woods, eyes flashing red as bloodlust threatened to take over. A sharp bite of fear that I hadn't been expecting had me jolting away, and for a second I wondered if he would tear through the trees looking for whoever dared to do this. It only took one glance at the forest to know that the fear didn't come from Eirik's rage, or from the rolling growl that shook my bones.

It came from the idea that he might leave me here alone, as silly as it was.

He didn't give me long to stew on the thought as he turned sharply away from the clearing, *flitting* through the woods and to the front door so quickly it knocked the breath out of me. The growl that had continued in Eirik's broad chest settled, sinking down into a low purr of what I could only assume was an apology.

He walked us through the door, the aroma of Adrian's newest concoction hitting me almost as quickly as his words.

"You guys are back soon. Figured you'd be out a little longer." Adrian's chipper tone was enough to get my attention as I jerked my head his way. His back was turned to us as he tapped at each of the cabinets softly, before leaning over his pan to smell the contents. His eyes were closed as he turned toward us, and he hummed softly before he spoke. "Eri bore you already—"

His eyes opened with a grin, but whatever he saw on our faces stopped the sentence flat in his throat. Eirik's growl quickly took up the silence, his hands tightening around me again.

My numbing, uncontrollable panic subdued, just enough for me to feel the pressure of his fingers, and I flinched. Eirik's jaw snapped closed, the sound audible as he hurried over to the table, the jerking movements forced. I felt the flex of his wolf as he set me down gently, his skin trembling under my fingertips. A grimace lit up his face, eyes such a deep blue they were almost black as he assessed my arms. A strangled noise fought its way up his throat before I could find the words to tell him I was fine.

"Osiris!" he snarled, snapping his head toward the stairs as he pulled away from me, his hands going to his arms, tightening until his skin went white under the pressure.

I tried to find the will to reach out, but couldn't, just as trapped in my own thoughts as he was in his. I glanced at the door, waiting for Prince to saunter through and tell me everything was alright.

But it wasn't. I could feel it in my bones. Something was wrong, terribly *wrong*. It made my stomach twist and my head spin, just as a shadow covered me.

"What happened?" Fallon asked, taking Eirik's spot in front of me.

I looked up at him, using his face as a point to focus on. Green eyes, pointed and cold if you didn't know what you were looking for, stared me up and down, checking for injuries he wouldn't find. But he must not have been searching for something physical, as a moment later his thin lips twisted, tightening in confusion and worry.

"Someone destroyed the wards," Eirik bit out, his elongated teeth clanking against each other as he spoke.

Fallon pinned Eirik with a cold stare.

"What do you *mean*, someone destroyed the wards?" he asked, and Eirik snarled again, snapping his mouth shut, and flashing his teeth.

"Can't get much clearer, pup." A growl broke Eirik's crisp words. His fangs were extended over his lip, though they were different than I remembered. Each tooth pointed and lengthened far past what was normal. The sharpness of his face only grew more pronounced as he slammed his hand on the island, his back flexing under his tattered jacket. I flinched again, unable to stop it. Eirik took it personally, his eyes flashing red as he grabbed at his throat like he couldn't breathe. "Osiris, get the fuck down here!"

Just as quickly as we'd arrived, Osiris appeared. His hair was wet, hanging around his head in soft waves. For once he wasn't wearing a suit, rather an oversized T-shirt I could tell wasn't his and a pair of gray sweats.

For a brief second, I forgot what we'd been so worked up about, too busy staring at a *normal* looking Osiris. He brushed his hair back, glancing at me and Eirik, the seriousness in his expression steeling my spine. His arms were exposed, something I hadn't seen before, and my eyes caught on the harsh ink at his wrists. He didn't breathe, the unnatural stillness in his chest only surging to make my instincts scream again.

"Explain," he said.

Eirik could only snarl, his hand pressing so hard against the island that the marble groaned. He tried to force words out, but nothing resembling speech materialized. So, I stood on shaking legs, smiling the best I could at Fallon as he looked at me like I was crazy. I took a few tentative steps toward Eirik, every person in the room seeming to hold their breath. I hummed softly when Eirik turned to face me. I reached my hand out to him and he grunted before setting his palm in mine. The familiar sky-blue of his eyes eluded me. Instead, they continued to swirl and clash like a turbulent ocean as he dipped his head, motioning for me to speak.

"When we got to the clearing, there were wood splinters scattered around," I started, glancing around the room. Just like before, a burst of cold made every hair on my body stand and goosebumps littered my arms.

Though this time, it didn't incite panic. Prince walked through the door only moments later, looking even more pissed than he had before; and slightly winded. Or at the very least, he was faking it for the theatrics, bent over with his hands on his knees, before he pointed accusingly at Eirik.

I let out a breath, smiling. Distraction was a tactic he'd used often, and even now it calmed some of the anxiety that had taken root in my soul. He lifted his hands, as he'd done before, hesitating. This time he didn't let his hands fall, as he crossed them over his chest in an 'X'.

Danger.

"Prince says ... it was someone dangerous," I whispered, never taking my eyes off of my knight.

"What does he mean by dangerous?" Osiris asked, and Prince flashed him an agitated glower.

He lifted his hands again, glaring at them as if willing them to speak for him. When he raised his hands again he shook his head, and again crossed his arms over his chest in a confident 'X'.

"I don't know," I said, worry sinking further into my stomach at Prince's expression.

I turned to Osiris, my entire body tensing when I realized he'd gotten closer. He was barely an arm's length away, his head tilted slightly to the left. I took a deep breath, focusing on the differing blues of his eyes. Osiris inhaled with me, his shoulders relaxing as his chest heaved. The dead stillness faded from his posture in a blink

"I wish I had more ... but we didn't really have the time to develop our communication past basic phrases," I mumbled, looking away.

"Had to have been magic. No scent left behind," Eirik said, his voice clearer, lacking the growl of his wolf.

"Who would be stupid enough to do something like this? Everyone knows Osiris is the head of the Pennsylvania territory." Adrian's disbelief caused a quiet to extend through the room.

"Could it be ... *him*?" Fallon hissed the word, thick arms crossed over his broad chest. The white of his suit flexed where his arms strained against the material.

Eirik stiffened, using our still-joined hands to pull me softly against him. He gave me plenty of time to pull away, though I wouldn't turn down comfort right now. My back pressed against his front, and his arms wrapped securely around me, holding me to his chest.

"No," he said, the word brushing against my skin.

"Can you be sure?" Fallon asked, and Eirik growled again.

"Aye. This stinks of old magic." He breathed deep, his nose twisting like he was clearing the smell of it out.

"And just when I thought we were done dealing with temperamental Sorceri for the week." Adrian groaned out the words from his place on the other side of the island, sourness sticking to every one. He leaned over the counter, tapping his hand against the marble. "This has Eternal written all over it, the damned bastards. Maybe one of them is trying to get rid of us to gain *his* favor."

I tensed against Eirik.

"Is there any chance it was an accident? The ward could have failed."

Osiris's words did little to help the racing of my heart, and a bitter taste settled on my tongue.

It wasn't an accident, I knew it. Though I couldn't seem to get the words past my lips. I looked to Prince again, my throat only locking down further as I watched him pace the length in front of the door, his gaze on the floor.

Never make noise.

My spine straightened, and my hands went numb at the silent uttering of my mantra.

"No, your magic was dead in the air. Someone canceled it out," Eirik said, cracking the ice that held me frozen, just enough for me to breathe. "They had to have been strong to break the ward and remove their trace."

Fallon cursed, ripping his hand through his hair, golden strands falling to the floor as his thin lips curled into a silent snarl.

"I don't like this. So close to the Eternium, this feels like a warning. Adrian, do you know of any Eternals that have issues with our Crypt?" he asked.

"Better question is which ones don't?" Adrian mumbled the words, rubbing the back of his neck. "Of the Eternals that I know, none would be brash enough to attempt an assassination on us."

A sharp push against my nerves had me biting down a cry. The need to run suddenly made my legs shake, and I pressed my hands into Eirik's arms to hold myself steady. He tightened his grip easily, tipping my head to look me in the eyes. I bit my lip and turned toward the others.

"Power does strange things to people ... They might not have before, but who's to say what they would do, given the right incentive?" I asked, ignoring the lingering ache in my bones as I thought about Castillion and Nox. They'd been doctors before the Ascension brought them on, people trained to *help*. Look where their greed had gotten them. "Maybe ... *he* didn't want his hands in this."

I didn't know their Maker's name, and with the way each of their eyes burned at just the thought of him, I knew I didn't need to. Each of them stiffened, heads tipping in silent contemplation.

"Maybe, but I doubt it. This isn't his style. This was meant to be found, like a calling card." Eirik pressed his nose to my hair as he spoke.

With everyone's focus so pointed, I wasn't surprised that they'd missed the way Osiris trembled, and grabbed his exposed wrist. His eyes flared wide for only a moment, before stark disbelief and numbness took over. Then there was nothing. I didn't have time to question it, the expression was gone so quickly I wondered if I'd seen it at all.

"Got something to add, Osiris?" Fallon asked, turning his head toward Osiris, oblivious to what I'd seen.

My chest ached, and I considered asking about it. What was it about that sentence that made him so numb? An instinctual need to flee skittered down my spine, pushing me to run just when Osiris caught my eye, and any words I had caught in my throat.

"No," he said with purpose. "I'll work on making a new ward. Shouldn't take more than a few days."

"Will we be safe that long?" Adrian asked.

Osiris hesitated for a moment before nodding. The others relaxed just barely, but enough for me to see the trust they held in his words.

"Okay," Fallon said, stepping away from the island, and toward the front door. "We should still check the area, see if they left anything behind. Eirik, you down for a hunt?"

Eirik only grunted, slowly unwinding his arms from around me, giving one more lingering touch to the top of my head before he moved toward Fallon.

"This feels wrong." I finally got the words out, past clenched teeth and the mantra that my mind kept screaming at me.

Never make noise.

"What do you mean, love?" Adrian asked softly, and I almost couldn't get anything else out.

They get more violent when they hear noise.

I pressed my palm to my chest, willing my heart to calm.

"I don't know ... but I think something's coming," I said, and clenching that same hand into a fist. "I can feel it."

Somewhere deep in my chest, I expected them to laugh and brush off my thoughts. Though I knew better than that, and Adrian only soothed my nerves when he nodded, a seriousness in his eyes, not quite the bubbly joy I'd grown used to seeing. I took a deep breath.

"We'll be ready. There are very few that can best us," Osiris supplied. I turned to glance at him just as the door clicked shut, and Fallon and Eirik ambled off into the woods.

I couldn't stop the fear that still lingered, but I nodded.

"I trust you," I said, meaning it with everything I was.

I reached up, grabbing the pendant that hung around my neck, taking comfort in the cool steel. Osiris watched me hold it, his hands flexing as his eyes fell closed. When he opened them again, it was only Osiris that I saw, clear aqua and royal blue, resolute. He locked his gaze on mine, a subtle question behind them.

He knew: knew that I'd seen the panic in his eyes. It only took one glance to know he was asking me to push past it, to place my trust in him. Trust that he would tell us if something was wrong, that he knew what he was doing.

It was easy, letting out the breath and pushing down the still-nagging sense of dread. I turned toward Prince, who had his eyes on Osiris. His jaw was tense, and his apprehension was bleeding into the air. Like always, he turned toward me without me needing to speak, worry still swirling in the endless white depths even as his lips tilted into a roguish grin. There was worry there ... but above all, there was *trust*, and it was that look that settled my decision.

I had to trust Osiris; I *did* trust him ... for better or worse, I had to believe that was the right choice.

Chapter 34

Adrian

I sighed, rolling my head side to side as I only barely listened to what Fallon was droning on about. Something about our next bet? Maybe the dreary weather? Ah, I know, how does one smile without scaring young children?

More than likely it was the wards that had more or less combusted into tiny bite-sized wood chips. Normally, I'd be more inclined to at least pretend that I was paying attention, be more stressed about our wards, or lack thereof. I was in charge of figuring out what happened after all, thanks to being the jolly information gatherer of our Crypt.

But today, I couldn't seem to focus on anything but the most basic of tasks, as I had a *headache*, something that I hadn't dealt with since my human years. It almost felt like I was getting sick, as absurd as that was. *Vampire*s couldn't get sick.

Right?

I sighed again, head tipping back, as Fallon, disgruntled with my lack of attention, snapped. Literally. The sound was audible as he snapped his fingers.

"You're insufferable," he bit out. "Our safety is at risk. You could at least pretend to give a shit."

I rolled my eyes as I pushed off the counter, waving my hand at

Fallon as I stalked toward the island that housed our blood fridge. The marble countertop was cold against my hand when I leaned down, and a shiver shot down my spine.

Strange. Was I cold too?

"And you're an asshole," I snapped back, searching through the bottles with mild discontent. Was it so hard for a single wine to taste reasonable? Really didn't seem like too much to ask. "And really, Fallon? Who exactly is going to come fuck with us, huh? Osiris would have anyone but Sebek strewn out Vlad the Impaler style, before they hit the yard. This is just some petty attempt to scare us before the Eternium."

A flash of white caught my attention, and I looked up at Fallon, who had moved over to where I kneeled. His eyes were narrowed, the white of his suit uncharacteristically ruffled as he leaned down and assessed me. I grit my teeth.

"Are you okay?" he asked.

Fallon wasn't one to outwardly care about anything that didn't involve a fight or his damn chocolates, so it knocked me off guard to see the worry in his eyes. I sighed, pressing my thumbs against my temples, flicking my gaze through the banal-sounding blood wines we housed in the small fridge. Each made my insides turn, and though the ache of hunger was ever-present, I couldn't force myself to pull out a bottle. It wasn't like the *Call*: a false hunger. It was real, and it grated at my stomach and made my head spin. Blood wine had been losing its effect for us over the last few years, but damn, this was brutal. We really needed something from the vein.

That thought brought something unbidden: the press of my lips against Aaliyah's soft throat, fangs sank deep into her skin. I shook it off violently, slapping my palm against my forehead to clear the thought.

"Yeah. Just a headache," I said, standing and closing the fridge, pretending like Fallon didn't just see me slap myself in the face.

As I glanced at him, I realized he didn't look much better than I felt, and the shallow air of scrutiny in his eyes told me he wasn't going to drop it now that I'd brought it up. But I didn't have the will to deal with one of his moods, not today. So, I sighed and forced a smile.

"Oh, don't look at me like that. I'm *fine,*" I said, patting him on the shoulder. "I'll be right as rain and ready to deal with your incessant droning in a few hours."

Fallon rolled his eyes but didn't let up, even as I turned toward the stairs intent on finding another way to distract myself from the pain. His even steps echoed behind me, his cool black oxfords creating a quiet click against the hardwood.

"Fine, Adrian? Have you been feeding?"

I scoffed and looked over my shoulder at him with a raised eyebrow, not stopping, though not moving quickly either.

"Define feeding?" I asked, rubbing my temples again. "I keep it down about as well as one would spoiled milk. We really need a hit from the vein. This bottled shit has really gone rancid."

Fallon's jaw tensed.

"Look, it'll be fine. I'm sure it's just stress. We've been through a lot these last few weeks."

"What if it isn't, Adrian?" Fallon pressed, following me as I walked up the stairs. He *flitted* past me, blocking my door.

I groaned and took a deep breath, having to stop myself from getting into a fight that I knew I wouldn't win. It was just a bloody headache, and his pressing attention was only serving to make it worse.

Though ... I knew what he was talking about. I wasn't daft. He was worried that our feeding issue was related to Aaliyah, but I just couldn't believe that. Our blood problem started several years back, and the fact he was even considering that it might be her made my blood boil.

"You are *not* blaming Aaliyah for our feeding problem," I said firmly, pushing Fallon out of the way and marching into my room. "A problem, mind you, we've had for *years*."

For the first time, I was thankful that the walls were a mute-gray, and that there weren't any windows to let in any stray moonlight. I looked at the comfort of my bed, and my body sagged at the thought of falling into its silky embrace.

"But it's gotten worse, Adrian. I can't even stomach blood wine anymore, even the taste has gone ashen." I barely heard his words, waving my hand over my shoulder as I turned away from the heavenly looking bed and walked toward my dresser. "That wasn't how it was three weeks ago."

I groaned, glaring at him over my shoulder. I wanted to sleep, which meant that I *needed* to move. It had been over a month since I'd last made use of our pool. If I was lucky, it would help.

Or at the very least get Fallon off my back for a few hours.

"I'm going to go take a swim," I said, before pulling my shirt off, folding it carefully and placing it on the bed. I glanced at Fallon again. His arms were crossed over his chest, eyes narrowed and pointed as I ignored him. "We can talk about this later, Fally."

Fallon shook his head, dropping his hands as he turned away. His scowl didn't let up, and his disappointment bled into the room.

"Ignoring this isn't going to fix it ... isn't that what you said after we brought Aaliyah back?" He didn't give me time to respond, *flitting* away from the door.

The sound of his own door slamming had me throwing my head back and running my hands over my face, groaning. Why did he have to be so pushy?

And goddammit, he couldn't use my own lines against me like that.

"Bastard," I mumbled as I finished dressing, throwing on a tight pink speedo that happened to be at the top of my stack before I turned around and strolled out of my room.

I made my way across the snowy ground, hating every second that I spent with my feet against the snow, and all but barreled into the covered swimming pool area to get away from it. The brush of heated air, thick with the smell of chlorine, was a welcome burn compared to the cold.

I stretched, sighing as my shoulders popped. Normally, this wouldn't have been an issue, as I was the only one that ever actually used the pool house. None of the others had the love of water like I did. Hell, Osiris couldn't swim at all.

But I hadn't thought about Aaliyah. I'd been too distracted, the ache in my skull taking up far more of my attention than it should. So, when my eyes opened, landing next to the pool ... there she was, mouth dropped open, cheeks a darling shade of pink.

Damn, I could get used to seeing that.

She always looked like someone pulled directly out of my dreams, the soft wave of her white hair and the shy way that she stared up at me from where she kneeled next to the pool. She didn't speak like I expected her to, her eyes wide as she traced her way down my face, dipping into the curve of my neck, and down, and down ...

I took a glance at myself and was quickly reminded of the fact that I was in a speedo. A vibrant pink, giving away everything, and rapidly tightening speedo.

Aaliyah swallowed, the sound clinging to the air, and I jerked my head up, catching her heated stare.

Confusion clashed with interest in her eyes, and the heat on her cheeks had spread down her chest, getting lost under the familiar fabric of one of my T-shirts. It was a mute-gray, and though it was smaller than the others she normally wore, it still stretched down over her bent legs. Her calves had a thin layer of water on them, sliding down the soft bare skin, taunting me.

I took a step forward, almost like I'd been *Charmed* to do so. Any words caught in my throat at the sight of her. Gods, she was beautiful. At that moment, nothing mattered. Not the headache, not Fallon's pressing words or our fucked-up wards.

Just her, and the innocent way her lip slid between her teeth. The curious tilt to her head and the blush that crept down her neck.

Innocent thoughts, Adrian. You can do it. Puppies, kittens.

"Evening, love," I finally said, clearing my throat as I sat down next to her. I kept the leg closest to her bent, so she wouldn't see my growing problem. "Fancy seeing you here."

I flashed her a smile, one that she surprisingly didn't return. She'd stopped her perusal somewhere over my chest, and her breath caught.

I knew my looks were above the average sort. After all, Sebek wouldn't have turned me otherwise. But knowing that the red on her cheeks and that the quickening of her breath came from seeing me?

Innocent. Thoughts.

"Sorry. I can go," she said, fiddling with her hands before she looked away.

She stared at the water like I did, with a longing for it. I stretched, one foot settling in the spring warmed pool.

"You sure? Looked like you were about to go for a swim," I responded casually.

She bit her lip again, and I couldn't look away from the abused flesh.

"I've thought about it," she whispered back, tense.

I couldn't tell from what. The water or me, maybe a mix of both. The gentleman in me told me I should move away, give her some space.

But the bastard in me wanted to lean in close, to turn and make sure she could see every inch of me. So I settled for somewhere in between, reaching out and pressing a stray hair behind her ear, a tremor shooting down my spine as she trembled against my touch. The heat of her breath touched my palm.

"Then come on, join me. Nothing like getting wet on a cool winter night," I said with a wink.

Aaliyah paused for a second, then shook her head, standing. Something akin to defeat clouded her eyes.

"I don't know if I can anymore," she whispered. "I know my dad taught me. I remembered that ... but what if I can't? What if I've forgotten how?"

I paused for a moment, cupping her cheek.

"And what if you haven't?" I whispered. "You worry that you've forgotten without trusting that you remember."

She took a deep breath, shuddering, and it was another breath before she responded.

"I don't have the best track record of trusting my memories." Her words were soft, like saying them was hard for her. "It's hard to trust something that doesn't always feel real."

"Then trust me. I'll keep you safe, Aaliyah. Always." I leaned in, pressing a kiss to her forehead, searing her taste onto my lips. I lingered there, only pulling back when she let out a shaky sigh. "And if you don't remember, then I'll teach you again."

I pulled back and slid into the water. It wasn't very deep, about six feet the entire length, so I could stand pretty easily. Instead of that, I treaded water and stretched my hand out toward her. She hesitated for only a moment, before reaching her hand out and settling it in mine. The shock of pleasure that came with her skin hummed inside of me as she joined me in the water. She gasped, her arms finding their way around my shoulders. Her breath, short and warm, skimmed my collarbone, and I lost my balance for a moment. Her legs paddled, brushing against me.

"See," I said, hands at her waist. "Told you that you could do it."

"Yep, you were right," she whispered, her face still pressed against my chest. "But please don't let me go."

I clutched her tighter, one hand at her waist, the other sliding up her back, over the shirt that now clung to her like a second skin. She was close, so close that I could hear the beating rush of her heart, and smell the lavender that defined her scent, the more subtle spicy undertone of cinnamon nearly dragging a groan out of my throat.

"Never, love," I said, and she laughed.

She didn't know how much I'd meant it, not yet, and that was alright for now. We were already bounds ahead of where I thought we'd be. She was in my arms, her head resting against my chest. I held her tighter, brushing a tender kiss against her forehead again.

Aaliyah looked up at me, a curious tilt to her head. Her bottom lip was bruised from her teeth and her cheeks were still flushed. She looked adorable and like sin at the same time. Her eyes slid over my face and dipped down ...

Innocent. Thoughts.

"Adrian ..." A breath of a whisper.

A man could only take so much. I slid my hand under her chin, keeping the one at her waist to keep her stable. She jolted under the touch, a ragged gasp destroying what control I had left. I leaned in and hovered over her lips for a breath, then two ...

She inched the rest of the way forward, the soft brush of her lips against mine, the heat of her skin searing even compared to the water. Her hands tensed on my shoulders, another sharp, needy noise driving me mad.

My grip on her hip tightened, and I leaned forward enough to press her against the side of the pool, supporting our weight with one hand, using the other to keep her pressed against me.

I didn't have to open my eyes to know they were red. I didn't need to see the familiar red sheen. It was as easy to recognize as the grace of fangs that had pulled at my gums. Excitement roared and dragged me to pull her closer, to see what other sounds I could get to spill from those perfect, pink lips.

But then I felt the tremble. Soft and barely there, the tension of confusion and the sour scent of worry.

I pulled back, shaking as her breath skimmed my face again. I moved up and pressed another kiss to her forehead, arms still shaking. Somewhere deep in my chest I knew that this was too fast, that with everything she'd been through she likely needed patience, or at the very least a damned conversation. I'd wanted to woo her, and only now with that red sheen of pleasure slowly fading, did I realize I may have gone too far. Pushed, too hard ... A fact that I was going to have to deal with.

But goddamn if this wasn't exactly where I wanted to be.

CHAPTER 35

AALIYAH

I'd come to the pool house hoping to distract myself from thinking about the wards, after spending hours in the library doing exactly that. Reading, even skimming through books in languages I couldn't hope to understand just to get a few brief seconds without the mind-numbing fight-or-flight state my body had been in since Eirik and I had told everyone what had happened. Now, it seemed like I finally got that distraction, and the only thought I could focus on ...

Was that Adrian's lips were surprisingly warm?

There was a slight chill, the same one that came with the rest of his skin, but it was like the spark that lit when I touched him seared straight through that cold the moment my lips hit his. They still tingled, and I had to stop and ask if that had actually just happened.

Did I just kiss Adrian?

My cheeks burned, hell, my entire *face* felt like it was on fire, and I found I couldn't look up at the man who still held me in his arms. I was pressed flush against his body, the tile of the pool against my back, his hand strong against my hip. He was firm under my touch, his muscles shuddering as I laid my hand flat against his cool skin.

Adrian's hand fell over mine, stopping me from trying to follow that tremble, a masculine groan echoing in my ear as he leaned forward, pressing a kiss against my neck. I could feel his fangs imprinted behind his closed lips, and I shivered. A trail of liquid fire slid down my body, ending between my legs, and I arched at the feeling of it, something hard against my core taking my breath away.

It was terrifying; an all-consuming ache that swallowed rational thought. I didn't know much about sex or anything that went along with it besides the short awkward conversations that I'd had with Eliza, so I had no idea if this was normal.

Gods, I hoped this was normal.

I gasped as Adrian's kisses trailed up my neck, forcing my head up with the gentle pressure. His breath tickled against my jaw, and my toes curled at the press of his hands against my waist, his fingers tightening.

"You're driving me mad, love," he said, pressing a last kiss to my nose, one that was so tender it had my eyes opening.

Adrian's eyes were red, heat buried in them. His lips, slightly parted as he breathed heavily, showed fangs. There wasn't fear, not like I was expecting, just more dull aches that made my skin numb and my bones turn to putty.

The imprint of his kiss still burned against me, and everything I wanted to say got stuck in my throat. I balled my hands into fists against his bare chest, my arms trembling, begging me to press my palms flat and chase that seductive heat.

What would I even say? What would make sense? That he'd just been my first kiss? That nothing in the world could have prepared me for how sharp the ache that followed it would be? Hell, I hadn't expected this, didn't expect anything like this because who in the hell would want to kiss *me?*

Say something.

But nothing came out. The aching in my chest that was currently threatening to swallow me whole only got worse. I grew dizzy at the heat that still burned my cheeks. Adrian pulled back more, something in his eyes that I didn't recognize, his arms still keeping us afloat as I gripped at his shoulders.

What if it was a misunderstanding? I mean, he'd leaned in, but maybe he didn't mean to kiss me? Was he not saying anything because he didn't want to hurt my feelings?

God, I don't know. Maybe he slipped?

"What's on that beautiful mind of yours, love?" A soft question, one that radiated down my spine and ended between my legs.

Beautiful.

Suddenly, the chill of his chest against my closed hands was all I could feel. His hand at my hip, the tilt of his lips. Overwhelmed didn't begin to describe how I felt.

I needed to talk to Eliza.

"I think we can make that happen. Want to call her tonight? It's still early in the evening." Soft amusement twinkled in Adrian's smooth words, and he pressed a soft kiss to my cheek.

I tilted my head, jaw dropping. Vampires couldn't read minds, and that meant that I'd said that out loud ... to Adrian. Who still looked at me with that sweet smile like I hadn't just buried myself in embarrassment hell.

"Sorry." I didn't know what else to say, couldn't force any other words out. Mortification mixed with everything else, and my senses imploded on themselves. All at once everything felt too close and seemed too loud.

"Nothing to be sorry for, love," Adrian said softly with a hum, still smiling down at me.

My lower lip slid between my teeth as I tried to find something to say, when I realized something ...

Adrian looked ... *off*?

I frowned, tracing the dark circles under his eyes, and the way he squinted at me. I knew what pain looked like, and he had all the signs of someone dealing with it.

"Adrian?" I said, reaching up and pressing a palm to his cheek. His eyes fell closed, and he leaned into the touch with a sigh. "Are you okay?"

He pressed his hand against mine and pulled back to kiss my wrist. The sway of the water against us sloshed as Adrian leaned his weight on the wall. When he opened his eyes again, they were that clear copper with touches of autumn amber.

"Yeah. I'm alright, just a headache."

I bit my lip, ready to question more when he shook his head, lifting me so quickly that I gasped. He set me on the edge of the pool as he pulled himself out. He looked troubled, his hand rubbing behind his neck. The air of our kiss faded, and I couldn't help but feel insecure as he stood, looking away from me.

I felt exposed, and the tingle in my lips turned cold.

"Maybe we should call it for the night. You'll want to ring Eliza soon, so you can catch her before she goes to sleep," he said hastily, helping me to my feet.

He shivered, his hand going to his head, wincing when he pressed his thumb to his temple.

"Adrian ..."

I didn't want to leave it like this. It felt wrong, but I could tell from the look on his face that I wouldn't be getting anything else out of him. He smiled. The brittle look was the last I saw before he was gone. I stood, shaking in the pool house, my lungs straining for air and my eyes burning. My body still sang where Adrian's hands had been.

I needed to talk to Eliza.

CHAPTER 36

AALIYAH

I fidgeted on my seat at the dining table, nervous as Adrian hummed about the kitchen, tapping at the black cabinets and talking quietly with Fallon as he prepped for our drive. The thought of leaving the Vivas house made me uneasy, but I needed to do this.

I *needed* to talk to Liz.

These last few days had been interesting, to say the very least, with my death and the destruction of the wards. I still felt that lingering panic, one I'd hoped would waver after a day's sleep. It hadn't, but at least I could breathe without flinching again. Osiris had assured me it was being taken care of, and if the sleep-deprived look in his eyes was anything to go by, I'd guessed that he was taking this attack far more personally than the others realized.

Still, I trusted him, and that thought helped to keep my mind on where we were going. Even a statue could tell that the dynamic of the house had shifted ... and I didn't mean just since the wards. No, this change had started around the time the guys had learned about Ascension Rising. *Drastically changed.* I'd been ignoring it, trying to stay blissfully unaware of what I was feeling. But I couldn't do that anymore, not after last night.

After the kiss I wasn't sure even happened.

I wasn't sure how to navigate this, how to deal with this twisting in my stomach. I hoped Eliza would have some advice. Because if she didn't, I was screwed. Wholly and fully screwed.

"Ready, love?" I jumped, dragged from my thoughts by the adoring quality in Adrian's voice as he appeared in front of me, extending his hand for me to take.

I'd expected today to be awkward, or at the very least, for him to say something about our kiss. But all evening he'd been the normal, cheery, blindingly handsome Adrian I knew. I could barely look at him without thoughts of last night taking over. It was all I could seem to think about. Hell, I still felt the cool press of his lips, and it was driving me crazy. But it didn't seem like it was the same for him, which only made my stomach flutter more. I wanted to ask, so I could understand what last night meant.

But I couldn't find the words.

I blushed as he winked my way. I took his hand, marveling at the icy touch that I didn't want to let go of as we walked toward the front door. His thumb skimmed the skin of my wrist, leaving a burning in my chest that twisted and swirled, making me breathless and star-struck all at once. It wasn't an unfamiliar feeling, per se. No ... it was one I'd dealt with for years, one that I hadn't been able to place before.

Because it was the same feeling I got around Prince. The warmth, the butterflies. The desire to spend as much time as possible with them, adoring their company in whatever form it took.

Once outside, we came to a stop in front of a sleek silver car, one that wasn't normally parked here. It was one of the few they kept in their off-ground garage, a building that I'd only been told about since they didn't need to drive often. The cold air skimmed my skin, and I shivered through the winter coat I wore, biting my lip, and only noticing Fallon's disgruntled glower when he tapped where my teeth sank. It startled me, and I clenched Adrian's hand, looking at Fallon with a tilted head.

"You're worrying yourself silly, Ali," Fallon said, the gruffness to his voice bringing a familiar peace. His nickname made me smile, and his lip twitched. "We don't have to go."

I chuckled, shaking my head at his attempt to give me an out.

"I need to see Eliza ... and from the sound of it, Eternal Ilenia needs to see me too," I said, and I found it hard to disagree with his scowl.

When I'd called last night, Eliza told me what her *baba* wanted, and I couldn't very well refuse the call of an Eternal.

As expected, Fallon's eyes fell closed, and I missed the frosty green. He'd been the most opposed to me meeting with the Siren Eternal and had vehemently disagreed. But in the end, he'd swayed when I told him he could come with me.

So here he was, looking out of place standing in the snow in his white suit.

"I don't like it, but I understand," Fallon said with a sigh, opening the car door for me, while running a hand through his golden hair. Adrian took a second to pull me to him, lifting my hand to his cool lips. He placed a soft kiss on it, lingering. I almost bit my lip again, looking to see if Fallon noticed.

His eyes were glued to where Adrian held me, a subtle heat in them, before he flicked his attention back to me. Swirling green and mixed with longing. My breath caught. Did he know about what Adrian and I had done? Did he know about the kiss? Suddenly, the hand in mine felt like embers, and I struggled to keep a hold of it. And it only became apparent as I fought for words that ...

... that it wasn't just Adrian that I had this strange feeling about.

"I won't let her hurt you, Ali. Eternal status be damned." Fallon's worry was a balm to my soul, and I reached out, slipping my hand from Adrian's grip to squeeze Fallon's hand before I slid into the car. His shocked look made me smile, and I nearly did it again just to see if I could get another stray expression to show up.

"I know. I trust you, Fallon," I said.

He nodded, eyes narrowing as he closed the door, mumbling something I couldn't hear. He and Adrian found their way into the car, clipping their seat belts in and starting the drive to Liz's *baba's*. Almost immediately, they started bickering over Adrian's driving.

"You missed the stop sign," Fallon grumbled, rolling his eyes as Adrian squinted, glancing at the rearview mirror.

"That wasn't a stop sign," Adrian said, shaking his head. "Probably just a figment of your imagination. You going senile in your old age, Fally?"

A vein popped on Fallon's jaw.

"If you aren't going to drive safely, then pull over. I'll drive."

"Fallon, last time you drove, you totaled Osi's '67 Firebird." Adrian laughed as he again narrowed his eyes on a sign that we passed, this time following what it said.

At least I think he did, based on how he slammed on the brakes. Fallon ground his teeth, looking like he was going to reach over and strangle Adrian where he sat.

"I didn't crash it. You ran in front of me and yelled *Chicken!* Would you rather I'd hit you?" Fallon looked like he was really considering doing the same again. "You were barely sixty years turned. It would have taken you months to heal had I hit you going seventy.'

Fallon glared and Adrian laughed maniacally. I didn't butt in, as much as I wanted to. Instead, I sank into the cured leather of the seat, the smooth material warming under my touch. I loved hearing them bicker too much to risk interrupting it.

"But you didn't have to hit the tree! God, you had Osi in hysterics, thought he was going to bust a god damned blood vessel. So rude, Fally." Adrian laid on the victim complex as he narrowed his eyes on Fallon, a wicked grin on his lips.

Fallon groaned and said what sounded like a prayer. For him or Adrian, I wasn't sure.

I just smiled, listening to Fallon's sharp directions and Adrian's feigns at innocence. Prince, who'd slid into the car next to me, looked at them with a similar amusement, his arms crossed and gaze flicking between the two. Every now and again he would laugh, the silent rise and fall of his chest dragging a few from my own.

All too soon, we pulled up to an unfamiliar house. It was buried in the woods, down an old dirt trail that went on for a few miles. The building itself looked like it was about to fall apart. It was covered in moss with plants strewn on every open space on the ground. There were no other homes in sight.

I bit down on my nerves, watching as the front door flew open, and a familiar face peeked through the opening.

"I was wondering when you were going to show up!" Eliza shouted from the stairs up to the door as we stepped out, waving her hand with a giddy smile on her face.

She shot down the stairs and I barely had time to laugh as she pulled me into her arms. I leaned into her embrace, comforted by the smell of the sea.

"*Himal*, it's been ages," she whispered, pulling back, checking me over, before she glanced at the guys.

Adrian smiled easily, his eyes on me. Fallon, on the other hand, leveled a glare at Eliza, buried anger still clinging to his gaze.

Baby steps.

"It's barely been a week, Liz," I said with a grin, hoping to calm everyone down enough to stop the fight that was brewing.

I really didn't feel like dealing with blood spatter today.

My distraction did enough, or maybe Eliza just realized that the guys weren't as bad as she thought, as she turned to me and smiled.

"Like I said, *ages,*" she said, exasperated as she grabbed my hand, pulling me toward the door. "Come on, the boys are waiting, and my *baba* made tea."

I nodded, fighting to keep the smile on my face at the thought of Eliza's *baba*. I wasn't exactly excited to meet the woman. She sounded intense, almost downright terrifying. But Eliza insisted, so here I was. I glanced back at the guys, who still stood by the car, obviously waiting for something. Eliza stopped for a moment before she sighed, sending a muted glare at Adrian and Fallon.

"You can come too," she mumbled, before dragging me up the stairs. "I humbly invite you into my *baba's* home."

She did a little bow, flaring her hand out. Adrian snorted and shook his head, walking behind us as we passed through the entrance. Fallon did as well, both men taking off their shoes as Liz and I did the same.

"Thanks, Liz," I said, laughing as she mumbled something about trying her best.

The house was decorated like it was directly out of the early seventies, with assortments of colors on the walls, swirled furniture, and the smell of salt in the air. It was chaotic, much like the herb house, with bits and bobbles strewn around the room.

"My *baba's* in the sitting room. Grigen should be in there soon. He wandered off a while ago to play, but I'm sure as soon as he hears you're here he'll come running. He's been off the wall since he found out you were coming." The thought of seeing GeGe had me bouncing, nearly pushing past Eliza. "Dezen and Carter are by the pool, if you guys want to go hang out with them."

Though her words were curt, I was glad that she was at least trying to include Fallon and Adrian. Eliza was a tough one to crack, but I knew that if she spent enough time around them, she'd come to understand why they meant so much to me.

"You ladies have fun," Adrian said, pulling my attention to him as he reached out, pushing a stray piece of hair out of my eyes. I shivered when his fingers crossed my cheek, a blush rising. His smile stole my breath from my lungs. "Come find us when you're ready to go, okay, love?"

"Thanks," I said, and he winked before pulling away, dragging a disgruntled Fallon with him.

Fallon looked ready to riot, and I laughed as Adrian said something about another bet. Eliza ignored them, likely pretending they didn't exist for her own sanity as she showed me to the tearoom. I didn't know what I was expecting when Eliza said that she would be at her *baba's* house. But I certainly wasn't expecting the woman in front of me.

She had long aqua hair, the strands thin and shiny. She had it pulled into a loose bun on the top of her head, but it was so long that the last few feet of it hung loose, trickling down her pale shoulders like water over ivory. She was young, looking barely older than Eliza, almost like my best friend's twin, though missing Eliza's signature red hair. Her eyes, a familiar blue, narrowed on me, and I was stuck to the ground, unable to look away as she assessed me.

I might be fucked.

"*Baba*, this is—" Eliza started, but *baba*, or Eternal Ilenia, just raised her hand, silencing Eliza.

A thick power, one that told of age and wisdom, choked me. In some ways, it reminded me of Osiris and how he felt the day of my *Rend,* though much more pointed.

Because Osiris didn't want me scared, not like she did.

"Aaliyah, I'm aware." She clenched her glass, swirling it as she tilted her head, jaw clenched tight. "Sit," she said, leaving no room for argument, and we sank into a couch that felt like it had been sitting there for decades.

The rest of the tearoom was much like the living room, covered in various shells and gifts from the sea. Soft-blue walls accented tan floors. There was only the couch I was on, two other chairs, and a small coffee table that separated me from the most terrifying woman I'd ever met.

Eternal Ilenia continued to stare with that unsettling scrutiny as I rocked side to side, trying desperately to keep the woman's steadfast attention.

This wasn't awkward at all.

Eliza poured us all some tea, shooting me an apologetic glance as she added sugar to her own cup and mine. We sat in silence, sipping tea like we were going to the gallows, when Ilenia finally spoke.

"Stupid girl, involving yourself with the spawn of Death's Butcher." Her words hit my chest like a physical blow. A vacuum, sucking my response out of my chest. "Where's your sense? Those boys are nothing but trouble."

I paused for maybe a second, trying to decide if she really just said that. An irrational anger lit up inside of me, and I clenched my teeth. She could make all the assumptions about me she wanted; she could even say whatever she wanted about *me*.

But she was not about to insult my men.

"*Baba—*" Eliza started, but I stood, cutting her off as I spoke.

"I may not know their Maker ... but I know enough to understand that none of them are like him," I said, trembling as I stared Ilenia down. In fact, I didn't know anything about him, not even his name ... and that was more than enough to tell me he wasn't a good man. "They don't deserve to be called *trouble* by someone who's friends with a man like Archon Sewire."

I didn't care if she was God herself, I wasn't about to allow someone I didn't know insult any of the men that had been nothing but kind to me; who'd let me into their home and kept me safe. Who made me feel like I might have a life to live again.

How dare she accuse them of being anything like the man that even *they* hated.

"Archon is not a friend. He was a tentative ally at best. Rest assured, he's paid for trying to sell my granddaughter." Ilenia's eyes flashed, and my knees quaked under the flood of her *Siren's Call* as it leaked into the air. "And ... no. Cruelty like *his* is hard to match. I'm not saying it to offend, girl. I'm telling you because you need to be careful. Death follows the Vivas name, no matter how much they try to avoid it."

Ilenia didn't cut words nor did she apologize, but there was a calculating worry in them. She stirred her tea, then shook her head.

"That is not why I asked you here, child. I need to know if Osiris plans to Challenge at the Eternium." Her words took me back, and my mouth opened.

Eliza tapped my hand, and I glanced at her. She was worried, her head tilted as she looked back at the couch. I took her direction, sinking into the cushions again, the ache in my legs suddenly taking up all my attention. Standing against Ilenia had been more taxing than my mind realized.

"I don't know ... I don't believe so. Osiris hasn't really mentioned it," I said finally, and Ilenia nodded.

"Osiris is a good enough Vampire ... Tell him I will back him should he decide to." I didn't like her emphasis on Vampire, like it defined him. Not that he was an amazing man who'd saved me; not that he could weave stories for hours.

Vampire. He was a Vampire, and that was all that ever seemed to matter to people. For a while ... it was all that had mattered to me.

How had I ever been that shortsighted?

"You have a long road ahead of you, Aaliyah. One that's going to test your limits, one that will seek to break you." Ilenia's words choked me, and Eliza clenched my hand as my grip tightened on hers. "I hope you're strong enough to make it through, for Eliza's sake."

Sharp eyes that would haunt my dreams seemed to dredge through my soul.

"And for your own."

I was nearly standing again when Eliza sighed.

"Baba—"

Ilenia raised her hand, silencing us both.

"Don't worry, dear granddaughter, I've said my piece."

I ground my teeth, intent on just leaving—consequences be damned—when a familiar voice echoed in the small room. One that I'd been nearly as desperate to hear as I had Eliza's.

"Aunty Ali!" That small voice, with the distinctly twisting 't' made me smile, almost stupid with glee as a small body hit me.

My agitation was forgotten as I pulled Grigen into my arms, holding him close as he laughed, hugging me so hard I felt it in my chest.

"Good to see you, GeGe," I said, laughing when he wiggled to sit more comfortably on my lap.

"I thought you were gone, Aunty! Momma came home without you." Grigen's eyes were full of worry, love brimming in the beautiful aqua. It made my heart melt.

"I'm okay," I said, pressing a kiss to his forehead. "I'm sorry I worried you."

He huffed, making an indigent noise as he pulled back. His tiny face pulled into a scowl.

"It's not okay! I can't protect you if you leave!" he said, exasperated.

His shaggy brown hair swayed, and I reached out, ruffling it. He huffed again, this time arid smoke slipping from his nose.

"Sorry I left without telling you, GeGe. Aunty was finding someone to help her," I whispered.

Grigen bit his lip, looking at his momma. Eliza smiled at her son, reaching out to mess with his hair as I had. He blushed, shaking off his mother's hand and looking up at me, childish innocence making his wide eyes seem even wider.

"You're still sick?" Grigen asked softly, reaching up and pressing a warm hand to my forehead.

His skin was hotter than mine, but I doubted he noticed as he continued his exam, pressing the back of his hand to my cheek next.

Too cute.

"I am, but I found some people who can help," I said, nipping at Grigen's hand, making him giggle again.

"Do you mean the fangs that my daddies were talking to?" My mouth opened in shock, and Eliza let out a choked sound.

"Grigen, don't use that word," Eliza said, covering her eyes as shame leached into her expression. "Remember what we talked about?"

"Yes ... Sorry Momma ..." Grigen whispered, and I grabbed his tiny hand, holding it tightly.

"Adrian and Fallon are two of them, yes. They are good men ... the best," I whispered, smiling.

"Like my daddies? And Prince?" My smile trembled, and I turned, facing the corner where Prince had floated when we walked in.

He flashed me a roguish grin, crows feet at the corners of his eyes. At that familiar look, guilt mixed with the strange joy that I'd slowly become accustomed to. I thought about him a lot last night too. About how much I wished I could hold him like I had Adrian, and I wondered if he felt the same. I hadn't realized what I felt for him was so deep that I would give up everything, even myself, just to feel him for a moment.

"Yes." I turned away, tears making my throat hurt as I kissed Grigen's forehead. "Exactly like them."

Grigen nodded, pacified for a moment, his focus not on my face as I struggled to reign in the onslaught of unexpected sadness.

"Do you have to go back with them?" Grigen asked as he hugged me close.

"Yes, until we can make me better." I tried to explain, hating when Grigen's eyes filled with tears.

"I can go with you, then! I'll make sure they protect you," he said, smoke blowing from his nose, his expression full of confidence.

My strong little dragon.

"Who will protect Momma then, GeGe? You need to help your daddies," I said, and his eyes widened.

He didn't have an answer, just leaned into my embrace. I waited some time for him to speak, and it wasn't long before his breathing leveled out. I rubbed his back gently, holding him close and swaying. I hummed under my breath; the tune coming naturally, one that I recognized as my mother's.

"I can protect you both," he whispered, after a few minutes, the soft lull of sleep in his words followed by a yawn. "I'm strong."

"I know. You're the strongest little man I've ever met."

He didn't respond, and the soft ring of his snore echoed in my ear.

"He's out like a light," Eliza said, humming as she brushed the hair out of his face. "He's been waiting for this for hours. Tuckered himself out."

"I'll take him to his room," Ilenia said, standing.

She was tall, easily as tall as Osiris, and she walked with a dangerous grace. Her green dress swayed, shifting like it was underwater, not affected by such puny laws as gravity. She lifted Grigen from my arms, cooing softly when he sank into her. A softness replaced that sharp edge that had been in her eyes before. She gave me one more long look, staring into my soul like she was picking me apart, before she nodded once, sharply. Then she was gone, and Eliza leaned into the uncomfortable couch cushions with a sigh.

"Well, that went about as terrible as it could have," Eliza said with a laugh, her head shaking in moderate disbelief.

That was an understatement, possibly the biggest one I'd ever heard. It was comical, straining and insane, having to deal with someone like Eternal Ilenia when all I wanted to do was talk about my *love life*. Everything seemed so inconsequential in comparison, and I couldn't hold back anymore.

I laughed too, laughed so hard I cried and my stomach ached. Eliza was right there with me, covering her mouth with a manicured hand. It felt easy, being able to laugh with her again. By the time we calmed down, I was wiping away tears.

"Really? I thought it went quite well," I mused.

"Well, she didn't turn you into soup after you stood up to her chastising, so I suppose that's a plus." Eliza whistled, before she laughed again at my widening eyes. "I'm kidding! *Mostly*." Eliza crossed her legs, leaning into her hands as she stared at me. "Now, why don't you say what you've been wanting to?"

"That easy to see?" I asked, sighing as I pulled my knees to my chest.

"Ali, you're an open book," Eliza said, laughing. "I knew when you called last night that something happened. Something that couldn't be discussed with your hunks of man-meat ... or when they were in the room."

I shook my head as she wiggled her eyebrows, snorting when she blew me a kiss.

"Well ..." I said, rubbing at the back of my neck.

How did I say this without sounding like a complete idiot?

You see, Eliza, remember those Vampires I decided to stay with? I think I may like them more than one would a friend.

"Okay, I can't believe I'm saying this," Eliza said, sighing as she stared at me. "You like one of them, don't you?" To my surprise, she kept her words neutral.

"I don't know," I answered, unsure if that was how I felt.

It sounded right, and the thought made that heat settle in my chest.

"Aaliyah, my dear, sweet, dense sister, I can see it in the way you looked at them earlier, all sickeningly lovey-dovey. You know *so much* that you needed to come talk to me about it."

I sighed again and nodded.

"Now, I'm not going to do anything, but I will say this as a friend. As someone who loves you." Eliza phrased her words carefully, reaching out and grabbing my hand in hers. "Be careful."

"Liz," I started, but she shook her head.

"I don't mean it because they're Vampires, Ali. I'm telling you because you always need to be careful with your heart. You only have one. I don't want you hurting yourself."

I bit my lip and forced the burn of tears down. She always knew what to say.

"So, which one is it?" Eliza asked, a mischievous glint in her eyes as she leaned back against the couch, her red hair bobbing as she did.

"What?" I asked, unsure exactly what she wanted.

She laughed, leaning forward and whispering. "Which one do you want to do the dirty with?" she asked, nearly bouncing off the couch, and laughing when I balked.

"Oh." I stuttered, and my cheeks heated so quickly that I nearly passed out.

It took Eliza one or maybe two seconds before she gasped, squealing like a little girl. "You already *did* the dirty?"

I hissed, covering her mouth with my hands, and she laughed so hard it made my arms vibrate.

"No. *No.*" I stumbled over the words. "We didn't *do the dirty.*"

I hesitated, and I looked Eliza in the eyes, before I took a deep breath.

"But I kissed one."

Eliza squealed again, pulling my hands off her mouth. She looked surprisingly happy for me, considering who we were discussing *doing the dirty with*.

"Which one was it?" she asked, leaning in, whispering the words like it was my darkest secret. She even wiggled her eyebrows again, and I grumbled.

"Wait, wait! Let me guess." She pulled back, finger tapping on her chin. "The tall brooding one? With the wicked tattoo? How was it? Was it rough and needy? Did he make the first move?" she laughed. "What am I saying? Of course he did. That man *screams* alpha male."

If I wasn't blushing before, I was now. I shook my head. Because no ... it wasn't Eirik.

But now I couldn't stop thinking about how it would feel to kiss him. How it would feel if he kissed *me*. That deep rolling voice, whispering my name ... The gentle way he'd hold me. He was so big, and for once the thought of someone towering over me didn't incite fear.

"Really?" Eliza asked, eyes wide, dragging me out of the fantasy that I should *not* be having. "Then who?"

I hesitantly looked at the door. It took Eliza maybe a second before she cursed.

"Oh, it was *not* Mr. Asscicle," she groaned out the words, glaring at the door like the man behind it might burst into flames, and I nearly choked on my tea.

"No, it wasn't Fallon," I said, coughing. "It was Adrian."

I whispered it, the heat on my cheeks drowning me as I glanced at the door, half expecting him to barge in with that wickedly handsome smile on his face. But he didn't, and Eliza hummed contemplatively.

"Hmm. Wasn't expecting that one. Seems too shy."

Shy was *not* a word I'd use to describe Adrian. Especially after last night. He'd been like fire, burning through me, making me question my sanity.

"So, what was it like?"

I shuffled in my seat, suddenly heated by the reminder of my encounter as I looked at my tea.

"It was ... amazing. But I don't know what to make of it. He hasn't said anything, and I don't know how to ask."

She hummed again, tilting her head. "Sounds like he likes you, *looks* like he likes you. Don't know if you've noticed, but the man never takes his eyes off you."

Eliza wore a wistful expression for a moment before she shook her head. She reached out, grabbing my hands in hers.

"As long as he makes you happy, I'll be happy." The sincerity in her voice had me choking up, and I couldn't describe how much her words meant to me.

But they weren't quite right.

"It's not just him, Liz. All of them. I like all of them." The permanent blush burned my face, and I swallowed as Eliza's mouth dropped open. She let go of my hands, sitting ramrod straight.

"All of them? You're kidding. You're *not* kidding." She laughed with disbelief so clear I could see it in her clear aqua eyes. "Are you trying to give me a heart attack?"

"You have two husbands, Liz," I said, defending myself, and she laughed again.

"Two husbands that fought tooth and nail to get me to even consider our arrangement. You have four scorchingly hot Vampires *and* a ghost to contend with," she said matter-of-factly, motioning around the room as she waved her arms in the air.

Prince did his part, flashing me a wink that made my cheeks flame. Lacking his usual smile, I had to swallow down my thoughts. Even without color or a voice to use, it was hard to miss the heat in his eyes.

"You're supposed to be helping," I mumbled and she shook her head, giving me a genuine smile.

"What do you need help with? How to get in their pants? Easy, ask. The two currently talking with Carter and Dezen look like they'd give their undead souls for you to hold their *hand*. They'd give you orgasms for days if you let them, I guarantee it. But, the important thing here is that both parties understand what's happening," Eliza said as I blushed so hard my face hurt. Even the thought of what she said made my temperature spike, not that she noticed, as she sighed, saying something in that old Siren dialect I'd heard her use from time to time. "And if you think your happiness is going to be with them, then go for it. What I think doesn't matter. I'll be here for you no matter what."

I froze at that, focusing on Eliza again.

"You mean that?" I asked, quietly.

I'd been expecting more backlash, knowing Eliza's anger toward Vampires. But she just shrugged, pulling me into a sideways hug.

"Of course, I may hate Vampires, but I can tell they care about you, Ali. Who wouldn't?"

"That's just it, Eliza, I don't know. The only other person I've felt this for is Prince." I looked at him. I had to, even knowing what seeing his face would do to me.

It lit up, that kind of love in his eyes breaking my heart as much as it filled it. Saying it out loud, how I really felt, still caused my chest to ache. I'd told him I loved him in the library, so he had to have known how deep this feeling went for me ... and if not, then it was on the table now, out in the open. I wasn't afraid of rejection, not from him. Even if he didn't feel the same, he was still my Prince.

He would *always* be my Prince.

His lips, trembling as he smiled at me, faltered for only a moment, like if he could cry tears, he would. It only took that one look to realize he loved me, too. I think that hurt more than questioning whether he liked me in that way at all.

"Just talk to them, Ali. They seem to understand that you aren't really used to this kind of thing. The best thing you can do is be honest."

Easy enough to say, but doing it sounded like my worst nightmare. I pulled away, staring at my now clenched hands.

"What if they don't feel the same?" I asked softly, and Eliza groaned.

"Ali, as a friend, they do. God, you can see the sexual tension in the air when they're near you." Eliza rolled her eyes, faking a gag and laughing when I reached out and pushed her. "But if for some unknown reason they say no, then you accept that. You wouldn't want a one-sided relationship anyway."

I nodded, taking in her words and what they would mean for me. I pressed my palms to the couch when Eliza cleared her throat.

"You could always test the waters first," she said, making a little swimming motion with her hand.

I bit my lip, not understanding what she meant.

"What does that mean?" I asked, and she shrugged.

"Watch them, see how they react to you. A brush of the arm, smile charmingly at them. Slam your lips against theirs and take what you want?" Eliza winked. "And see what they do."

I groaned, again flooded with thoughts of what happened in the pool with Adrian.

"I shouldn't have asked."

"It's perfectly reasonable advice. Hell, you've already gotten started, you animal," Eliza finally said, laughing, before wrapping me in another hug.

When she pulled back, she was smiling. Though it didn't last long. She ran a hand over my forehead, brushing the hair out of my eyes when she frowned.

"You okay, Ali? You're looking kind of pale." She pressed her hand to my forehead, and I squinted, confused.

I was tired, maybe hungry. Though I hadn't taken an actual moment to assess how I felt; something I was normally very good about doing. I was achy, and I had a slight headache, one that I hadn't noticed. But it wasn't the pressure of a *Rend*, and I didn't feel like I was about to be forced out of my body again. I glanced around the room out of habit and found Prince to be missing. I frowned, the sting of his absence making my heart hurt though I understood it. He was likely dealing with the same thing I was, the same ache in his chest. My heart went out to him, and I wished with everything that I was, that I could take that pain away.

Or, as Eliza said, 'slam my lips to his and take what I want'.

"Yeah, just tired. Kind of dizzy," I said, reassuring Eliza with a smile as she looped her arm in mine, waking us toward the door.

"Well, regardless, we should call it a day. Don't need you *Rending* again," Eliza said, worry obvious in her tone.

I nodded, leaning on her as we walked.

"Thanks, Liz. For listening," I said, and she beamed at me.

"Always, Ali."

The men were already in the main room when we walked through the doors, and the sight of Fallon greeted me, crouched down in front of a messy-haired Grigen. It was comical, Fallon stone-faced as he listened to Grigen's lispy words that were still hoarse from his rather brief nap, nodding seriously to every one.

"You'll protect her?" Grigen asked, arms crossed over his chest.

He looked just like Carter in that moment, and it made my heart clench when Fallon nodded again, looking nothing like the cold man who'd greeted me those first days with them.

"With my life," he said, such clear conviction in his words that my cheeks flushed.

Adrian must have heard us come in; he turned, flashing me an adoring smile. It was light and wispy as he turned back to Fallon.

"You'll make her smile?" Grigen asked, unrelenting.

Carter and Dezen watched on from the stairs, snickering at their son's antics, but seeming unfazed by his closeness to Fallon. I was glad that they'd seemed to mend their bridges, or at the very least, made them tolerable.

"Every day," Fallon assured, nodding.

"Give her chocolates?" Grigen asked quickly, shaking his finger like he was trying to be 'the boss'.

It was then that Fallon turned to Eliza and I, his forest green eyes catching mine. There was a beat, or maybe two, of silence before a smile lit up his face. Not a smirk or a tilt of the lips, but a full smile. The brash kind, the *winning* kind.

And it took my breath away.

"Always," he said, looking back to Grigen, who nodded, finally realizing we were here.

"Still think they don't have a thing for you?" Eliza whispered so quietly in my ear that I doubted they heard it.

I didn't have time to process as Grigen ran at me, wrapping his small arms around my legs, holding me close. I leaned down, hugging him to me.

"Love you, Aunty Ali," he whispered. "They'll protect you, I made sure."

The conviction in his words finally broke the dam of tears that I'd been holding back, and I held him tighter as I laughed through them.

"Thanks, GeGe. Love you too." I brushed his brown hair back out of his eyes as I stood, and he walked over to Eliza, who happily pulled him into her arms.

"You tell Osiris I'll support him at the Eternium," Ilenia said, moving from her spot by the table, narrowing her eyes on Fallon and Adrian, before she gave them a small smile herself.

It was cold enough to freeze the air in my lungs, but at least it was a smile.

"Thank you, Eternal Ilenia," Adrian said, flashing her a winning smile. "He will happily accept your support."

Then he turned toward me, extending a hand, and I took it, happily watching as his eyes lit up. I tried to look past what I'd thought that expression might be, to believe that there was a chance he felt that same heat in his chest, and I smiled.

"Ready, love?" he asked, and I nodded, stepping closer to him.

"Yeah, let's get home."

CHAPTER 37

PRINCE

I'd grown used to aching for Aaliyah. At first, it was for the young woman who'd faced torture that none should ever have to endure. I grew used to aching over my inability to do anything for her, to help her. Then I grew used to aching to see her smile again, to get her eyes to light up, to get her to say my name. The name she gave me and not the one I spent centuries building a reputation for.

I could've lived the rest of my undying days never hearing that name again, because it didn't matter now. Only she did. And she *loved* me. And Gods above, if I didn't love her too. I loved her with everything I was, everything I had been, and I cursed my cruel fate that I couldn't tell her as much.

That I couldn't ever hold her the way *they* did.

I floated around the upper rooms of Eternal Ilenia's home, only vaguely listening to the words being spoken below. There was no threat, not that I was worried. No one would be stupid enough to attack an Eternal's home while several powerful Naturals were inside. Though I did take a second to make sure I could hear Aaliyah's steady heartbeat.

After last night's scare, I couldn't be too careful. I wasn't sure what had destroyed the wards, but I could guess, and every option that had come to mind seemed worse than the last.

As the others had, I trusted that Osiris had made the right decision, based on the evidence. He could handle a fight, that much I knew.

So long as the other fighter played fair.

I shook my head as I ran a hand across the twisting designs on the wall, the aged paint fluttering from my light influence. I could see much of the seventies spin from the living room branched out on this floor, with swirling rainbow twists and psychedelic designs coating nearly every surface. The age of the house didn't go unnoticed either, smelling of cracking wood and lead paint. It wasn't what I was expecting, not from someone as straight-laced and 'holier than thou' as Ilenia. The Red Witch of the Atlantic wasn't known for her colorful personality, and even when I had been alive, I could barely tolerate her. She probably stole this home off some poor human and just hadn't gotten around to changing the decor yet, likely ate the poor bastard's heart and used his body as fertilizer for her garden. Wouldn't put it past her.

I checked each room, most looking the same as the last with varying degrees of furnishing. It was only when I slipped through an unassuming door at the end of a long hallway that my imaginary heart sped up.

Oh, this was going to be good.

It seemed I'd stumbled on a study, and I was more than happy to snoop. I only wished I could tell someone about whatever I was about to find. I was always one for a little drama. But, alas, my language with Aaliyah was minor, thanks to the near constant experiments those bastards had done on her and my lack of knowledge on sign language. I knew a few basic signs, nowhere near fluent, and I wasn't anywhere as good as Osiris was. Though, even had I been better, I doubted it would have mattered when it was so hard to find time to teach her such things.

Especially when they took to breaking the bones in her hands.

It was moments like these when I was glad to remember the state I'd found Castillion in, though I still wished it could've been me to put him in it.

I clenched my fists, shaking my head as I floated forward and truly looked around. Unlike the rest of the house, the room I stumbled into was a crisp white. In its center was a single desk, with papers neatly placed directly in the middle.

Even the damned pen was straight.

Interesting.

I hovered, looking at the bare walls and the bland bookshelves with several subjects ranging from ocean fauna to a dissertation on salt concentration in the Atlantic. It wasn't until I finally gave in and looked at the files on the white oak desk that a smile truly split across my lips.

You crazy old bat.

I chuckled, skimming a hand over the fresh ink, harsh black scratches over familiar names. I may not have been the biggest fan of Ilenia, but she was good for something.

She knew how to plant the seeds of rebellion.

It helped to settle my nerves, knowing that her intention to back Osiris was a well-founded one. Aaliyah was safe here, even with the old Siren's surly attitude. Appeased enough and calmer than I'd been when I'd left Aaliyah in the foyer, I slipped back through the door. The others were already leaving, Aaliyah's worried expression finding me for a moment before it faded, and her eyes warmed at the sight of me. I smiled widely, like always, before it faltered for a second, mouth already opening to tell her what I'd found. I forgot sometimes that speaking was useless, and that she wouldn't hear me. So instead, I shook my head and carried on.

It ached to not talk to her, and for a brief, selfish second, I allowed myself to consider what it would be like. The smell of lavender that the others spoke of, the brush of gasped breaths, or the feeling of her skin against my palms as I learned every inch of her.

And like always, that feeling died in the empty expanse of my chest and I continued to smile through it all. Because at the end of the day, it didn't matter.

The only thing that mattered was her. She *loved* me.

And that was enough.

Chapter 38

Aaliyah

"You feeling okay, love?" Adrian asked as he helped me out of the car, his steadying hand pressed comfortingly to the small of my back.

Before I had time to process it, he had me in his arms and into the house that had quickly become my home. Adrian set me gently on my feet by the island in the kitchen, only pulling back enough to run a hand over my forehead.

His cool skin helped to settle the ache I felt, the flush of my skin becoming even more noticeable. The dizziness had started at Eliza's just before we left, and it had only gotten worse. The tugging feeling of dread that I'd felt about the rather odd ache only added to my already flighty emotions.

One thing after another, it was like I couldn't catch a break. Nausea swallowed my words, and my eyes fell closed. All I really wanted to do was sleep, and that alone kept me from heading toward the stairs.

I was fine; I had to be.

Adrian's fingers lightly tapped at my cheek, and I opened my eyes again, catching his dazzling smile.

"Yeah, just dizzy," I said, brushing it off along with the sourness of my lie, before I reached up, running a hand over soft his copper hair, pushing it back out of his eyes. It was such an effortless move that I barely registered how strange it was for me.

To just touch him, to *want* to touch him.

His eyes crinkled at the corners as he smiled, his windblown hair glowing under the soft white lights of the kitchen. He grabbed my hand after a few seconds, his smile turning sinful as he kissed the inside of my wrist.

A shiver raced across my nerves, and I couldn't stop myself from looking at his smooth lips. They looked so firm, their defiant tilt defined as his tongue shot across them. But I knew differently.

Soft. They were soft.

"Not as soft as yours." A whisper, one that felt like it was screamed into my ear as heat exploded, and I trembled again.

Was now a good time to talk about what had happened at the pool? It didn't seem like it, with everything that was going on, still ... I looked closer, trying to catch an idea of what Adrian was really feeling past the playful trickster that I'd come to adore. But affection wasn't what I noticed, as the paleness to his skin really became pronounced. That dark undertone of his iris stood strong against the bags under his eyes, and the heat that burned in me was smothered out.

I frowned and took a step toward him.

"You're not looking the best either, Adrian. Are you sure you're alright?" I asked, carefully pressing my hand to the darker skin.

He kissed my wrist again slowly, like he was savoring the moment, before he pulled back.

"Absolutely. Just haven't fed today is all," he said, laughing it off just as I had.

But I didn't like the tension that was so clear in his shoulders, a tension I hadn't been paying attention to. It reminded me of the pool, when he'd rushed off ... because of a headache?

Was it the same now? Did he still feel sick?

I frowned, pressing my palms to his cheeks. His lips tilted at the corners, amusement smothering the pain in his eyes as he pressed both of his chilled hands over mine.

"Hey, don't worry. I'm fine, I promise." From his sigh, Adrian knew I still wasn't convinced. "Here. I'll grab something now. Why don't you go see what Eirik is up to? He's just in the training room. Something tells me he's missed you," he said knowingly, as he ran his thumbs over the top of my hands before pulling them away from him.

He raised them up, kissing each one slowly. The move sparked heat where his lips lingered, and my own tingled again.

"Really?" I asked, cautiously, and he nodded with a smile.

"Absolutely. I know I would." Some of the strain in my chest lessened, and the question that had been on my mind almost came out.

But Adrian didn't give me a chance, winking comically fast as he pulled back the rest of the way. I hated to see his acting, to see him straining to not look tired for me. But I didn't say anything else, just forced my own smile before I turned. I would let it go this time ... it was only fair considering I wasn't being as truthful as I could either. But if he wasn't better the next time I saw him, I wasn't going to let him just run away.

I turned, knowing that if I looked back, Adrian would already be gone. I knocked at the training room door before peeking inside.

"Eirik?" I asked, smiling slightly as I stepped inside the large open space.

There were several pieces of equipment sprawled about. I didn't know what most of them were for, but I figured each had its purpose there. Most of the room was white, contrasting the gray of the house. Moonlight trickled through the wall of windows at the far side of the room. They stretched across the entire surface, and I loved the look it gave.

Eirik had his back toward me, sitting on a small blue pad in the center of the floor. It was hard to miss the tension in his exposed skin, as the dark ink that lined his frame moved harshly with every hard breath. He took one more, like he was breathing in the room, which smelled distinctly of sweat and power. As quickly as I'd seen it, his shoulders lost their strain.

He turned toward me, his sky-blue eyes tracing me from head to toe. The intensity of his stare sent a shiver down my spine, and I struggled to stay still. I didn't miss the spark of the wolf behind his eyes as it watched me too.

"How was your visit?" he asked.

He didn't move from his spot on the floor as his eyes slid closed again, and he turned back around. I walked forward, sitting in front of him, crossing my legs under myself as he had. The mat he was on was warm, and with the moon to my back, a soft shadow was cast along Eirik's tanned skin.

"Good. Grigen gave Fallon and Adrian a good talking to." I laughed as I remembered the proud look on Grigen's face.

And Fallon's responses.

I smiled at that, my chest so full of warmth that it felt like it might consume me.

"It go alright?" Eirik asked, keeping his eyes closed.

His palms were sitting against the tops of his thighs. Well, less sitting and more pressing. The tension in his shoulders must have moved, as his fingers pressed so tightly against the muscle there were indents. His chest heaved in an even, steady breath.

"Yeah, no problems," I said, taking a rare moment to study him.

It was hard to get a good look at any of them, considering that they were *always* looking at me. Firm jaw covered in a trimmed dirty blond beard. The twisting ink across the left half of his face, a dragon crawling to reach the gem that was his eye. That same ink crawled along his arms, up his sides, fitting him like a second skin. Arms that were easily as thick as my head, a body that was built to intimidate. But that wasn't what I felt, even though something in me told me I should. No, a familiar heat tickled my stomach, and the space between my legs ached.

Eirik huffed a breath, a low growl echoing against the glass windows. It was different from normal, not quite a purr but not angry either. I hummed back, tracing down the corded muscle on his chest, across his defined abdomen ... the smooth skin tensed and I wanted to reach forward, and see if it was as hard as it looked.

"Good," Eirik bit out past thinned lips, that same growl sticking to his words.

The tension that had been clinging to him was back in full now, his head tipping left and right as he tried to release it. He was obviously doing something important. Was I distracting him? I fidgeted for a moment before pressing down on the mat to stand. I didn't make it very far as a hand shot out, grabbing my wrist. The familiar sharp jolt of pleasure that came with touching one of the guys nearly brought me to my knees.

"Stay." The hoarseness of the word told me it wasn't just him speaking, and I bit my lip.

His eyes slid open, the sky-blue now a rolling royal. It happened sometimes, and I now realized that it was likely his wolf coming close to the surface. Like Carter and his dragon. It was intense, like a different man was sitting in front of me, but it didn't scare me. I knew in my soul that the beast behind the eyes of this man wouldn't hurt me.

So I sank back down, and Eirik's eyes fell closed again. Though he didn't let go of my hand.

"What are you doing?" I asked, watching as his hand loosened before sliding down my arm. When he reached my fingers, he twined ours together.

"Meditating," he said, settling back down, and the pose he took up suddenly clicked.

"Why?" I asked, and shifted, sinking further into the seated position.

"To focus," he replied, cracking an eye open, tracing where I sat before he closed his eyes again.

"Meditating requires silence, right? I'm probably not helping," I said, laughing as I realized I was making *more* noise.

Eirik didn't seem to mind, shaking his head.

"This is the only time my wolf has been calm all evening," he mumbled, heat lacing his words.

Adrian's words from earlier came back to me: that Eirik had likely missed me, and I blushed.

"Stay. Meditating centers you. Might help with keeping your soul in check."

I hummed, but nodded. It wouldn't hurt to try. I looked at Eirik's stoic face again and settled in. There was a calmness about him that I was drawn to, one that helped to center me after the insanity that was my meeting with Eliza.

A chill, unnatural to anyone but me, filled the room just as I was getting ready to close my eyes. I smiled softly, glancing at Prince as he strode through the closed door. His lip tilted in a Cheshire smirk when he saw what we were doing. Settling by the door, he crossed one leg slightly over the other before dragging his hand over his face and closing his eyes. When he opened them again, he pointed to Eirik, stuck one hand out and brought the other down in a chopping motion.

Eirik is bad at meditating. I think that's what he was trying to say. When I looked at Eirik's knitted brow, I couldn't help but laugh.

Turned out I wasn't good at meditating either.

"No offense, but this doesn't seem like something you'd do," I whispered, smiling when Eirik's lip twitched.

"Learned it from Nero, been doing it ever since ... but you're right, I've never been much good at it," he said, a calm tone to his words that wasn't normally apparent when he spoke of Nero.

It was soft, like the idea of his brother didn't torture him, and that thought made me smile. I wanted to know about him, about the stunning man that had been such a big part of these men's lives. So, I took a deep breath in, setting my palms on my thighs as Eirik had, before I closed my eyes.

Heat bled from Eirik's large frame, his knees brushing mine. It was hard to ignore him, ignore his touch and the soft breaths he let out. I shifted my legs, trying to gain a touch of distance and I only managed to bring us closer. My hands tensed around my thighs, and I bit my lip just when Eirik smirked.

"You're fidgeting," Eirik said, shaking his head with an amused half grin. One I caught as I sighed and opened my eyes again.

"Sorry," I said, again trying to settle into the position that he had.

He surprised me as he moved, scooting a little closer until he was so near that I could feel the rumbling purr where our skin met. I shifted in place, eyes locked on the span of his legs, which was easily twice mine. He leaned forward, pressing one of his hands to my chest as I again realized how large he was. Thumb against one shoulder, fingers up by the other side of my neck. He carried it well, all of that muscle proportioned perfectly on his tall frame, a powerful kind of grace making him seem almost godly. He looked graceful, deadly, and *beautiful* all at the same time.

His heat seeped into my skin, and sparks of sporadic pleasure crept their way into me from his touch. It did with all of them, but after so much time around them, it was dulling from the surprising jolt it had been.

Now it was just warm, like my soul found comfort in theirs.

"Breathe. Feel it here," Eirik said, running his thumb over my collarbone, his fingers jumping against my skin when my heart thudded against his palm.

Look at him. I tried, I *really* tried. His eyes, that scorching blue that made heat settle between my legs, pinning me in place and rolling like waves. The tick of his jaw and how he breathed.

The thin line of his lips.

"Let that feeling move, focus on it, on how you feel and what you can smell, hear," he said, and I took an unsteady breath.

All I could sense was him, the soft scent of the sea that always told me he was near, the heat of his hand against my skin, the spark that lit up my nerves and made me want to lean forward and seal our mouths together.

Do it. Or ask him to do it. Do. Literally. Anything.

"Well?" he asked, a hoarseness to his voice.

There was emotion there, but what was it? *Was it affection? Love? Adoration?* I couldn't decide, too tied up with what I could sense, that I couldn't focus on what I needed. So I didn't. Didn't lean forward like everything in me was screaming to do, didn't try to find that want in the heat of his skin.

"Salt, fresh cut wood," I said, listing the scents that made Eirik him. "Your heart ... I can feel it against my chest, and I can hear you breathing."

Eirik's hand twitched against me, his gaze so heavy that the black of his pupils had nearly swallowed the blue. I shivered again, feeling like I was being hunted by the beast behind them.

"What else?" he asked, leaning in so close I could feel breath against my cheeks.

I swallowed hard, trying to find the words to describe it. I closed my eyes. I could feel *everything*.

And like it clicked into place, a chill shot down my spine. The soft scent that was Eirik faded away, and a smell that I could only describe as molten steel burned in my nose. Eirik's hand seared against my chest, like shoving a limb in snow and holding it there, but more pointed. Everywhere where there had been heat was now solid ice, and as the dark of the room closed in, I realized I was freezing too. The dark moved and ebbed around me, swallowing an unmoving Eirik until that dark hue was all I could see.

"Eirik?" I whispered.

"What?" he asked back, his voice echoing around me, sounding like it was right in my ear and yet miles away.

Confusion muddled the heat that was still in his words. I couldn't feel the beat of his heart against my palm, couldn't feel the warmth of his skin. I opened my eyes and met the silver room that had spelled my death.

"Not again," I gasped, slamming my eyes closed. "Please, *please* not again," I said, barely able to speak as I choked on tears that burned my cheeks.

Did this force a *Rend*? I couldn't breathe, couldn't get any more sound out as I trembled. Something shook me, but I couldn't look at it, couldn't risk seeing the room that could be my death one day.

One day soon, if my soul had anything to do with it.

"Open your eyes." Someone whispered those words, their breath like a freezing wind on my skin

Who was that?

Hands gripped my shoulders, digging in enough to feel the pressure of them. The dark morphed, shifting like an angry beast, strangling me.

"It's closing in." I gasped, trembling. I kept my eyes closed, refusing to drag them open, too scared of what I would find. "Please."

"*Elsken,*" the voice hissed into my ear.

Rough words, ones spoken in a language I didn't know, by a voice that breathed familiarity into my lungs.

"I can't breathe," I said, gasping.

The hands tightened again and I was shuffled, my chill driven away by the searing heat of whatever I was now pressed against. Still, the Void didn't let me go. It begged, pleaded against my mind for me to open my eyes ... like the brush of a gentle hand, and the pressing feeling of something that I *needed* to know. Not a memory, or even a thought that was my own. It was a presence, a word that had no place or meaning. I ached to push it away, just as I let it slip into my mind.

Bog. A whisper, one that was both shapeless and endlessly loud.

"Aaliyah, open your eyes!" The voice snapped into place.

Eirik.

Panic laced the sound of my name on his lips. It was enough to drag my eyes open, and I was face-to-face with Eirik. I was sprawled across his lap, his heart thundering under my ear that was pressed to his chest. His hands traveled over my face desperately as he finally caught my gaze. A strangled noise caught in his throat and he pulled me so tightly against him he was all I could feel, holding me so close that I couldn't move.

"I've got you," he whispered, and I couldn't respond.

I just looked around the room as much as I could, focusing on the walls, on the shadows that surrounded us. All I could see was the silver, the endless abyss that would claim me one day.

Prince flashed, worry brimming in the air as he flexed his hands. It was the last straw, and I let out a shuddering breath, clinging to Eirik as tears struggled past my burning eyes.

Please, no ... please let this be a dream.

I wasn't sure exactly how it happened, but sometime between the start of my extremely dignified crying session against Eirik's broad chest, and right now, I'd ended up in Eirik's room.

Eirik's room was the definition of rustic. Deep-reds clashed with soft brown pelts, each piece adding to the comforting feeling that reminded me of tea on a wintry day. It was crowded; bits and bobbles strewn about in an order that made sense to no one but him. I'd been curious what their rooms would look like.

I just hadn't expected this would be how I ended up in one.

I sniffled against his chest, grimacing at the cool feeling of wet skin. Panicked didn't quite express what I felt, and I could barely string together a few words after my trip to the Void.

Bog. What could it mean?

Eirik hummed softly, the tone light and airy, with a sense of familiarity to it. It only took a few verses to realize I *had* heard it before.

"You sang that to me," I whispered, the words coming out cracked and broken. His rolling words paused, and my hands balled into fists. "The day I died."

Eirik shuddered so hard it jolted me, and in my haze, I realized the cruelty of my words.

Death wasn't new to me. It hadn't been since I crawled out of the ground. But Eirik had only just seen it, and he was still coming to terms with the fact that my days were likely limited if we didn't find answers soon. It made me ache in a way I hadn't in weeks. I'd come to terms with death ... but the thought of leaving them behind soured my stomach and made tears rise again.

"My mother used to sing it to me when I was a boy." Eirik's words bounced around the room, and he pulled me a little tighter to him. His beast flexed as I opened my hands, pressing my palms against his warm chest. The tightness of his skin gave him away, just as a rumbling purr filled the space instead. "Warded off bad spirits."

"It's pretty," I mumbled, and the brush of Eirik's beard bouncing against my head told me he found amusement in my answer.

"Never been called pretty before," he said, his warm breath making me wiggle in his arms.

"I said the song was pretty," I said, daring a glance up. "You're rather ..."

How could I describe him? Were there even words that would be enough?

"Brutish?" Eirik said gruffly, and I frowned. "Beastly?" he added, the hand that had been rubbing slow circles on my back going still. His lips twisted in a grimace, and I reached up just as he spoke his last word. "Monstrous?"

I set my palm against his cheek, running a thumb across the scar that stretched across his face. It was harsh, brutal. But it was never what I noticed first when I saw him.

No, it was always his eyes.

"I was going to say handsome," I whispered before I could trick myself into staying silent.

I let out a breath, one that seemed trapped in my throat. That must have shocked him, as Eirik's eyes went wide and the gnarled grimace morphed into a confused stare. The sky-blue depths I'd grown to love swirled and darkened as the skin around his nose and lips tightened. The rumbling purr began again, and I sank into his embrace. When he spoke again, it wasn't Eirik's voice I heard, nor was it a word I could comprehend.

He went quiet for a moment after that, only the rumbling purr to fill the space.

"There are no words to describe what you are, *smár Valkyrja*," Eirik said, after a few seconds more of silence. The words sounded like they'd spilled from the maw of a beast, twisted and forced, each syllable sharp as a polished blade. "The best this one can find is ethereal."

I shivered and tilted my head to the side, Eirik following the move-ment as he did the same. It was a fluid motion, his pupils blown wide as his attention never lingered from me.

"This one? What do you mean?" I asked, startled by the return of Eirik's purr. It was louder than it had been, making my entire body vibrate.

He paused for a moment, head dipping to the side in a way that could only be described as animal. Then he smiled, with his teeth on full display in a breathtakingly roguish grin.

"This one ... the beast."

The beast. I held myself steady against Eirik's chest. Some part of my mind told me I should be terrified, or at the very least questioning my sanity given that I wasn't. Instead, I was curious.

"Are you not Eirik?" I asked softly, and warm familiar arms tight-ened around me, pulling me to a chest that smelled like the sea.

"I am the beast ... *Úlfheðinn*." His words were clipped, like the answer was obvious. He ran his nose over my temple in an easy motion, puffs of warm breath tickling me. "*We* are Eirik."

It took a second to process before it really clicked into place. They were two separate beings making up one body. It was strange, though not entirely surprising the more I thought about it. Carter used to speak of his dragon like it was another person, and I'd never made the connec-tion that it really was.

Eirik hummed, content to hold me.

"You are safe with this one, always." His hand rubbed at my back again, soothing me.

The warmth of his hand spread across my skin, and I sighed at the feel of it. That rumble began in his chest again, the one that shook me to my core and calmed me just as thoroughly. Though it wasn't quite enough to completely dissipate the panic from the training room. My hand shook as I pressed it against his bare chest. The rumble slowed.

"I know," I whispered back instead, and the beast chuckled again.

Eirik held me tighter for a moment. My conscience taunted me, saying that I should be scared, yet I couldn't find the will to be, or a reason. Not when I had so many other things to deal with, not when I knew that Eirik, the man, would never hurt me.

I trusted Eirik, and by extension I now trusted his wolf.

But that didn't mean I trusted myself, or the Void that still sought to swallow me. A sickening feeling of dread threaded with the nerves in my stomach, one that told me this wasn't over, that what had happened in the training room was the least of my worries. I almost opened my mouth to tell him what I'd heard, but for once, I held it back.

I needed a few minutes of peace, a few seconds to rebuild my walls, and then I would ask him if he had any idea what it could mean.

"He fights to get back to you," Eirik muttered sorrowfully, pulling me out of my thoughts. He growled, but didn't seem too upset as he started his purr again shortly after.

The ache from the training room and the numbness from my tears finally caught up with me, and I closed my eyes again.

"Rest now. We will keep you safe."

I tried to believe him, but that gnawing feeling didn't leave. I knew now to trust my instincts, and something was telling me to be wary, to be scared. The word from the Void echoed again, and I remembered the crispness of urgency that it had carried.

Bog.

It was important ... it had to be. The problem was, I had no idea how it would help us, or if it even could. I could only hope that Osiris got the wards back up before it was too late.

Before whatever was coming got to us.

CHAPTER 39

OSIRIS

I picked at the ivory keys of our piano, just light enough to indent, yet not make a sound. They mocked me with how they bounced back, and when I looked down, it wasn't my hands I saw. No, like always it was Nero's bruised knuckles that glared back at me, speckled with blood and moving over the keys like a dancer gracefully pirouetting.

How many times had I done this same thing? Sat at our grand piano and thought of every song that Nero and I had played? More than I could count in one lifetime, it seemed. I continued to hear each one and continued to pick out his laugh among the odd noises that an old house made.

The soft click of our front door opening, then closing, echoed softly. Nero's scarred hands faded from view, leaving me seated alone by the silent, dusty piano. It only took a second to decipher who had come home, the tapping of a hand against our kitchen cabinets giving Adrian away.

I nodded to no one, reaching up to touch the ward that was settled in my breast pocket. My eyes were heavy with fatigue, and the ache of day sickness still sank into my bones, but I was content knowing that it was worth it. The ward was done, and now all I needed to do was place it.

Giving the piano one last glance, I stood, lowering the key cover, letting the click of it follow me as I *flitted* downstairs to where Adrian was. He was crouched behind the island in the middle of the kitchen with one hand settled on the marble black top as he searched the wines in the small freezer hidden there, only peeking over to whisper a greeting.

I nodded back, moving to stand near the front door as he cursed, bottles clinking as he shuffled through the selection that felt more abysmal every day.

"Where's Aaliyah?" I asked as Adrian grunted and peaked over the counter again.

His eyes, dim even in the sharp lights of the kitchen, were sunken, and at that moment he looked like he was a human lacking sleep. The dark rings under them only accented the noticeably pale tint to his skin.

"Upstairs with Eirik," Adrian said, sighing as he finally pulled out a bottle. A chardonnay with Nymph. The sight of it made my gums ache just as the faint taste of ash slid over my tongue. "She meditated with him today. Last I saw, he was carrying her upstairs, trying to get her to stop crying."

I hadn't heard it, hadn't even thought to listen for the dual heartbeats that now seemed to thunder in my ears. Adrian wasted no time in pouring two glasses, walking over and handing me one. He grimaced as he downed his in one go. The faint taste of ash became overwhelming, and I had to do the same to stop myself from gagging. We needed something from the vein, badly.

"What happened?" I asked, setting the glass on our counter, using my pinky as a cushion for the bottom so the sound wouldn't echo.

"Don't know. But she was shaken up. Whispering about that night ..." Adrian said, wincing. "When she died."

He shook his head once, twice, then tipped it toward the stairs as he tried to catch any conversation. But there was none, only the echo of two heartbeats, so close to each other that they beat in tandem. Jealousy wasn't a feeling that I felt often, or one that I had ever paid much mind to. I didn't crave touch, could barely stand it enough to feed. And yet still my thoughts strayed where they had no right to be.

Would Aaliyah mind that the only warmth in my skin would come from her?

"Fallon?" I asked, pulling my hand back to my side, tugging at my cuff to hide the skin—and the brand—that suddenly burned.

"Ran off to town, not sure what he needed. Was just gone," Adrian groaned out, irritation clear in his words as he rubbed at his face. "You know him. Probably just needed to find someone stupid enough to fight him."

I nodded and continued my path out the door, feeling a similar need to get away, if only for a moment.

"Where are you going?" Adrian asked, and I almost didn't respond.

It was the vulnerability in his words that had me turning back. His copper eyes were innocent, reminding me he was just a youngling, that I had thousands of years of experience over him. I sometimes forgot he hadn't been around in the days of old, that he'd only lived this existence for a mere century. That he hadn't even been introduced formally to the rest of the Natural community. He didn't know what we were before, and it was clear to see as he looked at me for advice that I didn't have to give.

"To fix our wards," I said, not giving him a chance to respond as I turned away, guilt burning my words away as I closed the door softly behind me.

Some elder I was. Adrian looked to me for help, for anything, and the best I could give was sharp words and a closing door.

I walked for about fifteen minutes to the edge of our property, listening to the crack of leaves and the rustle of wildlife that was brave enough to stay outside with me near. I hadn't lied to Adrian, though it hadn't been the full truth either. I had made a new charm, and the weary magic that I had neglected over my immortal life ached even now, like a muscle that wasn't used to being trained. As far as I was concerned, that magic died with me when I turned. I didn't like to remember what it represented.

I only used it when it was necessary for our safety. Or, more recently, for Aaliyah's. I wished it was just that much, that I only wished to provide her protection, and not for her to gift me one of those small smiles, the ones that reached her eyes and allowed her soul to shine through them.

Lux mea.

I pushed past the ache and clutched the small pendant in my pocket. We *needed* our ward replaced, and this was where I planned to put it. But it wasn't all I was doing, and it wasn't our ward house I ended up in front of.

Laid out in one of the few clearings on our property were four unassuming flat stones, each meticulously placed and well maintained. Though their age was starting to show, with hairline cracks peeking through the meticulous finish and the once pointed edges dulled with time. Only one of them had recognizable markings, though that was a conscious choice. I reached out, brushing a hand against the familiar marble before taking a seat next to it. This spot, with all its speckled gravestones, was far more important than the surrounding woods let on. It had been where Nero had first landed in the country, where he planted our roots. Though our home's final location had moved, this spot would always be his.

His gravestone said as much.

I sat, and leaned against it. It was cold enough for me to recognize the chill as it spread down my arms, not unlike the snow that fell from the deep gray sky. I only took a second to glance at the other stones, the markers for Sebek's original three. Our other brothers, the ones that had been lost before my turn. I didn't feel the same dragging need to visit them as I did Nero, but I liked to keep their memory alive, even if their names and bodies were lost in time. Even Nero's wasn't here; instead in Rome, in the Familial crypt with the empty coffins of the others.

But it *felt* like he was here, scowling at my decisions, telling me to pull my head out of my ass and stop overthinking everything. I flexed my hands, fingertips scraping the ground, hard enough to stop me from reaching for the cuffs of my shirt. I could hear him now.

Maybe if you actually fucking talked *to her, you wouldn't feel this bad.*

"Though you wouldn't have used so many words," I mused, leaning back, sinking to the ground and staring up at the stars. The words settled in the back of my throat, the ache so sharp it burned my tongue. "Could use your level head and sharp wit right now, Nero. Could use your advice."

No response. No curling of a crooked smile or a raised eyebrow to meet me. I pressed my palm to the ground, closing my eyes. For a moment, it almost felt like the answer I was looking for was going to appear in the air, whispered from between dead lips. I would open my eyes, and Nero would be there.

But he never was. That didn't stop me from searching the woods for him.

"I can't stop asking myself what you would do, can't stop seeing you where you *should* be. It's driving me mad," I admitted, finally saying the words out loud.

They burned like I expected, searing my lungs and dragging pain to the surface. It had been there since the last day I had seen our brother alive, and skating around it had become commonplace. But my time with Aaliyah had brought it up again, forcing the thoughts to remain, no matter how fiercely I shoved them down. She wanted to know about him, about his feats and his life. I had seen the glow in her eyes at the bonfire, the joy that not only she held, but the rest of my brothers as well. They wanted to remember Nero how he was, how he *should* be remembered, his life full of adventure and crass joy.

A life that I drew short.

"You were a gladiator. You spat in the eyes of kings and laughed when they sputtered and raged." The crisp air turned frigid. "If I had thought for even a second that you couldn't handle it ... if I had just trusted your word over my own perceptions. Then, maybe ... maybe—"

I couldn't finish the thought, couldn't voice out loud what had been a weight in my chest. Because saying it would make it more real than I was willing to accept, even after a hundred years of denial...

Then maybe you wouldn't have died.

My hands ached, clenched so tightly that my joints protested, and a sharp burst of cold shot from my shoulder down my spine. Seemed even the weather was out to ruin my mood. I shook my head, patting the stone, brushing off some of the stray snow that had clumped on top.

"*Te desum*, brother." The whisper of Latin, his mother tongue, was too much to bear.

"Osiris." The familiar detached tone of Fallon's voice cracked at my name, shocking me, and I glanced at him from my spot on the ground.

He looked almost rabid, with his jaw clenched in a way that reminded me of Eirik before a shift. Green eyes were still sharp with the adrenaline that came with a good fight, and blotches of red splattered across his crisp, white suit. That alone was shocking, considering his distaste for blood stains. His knuckles were still mending, with flecks of bone that were not his own falling to the ground like hail.

It was when he was like this, just after a brawl, that I saw Nero in him. Saw that he was more than just animated ice.

"What?" I asked, canting my head toward him as my hand slid off the cold marble.

The dead leaves and twigs that littered the ground from the lingering fall bit into my skin, and it only took one look at me to realize how disheveled I was. Fallon gawked at me like one would a caged animal: with pity in his eyes. With surprise. I bit my tongue and nodded for him to say whatever had dragged him out here.

"I can see you're having a moment, or whatever the fuck you're doing ... but you need to come home," he said, glancing over his shoulder. Panic didn't suit Fallon, tension wasn't made for the way that he held himself, yet he looked no less terrified than a pig being led to slaughter. "Some psycho Sorceri showed up just after I got back, just appeared out of thin fucking air ... She's inside with Adrian."

He paused, and the closest I'd ever seen to genuine fear crept into the brawler's eyes as he flexed his hand, blood pooling in the open wounds and dripping down his fingers, painting the snow red.

It took longer than it should have, for me to realize what he was saying. My mind scrambled and my insides revolting. Sebek's words the night of Nero's death, cold even for him, echoed in my mind now.

Losing one's sense is a weakness. Mourning is a weakness. Do you really need another lesson so soon, Usire?

I lost Nero, a piece of my soul ... He lost only the time it took him to come to the states and deal with our grief.

"Osiris, we don't have time for this. She said she won't leave till she talks to you."

Fallon's words were quiet, like they echoed down a long hallway. It was too raw, burned too deep. And now someone was here, someone that wasn't meant to be. I took a deep breath, half expecting Sebek's sour scent of death, even with Fallon's words that our intruder was a Sorceri. Instead, I choked on the harsh scents of sulfur and brimstone. Dark magic. *Old* magic. My mind went to the broken ward, the one that I came out here to replace. And to the creeping thought that I hadn't even dared to consider as the truth, when we had first been told of the destruction.

And it all made sense.

"Kali Rourovic," I said, before Fallon could even open his mouth.

Kali Rourovic was in my home. In *my* home, around my brothers. *Aaliyah was there.*

I gripped my cuff, pulling so hard that the fabric tore as rancid bile rose up my throat, but the ripping of threads barely registered in my mind, and for the first time, the bloodlust I felt for the vile woman won over the fear that she brought. I clenched my jaw, suppressing every emotion but rage as I stood and brushed myself off.

My old master's lover: the one who had made me understand the meaning of hopelessness. She always had been good at exploiting weakness, and it figured she would find her way here when everything felt so broken.

And now she was in my home and none of my brothers knew the danger they were in. Rancid regret and guilt swallowed my words as I rolled my neck, forcing a looseness that I didn't feel. This was my fault, my doing. I had been distracted by Aaliyah, by Sebek ... by my own want to fade away from the world.

In doing so, I had done exactly what I'd promised I never would again. I had allowed death into our home. She broke our wards, and I turned a blind eye, begging for it to be anyone else so desperately that my mind made it true. Kali was a monster of monsters. I knew as much, because she'd taught me as much.

I reached into my pocket, fingers wrapping around a familiar charm. The ward was cold in my hand and the subtle pull of protection magic pooled at my fingertips. I traced a simple circle in the air, the charm glowing a bright blue. I looked down at the grave that would forever haunt me before reaching out and placing the ward on top. It was a slow build, the magic sluggish in its movements as it spread across our land, hitting our borders as I had made it to. The effect was immediate, and my thought was confirmed with the brush of blood magic against my barrier *from the inside.*

I moved past Fallon, the trailing of his steps behind me heavy and tense. This was going to deserve an explanation I wasn't prepared or willing to share, but it could wait until after we got Kali away from our home, away from Aaliyah. She didn't know who had just walked through the door. No one but Eirik did ... Another mistake on my part, one that left us all open to attack, open to the same fate as Nero. I cursed myself again, moving faster.

The Sorceri Eternal had come to visit.

To be continued ...

NEED MORE TO SINK YOUR TEETH INTO?

Then come and join my newsletter! You'll get exclusive chapters about how the guys found and built their home. Along with this, you can expect to be the first to hear about all things book related. Including being the first to see cover reveals, exclusive commissioned art, and new ideas in the works!

You can find the sign up on my website!: krrainbolt.com

Still craving more? Then stick around for a brief look at the second book in the Ascension Rising Series, Of Lavender and Ash. See you all soon!

Of Lavender and Ash

Book 2 of the Ascension Rising Series
Out Now!

What would you do to live?

The Eternium ball grows ever closer, and with it, comes old foes that threaten to shatter the already strained bond of the Vivas Crypt. Now, I'm left stumbling with a whole new set of problems, each more complex than the last.

Ascension Rising, the ones responsible for years of torture, is looking for me, and there's no telling what they'll do when they find me or how they'll punish me for escaping them.

My growing attraction to the Vampires who saved me, and the ever present reality that death is only one Rend away, drive us forward. We need to figure out what I am and find a way to survive the Eternium all in one breath. It will be a miracle if we all make it out alive.

And if I've learned anything ... ***it's that miracles don't happen to me.***

A Note for You, Dear Reader

If you've made it this far, then this is for you, dear reader. Thank you for jumping into this story and enjoying the twists and turns that Ali and the guys' adventure has taken so far. I hope, for a while at least, I gave you some place new and exciting to explore, and I can't say how excited I am to continue this series and this experience with you. You could have picked any other book to read, yet you chose this one! Being a debut author, with this being my first of hopefully many book babies, I'll forever be thankful that you took the dive.

Thank you for being you.

That being said, it would mean the world to me if you could take a second to leave a review on this book's Amazon or Goodreads page. Reviews are like lifeblood for many indie authors, me included, and your support—with even just a sentence—would help me leaps and bounds.

Thank you so very much for your support, I couldn't do this without you guys!

Acknowledgments

I've mulled over exactly how to put this for ages, and at the end of the day, I've decided that at the top of this list should be you, my lovely reader. Your support means everything to me, know that this book is only possible because of you. I've always wanted to share my stories, and I'll forever be thankful that you've taken a chance on me and picked up this book. From the bottom of my heart, *thank you.*

Okay, now I'm crying, moving on ...

Momma. You have been in my corner since forever, and I want you to know that this book wouldn't be around without you. You've supported me through everything. Getting my degree, moving across the country, and now this. You are the foundation of who I am, and I am so thankful for you every day. Love you forever, Momma.

Sara, my bestest buddy and partner in crime. You know I couldn't very well include this in here and not put you down! You have been by my side for years (and years, and years ...) and your constant support has been legendary. Thank you for always listening while I babble on about the same thing for hours. Thank you for picking me up when I'm down. Most of all, thank you for being you. Love you bestest buddy, couldn't have done this without you!! And don't think I misspelled your name... Sarah!

Henley, my very first fan, and one of my absolutely best friends. You were the first to read this book when it was just a whiff of an idea that didn't even have Prince in it yet (shocking; I know). You've been by my side through every change (and several re-readings), and you have no idea how much I appreciate that. Now that this is finally published I owe you all the Applebees, and a huge hug, as this book wouldn't exist without you. You were the first one to read it, and the first one to tell me

I had to finish it. Thank you for standing by my side, my dude. I'll never forget that. I don't say it enough, but I love you, lovely!

Gisele, my first beta. Though you started out as a beta, you quickly became one of my best friends, and before I knew it, I was sharing everything with you. Scenes, character art, life in general. You helped keep me sane during this crazed process, and I couldn't have made it through this without you. Because of you, I've been able to *just keep swimming.* You always knew what to say when I was in a funk, and worried about what people would think about my novel. Your kind words and endless energy kept me going when I just wanted to sleep (or cry). Thank you for everything!

Lærke, my beta turned friend. Thank you for always being there for me to bounce ideas off, your thoughts and suggestions have been beyond helpful and I can't thank you enough for always being there. You've been amazing, from helping to keep me up when anxiety is getting me down, to fangirling over anything and everything with me, and even picking out songs for my playlists! Thank you for giving my novel a chance and thank you even more for giving me a friend as badass as you! Thank you!

To the rest of my betas: Amanda, Amy, Gitte, Maria, Rachel, Rebecca, Nicci, Alexis and Phyllis. You guys gave me the confidence to keep moving forward. When I first sent my novel out to you I was terrified, and it was only because of your kind feedback, support and friendships that this novel is what it is today. You guys truly are the best, and I can't even begin to express how much you all mean to me. Thank you for taking a chance on a new author, and giving me feedback. I'll forever be grateful to you!

To the ARC readers, the first to take a chance at the finished product. If you made it this far, I hope you loved it. Thank you for giving this novel a read, and for giving it a chance. I'll forever be grateful for that!

To *BY THE BROOKE DESIGNS.* Thank you for giving me the cover of my dreams. It couldn't have turned out more perfect! Your endless kindness and willingness to work with me was so appreciated.

To Nic Perrins, for being the best editor that I could have asked for. You gave amazing critiques, helped me build up sentences that were lacking, and pointing out things that I never would have found otherwise. You were extraordinary, and I have you to thank for how this book shines. Thank you!

To Raeleen Nelson, for proofing this novel when you didn't have to. I'll forever be thankful to you for helping me when I was down. After finding out about my back issues, I didn't have the money to afford the final step in the process. You took me on anyway, and I'll never forget that. Thank you!

To the rest of my family and friends (as this is getting ridiculously long). To my dads for always being there when I needed you both, and for always picking me up when I was down. To my siblings for not killing me when we were younger, and for being some of my best friends now. To my nana and papa for loving me like your own and always making sure I was included. To everyone in between, thank you for always being on my side. I really can't thank you all enough. If you read this, I hope you enjoyed it. If you read it and didn't, then can we just all agree to not bring this up at Thanksgiving? Thanks. Love you guys.

And last, Dominic, the love of my life. As they say, *save the best for last.* You have stood by me from the start of this novel, and words can't describe how much that means to me. This has always been a dream of mine, and when you could have brushed it off or paid no interest, you engaged. You helped me along, listened to me spew useless facts about characters no one will ever meet, helped me pay for editors and cover art and everything that goes into making a novel, and most of all, you never told me it was too much. Thank you for always believing in me.

I love you, handsome, more than words can ever say.

ABOUT THE AUTHOR

Born and raised in the Wyoming Rocky Mountains, K. R. Rainbolt, or Kennady, is a lover of cakes and all things sweet. She also has a *minor* obsession with suits, but who doesn't love a nice crisp waistcoat, right? She has been crafting stories for as long as she can remember, and nothing makes her happier than bringing a character to life. Now, as a first time publisher, she's excited to share them with everyone else as well.

Kennady spends a lot of time writing, both for her novels and the occasional video game mod. When she's not immersed in one of her stories, she can be found spending time with the love of her life Dominic, or playing with her fur baby Marlie.

Kennady loves to bowl, fish, play video games, and watch movies (the spookier the better). Along with this she is big on the world of science and research, and as a Chemical Engineer she loves to include hints of her studies in her novels.

Lastly, a word of advice that her grandmother used to say: *Remember, live life.*

After all, you only have one, so you better spend it doing something you love!

Want to know more about Kennady? Then stalk her on social media! You can find her Official Facebook group, TikTok, Instagram and more on her Linktree: https://linktr.ee/k.r.rainboltauthor

Glossary

Latin

Vivas — To live

Lux mea — My light

Et in domum suam in solem — Home of the sun

Frater — Brother

Te desum — I miss you

Rex interfectorem — Kingslayer

Icelandic/Norse

Elskan — Darling (term of endearment)

Fífl — Idiot or Fool

Úlfhéðinn (singular)/*Úlfhéðnar* (plural) — Wearers of the wolf skin, or Odin's special warriors

Smár Valkyrja — Small Valkyrie, or tiny warrior.

Muna langt fram — Remember from a long time back

Dreyrugr — *Bloodstained*

Lítár hana — Look at her

Aboriginal Australian

Mob — Family

World Specific

Baba — Old Siren dialect meaning grandmother, or matriarch.

Charm — A Vampire ability.

Chronomancer — A Sorceri that can control the flow of time to a degree. They can often view into the future a short distance, and read someone's past with a touch. They can also slow and speed up time in an area.

Crypt — A grouping of Vampires, typically living together. A Crypt does not have to contain Vampires of only one Maker.

Echomancer — A Sorceri that can mimic the abilities of the other Sorceri classes to a degree. They are a jack of all trades, but master of none.

Eternal — A leader of a Natural Race. Each defined Natural Race has an Eternal.

Flit — A Vampire ability that allows them to move at very fast speeds. Their physical form warps when flitting, making them appear as little more than a burst of ashes.

Forgemancer — A Sorceri with the ability to enchant items, or craft magical items. They specialize in charm and ward making.

Hemomancer — A Sorceri with the ability to manipulate blood cells, and in some cases, other cells as well.

Himal — A figure that most Waterborn Naturals consider to be their primary deity.

Makers Call (often called The Call) — This is an undeniable pull that a Vampire Maker can place on his spawn. It is a Charm that they must follow. As time goes on, this pull can lessen, and they can resist it. It doesn't go away, unless the one that placed it dies.

Natural — The term for supernatural beings in this universe.

Rend — Aaliyah's affliction. The first part of a Rend is her soul leaving her body for a time. This time grows in length with each Rend she has. The second part of a Rend is the memory. Rends are often brought on by 'triggers' or events that remind her brain of something from the past.

Sirens Call — The Sirens ability to muddle minds. This often makes people forget periods of time or do small things at the Sirens' behest.

Sorceri — They are human wielders of magic, though are still considered Naturals.

Swell - A grouping of Waterborn Naturals (including but not limited to Sirens, Mermaids, Selkies, etc.).

The Flame — A gift passed down the Vivas bloodline from one of the original six Vampires, Ferrion.

PRINCE'S CODE

You okay? — Pointer finger to the nose while nodding.

Danger — Crossing arms over chest in an 'x' formation.

All clear — Pointer and middle finger pointed at the eyes.

Quiet — Pointer finger over lips in 'shush' motion.

Tell me? — Middle finger dragged from lips to left ear.

Sorry — Hands with interlaced fingers brought from chest to lips.

Forever — Hand settled over the heart, with the pinky and ring finger tucked underneath the hand.

Idiot — Swirling a finger around the ear.

Rend — Hands together, palms against one another, before they are pulled slowly apart.